Ma
Mankell, Henning, 1948-

Daniel

DANIEL

Henning Mankell

DANIEL

Translated from the Swedish by

Steven T. Murray

THE NEW PRESS

NEW YORK
LONDON

Requests for permission to reproduce selections from this
book should be mailed to: Permissions Department,
The New Press, 38 Greene Street, New York, NY 10013.

First published as *Vindens son* by Norstedts Förlag, Stockholm
Published in Great Britain by Harvill Secker, London, 2010
Published in the United States by The New Press, New York, 2010
Distributed by Perseus Distribution

LIBRARY OF CONGRESS CATALOGING-IN-PUBLICATION DATA

Mankell, Henning, 1948-
  [Vindens son. English]
  Daniel : a novel / Henning Mankell ; translated from the Swedish by Steven T. Murray.
    p. cm.
  Originally published in Swedish as Vindens son.
  ISBN 978-1-59558-193-8 (hc.: alk. paper) 1. Boys—Fiction. 2. San (African people)—
Sweden—Fiction. 3. Africans—Sweden—Fiction. I. Murray, Steven T. II. Title.
  PT9876.23.A49V5613 2011
  839.73'74—dc22

                                                                      2010027425

The New Press was established in 1990 as a not-for-profit alternative to the large,
commercial publishing houses currently dominating the book publishing industry.
The New Press operates in the public interest rather than for private gain, and is
committed to publishing, in innovative ways, works of educational, cultural, and
community value that are often deemed insufficiently profitable.

www.thenewpress.com

Printed in the United States of America

2 4 6 8 10 9 7 5 3 1

CONTENTS

In memory of Jan Bergman

PROLOGUE

SKÅNE, SOUTHERN SWEDEN, 1878

The crows were fighting. They dived towards the mud, flung themselves up again, and their cries cut through the wind. It had been raining a long time, this August of 1878. The restlessness of the crows was a portent of a long, hard winter. But one of the tenant farmers working below Kågeholm Castle, just north-west of Tomelilla, was bewildered by them. There was something strange about their agitation. And he had seen flocks of crows his whole life. Late in the afternoon he walked alongside a ditch that was filled with water. The crows kept squabbling, but when he approached too closely they fell silent and flapped off. And he, who had come to investigate what was bothering them, discovered at once what it was. A girl lay dead, half buried under the brushwood.

He realised at once that the girl had been murdered. Someone had stabbed her and slit her throat. But when he bent close over her face he noticed something odd, something that frightened him more than her slit throat. Whoever killed her had suffocated her with mud, which he had stuffed down her throat and into her nostrils. He had pressed so hard that he had broken her nose. The girl must have suffered an agonising death.

He ran back the same way he had come. Because it was obviously a murder, Chief Constable Landkvist in Tomelilla called for help from the investigative police in Malmö.

The dead girl's name was Sanna Sörensdotter and she was regarded by all, including the parish pastor David Hallén, as mentally retarded. She had been missing from her home in Kverrestad for three days before her body was discovered.

According to the doctor who examined the corpse, Dr Madsen of Simrishamn, she had apparently been sexually molested. But since her body was in a state of decomposition and the crows had done considerable damage to it, he had to admit that the truth might well be something else.

3

Many rumours flourished as to who had murdered her. One of the simplest claimed that a Polish sailor had been seen in the area just before Sanna disappeared from her home. Although a bulletin was put out all over Sweden, and even in Denmark, the man was never found.

The murderer remained at large.
Only he knew what he had done.
And why.

PART I

THE DESERT

CHAPTER 1

He had walked a long way in the intense heat. Several times in the last twenty-four hours he had been struck by vertigo and thought that he was about to die. It had filled him with fear, or perhaps it was actually rage, and he had struggled on in a fury. The desert was endless. He didn't want to die here, not yet, and he had urged on Amos, fat Neka and the other black men he had hired in Cape Town who were driving his three oxen and the wagon in which his entire life was packed and tied with ropes. Somewhere ahead of them, deep inside the blinding heat, there was a trading post, and if he reached it everything would be all right again. He would not die. He would continue to search for his insects, to look for a damned fly that no one had ever seen before, which he would name after himself, *Musca bengleriensis*. He couldn't give up now. He had invested everything in this hunt for an unknown fly. So he struggled onward, and the sand and the sun sliced through his mind like knives.

Two years earlier he had been sitting in his student room on Prästgatan in Lund and listening to the sound of horses' hooves clattering on the cobblestones outside, as he studied an incomplete German map of the Kalahari Desert. He traced his finger along the coastline of German South-West Africa, north to the border of Angola, south to the land of the Boers, and then inland, towards the centre of southern Africa, which had no name. He was twenty-seven years old then, in 1874, and he had already given up all hope of completing his university studies and passing his exams. When he first came to Lund from the Cathedral School in Växjö he had thought of becoming a physician, but he fainted and fell like a heavy tree on his first visit to the Anatomy Theatre. The lecturer, Professor Enander, had clearly explained before the doors were opened that they were going to dissect a homeless, unmarried woman who had drunk herself to death at a brothel in Copenhagen and been transported back to Sweden in a pine box. She was a Mamsell Andersson from Kivik, who had fallen into the sinful life and delivered an illegitimate child at the age of fifteen. She had sought happiness in Copenhagen, where there was nothing to be found but misfortune. He could still hear the almost salacious contempt dripping from Professor Enander's introductory words.

'We shall be cutting up a cadaver that was already a cadaver even in life. A whore's cadaver from Österlen.'

Then they had entered the Anatomy Theatre en masse, seven medical students, all men, all equally pale, and Professor Enander had begun to slice open her abdomen. That's when he fainted. He struck his head on one of the hard steel edges of the dissection table; he still had the scar, just above his right eye.

After that he had abandoned all thought of a medical career. He considered joining the army but could envision nothing but a meaningless ritual of marching and screaming young men. He had dabbled in philosophy, and thought about becoming a pastor when he sat drinking with his friends, but there was no God, and finally he wound up among the insects.

He could still recall that morning in early summer. He woke with a start, as if something had bitten him, and when he threw open the window the stench from the street below made him sick. As if aware of sudden danger he quickly threw on his clothes, grabbed his walking stick, and strode out of town to the south, towards Staffanstorp. Somewhere along the road he grew weary and stepped into the bushes to rest and perhaps masturbate in the shade of a tree. And as he lay there a gaudy-coloured butterfly settled on his hand. It was a brimstone butterfly, but it was something else as well. The play of colours kept shifting on its wings as they slowly opened and closed. The rays of sunshine falling through the foliage transformed the yellow to red, to blue, and back to yellow. The butterfly sat on his hand for a long time, as if it had an important message for him, and then, as it suddenly took flight and vanished, he knew.

Insects.

The world was full of insects which didn't have names and had not been catalogued. Insects that were waiting for him. Waiting to be sorted, described and classified. He had returned to Lund, sought admission to the Botany Department, and although he was already a senior student the professor was kind and accepted him. During the summer he visited his home in Småland, where his father lived as a man of independent means on the family estate outside Hovmantorp. His mother had died when he was fifteen; his two sisters were older, and since they were both married and lived abroad, in Berlin and Verona, only his father was there, with the old housekeeper. The house was decaying, just as his father was slowly rotting away. He had contracted syphilis in his youth when he was in Paris, and now he sat imprisoned inside an arbour in the summer, alone in his chair. The arbour was pruned so that one had to crawl inside through a hole quite close to the ground. In the autumn his father locked himself in his bedchamber and stayed there through the whole six months of winter, motionless, staring at the ceiling and grinding his teeth until the warmth of spring returned.

Bengler's grandfather had been fortunate in his business speculations during the Napoleonic Wars, and there was still some capital left, although it was much diminished. The estate was mortgaged to the rooftops, and every time he visited his childhood home he realised that this was all the inheritance he could expect. Nothing but the monthly allowances that made it possible for him to survive in Lund.

His father was a shadow and had never been anything else. And yet Bengler visited him in in Hovmantorp that summer to obtain his blessing. He had a vague hope that his father would be able to give him a little financial support for the expedition he was planning.

In addition, and this was the most important thing, he knew that it was time to say goodbye. His father would soon be gone.

From Växjö he got a lift from a travelling salesman who was going to Lessebo. The wagon was uncomfortable, the road was bad, and there was a strong smell of mould from the salesman's coat. He was indeed wearing a fur coat even though it was early June – not full summer heat yet, but already warm.

'Hovmantorp,' he said after an hour had passed. 'A fine-sounding name. But there's nothing there.'

Then they introduced themselves. That never would have happened when they met the night before, as he went round the inns in the little town looking for a ride.

'Hans Bengler.'

The travelling salesman pondered for several kilometres before he replied.

'That doesn't sound Swedish,' he said. 'But what is Swedish anyway, other than endless roads through equally endless forests? My name isn't Swedish either. It's Puttmansson, Natanael Puttmansson, and belongs to the chosen yet exiled people. I sell brushes and household remedies for barrenness and gout.'

'There's some Walloon in my lineage,' replied Hans Bengler. 'A bit of French. There's a Huguenot in the family too, and a Finn. And a French cavalry captain who served under Napoleon and took a shot through the forehead at Austerlitz. But my name is genuine.'

They rattled on further. A lake glittered among the trees. He's certainly not talkative, Bengler thought. Big forests either make people silent or make them talk incessantly. I'm thankful that this salesman who smells like mould is a man who keeps his mouth shut.

Then the horse died.

It stopped in its tracks, tried to rear up as though it had suddenly encountered an invisible enemy, and then collapsed. The salesman didn't seem surprised.

'Swindled,' he said simply. 'Someone sells me a horse under false pretences, and the only thing I've never learned to judge is horses.'

They parted ways without much ado. Bengler took his knapsack and walked the last ten kilometres to Hovmantorp. Since he was a man devoted to insects, he stopped now and then to study various creeping things, preparing himself to see his father. Just before he reached Hovmantorp it started to rain. He crept into a barn and masturbated for a while as he thought about Matilda, who was his whore and worked in a brothel just north of the cathedral. It was several hours before the rainstorm passed. He sat looking at the dark sky while his member dried off, thinking that the clouds looked like a caravan, and he wondered how it would be to live in a desert where rain almost never fell.

Why had he decided on the desert, anyway?

He didn't know. When he was studying the maps his first thought was of South America. But the mountain ranges frightened him, since he didn't like being up high. He had never even dared climb the tower of the cathedral to look out over the fields. It made him dizzy just thinking of it. The choice came down to the great steppes in the realm of the Mongolians, the deserts of Arabia or the white spot in south-west Africa. His final decision had something to do with German. He spoke German since he had hiked the country with a friend several years earlier. They had made it all the way down to the Tyrol. Then his travelling companion suddenly contracted a fever and died after violent attacks of vomiting, and Bengler hurriedly returned home. But he had learned German.

As he sat there in the barn with his member in his hand, he thought that he was actually an apprentice, sent out into the world by the dead master Linnaeus. But he also worried that he was not at all suited to the task. He had a low tolerance for pain, he wasn't particularly strong and he was scared of loud noises. Yet one thing could be counted as an asset for him, and that was his stubbornness. And behind his stubbornness lay vanity. Somewhere he would be able to discover a butterfly, or maybe a fly, that was not listed in the catalogues of entomology, and then he could name it after himself.

He went home. His father was sitting in the arbour soaking wet when he crept through the hedge. His father's jaws were grinding, he was crumbling away. He was bald, his skin hung loose and he did not recognise his son. It was a living death sitting there in the arbour, his jaws grinding like millstones with no grain, his whole skeleton creaking, his heart heaving like bellows, and Bengler felt that this pilgrimage to his childhood home was like stepping into a nightmare. But he still sat there for a while and chatted with his deranged father. Then he went up to the house, where the housekeeper was pleased to see him, but no more than that. She made up a bed for him in his old room and gave him something to eat. While she was clattering around in the kitchen he walked round the house and picked up any silver he found. He was taking his inheritance in advance, realising that he would be arriving in the African desert as a quite indigent entomologist.

*   *   *

11

During the night he lay awake. The housekeeper usually brought in his father at sundown and put him to bed on a sofa downstairs. Sometime in the night he went down there and sat in the shadows looking at his father. He was asleep, but his jaws kept on grinding. Something suddenly made Bengler upset, a sorrow that surprised him, and he went over and stroked his father's bald head In that instant, with that touch, he said his farewell. He felt as if he were standing and watching a coffin being lowered into the earth.

Afterwards he lay awake and waited for daybreak. There was no substance to this waiting, no impatience, no dreams, as though his insides were a flat, cold slab of stone.

He left before the housekeeper awoke.

Three days later he returned to Lund. During his first week back he travelled across the Sound and sold the silver in Copenhagen. Just as he had suspected, he didn't get much money for what he had to offer. The only thing that brought a good price was a snuffbox which had belonged to the ancestor who had his brains blown out at Austerlitz.

By the following year he had learned everything he now knew about insects. The professor had been friendly, and when he asked why a perpetual student had suddenly been gripped by a fascination for the tiniest creatures, Bengler replied that he actually didn't know. He had studied colour plates and examined the insects preserved in alcohol, floating weightless in the glass jars that stood on mute shelves in the halls of the Biological Institute. He had learned to distinguish and identify, had plucked off wings and dissected. At the same time he had tried to learn about deserts, about the African continent, which was still largely terra incognita. But in Lund there had been no professors who knew anything about deserts, or barely anything about Africa. He read everything he came across, and went over to Copenhagen a few times to seek out seamen in Nyhavn who had travelled to Cape Town or Dakar and who could tell him about Africa.

He had told no one but Matilda about his plans. She came to him every Thursday between four and six in the afternoon. Besides having sex, always in the missionary position, she also washed his shirts, and afterwards they would drink port and talk. Matilda was nineteen years old and had left her home in Landskrona when her father tried to rape and then set fire to her. For a brief period she had been a maid before she threw away the apron and the subservience and headed for the brothel. She was flat-chested but very nice, and he made no other demands on eroticism but that it should be nice, not troublesome or ecstatic. He told her about the journey on which he would be embarking the next year, early in the spring, when he understood it was not yet too warm in southern Africa. She listened, uninterested beyond the fact that now she would have to look for another steady customer.

Once he had suggested that she come with him.

'I refuse to travel by sea,' she replied vehemently. 'You can die there, sink to the bottom and never come up.'

And nothing more was said about it.

Winter that year was very mild in Skåne. In early May he moved out of the apartment on Prästgatan. He told his few friends that he was going to take a short trip through Europe and would be back soon.

A fishing boat took him to Copenhagen. For three weeks he lived in a cheap boarding house with sailors in Nyhavn. One Sunday he went to watch a beheading. He didn't go to the theatre or visit the museums. He talked to the sailors and waited. He had reduced his baggage to a minimum; everything was contained in a simple chest he had found in the attic of the building on Prästgatan. He had packed up his maps, colour plates and books, some shirts, a pair of extra trousers, leather boots. In Copenhagen he had bought a revolver and ammunition. That was all. He changed the money he had left into gold. He carried it in a leather pouch inside his shirt.

He also had his hair cut very short and started to grow a beard. And he waited.

On 23 May he found out that an English schooner, the *Fox*, would be sailing from Helsingør to Cardiff and then on to Cape Town. The same day he left his boarding house and took the post coach north to Helsingør. He paid a visit to the captain of the black-painted schooner and obtained a promise to be accepted on board as a passenger, although there would be no private cabin at his disposal. For the passage he paid about half the contents of his leather pouch.

On the evening of 25 May the *Fox* left Helsingør. He stood by the railing and sensed everything making headway within him. Inside his breastbone he had masts that were raising their sails. Something was pulling at him, as if a line had been lashed around his heart. He was seized by a desire to be a child again, just for a moment. To skip, babble, crawl, learn to walk right there on the scoured deck.

That night he slept heavily.

By dawn the next morning they had already passed Skagen at the northern tip of Denmark and were in another world.

That world was covered by a thick and immovable fog.

CHAPTER 2

On the ship he was liberated from his name. He was never called anything but 'the Passenger'. Without knowing how it happened, he underwent a ritual in which he was stripped of his former identity and became the Passenger. Among these pale but hard-working men he was the only one who did nothing but travel. Without a name, without a past, with nothing more than a bunk in the crew's quarters. And that was fine with him. When he lost his identity, the past disappeared. It was as though the salt water that splashed up over the railing penetrated his consciousness and corroded all the shadowy memories he carried. The sound of his father's grinding jaws ebbed away, Matilda became an indistinct silhouette and the house in Hovmantorp a ruin. Of his mother and two sisters nothing was left, not even the memory of their voices. When he was transformed into the Passenger he discovered for the first time that something existed which he had heard of but never before comprehended: freedom.

He would always remember the arrival in Cape Town as an extended and surreal dream. Or perhaps it was actually the end of one nightmare that imperceptibly slipped over into another? Even before they reached Cardiff, the captain, whose name was Robertson, had turned out to suffer from recurrent bouts of madness. He would come rushing into the crew's quarters with knives in his hands, slashing wildly in all directions. They had to tie him down; only when he began weeping some days later would they release him again. Bengler understood that the crew had great love for the captain. The schooner was actually a floating cathedral with a number of acolytes who were prepared to follow their master into death. Between his attacks, Robertson was very amiable and devoted both interest and time to his lone, taciturn passenger. He was in his forties and had gone to sea when he was nine. At sixteen he underwent a religious crisis, and then, when he became captain, shouldered an invisible mantle which was actually a pastor's robe and not a marine uniform. He told his passenger about many oddities from the African continent. But he had never visited the desert. He assumed an absent, almost sorrowful expression when the Passenger told him about his plans. He didn't reveal his deepest secret, about the mysterious butterfly or fly he would name after himself. But he did talk about the insects, how he was going to catalogue, sort, identify and carry out the arrangements that were necessary for a person to be able to live a decent life.

The talk about the desert, the expanses of sand, made Robertson depressed.

'You can't even drown in sand,' said Robertson.

'But you can be covered up by it,' replied the Passenger.

Robertson observed him for a long time before he made another comment.

'No one has ever seen a god arise from a grain of sand. On the other hand, the Devil has been known to spew burning sand from his maw.'

The Passenger didn't mention the sand again. Instead he enticed Robertson to tell him about the black people, the very short and the very tall, about the women who smeared dung in their hair, the violent dances that were nothing more than shadow images of erotic games. And the Passenger listened. Every evening, except during a heavy storm in the Bay of Biscay, he noted down what the captain had said. After he helped Robertson clean out a severely infected ear, their relationship had deepened. As a special favour, as if he were being allowed to take part in a holy sacrament, Robertson had taught him to use the sextant. The feeling that he was carrying the ship inside him rather than standing on its deck became ever stronger. Each morning he raised his inner sails, depending on the direction and force of the winds. In the evenings, or when a storm was brewing, he watched the crew clambering up the rigging and took the same measures inside himself.

On 22 June just at sundown, the lookout shouted, 'Land, ho!' Robertson let the vessel lie at drift-anchor that night. In the crew's quarters a strange silence prevailed, as if none of them dared believe that they had survived yet another journey to the distant dark continent. In low voices, as if they were confiding secrets to one another, they began to plan for the days they would spend ashore. He listened attentively to the whispers passing through the cabin. It was like a chant in which two things were murmured time after time: *women and beer, women and beer*. Nothing more. The last night on the ship he tried to reconcile his thoughts with all that he had left behind, but he could not even recall Matilda's face. There was nothing.

At dawn he took leave of Robertson.

'We'll never see each other again,' said Robertson. 'I can always tell when I'm saying goodbye to someone for the last time.'

It was as though Robertson were issuing his death warrant. It upset him because it made him fearful. Could Robertson see what lay before him, see into the unknown? He refused to believe that this was true, but Robertson was one of the most mysterious men he had ever met. What was he really? A mad preacher or a mad sea captain? Or a man who actually had the ability to discern the men for whom death was already waiting?

'Good luck,' said Robertson, stretching out his hand. 'Everyone has his path to follow. And that cannot be altered.'

Then he was rowed ashore. Tafelberg loomed high like a decapitated neck over the city that lay wedged at the foot of the mountain. On the quay there was great confusion; people yelled and shoved, some black men with rings in their ears began to tear at his chest and he was forced to defend himself with his fists. He spoke German, but nobody understood him; all around him English was being spoken. Robertson had given him two addresses, one for a boarding house which was usually free of lice, and one for an old English pilot who for some reason was the honorary consul for the Union of Sweden and Norway in Cape Town. When, after numerous difficulties, he found his way to the boarding house, he was drenched with sweat. The white woman who owned the establishment yelled at a fat mulatto and told her to give the new guest some water. He drank it, knowing that something was going to happen to his stomach. He was shown to a room where the sheet was ironed yet still wet. Everything seemed damp, the floorboards had pores, and he lay down on the bed and thought: Now I'm here and I have absolutely no idea where I am.

*   *   *

The next day, after he had succumbed to the first bout of diarrhoea, he looked up the Swedish-Norwegian honorary consul. This gentleman lived in a white house next to a road that climbed towards the mountains. He was admitted to the house by a black man with no teeth, and he sat waiting for two hours on a wooden chair until Consul Wackman had finished snoring and got up and dressed. Wackman was completely bald, had no eyebrows, and his protruding ears reminded Bengler of swallows' wings. His legs were short, his stomach held up by a piece of Indian fabric, and on his bare chest sat two bloodsucking leeches. He glanced over the letter that Robertson had written and then tossed it aside.

'All these Swedish madmen. Why do they always have to come here? What we need are engineers. Competent people who can solve practical problems, or have raw strength, or a little capital. But not all these madmen who either want to import revival or collect the dung that the elephants leave behind. And now this. Insects. Who needs flies and mosquitoes in catalogues?'

With his fat fingers he grabbed a small silver bell and rang it. A black servant, naked except for a thin loincloth, came in and knelt down.

'What would you like to drink?' Wackman asked. 'Gin or not gin?'

'Gin.'

The black man disappeared from the room. Outside the window Bengler could see that someone had hung up a vulture by its feet and was beating it with a wooden stick.

They drank.

'I had thought about making a living from ostriches,' said the Passenger, who was now slowly feeling his name returning. He was again on his way to becoming Hans Bengler from Hovmantorp.

Wackman regarded him for a long time before he replied.

'So, you're a madman,' he said at last. 'You think you're going to hunt ostriches and export feathers for ladies' hats. It won't pay. The feathers will rot before the ship has even left the harbour.'

With that, all discussion was over. Wackman did, however, exhibit a certain resigned kindness and promised to help him acquire some oxen, a wagon, and hire some ox-drivers. Then he would have to manage on his own. Wackman thought it would be advisable if he left a will with him, in case there was something to be inherited. Or at least the address of a family member who could be informed that his relative's bones were now resting in an unknown location in an endless desert.

They kept on drinking gin. He thought about the mellow port wine he had drunk with Matilda. That world now seemed like an enigmatic mirage. Now it was raw gin tearing at his throat. And Wackman, breathless, as if he would give up the ghost at any time, told him the strange story of how he, who was born in Glasgow, had wound up in Cape Town and came to be the owner of a brothel and represent the Swedish-Norwegian Union.

The story was about bears and a lithograph that he had once seen in his younger days in the window of a bookseller's in Glasgow. *Bear Hunting in Swedish Wermland*. He had never been able to forget that image. In his twenties he had made his pilgrimage, arriving in Karlstad in the middle of a terrible winter. Several times he had almost died from the terror that the cold aroused in him, not the cold itself. He never saw a live bear, even though he stayed in that awful cold for more than two months. On the other hand, he did see a bear skin at the home of a retired artillery captain who lived by the square. Then he had left Sweden as fast as he could, and by a circuitous route ended up in Cape Town, where he wanted to show his gratitude for seeing the bear skin by taking on the task of serving as the consul of the Swedish-Norwegian Union.

By late afternoon they were both fairly well intoxicated. Wackman ordered his carriage and together they rolled down the steep road and stopped outside the low cement building that housed his brothel. Half-naked black women melted into the darkness in the low rooms and there was a strong smell of unknown spices. Wackman vanished and Bengler suddenly discovered that he was entwined with black snakes: female arms, legs, feet, bellies, and he fled into the gin fog and didn't know whether it was actually Robertson's schooner that slowly sank towards the bottom of the sea, or the ship he carried inside himself.

The next day he awoke on the floor of a room with a veil beside his head. When he forced himself to stand up he discovered a blue spider which was busy weaving its web in the corner between two walls. He reminded himself of his mission and walked through the brothel, where everyone now seemed to be asleep, and found Wackman passed out in an antique rocking chair. Although Wackman was sleeping deeply, he seemed to have been waiting for him. When Bengler stood behind him he awoke with a start.

'I need nine days,' Wackman said. 'And all the cash or all the gold dust you have in that pouch that's bulging under your shirt, which by the way is filthy and should be washed. Nine days, no more. Then you can be on your way. And I will never see you again. But there is one piece of advice I would give you. Advice about the future.'

'What's that?'

'The pianoforte.'

'The pianoforte?'

'It's all the rage in England. It will spread over the entire continent. Those young mamselles play the piano. Black and white keys. Those pianos need keys. And the keys need ivory.'

Bengler understood. Wackman thought that he ought to go in for elephant hunting.

'I came here for the tiny creatures,' he replied. 'Not the big ones.'

'Blame yourself and die,' said Wackman. 'No one will miss you, no one will remember you.'

But Wackman, whose first name was Erasmus, kept his promise. On the ninth day everything was ready. For lack of anything better, Bengler had left Wackman the address of the housekeeper in Hovmantorp. In the event that he died, she would stuff the letter between his father's grinding jaws and the last memory of him would be eradicated.

And yet he knew this would not happen. Without being able to explain it, not to mention defend it, he was convinced he would survive.

The sand would not sneak up on him.

On one of the first days in July he set off from Cape Town.

The sluggish oxen moved very slowly. He had purchased a tropical helmet and hung a rifle over his shoulder. Insects buzzed around his face, lured by his sweat. He thought that they would lead him in the right direction. They were his most important travelling companions.

The compass, which had been made in London and was encased in brass, showed that his course was due north, perhaps with a deviation of a few hundredths of a degree to the west.

The first night he changed his clothes before he sat down to eat the dinner served by Amos, his cook. They had made camp by the bank of a small river. The starry sky was clear and close. Suddenly he saw the Big Dipper. It hung upside down. As a last farewell to everything he had left behind, he surprised his ox-drivers by standing on his head and looking at the Big Dipper as he had seen it as a child.

They thought he was praying to a god.

For a long time he lay awake and waited for a beast of prey to roar in the night.

But everything was very quiet.

CHAPTER 3

The next day, during the hottest hour of the day when the sun hung straight over his head, the fear came.

At first it was a creeping anxiety. A premonition which he initially dismissed by thinking it was something he had eaten. Or that he had forgotten something, a thought that glided past unnoticed, and he didn't realise was important. This uneasiness or anxiety was light. The fear came later. It was heavy and pulled at him like a powerful magnet.

They had stopped at the edge of some flat country where low bushes lay blanched in the sun. Neka had set up a parasol and placed his folding chair on a little rug. They had eaten rice, vegetables and a strong spicy bread which according to Wackman was the only kind that did not get mouldy during long expeditions. Amos, Neka and the other two ox-drivers, whose names he hadn't yet learned, lay sleeping under the wagon. The three oxen stood motionless. Their skin twitched when insects bit them.

It was in that instant the dry earth was transformed into iron. The magnet pulled and he felt the fear coming. He had just taken out his diary to make notes about the morning's events. He had decided to write three times a day: when he awoke, after the midday rest and before he went to sleep. Since he could not imagine keeping these notes only for his own sake, he had decided that the person he would direct his words to was Matilda. The fear came just as he had finished his account of the morning. They had struck the tent at sunrise. At nine o'clock they passed a dry riverbed where he had identified the skeleton of a crocodile. He calculated the length as three metres and ten centimetres. Just after ten o'clock they passed an area of dense, thorny thickets that made the oxen restless. Before they stopped for their midday rest, he had seen a large bird hovering motionless above his head, as if resting on an invisible pillar. Whether it was an eagle or a vulture he could not tell. After these practical matters he had added, *The feeling is very strong. From Hovmantorp I have come all the way here. I realise that the road is endless and life is very short.* That was when the fear came. At first he wondered what was causing it. He no longer had diarrhoea, his pulse was normal, he had no infections. There didn't seem to be any threats: no beasts of prey, no hostile inhabitants. Everything was actually quite idyllic. Motionless oxen, men sleeping under a wagon.

It's about me, he thought as he wiped the sweat from his brow with his sleeve. It's about me sitting here in the midst of an unreal idyll. He suddenly thought he saw Professor Enander before him and heard his words: We shall be cutting up a cadaver that was a cadaver even in life.

He thought about how he had fainted and that it had been his way of fleeing. To escape seeing how the belly would be slit open and the guts spill out. Now he sat in the middle of a strange place in the southern part of Africa, on his way to an unknown goal: a previously unnamed, uncatalogued, and unidentified fly, or perhaps a butterfly.

He could now look his fear right in the face. What he had decided to devote his life to, an expedition from which it was uncertain that he would return alive, was also a kind of flight. The same as when he fainted in the Anatomy Theatre. Now he was in a different kind of theatre. The African landscape, the motionless oxen, the sleeping men under the wagon, it was all a stage set. He was in the middle of a play about his own flight. From Hovmantorp and the grinding jaws, from his failed studies in Lund, his failed life. Nothing more.

He regarded the revolver that he had bought in Copenhagen, which was now loaded and lying at his feet. It would be very simple to take his own life, he thought. A few simple hand movements, a boom that I would never even hear. Probably the ox-drivers would bury me on the spot, divide up my belongings and vanish to the four winds. They might get into a fight over the oxen, since there are four of them and only three oxen. By then they would already have forgotten that I ever existed. And I would never learn how their names – the two whose names seem to consist only of consonants – are actually pronounced.

*   *   *

He got up and left the shade of the parasol. One of the oxen looked at him. The heat was very strong. He stood underneath a knotty tree, the only one at their resting place. I'm afraid because I don't know who I am, he thought. Whether all this has been a flight from the thoroughly meaningless life of a student or not, it has certainly been a flight from myself. I have sat drinking for nights on end and denied God's existence, but it was nothing more than drunken babble. I believe in a god, a god of wrath and judgement, who is everywhere. I was ashamed when I sat and masturbated in the ditches by the fields of Skåne. I knew that someone was watching me when Matilda sucked on me. I have pretended to be liberal, professed myself an adherent of the new world that the engineers and steam power will create. I was full of contempt when Pastor Cavallius in Hovmantorp claimed that railways were an invention of the Devil. I pretended to believe in the future, feigned a resistance to everything obsolete, when actually I am afraid of everything I can't predict. I am the least-suited person to be standing under this tree in Africa, as the leader of an expedition, on the hunt for an unknown insect. Wackman was absolutely right, of course. He saw straight through me, saw the madman behind the false earnestness.

He went back to the parasol. The fear sat like a knot in his stomach. He folded his hands and said a prayer. *I am looking for a truth that does not have to be big. Just so long as it exists. Amen.*

Neka, who was fat and shapeless, had woken up. He stood by the tree pissing, then he returned to the wagon and went back to sleep.

Bengler began to think about the English scientist and his theses that they had discussed during late nights at the Småland students' club. The man had travelled around the world with one of the British Admiralty's vessels and then returned to England and claimed that human beings were apes. Bengler had seldom said anything during the heated discussions. To a man, the theologians had stood on the side of God, and they had loosed volleys of Scripture against the attacking hordes of freethinkers. And the freethinkers had picked up Darwin's instruments and slit open the theologians' arguments with tiny scalpels. He had mostly sat on the sidelines and listened. Now he thought that

24

the fear had probably already been present back then. The fear that God would cease to exist. Whether his grandmother was an ape was not so important.

He could see everything very clearly now. The fear was like a spyglass that he could use to look backwards. And what he saw was nothing. A person from the interior of Småland who didn't believe in anything, who didn't really want anything, who in a manifestation of the utmost vanity was looking for a fly that he could name after himself.

At the same time he thought there might be a solution in this. He could use the expedition to try to find a meaning to his own life. He could choose whether there was a god or whether it was the engineers who shaped the world. Was God in a heaven or was He in the iron beams that held together the new factories, the new world? The path that led to the desert and then the desert without paths would give him the time he needed to find an answer.

Slowly he felt the fear receding. He closed his eyes. The sun continued to burn inside his eyelids.

They set off in the afternoon. He took turns walking in front, next to the wagon, or at the rear. The magnet had released its grip. He felt exhilarated.

They reached a swamp that they would have to go round to reach the low mountains beyond. According to the map, the mountains formed the extreme boundary of the desert which would then come slowly sneaking towards them. Then one of the wagon wheels broke. The wagon slumped over on its side, the oxen stopped, and he went to assess the damage. Behind him the ox-drivers stood silent. He tried to decide whether it would be possible to fix the wheel, but several of the rough spokes had broken off. They would have to use the spare wheel that Wackman had insisted he take with him, even though it was heavy and the wagon already overloaded. He explained to Amos, who he thought be might the leader of the others, by gesturing with his hands and arms that the wheel had to be changed. Then he called for his folding chair and parasol and sat down to watch the ox-drivers work.

The fear had been fierce. But the contempt that now consumed him was blazing. He watched the ox-drivers' clumsy attempts to brace the wagon, take off the broken wheel and replace it with a new one. Even though he had never used his hands for practical work he could still see how it should be done. After half an hour he was so upset at their clumsiness and slowness that he leapt up from the folding chair and began ordering them about. I've become a military man after all, he thought indignantly. And it's when some damned good-for-nothings can't manage to change a wheel. After he took charge he noticed that his agitation seemed to increase. He began to shout and point and push aside anyone who made a mistake. It surprised him that none of the men protested, or even showed the slightest sign of irritation at this treatment, and this increased his vexation. When the new wheel was in place he demanded that they pick up speed so that they could make up for lost time. But what time was actually lost? he thought. What path can't we reclaim tomorrow? What stretch of road do we have to put behind us today? This expedition has no goal.

And yet he forced the pace. His rage had now completely replaced his fear. For the first time in his life he felt himself to be the stronger one.

Just before sunset they pitched camp for the night. On the way he had shot an animal that looked like a hare. He lay down on his camp bed in the tent and smelled the aroma from the meat and the fire. I have instilled respect in these people, he thought. From now on there will be no doubt that I will make the decisions that are required. I'm still young, but these ox-drivers have understood that I have the power necessary to make the crucial decisions.

He ate the roasted meat. The ox-drivers kept their distance, by the fire. In the books he had read the previous winter, he had learned of some new theories, French and German, that seemed to coincide as if by chance. The noble savage did not exist. He belonged to the romantic world view of former eras, the time before the engineers, the iron beams and the account ledgers. He had read these theories which took a scientific view of skin colour and brains, noses and feet. He had read about subhumans and superhumans. At first he had thought that they could not be true, because all men had been created equal. But if there was no God, there didn't have to be equality either. Now he thought

26

he had managed to confirm this with his own eyes. The ox-drivers were another sort of human being. They had to be driven the same way that they drove the oxen. Even though he was only descended from a man with grinding jaws in Hovmantorp, in the depths of the poor, backward province of Småland, he was still the one who had to make the important decisions for these black people.

Just before he fell asleep, after placing the revolver under his pillow and the rifle on the ground next to his camp bed, he made his last notes of the evening. Once again he addressed himself to Matilda. *These people, unfathomably dark in skin colour, cannot be compared to us. They belong to something else; perhaps they are more like animals. But they remind me of the paupers in Sweden. Their submissiveness, silence, ingratiating attitude. Today I discovered the role I have to play in this drama. I am confirming my own freedom. The desert is still far off. Now, just before ten o'clock at night, it is still very warm. I have already noticed that I'm waking up more easily in this heat and that my dreams are different.*

Then he blew out the candle.

He didn't write anything about his fear.

He woke in the middle of the night, jolted out of a dream. His father's grinding jaws had been very close to him, like the jaws of a beast of prey. In the background he had glimpsed Matilda. She was naked, screaming that she was being raped by a group of soldiers with blue stripes glued to their naked bodies. She had seen him and called to him, begging him to help. But he hid, made himself invisible, and left her to her fate.

And yet it was not the dream that had woken him. When he opened his eyes in the dark he realised that he had been pulled out of sleep by something outside himself. He lay quite still and held his breath. The sweat was sticky on his body. It's the oxen, he thought. At once he was wide awake. He was not in Lund now, nor Hovmantorp. Africa was a continent where snakes coiled and big cats came sneaking out of the darkness and bit animals' throats. He fumbled for his rifle. When he felt the cold barrel he grew calmer. He listened in a different way.

27

But he hadn't been imagining things; the oxen were restless. He lit his lamp, pulled on his trousers and grabbed the rifle. The fire was blazing. He glimpsed the oxen in the shadows just outside the light of the flames. The ox-drivers lay curled up around the fire, but when he counted the bodies he saw that one of them was missing. He checked that the safety was off on his rifle, shook out his boots and pulled them on. Then he walked carefully over to the oxen.

He discovered Neka standing there. Fat, shapeless Neka. He had a whip in his hand. Slowly, as though he were driving the oxen in his sleep, he struck them on their backs. Bengler stopped. What he saw was utterly incomprehensible. One of the ox-drivers, in the middle of the night, naked with his fat belly jiggling, was slowly, as if in a trance, striking the oxen over and over. He thought he ought to intervene, snatch the whip from Neka's hands, perhaps wake the others sleeping around the fire, and then tie Neka to a tree and have him flogged. Wackman had explained that there were plenty of men, both drivers and bearers, to be found on this strange continent, but good oxen were expensive and uncommon. So oxen had to be weighed against men, oxen protected while men could be discarded. Yet Bengler didn't move. Neka seemed to be standing there striking the oxen in his sleep. He was staggering as if the blows of the whip were striking him, making his own flesh quiver and not the thick hide of the oxen.

Suddenly it was over. Neka dropped the whip and turned round. Bengler quickly retreated deeper into the darkness. If he were discovered he would have to intervene; punish Neka. But Neka hadn't seen him. He stumbled back to the fire, curled up and seemed to fall asleep as soon as he closed his eyes.

Bengler went over to the oxen. He stroked his hand along the back of one of them and got blood on his palm. Then he turned and went over to the fire. I could shoot these men, he thought. One by one. That's how the castes work on this continent. The ones lying here, curled up, unwashed, belong to the lower classes. While I, a failed student from Småland, am a member of the caste comprised of the strongest, those who have power.

He returned to the tent. A lizard sat next to the lamp, staring at an ant slowly approaching. Then its tongue lashed out and the ant was gone.

That night he made another note in his book. He wrote to Matilda: *Wish that tonight I had had the courage to flog open the back of one of my ox-drivers with the heavy whip. But I'm not quite at that point yet. If I struck him now it would bother me. Not until I know that the action won't cause me any pain, only the one who has the skin on his back flayed, will I do it.*

He rolled up the diary in the beaver skin that protected it against damp and insects, turned off the lamp and lay down.

I'm searching for an unknown fly, he thought. The way other people search for a god. In the desert I believe I'll find it. But Wackman with his brothel, his whores and his peculiar ears has no doubt already written to my father's housekeeper and reported that I failed, that I'm lying in an unmarked grave.

Even though he was very tired he lay awake until dawn.

The next day they continued past the low mountains and in the evening reached the Kalahari Desert.

CHAPTER 4

From a distance they saw a group of Bushmen pass by.

They were like black dots against the blinding sand. The fact that they were humans and not animals could be surmised from the oxen: the beasts had scented them but decided they were no threat.

They had then been in the desert for two months and four days. It was the first instance in all that time that they had seen any human beings. Before this they had seen only a small herd of zebras and the tracks of snakes that coiled below the crescent-shaped barchans of sand.

Bengler had lost more than nine kilos in weight. Naturally he couldn't weigh himself, but he knew that it was precisely nine kilos. His trousers flapped around his legs, his chest had sunk, his bearded cheeks were hollow. At night he dreamed that he was slowly being buried in sand. When he tried to scream there was no sound because his vocal cords had dried out.

Somewhere everything had gone wrong. According to the maps Wackman had got for him, they should have passed the chief town of Windhoek in German South-West Africa a week ago. But nothing other than bare mountains, sand and scattered bushes had lain in their illusory path. Twice they had come across waterholes, both times after they had seen swarms of birds rising and falling against the sky. Until now the ox-drivers had not complained, but Bengler realised that it would not be long. Every day the distance between them had increased. On two occasions he had been forced to raise the whip to get them to go on: he knew that the third time it happened he would have to strike.

Neka was still as fat as before. This amazed him. The ox-drivers' meals were even sparser than his own. But apart from Amos, who knew a few words of English, all conversation was impossible. As soon as he approached they were ready to take orders, perhaps receive a rebuke as he impatiently waved his arms or pointed at some detail that was not as it should be. He had assumed the habit of inspecting the wagon wheels every morning and evening since they could not afford to lose another one. He tried to evaluate the condition of the oxen, whether any were showing signs of illness or exhaustion. He also checked to see that nothing in the wagonload had disappeared. There were his jars and metal containers of alcohol waiting for insects, his drawing materials and provisions. As yet he hadn't been able to discover if any of the ox-drivers had begun stealing. Each time he made these checks he felt a surge of shame shoot up through his body. What right, really, did he have to mistrust these men, who were the reason that he made progress each day, who pitched his tent and prepared his meals? On several occasions, most often in the evenings, he wrote to Matilda about this. He nearly always used the word *caste*, as if it had become a sacred term in this connection. The caste who decreed, and those who took orders about what had to be done.

The two months they had been travelling through the desert had altered his entire perception of what the purpose of life actually was. He continued to believe resolutely in his idea that an unknown fly, or perhaps a beetle or butterfly, would provide a reason for his whole existence. Yet at the same time the sand, which was hopelessly incomprehensible, had forced him to look back at his life. The wagon rolled slowly onwards behind the oxen. Within him he was always walking backwards, or inwards, towards something, but he knew not what. Clarity? An understanding of what an individual could or should be? Each morning when they struck camp he selected an idea that he would work on for that day. Since he was poorly trained in philosophy, he had to formulate the big questions in his own mind as best he could.

One day he had pondered love, from the early morning until he fell asleep exhausted that evening. He was thirsty because from the beginning they had had to ration the water. To Matilda he wrote in his book that the grace of love was incomprehensible to him. But that the erotic game she had taught him could still fill him with strong desire.

That day the desert had filled him with hate, because there was nowhere he could go to and masturbate. And by evening, when he was alone in his tent, the desire was gone.

One night he was awakened by a strange silence. At first he didn't understand what it was. Then he realised that his father's jaws had stopped grinding. He lit the lamp, looked at his watch and noted the time in his diary. Without knowing it for sure, he was convinced that his father had died. He had been sitting on his chair in the arbour and when the housekeeper crept in to fetch him, his jaws were still and his heart dead. Bengler felt no sorrow, no pain or loss. But he did feel an impatience that was difficult to control. How long would it take before he could get confirmation that it was true? That his father had really stopped grinding his jaws on that very night?

After two weeks in the desert he had caught his first insect. It was Amos who found it. A very small beetle with a greenish-blue shell that was walking slowly through the sand. He identified it in one of the British entomological lexicons that he had brought along. To his astonishment he read that the Bushmen made a lethal poison from the secretion of this beetle. He stuffed it into one of his jars, filled it with alcohol and labelled it. Slowly he had begun to convert his wagon into a museum.

But the journey itself was still what was most important. He had decided that the trading post somewhere ahead of them would serve as the base for his expedition. From there he could organise his hunt for ostriches; from there he could plan, in an entirely different manner, his search for the unknown insect. There would be people he could converse with. He imagined that everything would be there that made a life possible. A hymn book, an old pump organ, ledgers and regular meals. He vaguely hoped that there would also be a woman waiting for him, someone who, like Matilda, might visit him once a week, sit on him and then drink a glass of port.

That had been among the last of his purchases in Cape Town before he said farewell to Wackman: two bottles of Portuguese port.

But the damned maps weren't right. Or else the constantly drifting sand was a landscape that was impossible to map. In vain he had sought along the horizon for a folded mountain range that was supposed to be there, according to the map. But he hadn't found it. He wondered whether there was some mysterious disturbance in the sand that made his compass unreliable. Sometimes he was confused at daybreak, thinking that the sun was rising over the horizon at a point where east had not been the day before. Since he had no one to talk to he started talking aloud to himself. So that the ox-drivers wouldn't think he was losing his mind, he disguised his conversations with himself as religious rituals. He folded his hands, and sometimes he knelt, while out loud he argued with himself about why in hell that mountain range wasn't where it should be. Why neither the landscape nor the maps were correct. During these sham rituals the ox-drivers would always keep their distance. Occasionally he would also remember to scold them for their laziness, for their unwashed bodies, as he knelt there with folded hands.

The days were uneventful. The sun burned with its blinding light from a cloudless sky. The oxen moved sluggishly, as if the sand were a bog. Now and then the silence was broken by the crack of a whip. The ox-drivers might also break out into incomprehensible songs that could last for hours or end abruptly after only a few minutes.

He wondered what they thought of him. How had Wackman managed to convince them to leave their families and follow him into the desert? What prophecy or payment did they think he would be able to give them? Their wages were poor, the food meagre, the water strictly rationed. And yet they followed him towards a goal that he had not succeeded in pointing out on the map. *One day it will come to an end,* he wrote to Matilda. *People can only put up with so much. When they realise that the journey is meaningless they may turn against me. There are four of them and only one of me. I have decided to shoot Amos first if they turn hostile. He seems to be their leader, the strongest one. I'll shoot him with the rifle. Then the important thing is not to miss the other three with my revolver. Every morning and evening I check my weapons to make sure no sand has got into the moving parts.*

He also wondered whether they could read his thoughts. More and more often the ox-drivers would halt the second before he had planned

33

to raise his hand to give the sign that it was time to stop for their midday rest or to pitch camp for the night. He had written to Matilda about this too. About the invisible language that had been created between himself and the four men who shared his existence.

Sometimes he tried to imagine that she could read what he was writing. Would she understand? Would she be interested at all? He felt a vague fear and a pang of jealousy when the only answer he could give himself was an image: the way she sat with her breasts bare and her dress pulled up, on top of some other, unknown man.

On the twenty-eighth day something happened that would have crucial significance for the man from Hovmantorp. (He had started calling himself that in his mind, a designation of a geographical starting point rather than a meaningless name. He felt that the name Bengler no longer existed. He was Hans Hovmantorp, or simply a man who had once run along the stream that flowed through that little, insignificant village in Småland.)

On precisely this day, the twenty-eighth since their departure from Cape Town, a strong wind had passed through during the morning hours. He had been forced to tie a handkerchief around his face and shade his eyes with his hand to keep out the sand. A little before ten o'clock the wind vanished and the silence returned. He had just taken off the handkerchief when the oxen suddenly came to a halt. Amos, who was guiding the leading ox, had made his whip whistle through the air, but the oxen refused to budge. Even after three or four blows on the lead ox's back, none of the animals moved. It was as if they had run into an invisible wall or were standing on the edge of a ravine. He saw that the unexpected behaviour of the oxen made the ox-drivers uneasy. He didn't know how best to intervene. There was no logic to what had happened, nothing in the path of the oxen. And yet they had stopped abruptly. He took the rifle from his shoulder and went over to them. They were standing quite still and he thought he could see fear in their big heavy eyes. But there was nothing on the ground before them: no snake, no crevasse. The sand was flat. There were some rocks sticking up. That was all. He called Amos over and threw his arms out as if to ask why the oxen weren't moving. Amos shook his head, he didn't know. Bengler felt

34

sweat streaming over him. Not the sweat that came from the burning sun, but sweat from his growing uncertainty. It was his responsibility to get the oxen moving. He walked around the animals and the wagon again, pretending to inspect the wheels as he tried to work out a solution. But there was no solution, because the problem was unknown. The oxen had stopped for reasons he could not discern.

By sheer chance he finally found the answer to the riddle. He had walked a few steps to the side, right in front of the lead ox, and kicked a rock that stuck up from the sand, revealing a piece of dark wood. With his foot he moved the sand and to his surprise found that what he was uncovering was part of a bow. He called the ox-drivers over and pointed at the tip of the bow. They immediately began an intense conversation with each other, first seriously, then more relieved, and finally they broke out laughing. Amos and one of the men he privately called the Consonants knelt down and began shovelling away the sand. Soon they uncovered the bow, a quiver, some arrows, braided leather thongs, and finally the skeleton. Now he understood that they had come across a Bushman grave. One evening at the brothel Wackman had told him that the Bushmen would bury their dead anywhere, and they returned to the area only when they could no longer remember exactly where the grave was located. The oxen had stopped because there was a grave in front of them. And they would have stood there until they fell over dead if the grave had not been discovered.

The grave belonged to a woman. Even though only parts of the skeleton remained, he could tell that it was a woman because he knew the difference between a male and a female pelvis. The teeth in the cranium were in very good condition. The seams in the skull's parietal bone indicated that the woman was young when she died. He was struck by a sudden desire to explain all this to the ox-drivers, but since he didn't have any language in which to communicate, he refrained. They dug a hole about fifty metres away, moved the skeleton, and filled it in. The oxen began to move again.

That evening he wrote a long letter to Matilda. *I have discovered that I am a very lonely person. When I stood before the open grave and saw the skeleton of the woman who apparently died very young, it was as if*

I had finally found companionship. The feeling is hard to explain, and I won't hesitate to say that it scares me too. For twenty-eight days I have conversed only with myself. In another twenty-eight days I need to meet a person with whom I can carry on a civilised conversation. Otherwise I'm afraid that it isn't the desert and the heat that will kill me, but my loneliness.

Nineteen days after they first sighted the Bushmen they again saw a group of them moving like black dots along the horizon. The next day the first ox died. They butchered it and camped at the place where it fell. That night they heard the hyenas laughing in the dark.

When he woke in the morning and stepped out of his tent, Neka and one of the Consonants had vanished. They had taken large amounts of meat with them and half of the remaining water. For the first time he succumbed to a fit of rage and fired his revolver. He aimed straight at the sun and fired three times. The oxen grew restless but Amos managed to calm them. To avoid being abandoned in the middle of the desert, he took forceful measures that night. He tied both Amos and the other ox-driver to separate wagon wheels. He did it carefully and was surprised that they let him do it. Several times during the night he woke and dashed out of the tent because he was afraid they had got loose. But the men were sitting by the wheels, fast asleep.

He realised that the desert had already partially vanquished him. Now he no longer followed the maps: they went where the oxen led them. Soon the water and food would be gone. He took inventory and then wrote down a calculation in a letter to Matilda. *The truth is now quite simple. If we don't reach the trading post within ten days the journey will be over. My visit to the Kalahari Desert will then be finished. The question is whether I will have the courage to shoot myself or whether I will end up lying in the sand, being burned to death by the sun.*

Apart from the beetle he had found only two other insects. A millipede that was close to twenty centimetres long, and a moth that lay dead next to the campfire one morning. He had identified both insects in his reference books. He forsaw that his museum would consist of these

36

three jars. Someone who might come across the wagon buried in the sand would wonder who the madman was who had wandered around in this hell collecting insects in glass jars from which the alcohol had long since evaporated.

He counted down the days. When they were three days from the end, when all the food and all the water would be gone, Amos came down with a high fever. For a day and a night they were forced to remain encamped. Amos was delirious, whimpering like a baby, and Bengler was sure that they would soon have the expedition's first burial. But by morning his fever had vanished as quickly as it came.

They pressed on. Just before the midday rest the second ox-driver began waving excitedly and pointing towards a spot that lay west of their route. It took a long time before Bengler managed to understand what the ox-driver had seen. At first it seemed that the sand was only quivering. But then he saw that there was a clump of trees and some houses. He heard a horse whinny in the distance. The oxen replied with dull bellowing.

At that instant he burst into tears. He turned away so that Amos and the other man would not see his weakness.

After a while he pulled himself together, dried off the traces of tears and urged on the oxen. They were now heading in a different direction. For the first time he had a goal.

Long afterwards he would try to recall what he had thought or felt at the moment they discovered the houses and heard the horse whinny. But there was only a vacuum of relief.

A little before three in the afternoon they arrived.

A man stood on the steps of the biggest house, waiting for them. He was missing two fingers on his right hand.

In resounding Swedish he said that his name was Wilhelm Andersson.

For him there was no doubt that Hans Bengler was Swedish.

No one but a Swedish shoemaker could have made leather boots as fine as those he was wearing.

37

CHAPTER 5

Wilhelm Andersson welcomed Bengler warmly. His handshake was so powerful that it felt like he was trying to crush his hand. Then Andersson took off his shirt, turned his back, and asked Bengler to cut open a boil between his shoulder blades that was inaccessible to his own hands. Bengler stared at the distended boil and recalled the time he had fainted in the Anatomy Theatre. He stroked the scar above his eye.

'It's probably best I don't. I can't tolerate the sight of blood.'

'There won't be any blood coming out, just greenish-yellow pus and maybe some worms or maggots.'

Andersson spat on a knife with an ivory handle and handed it to Bengler. His back was covered in odd cracks and swellings. It was as if the desert landscape had carved its presence into his skin.

'I've never lanced a boil before.'

'Stick the point in the middle and press. When it opens, cut downwards. And turn face your away so it doesn't squirt in your eyes.'

Bengler put the knife point against the purple boil, shut his eyes and pressed. Then he squinted quickly and cut downwards. A viscous mess ran down Andersson's back.

'Take this towel here and wipe it off. Then we'll eat.'

Still without looking, Bengler wiped off the mess and dropped the towel on the floor. Blood was trickling out of the incision now. Andersson gave him a piece of white cloth.

'Put this over the cut. It'll stick and stay on. The sweat makes it sticky.'

Bengler kept swallowing and swallowing so he wouldn't vomit. Andersson wriggled into his shirt and buttoned it wrongly so that one edge hung down. He noticed but didn't do anything about it.

Only now did Bengler realise that Andersson gave off a horrible stench. He tried to pull back a step and breathe through his mouth. But at the same time he remembered that he hadn't been anywhere near a bath in almost two months. Water for washing was the first thing he had rationed, only a week after they left Cape Town.

Andersson led him into a room that was filled with animal trophies. The odour of decay and formalin was very strong. In the middle of the room was a hammock, identical to the one Bengler had slept in during the passage on Robertson's schooner. It took a moment before he noticed that a short black man was standing motionless in the corner of the room. At first he thought it was a stuffed animal, but then he realised it was a live human being.

'My only form of homesickness,' said Andersson. 'Or possibly it's a sign of disgust. I've never been able to work out why I brought along a folk costume from Vänersborg and dressed my servant in it.'

This was a situation that Bengler had no background to help him understand. After two months in the desert he had reached a trading post where there was a Swede named Wilhelm Andersson who came from Vänersborg and dressed his valet in a Swedish folk costume.

'I've tried to teach him to dance the polka,' he said. 'But he refuses. They prefer to leap. I've tried to explain that God doesn't approve of leaping people. God is a higher being, higher than me, but we have the same view, that if there is dancing to be done it should take place in regular forms, in 3/4 time or 4/4 time. But they continue to leap and wiggle the most unexpected parts of the body.'

He offered Bengler a whisky and water. Bengler thought of his ox-drivers. Andersson instantly read his thoughts.

'They will be taken care of,' he said. 'They'll get water, food, conversation, be allowed to laugh, and at night there will be women who are warm and open. But you ought to shoot the oxen. You've driven the life out of them. Which brings me to the question: what are you doing here?'

Bengler felt the dizziness come as soon as he sipped the whisky. How can I explain something I can't even explain to myself? he thought. Then, surprisingly even for him, he excused himself by fainting.

When he woke up he was lying in the hammock. The black man in the folk costume was fanning him with something that looked like a piece of oxhide above his head. Somewhere in the distance he could hear Andersson singing a hymn, off-key and vehement, as if he hated the tune. Bengler closed his eyes and thought that in a sense he had now arrived. He had no idea where he was, nor did he have any idea who the strange man was whose boil he had lanced, but he had indeed arrived. He had crept ashore on a strip of beach in this endless sea of sand. I ought to say a prayer, he thought. One that's not as insincere as the hymn I'm hearing now. But who should I pray to? Matilda? She doesn't believe in God. She's afraid of God the same way she's scared of the Devil. She's just as terrified by heaven as by hell.

He didn't say a prayer. He tried to catch the eye of the black man fanning him, but his gaze was far away, above Bengler's head.

He suddenly had the feeling that he was in the very centre of the world. Right in the middle of something that for the first time in his life was completely real. Something that demanded he take a stand, have an opinion, make a choice.

He got no further with his thoughts. He noticed that the real reason why he had woken up was violent nausea. He leaned over the side of his hammock to throw up. The black man stopped fanning and cupped his hands to catch the vomit. Bengler didn't manage to turn away. He sensed a kind of love in the fact that an unknown man in a folk costume from Västergötland accepted his spew in his cupped hands. He knew that his conclusion was wrong, that he would eventually change it, but right now he believed it was love. It was a mercy to be able to throw up into another person's hands.

Exhausted, he sank back on the pillow. The black man wiped his face. Andersson was still out there somewhere bawling his hymn, which seemed to have an unlimited number of verses. Or was he repeating them? Or singing the hymn in different languages? Even though Bengler was very tired, very close to dropping off to sleep, he tried to listen. Then he realised that Andersson wasn't singing the proper text. He was filling the verses of the hymn with his own words. He yelled at some-body named Lukas, who was supposed to have fixed a fence long ago. Then he sang about a raft that he once built on Lake Vänern, but soon returned to cursing Lukas, and Bengler realised that Andersson was either insane or drunk.

And yet he felt utterly safe.

He had survived in spite of everything. He had arrived somewhere.

The magnet had loosened its grip. He had arrived at an unknown point where there were people, a bit of Sweden, something he could recognise.

He woke himself in the dark because he was snoring.

But when he opened his eyes the snoring continued. Andersson was asleep, rolled up in a zebra pelt next to a burning whale-oil lamp. Bengler crept carefully out of his hammock to take a piss. He fumbled his way in the dark towards a door or a curtain, and, without actually noticing how it happened, he found himself outside. In the distance some fires were burning. People were talking in low voices, shadows flickered, a baby cried softly. He shuddered from the sudden cold and the night wind. Then he took a piss. As usual he wrote some numbers with his stream of urine. This time a four and a nine. He finished half of an eight. Then he was done.

When he came in Andersson was awake. He sat wiping off soot from the glass of the whale-oil lamp.

'While you were sleeping I tried to figure out who you were. I went through the load on your wagon. All I found was a number of books and plates of insects and some jars with worms and beetles in them. That was all. It's like having a visit from a travelling insane asylum. Many people have passed through here, but none as crazy as you.'

He left the lamp alone and lit a pipe.

'In your catechism I read that you were from Hovmantorp. I looked on my old map of Sweden, but I couldn't find it. Either you're lying when you write in your notebooks, or Hovmantorp is an unknown place, even though it surprises me that there are still blank spots in a country like Sweden.'

'How long have you been here?'

'That's not a very precise question. Where is here? In the desert? In Africa? Or in this room?'

'In Africa.'

'Nineteen years. It amazes me every day that I'm still alive. It also astonishes all the blacks around me. It astonishes the oxen and the ostriches and perhaps even the wild dogs. But sometimes I think maybe I'm already dead. Without having noticed it.'

He picked up a bottle of beer and took a drink.

41

'If you hadn't lanced that boil I probably would have died. If it gives you any satisfaction, I would gladly say that you came through the desert like a gentle saviour and saved my life.'

'I was supposed to become a physician, but I wasn't good enough.'

'It's common for Europeans who weren't good enough to come to Africa. Here they can assert their skin colour and their god. Don't have to be able to do anything, or want anything. Here you can live well by forcing people into submission. Illiterates from Germany come here and suddenly they're the bosses of a hundred Africans whom they believe they are entitled to treat any way they like. East of this desert the Englishmen are doing the same thing; north of us sit the Portuguese, singing their sentimental songs and whipping the hide off their black workers. We export our skills to America. Those who come to Africa are either revivalist preachers or lazy brutes. And I'm neither a preacher nor a brute.'

'What are you?'

'I have foresight. I make deals.'

'I met a man in Cape Town named Wackman. He spoke of the importance of realising that the piano will create great fortunes in the future.'

'Exactly. For once that man is right. Wackman is a vile person. He slashes the soles of his whores' feet so they'll never forget him. His real passion is small boys with light brown skin. He rubs them with oil. Rumour has it that on one occasion, after having mounted such a lad, he found it so wonderful that he set fire to the boy. The oil made the boy burn very quickly.'

Bengler tried to assess whether Andersson was as cynical as he made out. How deep had the night cold and the loneliness actually penetrated him? Were there only frozen spaces inside, feelings embedded in blocks of ice, the same way that his beetles were drowned in alcohol? Or was there also something else?

'I was searching for another focus in my life,' Andersson said. 'My father was a pharmacist and thought I ought to exhibit the same passion for liniment that he did. But I was born with a hatred of all salves. So I left. Stowed away on a wagon taking Lidköping porcelain to Gothenburg. And from there out into the world. Until I drifted ashore here. I went home one time, to bury my father. I arrived six months after he died,

42

but they had left a hole in the ground so I could toss a little dirt on the coffin. Although I actually gave him desert sand. That was when I brought back the folk costume for Geijer.'

'Is his name Geijer?'

'I've forgotten his real name, but I christened him Geijer. A fine name. A clever fellow who wrote some poems that I still remember. Is he still alive?'

'Erik Gustaf Geijer is dead.'

'Everybody's dead.'

'You're living in the middle of a desert.'

'I hunt. I have the only trading post where the blacks are allowed inside. No Germans come here. They hate me the same way I hate them, because they know that I can see straight through them: their brutality, their fear.'

'You hunt elephants?'

'Nothing else. What were you thinking of putting in your empty glass jars?'

'I'm going to catalogue insects. Systematise and name them.'

'Why?'

'Because it hasn't been done yet.'

Andersson looked at him for a long time before he replied.

'That's an answer I mistrust. Doing something just because it hasn't been done yet.'

'It's the only answer I have.'

Andersson lay down and pulled a cover over himself.

'You can stay here. I need company. Somebody to eat with, someone to lance my boils.'

'I can't pay you much.'

'Company is enough.'

He stayed in the place that Andersson had named New Vänersborg. At the back of the room where he spent his first night there was another room where Andersson stored his elephant tusks. This room was emptied and cleaned, and he moved in. The ox-drivers were dismissed, the animals were slaughtered, and Andersson helped him find new draught animals and ox-drivers, although Bengler had a feeling that Andersson was using them to spy on him. Andersson knew everything he thought, all the plans he had. He also suspected Andersson of reading his diaries and rummaging through his clothing. They ate dinner and talked in the evenings. But now and then Andersson would withdraw with his bottles of beer when a very beautiful black woman came to visit. That's when Bengler would feel a fierce desire for Matilda. He resumed his habit of masturbating two or three times a day.

Sometimes Andersson disappeared and might be away for several weeks at a time. During these periods the place was supervised by Geijer, who never seemed to take off his folk costume. The trading post carried salt, sugar, some grains, simple fabrics and ammunition. No money changed hands, everything was done on the barter system. The black men who showed up like lone ships in all that white came bearing tortoise shells or tusks. He never saw anything else. Then they vanished with their fabrics and their sacks. With Geijer he could hold simple conversations in Swedish. Andersson had taught him the language. For some strange reason Geijer spoke in the Gothenburg dialect. But since his vocabulary was limited and he always seemed to be struck by sadness when he didn't understand what was said, Bengler never entered into very complicated discussions.

Besides, he had his insects. The jars were slowly starting to fill up. But after seven months he had not yet found any insect that he could say with absolute certainty was unknown.

One evening when he had been with Andersson for four months, he found a woman lying on the floor underneath his hammock when he went to bed. She was naked, with only a thin cover over her, and he guessed that she was no more than sixteen years old. He lay down in his hammock and listened to her breathing there below him. That night he slept fitfully and didn't properly fall asleep until dawn. When he opened his eyes she was gone. He asked Andersson who she was.

'I sent her for you. You can't be without a woman any more. You're starting to act strangely.'

'I want to choose a woman myself.'

'She'll stay until you've chosen. And she wants to.'

Andersson's reply made him angry. But he didn't show it.

For another night he slept in the hammock with the woman beneath him on the floor. The third night he lay down by her side, and after that he spent every night on the floor. She was very warm, with a kind of quiet affection that surprised him, because he had never experienced that with Matilda. She was always serious, kept her eyes closed, and only occasionally touched his back with her hands.

She seemed to fall asleep at the same moment he had his orgasm.

Her name was Benikkolua, and he never heard her cry. But she sang almost constantly, when she was cleaning his room, shaking his clothes, and carefully arranging his papers on the desk Andersson had given him.

He wanted her to teach him her language; not just the distinctive clicking sounds. He would point at various objects and she would pronounce the words. He wrote them down and she laughed when he tried to imitate her.

Every night he slipped inside her, and wondered who he actually was. To her. Was he committing an outrage or was she there of her own free will? Was Andersson paying her something that he didn't know about?

He tried to ask Andersson about it. But he kept repeating that she was there because she wanted to be.

Andersson's love life, on the other hand, seemed very complicated. He had a woman in Cape Town who had borne him three children, another family in distant Zanzibar, and several women who at irregular intervals came wandering through the desert to spend one or two nights with him.

All these women were black, of course. On one occasion as they were eating dinner, Andersson suddenly started talking about being in love with a preacher's daughter in Vänersborg when he was very young. But he fell silent as abruptly as he had begun.

The next day he took off into the desert to hunt elephants.

Nine months passed. Then Bengler finally found his insect. It was an insignificant beetle that he could not identify. Because it had short, possibly undeveloped legs he was not even sure that it was a beetle at first. But he was convinced by the time he stuffed it into his jar and screwed on the lid.

He had succeeded. He ought to return to Sweden and enter this new discovery in the scientific registers.

The thought upset him. How could he return? And to what?

He had found the beetle during an expedition that kept him away from New Vänersborg for two weeks.

When he returned he found Andersson inside the shop. A wagonload of salt had arrived.

But there was something else there as well. On the floor stood something that looked like a calf pen. In it lay a boy who stared at him when he leaned forward to take a look.

CHAPTER 6

When he saw the boy in the pen it was like looking at himself. Why, he didn't know. And yet he was sure: the boy who lay there was himself. He cast an enquiring look at Andersson, who was instructing Geijer on how to stack the sacks of salt to avoid the moisture, which in some strange way even reached this remote outpost in the desert.

'What's this here?' Bengler asked.

'I got him in trade for a sack of flour.'

'Why is he lying here?'

'I don't know. He has to be somewhere.'

Bengler felt himself getting upset. Andersson and his damned salt. When a boy was lying on the bottom of a filthy crate.

'Who would trade a live human being for a sack of dead flour?'

'Some relative. His parents are dead. There was apparently a clan war. Or maybe a feud. Maybe it was the Germans who arranged to hunt down some natives. They often do that. The boy has no one. If I had said no to the trade he would have just disappeared in the sand.'

'Does he have a name?'

'Not that I know of. And I don't know what I'm going to do with him either, so he'll have to stay here. Just like you. A temporary visitor who ends up staying.'

Bengler realised at that instant what he had to do. He didn't need any time to think it over. Now he had found his beetle, he would return to Sweden. The dream of insects no longer excited him, but the boy lying there in the crate, or animal pen, was real.

'I'll adopt him. I'll take him with me.'

For the first time since the conversation began, Andersson was interested. He set down a sack of salt on the planks and looked at Bengler with distaste.

'What did you say?'

'You heard me. I'll adopt him.'

47

'And?'

'There isn't any "and". There's only the future. I'm going home. I'm taking him with me.'

'Why would you do that?'

'I can give him a life there. Here he will perish. Just as you said.'

Andersson spat. Instantly Geijer was there, wiping it up with a rag. Bengler recalled with shame how he had once let himself vomit into Geijer's hands.

'What sort of life do you think you can give him?'

'Something better than this.'

'You think he'll survive? A journey by sea? The cold in Sweden? The snow and the wind and all the taciturn people? You're not only crazy, you're conceited too. Have you found that insect yet?'

Bengler showed him his jar. 'A beetle. With peculiar legs. It hasn't been named.'

'You're going to kill the boy.'

'On the contrary. Tell me how much you want for him.'

Andersson smiled. 'A promise. That some day you come back and tell me what happened to him.'

Bengler nodded. He promised, without thinking it over.

'I'll keep the crate,' said Andersson. 'You can have the vermin free.'

He motioned to Geijer to lift the boy out of the pen. He was very small. Bengler guessed that he was eight or nine years old. He squatted down in front of him. When he smiled the boy closed his eyes, as if he wanted to make himself invisible. Bengler decided to give the boy a name. That was the most important thing of all. A person without a name did not exist. He thought first of his own last name. What would go with it?

'You can call him Lazarus,' suggested Andersson, who had read his thoughts again. 'Wasn't he the one who was raised from the dead? Or why not Barabbas? Then he can hang by your side on the cross you nail together for him.'

Bengler felt like killing Andersson. If he were strong enough. But Andersson would only shake him off like an insect.

'You don't think Barabbas is a good suggestion?'

Bengler could feel himself sweating. 'Barabbas was a thief. We're talking about giving an abandoned child a name.'

'What does he know about what's written in the Bible?'

'One day he will know. Then how will I explain why I named him after a thief?'

Andersson burst out laughing. 'I believe you mean what you say. That you'll take the boy across the sea and that he'll survive. To think that I've had such a damned idiot under my roof.'

'I'll be leaving soon.'

Andersson threw out his arms as if in a gesture of peace.

'Perhaps I could call him David,' said Bengler.

Andersson frowned. 'I don't remember him. What did he do?'

'He fought Goliath.'

Andersson nodded.

'Might be suitable. Because he will have to fight against a Goliath.'

'Joseph,' Andersson said suddenly. 'The one who was cast out. Joseph is a fine name.'

Bengler shook his head. His father's middle name was Joseph.

'No good.'

'Why not?'

'It brings back unpleasant memories,' Bengler replied hesitantly.

Andersson didn't ask why.

While they were speaking the boy stood motionless. Bengler realised that he was waiting for something terrible to happen. He expected to be beaten, maybe killed.

'Did he see what happened to his parents?'

Andersson shrugged his shoulders. He had returned to the salt. Geijer was balancing at the top of a ladder.

'It's possible. I didn't ask much. Why ask about something like that when it's better not to know? I've seen the way the Germans hunt these people the way you hunt rats.'

Bengler placed his hand on the boy's head. His body was tense. He still had his eyes shut.

At that moment Bengler knew.

The boy would be called Daniel. Daniel who had sat in the lions' den. That was a fitting name.

'Daniel,' Bengler said. 'Daniel Bengler. It sounds like a Jew. But since you're black you can't be a Jew. Now you have a name.'

'He's crawling with lice. And besides, he's undernourished. Fatten him up and wash him. Otherwise he'll be dead before you even get to Cape Town. Before he even knows that he's been given a Christian name.'

That night Bengler burned the boy's clothes. He scrubbed him in a wooden tub and put one of his shirts on him that reached to his ankles. Benikkolua was always close by. She had wanted to wash the boy but Bengler wanted to do it himself. That way the boy's mute fear might subside. So far he hadn't said a single word. His mouth was closed tight. Even when Bengler wanted to give him food he refused to open it. He thinks that his life will fly away if he opens his lips, Bengler thought.

He asked Benikkolua to try. But the boy still wouldn't open his mouth.

Andersson stood aside and watched it all.

'Take a pair of pliers and prise it open,' he said. 'I don't understand this coddling. If you want to save his life you can't treat him with kid gloves.'

Bengler didn't reply. It would be a relief to get away from Andersson. In spite of all the help he had received, Bengler realised that he hadn't liked him right from their very first meeting, when he was forced to poke a hole in the boil on his back. He thought that Andersson was no different from the Germans or the Portuguese or the Englishmen who tormented the blacks and hunted them like rats. Except that Andersson exercised his brutality with discretion. What difference was there between clapping a person in irons and dressing someone up in a ridiculous Swedish folk costume? He thought that he ought to tell Andersson all this, to show him, in parting, that he saw right through him. But he knew that he lacked the courage. Andersson was too strong for him. Compared to him, Bengler belonged to an insignificant caste that would never have power over the desert.

That night Benikkolua had to sleep outside the door. Bengler left the boy alone on the mattress with the plate of food by his side. Then he put out the lamp and lay down in his hammock. Unlike Benikkolua, whose breathing he could always hear, the boy was silent. A sudden apprehension made him get up. He lit the lamp. The boy was awake, but his jaws were still clamped tightly shut. Bengler placed a beam across the door and returned to his hammock.

*   *   *

In the morning when he woke the boy had eaten all the food. Now he was asleep. His mouth was slightly open.

Three days later Bengler made his last preparations before leaving. He had loaded and lashed down his possessions on the wagon. The boy had still not said a single word. He sat mute on the floor or in the shade with his eyes closed. Bengler stroked his head now and then. His body was very tense.

Bengler had tried to explain to Benikkolua that he had to leave. Whether she understood or not he couldn't tell. How could he explain what an ocean was? Like expanses of sand but made out of rainwater? What was a distance, really? How far away was Sweden anyway? He realised that he would miss her, even though he didn't know a thing about her. Her body, he knew, but not who she was.

He spent his last evening with Andersson. They ate ostrich meat boiled in a herbal stock. Andersson had brought out a pot of wine. As if to indicate that it was an important day, he had put on a clean shirt. The while time that Bengler stayed at the trading post he had never seen Andersson wash, but he had grown used to the stench and didn't notice it any more. Andersson soon got drunk. Bengler drank cautiously. He was afraid of having a hangover the next day when he set off across the desert.

'I just might miss your company,' Andersson said. 'But I know that sooner or later some other Swedish madman will come marching this way. With yet another meaningless task to perform.'

'My task has not been meaningless. Besides, I've acquired a son.'

'The hell you've acquired a son. You're going to kill that boy. Maybe he'll survive the boat trip. But then? What are you going to do then?'

'I'll see to it that he has a good life.'

'How are you going to do that? Are you going to pin him down the way people pin down insects? Are you going to paste him into one of your volumes of prints?'

Bengler wanted to counter these shameless accusations, but he didn't know how. Andersson was still too strong for him. It was their last evening, and these accusations or insults would never be repeated, they would merely fall lifeless when his wagon rolled away. Yet he would have liked to have resised him more firmly.

'Your life is not merely peculiar,' he said. 'Above all, it's miserable. You pretend to oppose what is going on in this desert. This hunting down of people who have done nothing but live in this place. You pretend to be upset, pretend to love your fellow man, pretend to be a good person. But from what I've seen you're just as rotten as all the other whites here. Except for one person: myself.

'I very seldom whip my Negroes. I don't pinch them with tongs, don't box their ears, don't teach them the catechism. I do keep order, it's true. But I don't rip them up by the roots so they'll fall dead in the snow of Sweden. I ask you a very simple question: which is worse?'

'I'll prove you're wrong.'

'You have given me your promise. To come back. And tell me.'

They ate the rest of the dinner in silence. Andersson was soon so drunk that his gaze began to wander beyond the light from the whale-oil lamp. It struck Bengler that he resembled a confused insect at night, searching for a point of light that should not have been there.

That night, as his last note to Matilda, he wrote: *Tomorrow I set off. Andersson fluttered like a moth around the lamp. I don't know if he is an evil man. But he is a foolish man. He refuses to see through his own actions. Because I drank two glasses of wine I began to fantasise that he was actually an insect that I had pinned down on a sheet of white paper.*

He still hadn't made a single note about Daniel. He had decided to wait until they left. When the trading post disappeared behind them he would begin to write about him.

Daniel was sleeping on the rug. His mouth was still shut tight. Bengler wondered what he was dreaming about.

Despite the fact that he was tipsy and had also had to drag Andersson to bed, he managed to have one last moment of love with Benikkolua that night. He had stumbled out of the room where the ivory was once stored and tripped over her where she lay on her raffia mat. As usual she was naked under her thin cover. He was surprised that she never seemed to be chilly in the cold desert night.

In the morning he woke very early. The sun had not yet risen. Daniel was asleep. Bengler went silently out of the door. Benikkolua was gone. She had taken her raffia mat with her. But she had hung up the thin cover on a projecting edge of the roof. It waved like a farewell to him, Benikkolua's flag. It brought tears to his eyes and he thought it was as crazy for him to leave as it had once been to come here.

He had just as many questions, and just as few answers.

He was sure of one thing. The responsibility he had assumed for the boy lying in Andersson's pen was something he did not intend to regret. What he wasn't able to give himself perhaps he could give to someone else.

Bengler waited until Daniel woke up, then he smiled, put his best shirt on him and carried him outside. When Daniel caught sight of the wagon with the oxen hitched up, he suddenly began to shriek and flail about. Bengler held him tight, but the boy was like a wildcat. When he sank his teeth into Bengler's nose he had to let him go. The boy ran straight out into the desert. Bengler followed him with blood running down his face.

For an instant he thought he would have to hit him, but when he caught the boy the thought was already gone. He was still howling and flailing his arms but this time Bengler didn't let go, and dragged him back to the wagon. He tied him down with the baggage, just as he had once bound Amos and the other ox-driver to the wagon wheels. The boy pulled and tore at the rope, and his screams cut through Bengler like knives, but he couldn't change his mind now.

Andersson had come out onto the steps and was watching the commotion.

'I see you're leaving,' he shouted. 'A quiet departure. I just don't understand why you have to torment the boy. What has he done to you?'

Bengler rushed towards Andersson. Now he had no more fear.

'I intend to save him from you.'

53

Then he threw himself on Andersson. They rolled about in the sand. Andersson had met the attack with a roar. Around them stood black people silently watching the white men fighting like madmen.

Then it was over. Andersson knocked Bengler to the ground with a punch to the stomach. It took several minutes before he caught his breath.

'Leave now. But come back and tell me how the boy died.'

Andersson turned and went into the house. In the wagon the boy continued screaming and tearing at the rope. Bengler wiped the blood off his face and called to the ox-drivers.

The black men stood silent.

For a moment Bengler thought he had made a mistake.

But he quickly dispensed with the thought.

The boy didn't stop crying until late in the afternoon. He fell completely silent suddenly, without warning, and closed his eyes with his mouth shut tight.

Will I ever understand what he's thinking? Walking beside the wagon, Bengler watched him for a long time. Then he loosened the rope. The boy didn't move. He knows that I wish him only the best, thought Bengler. It will take time. But already he is beginning to understand.

When they reached Cape Town a few weeks later, Bengler heard that Wackman was dead. He had had a stroke at his brothel, which had now been taken over by a man from Belgium.

Daniel had stopped shrieking. He didn't speak and never smiled, but he ate the food Bengler gave him. Yet Bengler was still uncertain whether he might try to escape again, so he always tied him up at night and kept the end of the rope wound around his own wrist.

In early July they boarded a French freighter, a barque, that was bound for Le Havre. The captain, whose name was Michaux, promised that there would be no difficulty in finding a ship there to take them to Sweden. The money that Bengler got for the wagon and the oxen paid for their passage.

* * *

Late in the evening of 7 July 1877, they set sail from Cape Town. Bengler was afraid that Daniel would throw himself overboard, the way the slaves used to do, so he made sure he was tied up when they were standing by the railing.

Daniel kept his eyes closed.

Bengler wondered what he was seeing behind those eyelids of his.

CHAPTER 7

The ship was called the *Chansonette* and had come most recently from Goa on the Indian peninsula. Steamy aromas of mysterious spices that Bengler had never smelled before wafted up from the holds. When he took a promenade on deck he discovered some strange iron fittings screwed into the planks. At first he couldn't identify them other than as vague images from his memory. Then he remembered that he had once seen them in a comprehensive English book of plates that illustrated in detail the instruments and tools with which slaves were held captive during the journey to the West Indies. So he found himself on a former slave ship. It aroused a violent discomfort in him. The scrubbed deck was suddenly filled with blood that smelled stronger than the spices loaded in sacks and barrels down in the holds. He looked at Daniel, whom he was leading on a rope. So that Daniel wouldn't tear himself loose in one of the quick and always unexpected lunges he made at irregular intervals, Bengler had designed a harness for him. He had explained to the captain that Daniel was his adopted son and was going with him to Europe. Michaux hadn't asked any questions or shown the least sign of curiosity. Bengler asked him to inform the crew that Daniel's unpredictable moods made it necessary to keep him in a harness: it was a safety measure, not a display of cruelty. Michaux called over one of his mates, a Dutchman named Jean, and asked him to tell the crew.

They had been given a cabin near the stern, right next to the captain's quarters. After attempting to break free in a violent fit of desperation, Daniel had sunk into apathy. To calm him, Bengler had strewn a thin layer of sand on the floor. He had tried to explain that the ship was big and safe. The sea was no monster, the slight motion of the hull nothing more than the same motion that Daniel must have felt when he was carried around on his mother's back.

* * *

A young ship's boy, barely fifteen years old, had been assigned by Michaux to take care of the five passengers on board. Along on the journey were an elderly bachelor who had terrible smallpox scars on his face, and a very young lady who immediately became the object of the crew's lustful glances. Except for the fact that the man's name was Stephen Hartlefield, Bengler knew nothing about him or to what he had devoted his life. Captain Michaux had brusquely informed Bengler that the pockmarked man was an Englishman with cancer in his belly, and he was going home to Devonshire to die.

'He came to Africa when he was two years old,' said Michaux. 'Yet he still talks about travelling home to die in a country that he has no memory of. Englishmen are very strange creatures.'

The young lady, whose name was Sara Dubois, had been visiting one of her sisters who lived on a big farm outside Cape Town. She belonged to a well-to-do merchant family from Rouen and had a chambermaid with her.

The cabin boy's name was Raul. He was freckled, cross-eyed and alert. Bengler noticed that Daniel watched him for a moment, and caught his eye.

Raul asked why Daniel was being restrained.

'Otherwise he might jump overboard,' Bengler answered, feeling despondent about his reply. Something made him feel ashamed that he had to keep a fellow human being tied up. A human being that he regarded as his son.

'Will he always be tied up?' Raul asked.

Instead of replying, Bengler called over one of the mates and complained about the cabin boy's nosy curiosity. The mate boxed him twice on the ears.

Raul didn't cry, even though the blows were very hard.

They left Cape Town in the evening. Heavy rain clouds swept in over Tafelberg. Bengler had decided to keep Daniel in the cabin as they pulled away from land and not let him out until they were on the high seas. The sea was very calm that night and slow swells bore the ship away from the African continent. Daniel slept in the hammock. Bengler had tied the rope to one of the ceiling beams. Even though it was a low ceiling, Daniel wouldn't be able to reach the beam and untie it. Bengler had also checked that there were no sharp objects in the cabin that he could use to cut himself loose.

When Bengler placed a blanket over Daniel he discovered that in one hand, which was clenched tightly, he held some sand that he had picked up off the floor.

That first evening Bengler began to sew a sailor's costume for Daniel. He had procured the cloth from a nautical outfitter recommended by Michaux. Since he had spent all his money on the passage, he bartered for the cloth with the revolver he had bought in Copenhagen. It had also sufficed for buttons, needle and thread. He borrowed scissors from the sailmaker on board. He spread out the cloth on the table in the cabin and then pondered for a long time over how he could actually make a pair of trousers and a sailor's blouse. It took a while before he dared begin cutting. He had never before in his life made anything like this. The work proceeded slowly, and he pricked himself with the scissors and the needle that he used to sew together the various pieces. Late that night, as he crept up into his hammock next to Daniel, he hid the scissors in a cavity between two timbers up in the ceiling.

Before he went to sleep he lay still and listened to Daniel's breathing. It was irregular and restless. He felt Daniel's forehead but could detect no sign of fever. He's dreaming, he thought. Some day he'll be able to tell me what he was thinking when we left Cape Town.

The odours from the holds were very strong. In the distance he could hear some of the sailors laughing. Then it was quiet again apart from occasional footsteps on deck and the ship creaking against the swells.

The journey to Le Havre took a little over a month. They went through two storms and were becalmed for six days in between them. The African continent could be glimpsed now and then like an evasive mirage in the east. The heat was relentless. The captain was worried about his cargo of spices and several times went below deck to check that nothing was getting damp.

*   *   *

On the very first day Bengler had decided that Daniel needed a routine. After eating the breakfast that Raul brought in to them, they began taking walks on deck. The man from Devonshire seldom appeared. According to Raul he was in severe pain and ate almost nothing but strong medicines, which left him constantly in a trance-like state. The merchant's daughter from Rouen played badminton with her chamber-maid when the weather permitted. Bengler noticed that the ship then seemed to breathe in a different way. The crew devoutly hoped that the girls' skirts would blow up and expose a leg or perhaps a bit of their undergarments. During their walks, Bengler talked to Daniel constantly. He pointed and explained and alternated speaking German and Swedish. Slowly he thought he could feel the tension in Daniel begin to relax. He was still somewhere else, with parents who were still alive, far away from Andersson's pen and the ship that rose and fell, but he's getting closer, Bengler thought. The further away from Africa, the closer to me.

Bengler realised that he had to show Daniel that the harness was a temporary solution for what he hoped would be an equally temporary problem. The rope situation could only be solved by a growing trust. On the second day aboard, Bengler left the scissors he had borrowed from the sailmaker on the table and let Daniel stay alone in the cabin. He waited outside the closed door, ready for Daniel to cut the rope and then rush out of the door to try to cast himself into the sea.

After half an hour nothing had happened.

When Bengler went into the cabin the scissors lay on the table. Daniel was sitting on the floor drawing with his finger in the sand that still covered the floorboards. Bengler decided to take the harness off the boy. The feeling that he had committed an injustice filled him once again with discomfort. But he also experienced something that could only be vanity. He didn't want to admit that Wilhelm Andersson was right. That he should not have taken the boy with him. He didn't want to have his good intentions questioned, even if only by a man he would never meet again. A man who lived in the midst of far-reaching hypocrisy at a remote trading post in the Kalahari Desert.

*   *   *

59

Bengler went out on deck. The *Chansonette* was sailing in a light wind. The sails were full. He remembered how it had been when he came to Africa on Robertson's black schooner, when he had felt masts and sails inside himself. He stood by the railing and looked down at the water. The sails flapped like birds' wings above his head, a play of sunshine and shadow.

For the first time he seriously asked himself the question: what would he actually do when he got back to Sweden? The beetle with the peculiar legs lay in its jar. And he had Daniel too. In two big leather trunks he had 340 different insects he had collected, prepared and arranged according to Linnaeus's system. But the question remained unanswered. The thought of returning to Lund was not only repugnant to him, it was impossible. It was tempting to see Matilda again. But it also frightened him, because he was convinced that she had already forgotten him, forgotten their hours of lovemaking, which were never passionate, and the port wine afterwards. He didn't even know if she was still alive. Maybe she had wound up under Professor Enander's scalpel too. He didn't know, and he realised that he didn't want to know.

The only thing he knew for sure would be waiting for him was the obligatory trip to Hovmantorp to confirm that his father had really died the same night he had the premonition. But then what?

He sought the answer in the sea foaming in the wake of the *Chansonette*.

A seaman had silently stepped up next to him. He scratched out his pipe, spat, and stared at Bengler. The skin on his face was like leather, his nose was wide, his mouth dry with cracked lips and his eyes squinted.

'What do you want that damned boy for?' asked the sailor.

He spoke Norwegian. Bengler had once been friends with a young man from Røros who studied theology in Lund. He had been amused by the language and had learned to imitate it.

He thought he ought to ignore the question, which largely came from the squinty eyes and not out of the cracked lips.

'Are you going to kill the boy?'

Bengler considered complaining to the captain. As a paying passenger he shouldn't have to associate with the crew except on his own terms.

'I can't see that it's any of your business.'

The sailor's eyes were steady. Bengler got the feeling that he was facing a reptile that might strike him at any time. Just as Daniel had sunk his teeth into his nose.

'I can't bear it,' said the sailor. 'Africa is a continent from hell. There we make our whips whistle, we cut off the ears and hands of people who don't work at the pace we determine. And now we're starting to drag home their children even though slavery is forbidden.'

Bengler grew angry.

'He has no parents. I'm looking after him. What's so bad about helping a person survive?'

'Is that why you have him on a lead like a dog? Have you taught him to bark?'

Bengler moved off down the railing. For a brief moment he felt dizzy. The sun was suddenly very strong. He wished he had his revolver. Then he would have shot the damned Norwegian. The sailor was still standing there, his eyes squinting. He had on a striped jumper, trousers cut off just below the knees, and shoes with gaping holes in them.

'The times are changing,' said the sailor, moving closer.

'You have no right to bother me like this.'

'Let me guess: you bought him. Maybe to exhibit him at the variety show? Or in marketplaces? A Hottentot. Maybe you're intending to make him puff himself up like an ape. Could be money in that.'

Bengler was at a loss for words. He thought the sailor must be a revolutionary, a rock-thrower, an iconoclast. Maybe he belonged to that new movement they had discussed during the late nights in Lund. An anarchist? Someone who didn't throw bombs but flung words at him with the same power?

The sailor lit his pipe.

'One day people like you won't exist,' he said. 'People have to be free. Not tied up like lap dogs.'

During the rest of the journey to Le Havre Bengler did not exchange another word with the sailor. He found out that his name was Christiansen and was regarded by most as a competent and friendly man. He also had the virtue of never imbibing strong drink. This information was gathered by Raul, who Bengler had soon learned was a reliable reporter.

When he took the harness off Daniel he imagined that there would be a reaction of joy, of liberation. But Daniel's only response was immediately to crawl up into the hammock and go to sleep. As always he had some grains of sand gripped in his fist. Bengler was puzzled. If he saw himself in Daniel, how would he decipher the fact that the boy was sleeping?

A great pain has left him, he thought. It's natural to rest when an affliction is over, be it a toothache, colic or headache. That's what he's doing, sleeping it off now that the pain has left him.

Two days before they docked at Le Havre, the man with cancer who was going to Devonshire died. Since the captain was worried about his spices and they were becalmed that day, a burial at sea was arranged. Bengler was very depressed when he thought that the man would never return home. During the funeral itself he locked Daniel in the cabin.

Besides their regular promenades, Bengler had given Daniel instruction every day. There were two subjects. First, he had to learn Swedish if possible. Second, he had to learn to wear shoes. Initially Daniel was amused by the shoes, but after a while he grew tired of them. On one occasion he flung one of the simple wooden shoes over the railing. Bengler was angry but managed to control himself. He had been given another pair of small worn-out shoes by a carpenter, and he started again. Daniel showed no interest whatsoever, but he did not throw the shoes overboard.

With the language, on the other hand, no progress was made at all. Bengler realised that Daniel simply refused to take in the words. And he could find no way to counter his refusal.

When they docked at Le Havre on a foggy morning in early August, Bengler felt a growing unrest inside. Why in hell had he let his impulses get the better of him and dragged this boy along?

At first he had been afraid that the boy would jump overboard. Now he was afraid that he would throw the boy overboard himself.

*   *   *

62

The last thing he saw when he went ashore was the sailor squinting at him. His look was as cold as the fog.

In the middle of August Bengler and Daniel boarded a coal lighter heading for Simrishamn. Bengler was granted passage if he helped with various tasks on board. The ship was dilapidated and smelled foul. For the entire trip Bengler worried that they would never arrive.

On 2 September the vessel docked at Simrishamn. By then Bengler had been away from Sweden for almost a year and a half.

When he stepped ashore he realised that the fear he felt was shared by Daniel.

They had grown closer to each other.

CHAPTER 8

The day they landed a strange thing happened. For Bengler it was a sign. For the first time he seriously thought he had deciphered something from all the unclear and often contradictory signals that Daniel sent out.

From the dock they had walked straight across the muddy harbour square and into a little inn located in one of the alleyways leading down to the water. The innkeeper, who was drunk, had looked in consternation at Daniel, who was standing at Bengler's side. Could it be a little black-coloured monster that had hopped out of his delirious brain? But the man standing next to the boy spoke in a refined manner. Even though he had arrived from Cape Town, he didn't seem to be infected with any tropical disease that might prove worrisome. The man gave them a room facing the courtyard. The room was very dark and cramped. It smelled of mould, and Bengler searched his memory; somewhere he had smelled exactly this same smell. Then he recalled that it was the coat worn by an itinerant Jewish liniment pedlar he had met during his last visit to Hovmantorp. He opened the window to air out the room. It was early autumn, just after a heavy rain, and there was a wet smell from the courtyard. Daniel sat motionless on a chair in his sailor suit. He had kicked off the wooden shoes.

Bengler poured himself a glass of port to muster his courage for the future and to celebrate the fact that the coal lighter had not sunk during the voyage from Le Havre. In the courtyard children could be heard shrieking and laughing. He was sitting on the creaky bed with the glass in his hand when Daniel suddenly stood up and went over to the window. Bengler started to move from the bed because he was afraid the boy might jump out, but Daniel walked very slowly, almost stalking as if on the hunt, cautiously approaching a quarry. He stopped by the window, half hidden behind the curtain, to watch what was happening in the courtyard. He stood utterly motionless. Bengler cautiously got up and stood next to him.

Down in the courtyard two girls were skipping. They were about the same age as Daniel. One of the girls was fat, the other very thin. They had a rope, possibly a line from a small sailing boat which they had cut off to a suitable length. They took turns jumping, laughing when they stumbled, and then starting over again. For a long time Daniel stood quite still, as if turned to stone. Bengler watched him and tried to interpret his attentive observation of the game in the courtyard.

Then Daniel turned to him, looked him straight in the eye, and his face broke into a grin.

That was the first time Bengler saw his adopted son smile. It was not a broad, pasted-on mask, but a smile that came from within. For Bengler it was as though a long-awaited miracle had finally occurred. At last Daniel had severed the invisible line that bound him to the pen at Andersson's trading post. A line that bound him to memories which Bengler knew nothing about, except that they contained blood, terror, dead bodies, chopped-up body parts, desperate screams, and then a silence in which all that was heard was the sand rustling in the desert.

They went down to the courtyard. The girls stopped skipping when they caught sight of Daniel. Bengler realised that they had never seen a black person before. He knew that there was a brand of shoe polish whose lid was decorated with a black man with a broad grin and thick lips, but now these young girls were looking at a real live black person. Here in this dirty courtyard Bengler discovered something that might be a new task for him. To show the unenlightened Swedes that people actually existed who were black. Living people, not just decorated lids on tins.

He began talking to the girls. They were poorly dressed and their constant jumping had made them smell strongly of sweat. He asked their names and had a hard time understanding what they said. One of them was named Anna, the thin one, and the fat one was called Elin or possibly Elina. Bengler explained that the boy next to him was named Daniel and that he had just landed in Simrishamn from a faraway desert in Africa.

'What's he doing here?' asked the girl called Anna.

Bengler was at a loss for words. To this simple question, he had no answer.

'He's on a temporary visit to Sweden,' he said finally.

He wasn't sure if the girls really understood what he said because of his thick Småland dialect.

'Why does he have such curly hair? Did he have it curled?' It was still the girl called Anna who was asking.

'It's naturally curly,' Bengler replied.

'Can we touch it?'

Bengler looked at Daniel. He was still smiling, so Bengler nodded. The girls came forward warily and touched Daniel's head. Bengler was constantly on guard, as if he were watching a dog that without warning might turn hostile and bite. But Daniel continued to smile. When the fat girl who was maybe named Elin put her hand on his head, he stretched out his hand and carefully stroked her mousy-coloured hair. She gave a shriek and jumped away. Daniel kept smiling.

'He wants to watch while you skip,' said Bengler. 'Won't you show him?'

The girls skipped. When the fat girl stumbled Daniel started to laugh. It was a lusty laugh that came from deep inside, a dammed-up volcano that had finally found its release.

'Can he skip?'

Bengler nodded at Daniel and pointed at the rope. Without hesitation Daniel took it in his hands. He jumped very lightly, did double hops and turned the rope backwards and forwards at a rapid tempo. Bengler was astonished. He had never imagined that Daniel could skip. The experience filled him with shame. Had he really believed that Daniel could master nothing but silence and introversion? Had he regarded him more as an animal than a human being?

'He doesn't even get sweaty,' shrieked the fat girl.

Daniel kept on skipping. He never seemed to tire. Bengler had a feeling that Daniel wasn't really hopping up and down, but that he was on his way somewhere, as if he were actually running.

He's back in the desert, thought Bengler. That's where he is. Not here, in a filthy back courtyard in Simrishamn.

When the game was over, Daniel wasn't even out of breath. He put down the rope and took Bengler's hand. That was something that hadn't happened before either. Before it was always Bengler who took his hand. Something has happened, Bengler thought. From now on something will be different between us. But what has changed, I don't know.

That evening, after Daniel had fallen asleep, Bengler started a new diary. He decided to call it 'Daniel's Book' and printed the title carefully on the cover. From a nearby inn he could hear a tremendous racket of bellowing voices and a screeching fiddle. Daniel was asleep. Through the thin walls Bengler could hear a couple making love in the room next door. He tried to shut out the sounds, but they were loud and he started to feel excited. He tried to imagine the bodies, the man grunting and the woman squealing, picturing himself in there with Matilda or Benikkolua. After he had printed the title he took off his trousers and masturbated. He tried to follow the rhythm from the creaking bed and came at the same time as the squealing and grunting reached a crescendo.

Then he began to write. The book was going to be a study of the encounter between Daniel and Europe. The starting point was a distant desert and a dirty courtyard where a black boy was skipping with two girls.

What is a human being exactly? Bengler wrote at the top of the first page. That question could not be answered. God was inscrutable, He was a mystery, in the same way the Holy Scriptures were labyrinths and riddles that concealed more riddles. The only answer that existed was that which could be proven, which could be deduced from observations.

The example of Daniel, he continued. *Today, 2 September 1877, I have seen a black boy from the desert playing with two girls in a back courtyard in the town of Simrishamn. From this point a journey begins, perhaps it can be called an expedition, which deals with Daniel and his meeting with a specific country in Europe.*

That night Bengler slept peacefully. In his dreams the bed moved as if he were still on board a ship. Occasionally he woke up and opened his eyes. In the light autumn night he could see Daniel's face quite clearly against the white sheet. He was sleeping. His breathing was calm. Just before three o'clock Bengler got up and sat next to Daniel and took his pulse.

It was regular, fifty-five beats per minute.

*   *   *

After a difficult and bumpy journey they arrived in Lund two days later. During the trip Bengler had been struck several times by acute diarrhoea. His stomach had always been the most sensitive organ in his body. At the slightest sign of anxiety it rebelled. He remembered this from when he was very small: from the fear of certain teachers at Växjö Cathedral School to his years at the university in Lund. Without explanation, these stomach cramps had almost entirely vanished during his time in the desert. But now that he was approaching Lund the pain and cramping were coming back. Daniel sat next to the cart driver and a few times was allowed to hold the reins. Sometimes he ran alongside the cart, sometimes in front of the horses. Bengler realised that something decisive had happened to Daniel since he had skipped in the back courtyard in Simrishamn.

He still didn't speak, but now he had a smile on his face, a smile that came from very far away, and Bengler believed that he would understand soon enough what sort of miracle had played out in that back courtyard. Even if there was a rational explanation, if Daniel was simply happy to meet some children his own age, Bengler suspected that the boy's reaction was based on something alien. Something which he did not as yet understand.

Just before they reached Lund it began to rain. A heavy thunderstorm was passing through. They stopped at a dilapidated inn and took shelter from the weather. People gaped at Daniel, as usual, but he didn't seem to notice. Not even when a drunk farmhand came up and stood there staring at him.

'What the hell is this?' he asked. 'What the hell is this?'

The farmhand stank of dirt and aquavit. His eyes were red.

'His name is Daniel,' replied Bengler. 'He's a foreigner on a visit to our country.'

The farmhand kept staring.

'What the hell is this?' he repeated.

Daniel looked at him and then continued drinking the glass of water in front of him.

'Is it some kind of animal?'

'He's a human being from a desert in Africa called the Kalahari.'

'What's he doing here?'

68

'He's on the way to Lund in my company.'

The farmhand kept on staring. Then he placed his rough hand very lightly and carefully on Daniel's head.

'I've never seen anything like it,' he said. 'I've seen dwarfs and giant women and Siamese twins at fairs. But not this.'

'He's here so that we can look at him,' said Bengler. 'Human beings are made in different forms. But they're all the same inside.'

An hour later, just before five in the afternoon, the thunderstorm moved on. They continued into the city. The farmer, who had let them ride along for free, dropped them off near the cathedral. Bengler had no more than a few copper coins in his pocket. He had left his baggage in Simrishamn as a guarantee that he would return and pay the bill. He took Daniel with him into the grove of trees by the cathedral. Since the ground was wet he spread out his coat for them to sit on.

'What we need now is money,' he said to Daniel. 'The first thing we need is money.'

Daniel listened. He seemed preoccupied, but Bengler suspected that he must have begun to understand a few words.

'Before I travelled to the desert I learned many things from a professor of botany named Alfred Herrnander,' he went on. 'He was a good man, an old man. I'm considering asking him for a loan. We can only hope that he's still alive.'

Bengler had visited Herrnander once at his home north of the cathedral. They went there now. People passing by stopped and turned round.

'Everyone who sees you will remember you,' Bengler said. 'They will tell their families tonight about what they saw. You're already famous. Merely by walking down the street you've become a well-known person. You will be the object of curiosity, suspicion and, unfortunately, also some ill will. People are afraid of what's foreign to them. And you are foreign, Daniel.'

They stopped outside the low grey house. When the door was opened by a serving woman with a limp, Bengler prayed that Herrnander was still alive.

He was.

But the year before he had had a stroke, the serving woman told him.

69

'He's not seeing visitors. He just lies there drumming his fingers on the blankets.'

'Does he grind his jaws?' Bengler asked.

The serving woman shook her head.

'Why should he do that?'

'I don't know. It was only a question. But please go in and tell him that Hans Bengler is out here on the street. In his company he has a boy from the San people, nomads who live in the Kalahari Desert.'

'Am I supposed to remember all that? All those strange words?'

'Please try.'

'Wait just a minute.'

She closed the door. Daniel jumped. Bengler thought that a door being slammed might remind him of a gunshot.

Then she was back with a pen and paper. Bengler wrote everything down. She did not invite them in.

'The boy has oversensitive ears,' said Bengler. 'I would appreciate it if you would not slam the door so hard when you close it.'

They waited. By the time the door opened again, Bengler had begun to lose hope.

'He will see you. But he can't speak; with great effort he can write a few words on a slate.'

'If he can listen that will be sufficient.'

Herrnander lay on a sofa of dark red plush in his study. The curtains were drawn and the room was low-ceilinged, cramped and stuffy. There were bookshelves up to the ceiling, full of etchings and manuscripts. Herrnander looked like a bird under the covers. On a table next to the sofa stood water and a brown bottle of medicine. It took a while before he noticed that they had come into the room. He slowly turned his head; his eyes scanned Bengler's face and then stopped at Daniel's. The serving woman who had followed them into the room stood guard by the door. Bengler made an effort to be firm and motioned for her to leave, which she reluctantly did. But she left the door ajar, so Bengler went and closed it. Then he stuffed his handkerchief in the keyhole and returned to the sofa. In order not to tire Herrnander, he summed up his journey in as few words as possible. The whole time Herrnander was gazing at Daniel's face.

*   *   *

How could he convince Herrnander that it would be a good idea to give him a temporary loan so that he could get on with reporting his insect finds? He would write a scholarly article about the beetle and he would dedicate it to his mentor and teacher. But in order to be able to do this, he needed a small loan. A loan that could equally be regarded as an investment in the progress of science. Of course the loan would be paid back. Papers would be drawn up, signatures notarised. Everything would be done properly. He really needed this loan. And besides, there was the boy to consider. He had a person with him from a distant land: a person who was his responsibility, a celebrity to display.

When Bengler finished speaking his piece there was a long silence. He wondered whether Herrnander had understood anything he had said. Carefully he repeated the words: small loan. No great amount. For science and the boy.

One of Herrnander's hands dropped to the edge of the sofa. Bengler thought it was a gesture of great weariness. But then he saw that a finger was beckoning. Herrnander was pointing at a portfolio that lay on the floor. Bengler lifted it up. With infinitely slow movements Herrnander opened it and pulled out a wad of notes. When Bengler asked if the money was for him, Herrnander nodded. Bengler started talking again about the importance of written agreements and signatures, but Herrnander struck the portfolio so that it fell to the floor. Bengler could see his irritation. He didn't want any papers drawn up and signed. Next to the pillow he had his slate. He pulled it over and slowly scrawled one word. Bengler read it. *Why*. Nothing more. No question mark, just the single word *why*. Bengler was sure that the question had nothing to do with the money. This *why* was about Daniel. Bengler told him briefly what had happened before he found Daniel in Andersson's pen. But Herrnander shook his head impatiently. His 'why' was still unanswered.

He wonders why I brought him here, Bengler thought. There was no other explanation. He told him about the need to show mercy, the simple Christian message not to refuse a fellow human being who was in trouble. But these words seemed to annoy Herrnander even more.

Bengler abandoned the Christian argument and shifted to science. He wanted to make a study of Daniel and at the same time observe how Swedes reacted to their meeting with this foreigner.

Herrnander groaned. Slowly he crossed out the word *why* and replaced it with another one. Bengler read it: *crazy*. When he started to speak again Herrnander closed his eyes.

The conversation was over. Bengler felt insulted. What entitled this old man, with one foot in the grave, to criticise him? He stuffed the money in his pocket, took the handkerchief out of the keyhole and opened the door.

The serving woman came towards them from an adjacent room.

'You stayed far too long,' she said impatiently. 'Now he'll be restless all night.'

'I promise we won't come back,' was Bengler's friendly reply. 'We have completed our business.'

When they were out on the street Bengler took a deep breath and looked at Daniel.

'Now we have the most important thing a person can have,' he said. 'Capital. You don't know what that is. But one day you'll understand.'

Daniel could see that Bengler was calmer now. His eyes no longer flicked back and forth.

He stroked Daniel's hair.

'Tonight we're going to live the way we deserve. We'll eat an excellent dinner. And we'll stay at the Grand Hotel.'

He stretched out his arm to point in the direction they were headed.

'I knew it the whole time,' he said and laughed. 'I'm born to be a commander. Even if my army consists only of you.'

Daniel didn't understand the words. But he felt that the most important thing was that the man walking in front of him no longer seemed worried.

CHAPTER 9

They took a corner room on the third floor. The man in the lobby had regarded Daniel with displeasure, but he hadn't asked any questions. The room had thick curtains and smelled strongly of tobacco smoke. Daniel recoiled when he stepped over the threshold. Bengler thought it felt like stepping into a musty crypt. He was secretly ashamed that Daniel would have to sleep in this heavy smoke. He pulled back the curtains and opened the window. Daniel came over and stood next to him. He was afraid when he saw how high above the ground they were. Bengler realised that for Daniel there was probably no connection between the stairs they had climbed and how high the room was: for Daniel a staircase was a hill going up, not something that left the ground far below them.

'Tonight we shall sleep here,' Bengler explained.

He pointed at the bed. Daniel went over to it and lay down.

'Not yet,' Bengler said. 'First I have to give you a wash. Then we'll go down to the dining room and eat dinner.'

Bengler gestured to Daniel to get undressed. He took off his clothes too and hung up the worn suit on a clothes hanger. Daniel was very thin. Just below his right nipple he had a scar that shone white against his black skin. Bengler looked at his member. It was still undeveloped, but very long. On an impulse he couldn't resist, he touched it. Daniel at once did the same to him and Bengler gave a start. Daniel gave him a worried look. Bengler thought it was like having a puppy for a companion. He poured water into the washbasin and told Daniel to sit down on the bed and watch how a person washed properly. Bengler placed a towel on the floor and washed himself carefully. He reminded himself of how he had been washed as a child and concluded by scrubbing his buttocks with a brush. Daniel watched him intently. Bengler felt like a heavy and shapeless animal standing naked in front of the basin. When he had dried himself he rang a bell. It took a few minutes

73

before there was a knock on the door. A girl in a starched apron stood there and curtsied. She gave a start when she saw Daniel and quickly looked away. Bengler gave her the empty water pitcher and asked for some more hot water. He wrapped Daniel in the bedspread. When the girl came back with the hot water he gave Daniel the brush and sat down on the edge of the bed. Daniel washed himself. To Bengler's astonishment the boy had memorised in detail how he had washed himself. First the right leg, then the left arm, armpit, belly and then the left leg. Daniel repeated the movements.

'You learn very fast,' said Bengler. 'You've already mastered the art of staying clean.'

When they had dressed they went downstairs to the dining room. It hadn't changed since the last time Bengler was there. The kerosene lamps shone, on the tables stood candelabra, and Bengler felt a sense of anticipation: would there be anyone here he knew? They were greeted at the door by the maître d', who regarded Daniel with an astonished expression. He had a Danish accent. Bengler looked around the dining room. On this autumn evening the patrons were sparse: lone bachelors hunched over their bottles of arrack punch; a few small groups. Bengler asked for a window table. As they walked between the tables all conversation stopped. Bengler suddenly felt that he ought to tap a glass and give a brief speech about his trip through the Kalahari Desert, but he refrained. They sat down at the table.

'He's short,' said Bengler. 'Give him a cushion to sit on.'

The maître d' bowed and motioned for a waiter. Bengler didn't recognise him and wondered where all the waiters who were there before had gone. After all, he had only been away for a little over a year. Daniel was given a velvet cushion to sit on. Bengler studied the menu, shocked at how much the prices had gone up, and then ordered pork chops, wine, water for Daniel and orange mousse for dessert.

'Would the gentlemen care for an aperitif?'

The waiter was old and rheumatic and had bad breath.

'A shot and a beer,' replied Bengler. 'The boy won't have anything.'

When Bengler had received his shot of aquavit and tossed it back, he at once ordered another. The liquor warmed him and inspired a restless need to get seriously drunk. Daniel sat motionless across the

74

table and followed him with his eyes. Bengler raised his glass and said 'Skål' to him.

At that moment he noticed that a man had got up from a table next to the wall and was on his way over to them. As he approached, Bengler saw that it was an old perpetual student they called the Loop. He had been in Lund as long as Bengler had attended the university. Once in the late 1860s he had tried to hang himself outside the cathedral. But the rope, or maybe it was the branch, had broken and he survived. One of his cervical vertebrae had been damaged, which crooked his head rigidly to the left, as if his soul had been given a list that could never be righted. He stopped at their table. Bengler could see that he was extremely drunk. The Loop owed everyone money. When he arrived in Lund from Halmstad in the late 1840s, rumour had it that he was living on an inheritance. The first few years he had attended lectures in the theological faculty, but something had happened that led to the tree and the broken branch. It was intimated that it was the usual matter, an unhappy love affair. But no one knew with certainty. Since that day, the Loop had lived in a wretched garret on the outskirts of Lund. He broke off his studies and didn't read anything any more, not even the newspapers. He was always borrowing money, could tell a good story from time to time, but for the most part sat hunched over his glass and his bottles and held mumbling conversations with himself. Sometimes he would wave his arms about as if he were bothered by insects, and then sit in silence until the last patron was thrown out. Now he was standing by their table.

'There's been talk of an expedition to a faraway desert,' he said. 'And one never expected to see the explorer return. Now here he sits as though nothing had happened. He has a black creature sitting across the table. A boy who looks like a shadow.'

'His name is Daniel,' replied Bengler. 'We're only passing through.'

'So one's studies shall not be resumed?'

'No.'

'I don't wish to intrude,' the Loop went on. 'But the explorer, whose name has unfortunately slipped my mind, might possibly see his way clear to a small loan of a tenner.'

Bengler felt in his pocket and pulled out two ten-kronor notes. It was too much but the Loop had recognised him. The notes vanished in the Loop's hand, though he didn't bother to see how much he had got. Nor did he bother to say thank you.

'Everything is the same here,' he said. 'Maître d's come and go, as do the waiters. The students grow younger and younger, the weather worse and worse, and the knowledge that is taught is more and more difficult to respect.'

He expected no reply so turned and made his way back to his table.

By the time the orange mousse was set on the table Bengler was quite tipsy. He waved the maître d' over.

'Is it possible that the hotel could provide someone to watch the boy for a while?' He pointed at Daniel. 'I'm thinking of spending a few hours in the smoking room. It's not a suitable environment for a child.'

The maître d' promised to enquire at the front desk. Daniel had finished all his food. During the long passage from Cape Town, Bengler had taught him to use a knife and fork. He could see that Daniel had to make an effort to do as he had been taught, but he didn't spill anything or cram the food into his mouth. The maître d' returned.

'They think it would be possible to have one of the chambermaids watch him.'

Bengler paid the bill and stood up. He took a step sideways. Daniel smiled. He thinks I'm playing, thought Bengler. An intoxicated person is someone who's playing, nothing more. They left the dining room. The Loop had disappeared. Conversations stopped again as they passed various tables. Once more Bengler got the feeling that he ought to say something. But what would he say? What could he actually explain? Or did he somehow feel a need to excuse himself for breaking an invisible rule of etiquette by bringing a black boy into a public dining room?

It turned out that the girl who was sent to look after Daniel was the same girl who had brought the hot water earlier.

'All you have to do is stay here,' said Bengler. 'You don't have to talk or play with him. Just stay here. What's your name?'

'Charlotta.'

'Just see that he doesn't open the window,' Bengler went on. 'Or go out of the door. I'll be down in the smoking room.'

Daniel seemed to understand what he said. He sat on the edge of the bed and looked at Bengler.

The room beyond the dining room was just as he remembered it. The tobacco smoke that hovered like a motionless fog, the sweet smell of arrack punch, the dim light from the kerosene lamps. He stood in the doorway and looked around. It was as if he recognised all the faces even though the people there were strangers to him. A chair right next to one of the windows was free. He went over to it. The thought of punch didn't appeal to him so he ordered cognac. For the first time in ages he felt free. Daniel was a burden. He had taken it on himself, but still the boy was a burden. Had he ever thought about what a responsibility he had shouldered? The cognac muddled his thoughts. All he knew was that he had to take Daniel with him to Hovmantorp. Then he would present his desert finds and, based on that, attempt to find a way to make a living. What that would involve he had no idea. He could travel around and give lectures. But who would be interested in insects? He ordered another glass of cognac. In one of the darkest corners of the room two women sat drinking with some students. Suddenly he saw Matilda before him. A powerful desire filled him, now he had returned. Matilda must be nearby, if she was still alive, if she hadn't left for Denmark or Hamburg. One of the women on the sofa got up. She was not beautiful; her face was ravaged. She disappeared through the draperies. Bengler followed her. She was standing in front of a mirror and straightening her hat.

She smiled when he stopped next to her. For sale, he thought. She wasn't in Lund when I left. Now she's here, she's come from somewhere and she's for sale. The same way Matilda had come from Landskrona after her father violated her.

'I'm looking for a woman,' said Bengler.

She smiled but with her lips pressed together. Bengler knew what that meant: she had bad teeth. Or perhaps she had syphilis, which could be seen on the tongue.

'I'm already engaged,' she said. 'But some other evening. Gentlemen are so unpredictable. The one sitting in there wants to marry me. But what he'll want to do tomorrow, nobody knows.'

'Her name is Matilda,' said Bengler. 'Matilda Andersson. She used to keep me company. Then I left on a long voyage. Now I've come back.'

The woman at the mirror continued straightening her hat. Bengler looked at her breasts under the tight-fitting blouse. He could feel his excitement growing.

'Matilda is a common name. Just as common as mine, Carolina. Describe her for me.'

Bengler didn't know what to say. He could describe her naked body, the shape of her breasts and thighs, but how had she dressed? He tried to remember. But he saw her only without clothes.

'I can't,' he said. 'She had blue eyes, brown hair. Maybe it was naturally curly, maybe she had it curled. She smelled sour.'

The woman was finished with her hat. She moved close to him.

'What do I smell like?'

'Like liquorice root.'

'Forget her. Tomorrow I can keep you company.'

She gave his face a quick caress. He couldn't help grabbing her breast. She laughed, twisted away and then vanished back through the draperies. Bengler walked through the lobby and out in to the street. It was warmer now after the downpour.

Somewhere he heard a horse whinnying. He looked up at the corner room where Daniel had probably fallen asleep by now. The desire for a woman was very strong. He thought about Benikkolua. Why couldn't he have taken her along as well as Daniel? The thought of the woman in front of the mirror suddenly made him sick. In the cool autumn evening he began to hate this town. If it hadn't been for the money he would never have come back. Matilda wasn't even a memory, only a mirage, just like there in the desert. What had been was no more. Now it was only him and Daniel and the cognac, which made him feel like he was standing on the heaving deck of a ship again.

He went back inside, paid for his drinks, and heard the women laughing in the dark when he left through the draperies. I'm a person who's doing a lot of different things for the last time, he thought. I will never come back to this room.

When he came upstairs to the corner room the chambermaid was asleep in a chair. Daniel was also sleeping. The girl jumped when Bengler

78

touched her shoulder. Once more he felt desire flare up. How old could she be? Sixteen or seventeen, hardly more. She was very pale.

'I'll pay you,' he said. 'Did he go over to the window?'

'He sat on the edge of the bed playing with his fingers.'

'Is that all?'

'Then he played with his feet.'

'And then?'

'Then he went to bed. He never looked at me.'

'He seldom looks at people,' said Bengler. 'On the other hand, he does sometimes look straight through people who cross his path.'

Bengler had taken out a riksdaler coin. That was too much. Without really wanting to, he took a note out of his pocket.

'There will be more money to be made,' he said. 'If you're nice to me.'

She understood and jumped up. She ought to slap me, Bengler thought. Instead she blushed.

'I have to go,' she said. 'You don't have to pay me for this. I didn't do anything. Just sat here.'

Bengler grabbed her arm. She tensed up.

'I have to be careful,' he said.

She started to cry. Shame crashed furiously over Bengler. What in hell am I doing? he thought. I'm trying to buy this girl who doesn't even know what love is, knows nothing besides cleaning, curtsying and being pleasant.

'I didn't mean any harm,' he muttered. 'Take the coin.'

But the girl fled and he was left standing with the coin in his hand. His shame was raging. He went over to the window and looked down at the street. The students were leaving with their women. He watched the woman with the hat and thought: I have to get out of here. His old life was gone. He had left it behind in the desert. Now he had his insects and Daniel.

He undressed and sat down in the chair where the chambermaid had been sitting. Without inviting it, the feeling of arousal returned. Matilda was gone, just like Benikkolua. Only the woman with her lips pressed together was left. Daniel was asleep. He sat down at the desk. The kerosene lamp burned with a low flame. He turned it up and then took out 'Daniel's Book'. But the words wouldn't come. Instead he drew something, and at first he didn't know what it was. Then he realised that he was trying to depict the wagon and the oxen when the wheel broke and he had been forced to take charge. He drew poorly; the wheel was oval, the wagon sunken in, the oxen looked like sway-backed cows and the ox-drivers only thin lines. He closed the book, turned off the lamp and crept into bed next to Daniel. In the morning we have to be off, he thought. The money I have will get us to Hovmantorp and then on to Stockholm. Beyond that I can't imagine what will happen.

He turned his head and looked at Daniel lying curled up with his back to him. His breathing was very calm. Bengler carefully pressed two fingers to his carotid artery and counted silently to himself.

Fifty-one. Daniel's pulse was very regular. And he still wasn't in the deepest sleep: then his pulse would be between forty-five and fifty.

Bengler closed his eyes. The woman who was inside him pressed her lips together. Slowly he returned to the desert. The sun burned in his dreams.

Daniel lay wide awake at his side. When he was sure that Bengler was asleep he got up and carefully opened the notebook lying next to the kerosene lamp. The drawing depicted nothing. It was like an unfinished petroglyph on a rock wall.

PART II

THE ANTELOPE

CHAPTER 10

The one who had taught him about the dreams was Be. They coiled like tracks through people; the paths were not footprints they trod in the desert, but something that was inside them, in the spaces where only the gods had access. Be was his mother; her smile still burned inside him, even though the last thing he remembered was the blood that ran from her eyes and the scream that was abruptly cut off.

The boy named Molo lay awake by the side of the man whose eyes were always shifting. He was no longer afraid of him, afraid that he might have a spear hidden somewhere behind his back, like the ones who killed Be and Kiko. Besides, this evening he had been funny, almost tempting him to laugh. They had been sitting in the big room eating and he had drunk something that made his feet move the way they did when they were on the ship. He didn't know what was in the bottles, but he stored it in his memory. In this peculiar country where the sun never seemed to go down, the rolling waves of the sea were kept in bottles. He had memorised the labels in his head for the day when he would be able to go back across the water and return to the desert.

He lay quite still in the bed. The man next to him hadn't begun to snore yet. He still lay on his side. It wasn't until he turned over on his back that he started snoring. Molo listened in the darkness. Someone laughed down on the street. Shoes clacked on the paving stones. He thought about all the sounds he was forced to house in his head. In the desert people's footsteps were never heard. The wind might whine, but footsteps were always silent. They could hear voices at great distances and the antelope bucks bellowing with what Be called rut, which meant that they were looking for females to mate with. Molo thought about the shoes he was forced to learn to use on board the ship. Big and heavy, made of wood. His feet had cried in the shoes, curled inward like animals that would soon die, and he wondered why he wasn't allowed to go barefoot as he had always done. His feet didn't want to

83

have shoes, and the shoes didn't want to have his feet. That's why he had flung one of them into the sea, to placate his feet and himself and to show that he didn't need to have anything on his feet to be able to walk. He didn't want to shuffle along, didn't want to lose the joy of walking. But he had made a mistake. That was the first time the man who was still not snoring had got angry. A line had appeared on his forehead right above his eyebrows. His eyes grew narrow and Molo thought the man was going to hit him, maybe throw him overboard. But nothing happened except that the next day he got new shoes that were even heavier. Then he thought of something that Kiko had told him, about the slave caravans he had once seen when he was young at the far northern end of the desert. Hiding behind a rock, he had seen a white man whipping people who were chained together, all black, driving them towards the coast. When he came back he told Be about it. Much later, when Molo was born, he was told the story too. The memory had returned when he was forced to wear the shoes that made him heavy and lose the desire to move.

Molo got up from the bed and walked carefully over to the door. He had drunk a lot of water at dinner. Now he had to pee. In the desert you could pee anywhere, just not in the fire or anywhere Kiko was flaying an animal or Be was preparing food. But here it was different. On the ship he had stood by the railing. The man next to him had always held on to him. Molo had wondered if he was stupid enough to think that he would jump overboard. When they came ashore, peeing became a big problem, not to mention when he had to relieve himself of heavier things. There were special rooms with small wooden boxes where he was supposed to sit. He hadn't seen any box like that here in this house. He had learned that you had to pee when no one was watching and that you should pee in such a way that all traces disappeared instantly. He stood naked in the middle of the room and looked around. There was a potted palm on the table. He stuck his finger in the pot and sniffed. The dirt was wet and smelled of rain.

If he peed there it would surely run over the edge and the man would be angry when he woke up. The white pitcher that had water in it earlier was empty. He could pee there. But the pee would still be there the next day. If he tried to pee out of the window the man

84

who was sleeping would wake up and think he had turned into a bird. He went carefully over to the door and opened it. There was a kerosene lamp on the wall in the corridor. He closed the door behind him without a sound. That was something else he had learned. Doors were supposed to be opened so they were heard but closed without a sound. The corridor was empty and all the doors were shut. He walked carefully along the soft carpet. It was like walking in sand, he thought. Behind a door he heard a woman crying. It sounded like Be when she had given birth to a dead baby, the last one she bore before the man with the spear came and killed her. He stopped and peed on the carpet. The fabric would soak up the urine, the same way sand did. Then one of the doors suddenly opened. A man without a shirt and a big paunch that hid his sex came out. He had a bottle in his hand. He gave a start when he caught sight of Molo. Then he started to yell. Molo tried to stop peeing but he wasn't finished. Other doors opened; a man came running up the steps. Everyone stared at him. He still couldn't break off the stream. He wondered what was so strange. Didn't children pee in this country? Then he heard a door open behind him. It was the sleeping man who had woken up. He finished peeing.

'What the hell are you doing?' asked the man excitedly. 'Are you pissing on the hotel's carpet?'

Molo didn't understand what he said, just that he had made another mistake. The fabric under his feet wasn't like the sand. The man grabbed hold of his arm so hard that it hurt, and dragged him back into the room. He sat him down on the bed. Molo understood that he wasn't allowed to move. The man went back out of the door. Molo could see that the man gave money to someone who came running up the stairs. Molo thought that the best thing he could do now was to get in between the sheets and pretend to be asleep.

The man came in and closed the door silently. But Molo knew that he was angry and shut his eyes tight. He felt the man's breath close to his face. It smelled sweet. Molo knew without opening his eyes that the man was thinking about hitting him. His breath grew more sour, more dangerous. Molo tensed. But nothing happened.

'Damned kid,' muttered the man.

Molo didn't understand the words. Sometimes he thought that the language the man spoke was like the sound of an axe splitting old dried wood. Sometimes it sounded like Kiko hitting a rock with a tree branch to see if there were any hollows in it where snakes could hide.

The man crept into bed and sighed. Molo waited until his breathing grew calm. Soon the man would start to snore. Molo opened his eyes again. He was tired. He didn't know what awaited him in the morning. But Be had taught him about the dreams. They were not only hiding places, they could also predict what was going to happen. Molo searched among the images streaming through his head. He stopped when Kiko appeared before him.

It had been the last time he was allowed to accompany Kiko to the rocks that stuck up out of the sand and looked like a resting lion. He knew that the hills were sacred. A long time ago the gods had lived among these rocks. They had lit their fires and sat there, and one evening after they had eaten their fill and were in a good mood, they had decided to create a new kind of animal, which would later be called a human being. Kiko had told the story very precisely and kept asking if Molo had understood. He had repeated the same thing several times, talked about the gods in different ways, as if he were a bird who saw everything from above, or a snake who silently coiled around their legs. Molo had understood. It was among these rocks that everything had begun. Gradually the gods had tired of the humans, let them take care of themselves, and left for other hills. But so that the gods would not become impatient and take their food from them, or the rain, the humans had carved their images into the rocks.

Kiko had been working on an antelope the last time they went to the hill together. Anamet, the old man who had died the year before, had started carving the antelope, but when he withdrew, slowly isolating himself from life, and finally stopped breathing, Kiko was chosen to continue. He was not as talented as Anamet, nor would he ever be. Anamet had had a special ability to depict animals so that at any moment they might tear themselves loose from the rocks and vanish among the sand dunes. Kiko had coloured the animal's body this last time. The antelope was in the middle of a leap. Anamet had made the eye very large, and Kiko worried for a long time about whether to make it red from the colour of a crushed beetle or to make it yellow with the sap from a bush that grew near the hill. Kiko could be taciturn sometimes when he was working on the antelope. He was the least talkative in the entire group of seven families who lived and travelled together. In contrast to Be, who was always talking and laughing, Kiko could be silent so long that they wondered if he had been taken ill. Molo also knew that it was only wise to ask Kiko questions occasionally. Sometimes he would answer, but if Molo chose the wrong time, Kiko might grow tired, maybe even angry. But this last time they went to the hill together Kiko had been in a good mood. Molo knew that it would be a good day, when he could ask all the questions he wanted.

They set off early at daybreak. When they reached the hill and the crevice in the rocks where the antelope was carved, the sun had just begun to pour in. It looked like the antelope was on fire.

'Anamet was very skilled,' said Kiko. 'He not only knew how the hands should shape the antelope, he also thought about which spot on the rock he should choose.'

'What does it mean to be skilled?' asked Molo.

Kiko didn't answer. Molo knew that this was an answer too. If Kiko said nothing it meant that the question had no answer.

Kiko decided that the antelope's eye should be red. In a little leather pouch he had brought along some of the beetles that made the colour. He poured them onto the ground and the beetles tried to crawl off. He crushed them with a rock and began to squeeze out the colour in the shell. With a twig he then carefully filled in the incisions that Anamet had carved with his little chisel. Molo watched his father. The rays of the sun were slowly rising. The light was coming from below. The antelope's eye glistened.

'Where are the gods?'

Kiko laughed.

'Inside the rock,' he replied. 'Their voices are the heart that beats in the antelope's body.'

'I try to draw in the sand. Antelopes, zebras. But they aren't any good.'

'You're too impatient. You're only a child. The moment will come some day when you only see in one direction at a time. Then you'll be able to make an antelope too.'

Kiko worked all day. Not until it began to get dark did he put down the red-coloured twig.

'It'll be done soon,' he said. 'One day when you're older the colours will have disappeared. Then you can come here and fill them in again. It will be your turn to make the antelope come alive.'

They returned to the camp. From a distance they saw the fires and smelled the meat cooking. The day before, the hunters had managed to kill a zebra and now they had meat for several days. That's why Kiko had time to devote to the antelope.

'Tomorrow we'll continue,' said Kiko. 'And the next day too. Then the food will be gone and we'll have to hunt again.'

But did they ever go back to the hill? Molo lay with his eyes open next to the man who still hadn't started snoring. He could no longer remember.

He had been asleep when the men with the spears and rifles came. They had horses and white helmets, though not all the men had white skin, some were black. They surrounded the camp during the night and when the women woke up in the morning the shooting and slaughtering had begun. Molo had been drenched with blood and looked as though he was already dead. Through half-closed eyelids, with his heart pumping in his body as if he were in wild flight, he saw Be impaled by a spear and Kiko shot through the head.

The men who attacked them had laughed the whole time; they had acted like they were out hunting animals. And when everything was silent and everyone was dead except Molo, they drank from their bottles, cut off a few ears, and then rode away until they were swallowed up by the sand and the sun.

Molo had no memory of what happened next. When he woke to life again he was lying on boards of a shaking wagon. Andersson was leaning over him, and Molo thought that he must be dead and that it was Evil himself who was looking down at him.

He gave a start. For a brief moment he was in a landscape that was somewhere between dream and reality. Then he noticed that the man next to him had started to snore. Molo turned over on his side. He was tired now. The meeting with Kiko and the dream about the antelope had been exhausting. He curled up and fell asleep after he finally managed to change his insides to a white and completely empty desert.

* * *

In the morning when Bengler woke he had a headache and was very thirsty. He recalled what had happened the night before and decided not to discuss it with Daniel for the moment. But there was something else he knew couldn't wait. Daniel had already got up and dressed. He was sitting still on a chair by the wall. Bengler drank some water and then leaned back against the pillows. He made a sign to Daniel to come and sit next to him.

'You are my son,' said Bengler. 'Your name is Daniel and I am your father. And that's what you will call me from now on: Father.'

Daniel looked at him.

'Father. That's what you must call me. Father.'

'Faather.'

'Don't draw out the letter "a". It should be short. Father.'

'Faather.'

'You're still drawing out the "a". One more time. Father.'

'Father.'

'That sounds better. I am your father. So that's what you have to call me. We two are Father and Daniel.'

'Faather and Daniel.'

'You're having a hard time with the letter "a", but it will get better. Now you can go back to the chair.'

Molo didn't move. Bengler pointed at the chair. Molo got up. When he sat down on the chair he knew that his name would be Daniel from now on.

Then the man he had to call Father lay down and watched him with only one eye open.

'This damned town,' he said.

Daniel nodded. He didn't understand the words, but he knew Father didn't like something. Daniel was always on guard when Father started chopping with his mouth like an axe against dry wood. Was he talking about him or to him? He never knew for sure.

This morning it was taking a long time for Father to get out of bed. Daniel sat on his chair and waited. After they ate breakfast Father took him into town. It was warm and Daniel carried the shoes in his hand so he could walk more easily. They stopped outside a house quite near to the hotel. There were pictures of people in a window.

They stared straight at Daniel. Father opened the door. A bell rang. Inside it was dark, just like at Andersson's trading post or on board the ship. White people live in dimly lit rooms, Daniel thought. Everywhere there were doors that had to be opened or closed, walls to keep people from seeing, ceilings that hung heavy as blocks of stone over people's heads.

They entered a room where a lone chair and a table stood in front of a grey wall with painted flowers on it. Father sat down in the chair and placed Daniel next to him. The man who greeted them disappeared underneath a black cloth that hung on the back of something that looked like a cannon. Daniel had seen one of those once, the year before Kiko and Be and the others were killed. They had travelled through the desert and seen white soldiers dragging these weapons behind oxen. Daniel cast a glance at Father. Were they about to die? Father sensed his apprehension.

'We're only going to be photographed,' he said.

Father smiled and said something to the man under the cloth, who laughed. We're not going to die, thought Daniel. I'll have to put up with all this while I wait for an opportunity to return home. I'll think about the antelope that could break loose at any time from the rock face and become prey that we could kill and eat. I'll wait until I can take the same leap as the antelope. Or see wings grow from my back.

There was a flash of lightning. Daniel crouched down but Father just smiled. For an instant Daniel was afraid that Father could read his thoughts, but he had already got up from his chair and was busy talking to the man who had hidden underneath the cloth and fired the shot that didn't hit them.

Late that afternoon they went back to the shop. They stopped outside the window. Daniel saw his own face inside. It was staring right into the muzzle of the cannon.

I don't recognise myself, he thought. My eyes are those of another person. The man who hid under the cloth fired a shot at me that reminded me of when Kiko had his head blown to bits.

I'm dead too.

I just haven't noticed it yet.

CHAPTER 11

It took some time for Daniel to understand that the terrible land they had come to was the place on earth where Father had been born. After they left the town where the cannon was aimed at his face, they travelled through endless forests for weeks. Father had bought a horse and wagon, but Daniel realised very soon that he didn't know how to handle the horse, which mostly did whatever it wanted to do. It rained almost the whole way. The wagon was open and Daniel lay underneath something that was like sailcloth along with the boxes where Father kept his insects, his books and his instruments. Father caught a fever and a bad cough from all the rain. For about ten days they had to stay in a town called Växjö, where Father was put to bed and sweated hard in a house called an *inn*. Daniel bathed his forehead and gave him water. On several occasions he was convinced that Father was going to die. A medicine man in a dark coat visited him and watched Daniel with great curiosity. He gave Father a bottle that he was supposed to drink from when the cough grew too severe. Every time he visited Father he ordered Daniel to take off all his clothes. Then he squeezed his body, looked in his mouth, counted his teeth and cut off a piece of his hair.

During this time Daniel made friends with the horse. If Father died, the horse would be all he had.

While Father was sick a strange thing happened. When Father was delirious from the fever, Daniel understood what he said for the first time. Before, he could only identify certain words in the language, but now he understood whole sentences. It was as if he could look into Father's troubled dreams, and only then did the words take on meaning.

He still had a hard time understanding the new name he had been given. *Daniel*. His real name was Molo. But no one, neither Andersson nor Father, had bothered to ask. They had simply given him the long name Daniel, which meant nothing and which he could pronounce only with great difficulty.

The other word he was quite sure of was the word *damn*.

It could be pronounced quietly or in a yell, snarling or with great anger. Daniel understood that it was a holy word for Father, a word that meant he was talking with some of his gods. Since the horse was the most important thing for Daniel, he gave him the name *Damn*. He would stroke him on the muzzle when he gave him hay and whisper *Damn* in his ear.

Father did not die. Eighteen days after they left Lund the fever began to abate. He stopped raving and sank into a deep sleep. Daniel waited. He gave hay to the horse and got soup from the woman who ran the house where they were living. Often people came, some of them very drunk, to look at the boy as he sat watching over the sick man. They would stand in the doorway, breathing heavily as if he made them excited, and then go away.

After eleven days had passed they could resume their journey. By then it had finally stopped raining. Once again, Father's words became incomprehensible to Daniel. The clarity he had experienced when Father was delirious had evaporated.

The horse pulled the wagon into an almost impenetrable forest. The road was very narrow, they encountered no one, and Daniel looked around incessantly because he was afraid that the forest would swallow up the road behind them. When he wasn't sitting on the driver's seat next to Father he walked alongside the wagon. He had made a skipping rope from a rope he had found in the stable at the inn. Occasionally Father would start to sing, but he stopped when he began to cough. Sometimes Daniel would venture a few metres into the thick trees. He studied the ground carefully before he dared set down his feet. He suspected that the snakes in this country were very poisonous.

They stayed overnight in leaky barns and lived on dry bread and dried meat. They found water to drink in streams that ran next to the road. Daniel was always searching for signs that there was sand somewhere. Since they had travelled so far, surely they would have to come back to the desert soon. From Kiko he had learned that a long journey always ended at the point where it began. But he found no sand, only brown earth that was full of grey stones.

* * *

Late one afternoon, what Daniel had been waiting for finally happened: the forest opened up. The landscape brightened. Father pulled on the reins. Daniel watched his face. It was as if Father was airing out. He perked up, his eyes searched. Then he turned to Daniel.

'My desert,' he said. 'This is where I was born.'

He didn't think that Daniel had understood what he said. He handed him the reins and shaped a baby in the air and rocked it. Then he pointed to himself.

Daniel looked around. A green meadow stretched before him with a broken-down, crooked gate.

Then he saw the house. A whitewashed wall was visible behind a clump of tall trees. Father pointed at the gate and Daniel hopped down and opened it for the horse. When he tried to close it the gate fell off the rotten post. Father didn't seem to care, and Daniel hopped up on the wagon again. They stopped in the courtyard. Father sat still on the driver's seat. Daniel noticed that he was holding his breath. Then the door opened and a woman came out. In her arms she was carrying a little pig. Her clothes were ragged and her back was hunched as she walked over to the wagon.

'There's nobody home,' she squawked 'They're all dead.'

'I've come back,' said Father.

The woman didn't seem to hear what he said.

'Dead,' she yelled. 'And I'm not buying anything.'

Father shook his head.

'I knew it,' he muttered, thinking of the night he woke up when his father's grinding jaws suddenly stopped.

He climbed down from the wagon.

'It's me,' he yelled into the woman's ear. 'Hans.'

The pig jumped in fear and wriggled loose. It ran off squealing and vanished among the bushes. As if Father had stolen the pig from her, the woman started hitting him, pounding furiously on his chest.

Daniel held the reins. The horse didn't move. Father took hold of the woman's wrists.

'Hans,' he shouted in her ear. Then he turned her round and shouted in the other ear.

She stopped yelling but began hitting him again.

'Why have you come back?' she shouted. 'There's nothing here to come back to.'

93

'My father?'

'He's dead.'

Then she caught sight of Daniel and shrieked as if another pig had escaped.

'What in the Lord's name is that you're dragging with you?'

'His name is Daniel. I've adopted him. He's my son.'

The woman began rushing around the courtyard and making sounds as if she were a pig herself. Daniel laughed. Finally he had found a person he thought he could understand. She was playing the way Be had played, and Anima, her sister, and all the other women, unless they were so old that they were about to go away to die.

'Leonora,' said Father, pointing at her.

Leonora, thought Daniel. That's her name. Just as long, just as hard to pronounce as Daniel.

The woman vanished with a wail into the bushes. Father gestured to Daniel to climb down from the driver's seat. They went inside through the draughty door. Torn curtains hung in front of the windows, chickens had nested in the rafters and under the stairs, and shabby cats lay on chairs and sofas. The floor was covered with excrement. Both Father and Daniel grimaced at the stench. In the far corner stood a calf. Daniel broke out laughing again. He had come into a house that was alive.

But Father was angry.

'This damned misery is nothing to laugh at. It's enough to make me cry.'

Damn. There was that word again. Daniel cringed from the blow he was sure Father was about to give him. But instead he grabbed a shovel that was leaning on a sofa, which had once been red but was now greyish-white from chicken shit. He started swinging at the cats and the chickens. They fled hissing and cackling in every direction. The calf slipped on the filth and Father kicked open the door and chased the animals out until only one hen was left, which flapped up onto a rafter. The effort had made him start coughing and the attack was so violent that he staggered outside to the courtyard and threw up. Daniel followed him. When it was over, Father sank down on the front steps.

'I shouldn't have come,' he said. 'That damn old woman has gone crazy.'

He lay on his back and covered his face with one arm. Daniel went

94

over to the horse, removed the traces and led it to the grass. The woman was gone. The horse looked at him with weary eyes. On the steps behind him Daniel could hear Father muttering like a child.

Father sat up with a bellow. His clothes, which were dirty to begin with, were now filthy from the dung of the animals. He started crawling on all fours across the grass. Daniel followed at a distance with the horse. They reached a clump of dense bushes. There was a hole in it. Father crawled in among the bushes and disappeared. Daniel wondered if he wanted to be alone. But in his experience crying, crawling people seldom wanted to be alone. He crept into the hole in the bushes. Inside there was a space with no roof. For the first time Daniel realised that in this country rooms could be found without doors, and open to the sky overhead. Inside among the bushes, stood a rickety wooden table and a chair. Next to the chair on the ground lay a white clay pipe, the same kind Daniel had seen Geijer smoke at Andersson's trading post. Father pulled himself up onto the chair. Tears were running down his cheeks. Daniel supposed that this visit was a ritual, perhaps a method of sacrificing to a god. The woman who had run off screaming and the animals that lived in the temple were part of this ritual. The chair where Father was now sitting was a throne. And one of the gods must have forgotten his pipe.

This is a land where all the gods have fled, Daniel thought. They don't hide behind the rocks, their hearts don't beat behind these bushes.

Father coughed again, hacking and hoarse. Then he wiped his face with his dirty shirt.

'This is where my father sat,' he yelled. 'My father. Can you understand? My father, old Bengler who was good for nothing, sat here with his wasted life, with syphilis all through his body. Syphilis. And I yearned to come back to this hellhole. When I was wandering about in the desert I longed for this place. In my dreams, while the mosquitoes bit me, I longed for this place. Can you understand that, Daniel? Can you understand?'

Father was talking very fast. Daniel assumed he was saying some kind of prayer.

Father sat still on the chair until evening fell. Insects began to suck blood from Daniel's arms. Father was asleep. Daniel waited.

*　*　*

95

They stayed at the farm in Hovmantorp until the middle of October. With an energy that resembled rage, Father, with the help of the bent woman, cleaned the filthy ground floor. Daniel was given his own room upstairs. Father nailed a lattice of planks in front of the two windows, and every night he locked the door. Before they started the cleaning they had visited a churchyard and a gravestone shaped like a cross. Daniel understood that the ones who lay dead with their names on the cross were Father's parents. He was amazed by this churchyard, where dead people lay in rows beneath stones and crosses. The dead wanted to be in peace, they didn't want any traces to be left. No one was supposed to return to a grave in the desert until he had forgotten where it was. Kiko had taught him that. Here it was just the opposite. Father had also behaved strangely at the grave. He had wept. Daniel didn't understand why. You could cry for people who were sick or had been injured by some animal – they were in pain – but the dead had only gone their way.

The bent woman named Leonora had changed after her screaming fit on the first day. She never came near Daniel, never touched him, but she gave him food and sewed a new sailor suit for him, and she didn't yell at him when he went barefoot. She let him spend time with the chickens, the cats, the calf, the horse and the pigs. After the house had been cleaned and the stink faded, Father began unpacking his wooden cases. Daniel was astonished at all the insects he had dragged home. Why did he need all these dead creatures? He began to wonder if Father was a sorcerer, whether he had a special relationship to the powers that controlled people's lives. Could he talk to the dead? Daniel watched him as he arranged the insects in various groups, pinned them down and built display boxes with glass tops.

Father began to teach Daniel his language in earnest. Every morning and afternoon they would sit in the arbour, or in an upstairs room if it was raining. Father had great patience, and Daniel fell that he had nothing to lose by learning the odd language. He let the axes drop inside his throat, learned the words, and realised there was something there that even he could comprehend. Father never lost his temper or scolded him. Now and then he would stroke his hand over Daniel's cheek and say that he was learning fast.

*   *   *

Besides the language, Daniel also had to learn how to open and close doors. The practical training was done with the door that led into Father's workroom. By the time the practice sessions began, Daniel was already starting to understand the language.

'Door are just as important as shoes,' Father said. 'People wear shoes on their feet to protect them from the cold and wet. But they also have shoes to show their dignity as human beings. Animals don't have shoes, but people do. The same is true of doors. You knock before you walk through a door. You don't go in if you don't receive an answer. Then you knock again, possibly a little harder. But not impatiently, not at all. You can even knock a third time without losing your patience. Go ahead and try it. Knock, wait for an answer, open the door, bow, close it behind you.'

Daniel went out and closed the door. Then he knocked and opened it.

'Wrong,' said Father. 'What didn't I do?'

'The gentleman said nothing.'

'You mustn't call me the gentleman. I'm your father. So call me that. Father.'

'Faather.'

'Don't draw out the letter "a". How many times have I told you that? One more time.'

'Father.'

'That's better. Practise with the door again.'

Daniel went out and closed the door. Once again he caught a quick glimpse in his mind of how Kiko had painted the eye of the antelope red, then he knocked on the door again. There was no answer. He knocked again.

Father opened the door.

'Too hard,' he said.

He showed Daniel how to do it.

'It has to be like a determined drumbeat. Not like a bird pecking.'

Father closed the door. Daniel saw the antelope again and knocked. Father answered. Daniel opened the door, went in and closed the door behind him.

'You forgot to bow this time,' said Father.

*   *   *

97

They continued practising every day. When Father was busy with his insects, Daniel spent his time with the animals. The bent woman still didn't speak to him, but she let him feed the animals, wash the horse and lock up the chickens in the evening.

During this time Daniel wondered why there were no people around. He never saw anyone except for the man who was called Father and the bent woman. He realised that the people who lived in this country had very small families but that their deserts covered with forests were unimaginably vast. Behind the house there was a hill where he would sometimes stand and listen to the wind. The forest was everywhere, and it never seemed to end. He tried to listen for sounds that he recognised. The wind that passed through the trees was different from the wind in the desert. He found a tree that made the same rustling sound with its leaves that the sand made when it passed over a rock. He asked Father to say the name of the tree and found out that it was called *aspen*. He decided to venerate that tree. Every day he ran to it and peed next to the trunk. But there were other sounds he didn't recognise. Even the rain that fell so frequently in this country had a different sound. He listened to the birds he glimpsed among the trees, but their songs were not like any he had heard before. He wondered if his ears were still too small to catch the familiar sounds that must exist here. The sound of the drums, of the women laughing, the men telling their stories, and the occasional roar of a lion. Sometimes he thought he heard the distant sound of a drum, but he could never tell where it was coming from. And then there were the birds that Father had called *crows*; they broke apart the sounds he did manage to distinguish.

Almost every night he dreamed about Be. Sometimes Kiko was there too, but most often it was only Be. She was very close to him in the dreams, so close that he could feel her breath, touch her hair, see her teeth, lie close to her on the raffia mat where they slept. She spoke to him and said that she missed him.

Daniel woke up early every morning. He always woke when day was breaking and the bent woman and Father were still asleep. Since the door was locked he couldn't get out; he would lie in bed and think about what he had dreamed. Be had spoken to him and said that she missed him. I'm a little boy, he thought. I have travelled much too far away. My parents and the other people I lived with are dead. And yet they live. They are still closer to me than the man called Father and the woman who doesn't dare come close enough for me to grab her. My journey has been much too long. I am in a desert I do not recognise, and the sounds that surround me are foreign.

In the mornings Daniel often wondered whether he shouldn't just die too. Then he could search for Kiko and Be and the others. In his dreams he could always feel the warm sand under his feet. The only sand he had here were the grains he had found in the crates with the insects.

He often cried himself awake in the morning. He decided that he would have to tell Father how important it was that he go home as soon as he had learned to chop the right words with the right axe. Father would have to understand. He didn't want to end up like all the strange insects, pinned behind a pane of glass. The difference between the locked door and the glass that covered the insects was very slight.

When he heard the door being unlocked he usually pretended to be asleep. Only when he felt lonely again would he sneak out of the door, down the stairs and out to the animals.

A black cat with its tail missing had become his friend. She followed him wherever he went, when he pissed by the tree or gave hay to the horse.

By the middle of the month called October he had learned the language well enough that he would soon be able to explain to Father that he had to set off for home. It was now beginning to get dark early in the evenings.

He slept more and the dreams became drawn out, and more distinct. He had long conversations with Be, who was beginning to worry that he would never come back. Sometimes he also followed Kiko to the rock where the antelope was frozen in its leap.

One morning Father explained that his work with the insects was done and they would be leaving in a few days.

'Shall we travel back?' asked Daniel and felt his heart start pumping faster with joy.

'Back where?'

'To the desert?'

'You will never return to the desert. Your life is here. You will learn to speak, you will learn to knock, bow and enter when you are invited in. Now we are going to travel to a city where I shall exhibit my insects. But I'm also going to exhibit you.'

Daniel did not reply.

That night, the last before they were to depart, he decided that he had to keep his thoughts to himself. He wouldn't tell anyone that he planned to return to Be and Kiko even though they were dead.

He realised, though, that he lacked the knowledge he needed.

In order to return he would have to learn to walk on water.

CHAPTER 12

In Stockholm Daniel learned that a person's life is not only organised according to his relationship to doors, but that the movements of light and dark also require rituals that must be followed precisely.

Nearly a month had passed since they left the bent woman and the cat with no tail. With the horse and wagon they travelled towards the east, and finally the forests had reluctantly opened, and they had come to a town called Kalmar. There Daniel had seen the sea again. Father showed him where they came ashore on a map and how they had travelled in the shape of a horseshoe until now they were back by the sea.

The town was small and cramped. When they rolled in past the low houses, the streets were flooded after the long rain, and with the utmost difficulty they made their way down through the clay mud to the seafront, where they took a room in a stone house. Father asked Daniel to see to it that the skinny horse ate plenty of hay, with oats too, and to wash and groom the animal carefully. Then they would sell it and with a little luck perhaps get something for the wagon too. They needed the money to pay for the boat passage to Stockholm, Father explained. It was going to depart in six days, and after the horse had been well fed for four days they would sell it.

The first night they went and looked at the fortress that was located in the town. Daniel was more interested in the water. On this particular evening it lay utterly still and he thought that it might not be too hard to learn to walk on its shiny surface. But he still said nothing to Father. He doubted it would ever be possible to say anything. Father wouldn't understand. He might go back to tying him up, as he had during their first journey and keeping the doors locked, even though Daniel had learned how to knock, wait, open, bow and close.

On the second night they spent in the town, Father again drank one of the bottles that changed the ground beneath his feet into a ship's

101

deck. He slept on top of the bed without undressing and even forgot to lock the door and put the key in his pocket.

Daniel waited until it got dark. Then he sneaked out of the room, down the creaky staircase and out to the street. It was raining. Even though the mud was cold under his feet he went barefoot. He hurried through the darkness down to the water. A fire shone by the fortress, and in a house he heard a man yelling and singing by turns. He sounded exactly like Andersson, and Daniel thought that maybe it was someone who knew him, because their voices were so much alike.

He stood for a long time by the shore. Then he raised one foot and placed it carefully on the surface of the water. It held. But when he shifted his weight to the other leg he trod through the water. He wasn't yet able to make himself light enough through willpower alone for the water to bear him. It was still too soon. He hurried back to the house where they were staying. He was worried that Father might wake up and notice that he had left. But when he cautiously opened the door without knocking, Father was snoring heavily in the bed. Daniel undressed, wiped his feet and crept between the damp sheets.

Two days later they sold the horse to a very fat man who was missing three fingers on one hand. Father explained to Daniel that an angry horse had bitten off the man's fingers. After that he was known to torment horses. But since he paid better than the others, they were still going to sell the horse to him.

'Torment? What does that mean?' asked Daniel.

It was a new word he hadn't heard before.

'Like Andersson,' Father replied. 'Do you remember him? The one who kept you in a pen?'

Daniel tried to understand what the similarity was between the man who bought the horse and a man who kept him in a pen. He thought he ought to ask, but Father probably wouldn't answer.

He would miss the horse. He would have liked to take it with him when he learned to walk on water. People could tame animals. Maybe it was possible to teach a horse to walk on the surface of the water without breaking it.

*   *   *

The next day they boarded a small black-tarred coaster. They hadn't managed to sell the wagon and left it abandoned on the quay. The ship's hold was filled with dried fish and a large tub full of live eels. Father had supervised the loading of the crates which held his insect displays. He yelled at the crewmen to be careful. In Daniel's mind they were changed from men in ragged trousers and wooden shoes to ox-drivers in the desert: those who were forced to haul and carry every-thing the white men needed for their expeditions.

Once, and this was one of his earliest memories, Kiko and Be and the others had passed an expedition of white men who had pitched camp for the night at the edge of the Mountain of the Zebras. He was so small that Be was still carrying him on her back when he couldn't walk any further. But he remembered quite clearly how the white men had pitched their tents. Between the tents stood tables with white tablecloths. Kiko, who at that time was the leader of the group, chose to skirt round the camp cautiously because sometimes white men in the desert would suddenly start shooting as if they had discovered a herd of animals and not a group of human beings.

The bearers sat by their own fires. When the white men called to them they came running at once. There was a submissive haste about them, and their every movement was an expression of fear. This was something Daniel had understood even though he was so young. When he saw the sailors and heard Father shouting he recognised their behaviour. He was very surprised to see people who had fear in their arms and legs in this country too.

The captain of the ship wore no uniform. He had wrapped a shawl round his head because he had a toothache. He always had a bottle in his hand or on a cord around his neck. Daniel understood that at first the captain had been unwilling to take him along. Later father angrily explained that the captain was superstitious, believed in supernatural evil, and feared the ship would sink if they took aboard a person who looked like a black cat. Finally he had relented, though Father had been forced to pay double fare for him, and they were given a tiny cabin in the stern that stank of rotten fish. Father tossed out all the mattresses and blankets because they were full of fleas.

'Better that we sleep in our clothes,' he said. 'Otherwise we'll be eaten alive and won't have enough blood left when we arrive.'

Late that afternoon, when a light breeze was blowing from the south, they cast off the lines, hoisted the sails and left the harbour. They sailed up a strait where an island extended to the east of them. Daniel stood on deck and watched as the sailors pulled and hauled on the lines. They spoke in a dialect that was incomprehensible to Daniel, but he knew they were talking about him and that the words weren't kind. In the bow he found a worn-out rope. He transformed it at once into a skipping rope and began to skip. The sailors and the captain with his shawl looked at him with great misgivings, but no one said a word.

At dawn the next day, when Daniel went on deck, the island was gone, but the land to the west was still there. A cool wind was blowing. Daniel shivered as he walked across the wet deck. The boat rocked slowly, as if it were actually hanging on the back of the sea like a newborn child. Daniel closed his eyes and thought about Be. His memories awoke.

He was hanging on her back. If he kept his eyes closed he would be in the desert when he opened them. It would be before everything happened that made Be and Kiko lie in the sand with bloody faces and leave him behind.

He gave a start and opened his eyes. A musty smell overpowered him and drove away the memories. The captain was standing there. He had red eyes and his cheeks under the shawl were swollen.

'Have you ever seen anything so bloody awful?' he said, opening his mouth wide.

Daniel understood that he was supposed to look in his mouth. He stood on tiptoe to see. The teeth in the captain's mouth, the few that were left, were either black or rotted stumps.

'It's like having a snake in your jaw,' said the captain. 'Do you think that the man you're travelling with could pull it? He's a scientist, if I understand rightly.'

Daniel went back to the cabin. Father lay yawning in one of the two bunks with no mattresses.

'The captain wonders if Father can pull a tooth,' he said.

'Only if he pays us back and lets you travel free.'

Father got up and rummaged through his bag of instruments and finally found a pair of pliers that he used to bend the nails which fastened the back plates of the insect boxes. The captain sat on a hatch, swaying back and forth. He was in severe pain.

'I can pull the tooth,' said Father. 'I could also rip out your tongue if you like.'

'The tooth will suffice.'

'The price is free passage for Daniel.'

'Agreed.'

The captain opened his mouth wide. Father looked.

'A molar,' he said. 'Someone will have to hold on to you when I pull.'

The captain called over a crewman who was almost two metres tall and had powerful biceps.

'You have to hold me tight,' said the captain. 'And don't let go no matter how much I howl.'

The man muttered something in reply and then took a firm hold around the captain's body from behind. Father stuck in the pliers, found a grip and pulled. The captain roared but at last the tooth came out. The crewman released his hold, the captain spat blood, and Father asked Daniel to rinse off the pliers.

'I've seen his teeth,' the captain said. 'I've never seen anything so white. And strong, like the teeth of beasts of prey.'

'That's only your imagination,' replied Father. 'The reason is the absence of sugar in his diet.'

'I thought blackies were like children and loved sweets?'

'Then you thought wrong.'

The captain kept on spitting out blood. The cook announced that breakfast was ready, and Daniel returned the cleaned pliers to the bag.

That evening Father sat down to have a drink with the captain. Daniel stayed on deck, even though the wind was cold. The tall sailor stood at the helm, while another man who was his complete opposite, short and thin, lit the lanterns and then sat in the bow on watch. Daniel saw lights glimmering somewhere out in the dark. From the aft cabin he heard the captain's loud laughter. The thought struck Daniel that Father must actually be quite fond of him. Although it had certainly been a lot of trouble, he had brought Daniel with him on this long journey.

He had had clothing sewn for him, taught him the language, and above all instructed him on how to open and close doors. Even though Be and Kiko came to him at night, Father was there in the day and took care of him. He had even tied him up so he wouldn't vanish into the sea. It wouldn't be fair if Daniel didn't tell him, when the time was ripe, that he had learned to walk on water and that he intended to go back to the sand and the warmth under his feet. He would promise him never to forget how to open and close doors, even if there were few doors at the places where they pitched camp.

The sailor who lit the lanterns came over to Daniel.

They stood by the railing.

The starry sky was crystal clear.

He said his name was Tobias. Tobias Näver. He had been a soldier, he told Daniel, but he had been stricken from something called the rolls because during training he had taken a bayonet through his thigh and almost bled to death. After that he had become a seaman. Once he had sailed very far, to distant Australia, on an English barque named the *Black Swan*. He had almost decided to stay in Australia but changed his mind at the last minute and came back. After that he had only worked on small coasters working the inland sea called the Baltic.

Daniel listened. Tobias Näver spoke slowly and Daniel understood almost everything he said.

'You're far from home,' he said. 'If I understand rightly, you are the foster-child of the man sitting and drinking with the captain. What happened?'

Daniel thought about the fact that this was the first time anyone had asked him who he was. He bowed and said thank you.

'You don't have to bow and say thank you.'

'I'm going to learn to walk on water,' said Daniel. 'Then I'll walk home.'

'Nobody can walk on water,' Tobias replied, astonished. 'The fools who try just sink. There was only one man could do it. If what they say is true.'

Daniel perked up. 'Who was that?'

'Jesus.'

Daniel knew who Jesus was. Be and Kiko had sometimes talked about the odd habit white people had of nailing up their gods on

106

boards. That's how enemies who had committed terrible deeds should be treated. To nail up a god on a pair of crossed boards was both peculiar and frightening. Especially since the whites believed that it was the only god that existed. Daniel had seen pictures of the emaciated man with the crown of thorns but he didn't know that he could supposedly walk on water.

'Of course no one knows if it's true or not. It's called a miracle. And certainly the impossible can happen. We once ran aground on a reef in the *Black Swan*. We knew that we were going to go under in the storm. But suddenly it died down, and when we got the ship loose it stayed afloat.'

Tobias spat a stream of tobacco juice over the railing.

Daniel felt a great anxiety. It sat like a knot just below his heart. Could a person walk on water if a god did?

One of the lanterns went out. Tobias went over to relight it. From the aft cabin shouts were heard. Father was drunk now, Daniel could hear. His voice was harsh and he laughed joylessly.

Tobias came back.

'You can always perform at fairs,' he said. 'People would pay for that.'

'What's a fair?'

'A place where they exhibit deformed people, fat ladies, men with hair all over their bodies, men who can lift horses, children that are attached to each other, calves with two heads.'

Daniel still didn't understand what a fair was. But something made him decide to hold back his questions.

The wind had subsided. It was colder too. Daniel went to the cabin and lay down on his bunk. He decided to tell Be in his dreams about what Tobias had said, that the man on the boards was able to walk on water.

But Be was not in his dream that night, nor the next. When he woke in the morning he couldn't remember anything but darkness. It was as if an invisible mountain range had been raised inside his head. Somewhere behind it were Be and Kiko, but he couldn't see them.

On the fifth day they turned in towards land. They sailed among islands, across fjords and down narrow straits. Daniel noticed that Father had begun to grow restless and worried that it was because of him, that it might be because of something he had done. To show that he liked him, Daniel put on the heavy wooden shoes, but Father didn't even seem to notice. Several times when Daniel entered the cabin he was sitting counting the money that was left from the horse. Daniel had also heard him arguing with the captain about the money he was supposed to get back for pulling the rotten tooth.

They sailed through a strait and Daniel could see a tower in the distance. Father appeared by his side at the railing.

'What's that?' Daniel asked, pointing.

'A church tower. The capital. Stockholm.'

Father sounded irritated when he answered. Daniel decided not to ask any more questions.

They tied up next to another coaster in a forest of vessels. Far off, between the sails and the hulls of the ships, Daniel saw tall houses, and he counted five church towers. Because it was already evening, Father decided that they would stay on board for another night. Daniel wondered what would happen after that, but he didn't ask. When he lay down to sleep he hoped that Be would come. But the next morning too he woke with no memory but darkness.

They left the ship late in the afternoon.

Father had been ashore and two men came aboard to fetch his crates. When everything had been loaded onto two handcarts, Daniel was allowed to go ashore. He noticed at once that everyone was staring at him. But something was different; here they stepped forward, stared him right in the face, touched him, pinched his arms, and commented on his hair and his skin. He felt embarrassed and afraid, and he did something he had never done before: he took Father's hand and burrowed his head into his stomach. Father was astonished but stroked his hair.

'These are riff-raff,' he said. 'They work here in the harbour. Riff-raff who don't know any better.'

'What are riff-raff?' muttered Daniel.

'Uneducated people. Stevedores. Sump cleaners. People will look at you, Daniel, but these people stare. That's the difference.'

Father lifted him up onto the cart and shouted at the staring people to leave him in peace. Then the two men who had carried the heavy crates ashore pulled the carts away from the harbour. There were stones in the road that made the carts bounce and shake. Daniel had to hold on so he wouldn't fall off. They pulled the carts down a narrow street where the houses were very tall. Daniel had to breathe through his mouth because the smell was terrible.

Suddenly he couldn't bear to see any more. He shut his eyes and kept them closed as tightly as he could. The wheels rattled and clattered, people shouted, dogs barked, and Father bellowed at the men pulling the carts to be more careful. The sounds grew into a strong wind inside Daniel's head, but he couldn't make out what they meant. Somewhere far away he thought he could hear Kiko's voice, and Be's.

It was 3 November 1877.

Daniel had arrived in Stockholm. He shut his eyes as the cart full of insects rolled through the alleyways of the old town, Gamla Stan.

CHAPTER 13

Daniel opened his eyes when the cart came to a stop. Father touched his shoulder. The alleyway they were in was very narrow. In front of them was a church. The light had begun to dim. They moved into a little attic room at the top of a steep stairway. From the window Daniel could look straight in through another window across the alley. A candle stood on a table, with a great number of people sitting around it shovelling down food from a wooden trencher. Suddenly a boy his own age caught sight of him. He shrieked and pointed. Daniel quickly moved away from the window. Father came through the door after arguing with the men who had pulled the carts about how much they should be paid. The crates stood stacked in the room and it was almost impossible to move. Father looked around in disgust.

'If a fire starts here, everything will be in vain.'

He set down a little wooden box right next to the door.

'This must be saved if there's a fire. There's a beetle in it that no one has ever seen.'

He then proceeded to examine the bed. He shook the blankets and shone a candle between the boards.

'There are lice here,' he said. 'We're going to get bitten. But we'll only stay a few days. Then everything will be better.'

He set the candle on the table and sat down on a rickety chair.

'Living in this city and being poor is like living with an iron lid over your head. The only consolation is that we came at the right time. They had a smallpox epidemic here last year but it seems to be over.'

He took out his money pouch and poured the contents onto the table. There was one banknote and some coins.

'I'll leave you here,' he said when he finished counting. 'You have to keep watch. If a fire starts, you have to save the little box. I'll go out and find something for us to eat. I won't be gone long.'

He got up from the table. Daniel wasn't sure whether he was angry or worried. Then he left the room and his footsteps disappeared down the stairs.

Daniel was alone. Father hadn't locked the door when he left. Daniel could hear someone singing and someone else crying downstairs. The odour of food wafted up through the floor. It smelled rancid, like old animal fat. Daniel peeked cautiously out of the window. Across the alley a woman was making a bed for two children on the table where the wooden trencher had stood. Daniel had never seen this before, that a table could also be a bed. The people in this country live in strange ways, he thought. Either they live alone or they are so crowded together that no one has any room. Daniel carefully opened the box that he was supposed to save if a fire broke out. A beetle was pinned to a piece of stiff white paper. He had seen beetles like it many times when he searched for roots, snakes and small creatures with Be and the other women. They used to call the beetle the Sand Hopper, because when it was alarmed it would stop crawling and throw itself to one side. Be had been very skilled at catching them. It was like a game: hold out your hand and guess precisely where it would land. Daniel tried to understand why it was so important to save it. A little dead animal pinned to a piece of paper. It wasn't edible. Nor did it have any poison that was good for putting on arrowheads. Father was a very strange man. He was on a journey and had taken Daniel with him. People were always on the move. Travel meant the constant search for food. Now Father had gone out to find some. But where were they actually headed?

Daniel felt confined in the room. The ceiling was low; there were people beneath him that he could hear but not see. He searched for his skipping rope to keep himself from worrying. He began to skip, first slowly, then faster. The rope slapped on the floor in an even rhythm. It was like walking. He closed his eyes and imagined that the heat had returned. Somewhere he could hear Kiko's voice, his sudden laughter, and Be who talked so fast and always had a story to tell.

He was interrupted by banging on the door. He decided not to say anything so that whoever was standing outside would go away. But the door was flung open and a big man with a bare torso stood there staring at him.

'I didn't say "Come in".'

Daniel still spoke the language poorly. But he could pronounce some words.

The man stared at him.

'I didn't say "Come in",' Daniel repeated.

The man exuded a foul smell: from his body, his clothes, his mouth. Daniel breathed through his mouth so he wouldn't throw up. He was afraid. He hadn't said that the man could open the door and come in and yet he had done so. Daniel had thought that was a rule that no one could break.

'My head is pounding,' said the man. 'There's pounding from up here too. Are you the one who's stomping on the floor?'

Daniel looked at his skipping rope. It had been hitting the floor-boards.

The man followed his look.

'Are you completely possessed? A little black devil who skips on my head?'

He took a step forward and snatched the rope. Daniel tried to hold on to it, but the man was very strong and Daniel knew that he would lose it if he didn't use his teeth. He leaned forward and bit the man's hand. The man yelled in pain, but Daniel couldn't let go. He had a cramp in his jaws. The man howled and thrashed. Finally Daniel managed to loosen his jaws. The man stared at his hand, which was bleeding profusely. He had dropped the rope, and it now lay on the floor.

He's going to kill me, Daniel thought. He's going to bite me in the throat and shake me until I'm dead.

The man was breathing in heavy, panting gasps. He looked at his hand as if he didn't comprehend what had happened, then turned and staggered out of the door. Daniel closed it and wiped the blood from his mouth. There was no sound below him now. He didn't understand what had happened. Why did the man open the door without having permission to come in?

He stood still in the middle of the room.

From the street he heard a horse whinny. Then a dog barked and a girl shrieked.

He heard footsteps on the stairs. He recognised them at once. It was Father coming back. He was walking slowly, putting down his feet carefully, not stamping. There was a knock on the door.

'Come in.'

Father stood in the doorway smiling.

'You've learned,' he said.

Before Daniel could reply there was a racket on the stairs. The man Daniel had bitten stood in the doorway with a bloody rag wrapped round his hand.

'Are you the one who dragged this troll from hell here? He tried to bite off my hand!'

Father looked confused. He had a greasy brown-paper packet with him that smelled like food.

'I don't believe I understand,' he replied.

The man pointed at Daniel in a rage.

'That black monkey tried to bite off my hand. Look!'

He unwound the bloody rag and showed him the wound, which dripped blood onto the floor.

Father stared at his hand and then at Daniel.

'Did you do this?'

Daniel nodded. His tongue had swollen in his mouth. He couldn't squeeze out any words.

'I'm a coal carrier,' said the man. 'I work twelve hours a day. The sacks can weigh up to two hundred kilos. I carry them and I drag them. And I have to sleep. Then this thundering starts up here.' He grabbed the rope from Daniel's hand. 'He's skipping. As if he was hopping on my forehead. I have to have quiet if I'm going to get any sleep.'

Father still didn't seem to grasp what had happened.

'He's not used to things,' he said. 'He's not used to floors and walls and ceilings. It won't happen again.'

The man wrapped the rag round his hand. Slowly he seemed to be calming down.

'He looks like a human being. But he has teeth like a wild animal. I've been with women who have bitten me, but nothing like this.'

'He's a human being from another part of the world. He's on a temporary visit.'

The man looked at Daniel. 'Does he eat human flesh?'

'Why would he do that?'

'It felt like he was trying to tear off a piece of my hand.'

'He eats exactly the same food as you or I.'

The man shook his head. 'Life gets odder and odder. All this work. And then one night you meet a black boy who's skipping on your head. Will it ever end?'

'Will what end?'

The man shrugged his shoulders and cast about with his bandaged hand in the air, as if searching for a word that was actually an insect.

'Life. Which doesn't make much sense as it is.'

Then another thought occurred to him.

'He isn't sick, is he?'

'Why should he be sick?'

'What do you know about the diseases he might be carrying? Last year smallpox raged through the city, and this spring the children were shitting themselves to death.'

'He's not infectious. You won't turn black if you touch him.'

The man shook his head and disappeared down the stairs. Father closed the door.

'I can understand that you were scared but you mustn't bite people.'

'He came in and I didn't say "Come in".'

Father nodded slowly.

'You still have a lot to learn,' he said. 'But I'll protect you as best I can.'

In the packet he had fish that tasted strongly of salt. Daniel almost threw up after the first bite.

'You have to eat,' Father said. 'I don't have any other food.'

Daniel took another bite. But when Father turned away to sneeze, he spat the food into his hand and kept it clenched under the table.

After the meal Father lay down on the bed and stared at the ceiling. Daniel tried to enter his head and see his thoughts. He knew it was possible, Be had told him about it. A person you knew well did not have to say much, you could work out what she was thinking.

But Father was far away. Daniel imagined he could see him lying stretched out on a mattress in Andersson's house, in the room that had smelled so rank from the ivory.

The light from the candle flickered over his face. Daniel wondered about the pinched and often so sombre faces he encountered in this country. The girls who had skipped in the courtyard had laughed, even

114

the one who was very fat, but the grown-ups here were not like Be or Kiko. Life must be hard if they couldn't even manage a smile. Or their thoughts made it impossible for them to laugh.

But he knew that this wasn't true. From the street he kept hearing people laughing. He thought about Kiko, who sometimes grew tired of all his questions. Now he felt that he was growing tired of himself. He could have been lying there in the sand, with his limbs hacked off and the blood flowing, but he was alive, and one day he would finish painting the antelope that Kiko had started. The gods were waiting there inside the rock, and he couldn't forsake them. That would be like forsaking Be and Kiko and the others who had been killed, or all those who had died before them.

The candle had almost burned down. Father was asleep. Daniel blew out the flame, waited until its glowing wick was swallowed up by the darkness, and then undressed and crept into bed. Far below him he could hear a man snoring. He didn't regret biting the man on the hand. It had been necessary to defend his rope. But maybe he had bitten too hard.

The next day Father led him through the narrow, stinking alleys to a square where a man was sitting on a horse.

'That's a statue,' Father said. 'A man who will never move. He will always sit there and point. Until someone tips the statue over one day.'

They cut across the square and went through a big, tall gateway. The staircase was very wide. When they got halfway up the stairs Father stopped and put his hands on Daniel's shoulders.

'The most important thing now is to get some money,' he said. 'A man lives here who wants to measure and draw you. For that he will pay us money. I wrote to him from Hovmantorp. He's waiting for us.'

Daniel didn't know what the word *measure* meant, Or the word *draw* either, but he knew that what he was supposed to do now was something good. Father looked at him with a smile. His eyes were wide open now, not absent-looking as they were so often when he spoke to him.

They entered an apartment that was very large. A woman in a white apron asked them to wait. She gave a start when she first saw Daniel, even though he remembered to bow.

After a while a man in a long red dressing gown with a pipe in his mouth came in through a curtained entrance. He moved sound-lessly. Daniel discovered to his surprise that the man was barefoot. He had no hair on his head but his face was covered by a beard. He smiled.

'Hans Bengler,' he said. 'Six years ago we sat on a bench outside the cathedral in Lund.'

'I remember.'

'I told you the truth. Do you remember?'

'I do.'

'That nothing would ever become of you.'

Father laughed.

'You had no dreams. You didn't want to do anything. But some-thing must have happened.'

'I began to take an interest in insects.'

'I read what you wrote in your letter. Is your vain father dead?'

'He is gone.'

'And you inherited?'

'Almost nothing.'

'That's a shame. Parents who don't leave anything to their children are worthless. My father was a very unimportant man who neverthe-less was clever enough to speculate in British railway stock. That's why I can now forgive him for his otherwise wretched life.'

The man with no hair knocked his pipe out in a silver bowl.

'I said back then that you would never amount to anything.'

'Nor have I. But I did discover a hitherto unknown insect in the Kalahari Desert.'

'And you have a black boy with you. Do you sleep between his legs?'

Father was upset. Daniel didn't understand why.

'What do you mean by that?'

'Just what I said. Some men prefer their own sex. Particularly if they're exotic young men. I had a professor of geology who was forced to cut his own throat. Stable boys used to be called up to his flat. The matter was hushed up, naturally. But everyone knew about it.'

'He's an orphan. I've adopted him. There's nothing improper in what I'm doing.'

'I'm known for asking impertinent questions. Surely you haven't forgotten that?'

116

Father threw his arms out and then put one of them protectively around Daniel's shoulders.

'I'm leaving him here.'

Father squatted down in front of Daniel and said to him, 'This man's name is Alfred Boman, and he's an artist. He does pictures of people. He draws them. He is also interested in how people look in another way. A scientific way. He measures their heads, the length of their feet, the distance between their mouth and eyes. I'll leave you here and you must do as he says. I'll come to get you this evening.'

Then he was alone with the man named Alfred. He smiled and walked all the way round Daniel. Then he turned and went back the other way. His pipe smoke smelled rank. The man was also surrounded by a smell of perfume, but above all he was barefoot. Daniel had sores from the new shoes he had been given before they left the house in the forest.

'Let's go inside,' said the man.

Daniel followed him. The walls were covered with pictures. Stiff, pale people stood on some tables, but compared to the man on the horse they were small and white as if their skeletons had come out through their skin. They entered a room with a big window in the ceiling. Along the walls hung various pictures. On a table lay paints in tubes and tins.

Daniel noticed that one of the pictures showed an animal that resembled the antelope that Kiko had worked on. Unlike the picture that Kiko had carved into the rock, this animal was utterly still. Its face was turned towards Daniel and it looked directly into his eyes. The man who had made the picture was very skilled.

'A stag,' said the man. 'I painted it when I didn't have anything else to do. I only paint animals when people make me too discouraged.'

Daniel couldn't tear himself away from the picture.

'It's telling you something,' said the man with the pipe. 'The only question is what.'

Daniel didn't reply. He cautiously touched the picture with his fingertips. The eyes were very dark, not red like Kiko's antelope.

Suddenly Kiko was there with him. Daniel could hear him breathing. Then a cloud of smoke from the pipe hit his face and the breathing was gone.

'You must stand on this blue cloth,' said the man, who had put down his pipe. 'You can put your clothes there on the chair.'

Daniel undressed. There was a fire burning in a stove right next to where he was supposed to stand. The man had put on a pair of gloves and was holding a paintbrush in his hand. He walked around Daniel again, touched his arm, and asked him to stand with his legs further apart.

'Humans are strange animals,' he said. 'I think I'll call this picture *Black Saviour*.'

Then he grabbed a piece of paper, stretched it on a wooden easel, and began choosing among drawing pencils and paintbrushes. Daniel stood motionless. Now and then he was given a chance to rest. The woman who had answered the door brought in some food. She avoided looking at Daniel's naked body. Daniel was hungry, so he ate a lot very fast. The man, who kept smiling all the time, observed his appetite.

'If I could, I'd help you go back,' he said. 'Here you'll be merely a strange creature that other people pay to look at, not a human being who really exists.'

He kept drawing. Daniel tried to understand what he meant. But it was taking all his strength to stand still.

Late in the afternoon the man put down his brushes and fetched some instruments that he fastened on various parts of Daniel's head. He made notes in a book, asked Daniel to open his mouth wide, stuck his fingers in his armpits, tickled him on the soles of his feet, spread his buttocks, and pulled on his member to see how long it could stretch, and the whole time he took notes.

Afterwards Daniel was told to put his clothes on. He left off the shoes. The man nodded to him to come and look at what he had drawn.

Daniel went over to the easel. He saw his own face and body.

There he was on the paper. Under his feet was the blue cloth. It was his hair, his eyes, his mouth.

Now I'm like the antelope in the rock, he thought.

I am untouchable.

Behind me are the gods. And they are waiting for me to come back.

CHAPTER 14

On their second night Daniel left the room in the attic, slipped like a shadow down the stairs and vanished into the darkness outside. Father had not locked the door. He had come home late with shiny eyes and he was reeling. With a guilty conscience he looked at Daniel, but he didn't say a word before he tumbled into bed, as if he had returned from a long, unsuccessful hunt. Daniel realised that he had to start preparing for his journey back to the desert very soon. The antelope was crying to become complete inside him, and he had to learn to walk on water, before he was completely swallowed up by the world where he was now. He went out at night to look for the water. Each time Father took him out he tried to memorise the many streets, and where the water glistened and where it was swallowed up by the tall buildings that spread out like a shapeless mountain range. He had understood that he was in a ravine; the people in this country lived in caves hollowed out of cliffs which they seemed to build themselves. They hadn't risen up from underground, hadn't been cast out of the gods' invisible ribcages, like the mountains he had known before. He had to find his way out of the ravine, he had to do it himself, and he needed water so he could practise walking on the thin surface.

When he reached the cobblestone street he stopped. The air was cool, in a different way from what he was used to. The nights in the desert could be cold, but there was always the lingering scent of the sun that sooner or later would come up on the horizon and spread warmth again. Here he couldn't find that scent. The cold came from underground, beneath the soles of his feet. For a moment he almost changed his mind. He would get lost in the dark and the cold, maybe never find his way back. The hissing gaslights illuminated patches of the street. A rat ran quickly past his feet and vanished into a hole in the cliff. He took care not to enter the circles of light. The people who stared at him in the daytime might think he was an animal at night and chase him.

He stood utterly still and tried to remember where the water was. The shortest way was to follow the street in the direction it sloped. He had gone there earlier in the day when Father took him along to a cellar to get food. Just before they went into the cellar he had glimpsed the water. He hadn't been that close since they arrived in the city.

He huddled up against the stone wall when a horse and carriage rattled past. The man on the coach box was asleep. The horse walked slowly with its head down. Then two men came staggering the way Father did. They groaned and leaned against the walls of the buildings, as if they were sick or wounded by spears or snakebite.

Daniel picked up the smell from their bodies. It was a sweetish stench, as from dead animals.

Afterwards it was quiet. He cautiously started down the street, watching carefully where he put his feet. Even in this ravine there could be snakes, poisonous lizards, or scorpions. He hadn't seen any yet, but in the desert he was used to animals who only came out at night. He stepped in something slimy and saw that it was excrement, but not from an animal. He could tell from the smell; it wasn't a dog, but a person. In the desert they always covered up their leavings. Why did they have to put stones on the streets so people couldn't hide their excrement? He didn't understand, and he knew that Father wouldn't be able to explain it to him either. He dipped his foot in a puddle of old rainwater and scraped it clean against the rough stones. Very close to him, across the street, someone coughed. Again it was as if Kiko were right next to him. He thought he could hear him breathing into his ear. But there was no antelope carved into the wall, only a god who sat there coughing.

Daniel went on.

Under one of the hissing lamps he glimpsed a lone woman. She was walking back and forth, as if she were waiting for someone. Her clothes were dirty but had once been colourful. She reminded Daniel of a bird in a cage, like those he had seen at Andersson's: chickens before they were sold or slaughtered. She was wearing a hat with a plume, and he could see from her face that she was very young, but she had dressed like someone who wanted to seem older. When she turned her face away and for a brief moment stepped out of the light, he hastened on. He noticed that he had begun to shiver. Maybe there were already hunters after him that he couldn't hear. He picked up speed. He was at the cellar now, where they had gone down to eat. It was lit up and smelled of roasted meat from the door that stood ajar. Now he had to turn left, follow a ravine that was very narrow, and then he would be at the sea.

He hurried on and soon picked up the scent of the water. There were vessels packed tightly along the quay. On some of them there were men pulling on lines to keep the boats moving. Earlier in the day Father had explained that there were fish in those boats, fish that looked like snakes, which would die if the boats didn't rock back and forth and fresh seawater didn't flow in through the holes in the hulls. Lamps with flickering lights hung on the masts. Daniel almost stumbled over a man who lay sleeping next to some barrels. He moved carefully along at the edge of the light from the fires on the quay where men were sitting and playing cards. At last he found a staircase among the stones that led down to the water's surface. Close by there were some small rowing boats tied up. In one of them lay an old woman curled up asleep. Daniel moved cautiously so he wouldn't wake her. He felt the water with his hand. It was cold. He tried to make his hand light, turn his fingers into feathers, so that they wouldn't sink into the water. Then he tried with his foot. The water is like an animal, he thought. I have to be able to caress its pelt without making it twitch. Only then will it let me walk without everything breaking and me falling through. He still hadn't mastered the art. The animal's pelt kept twitching. His hand was like an insect irritating the animal. He realised that it would take a long time for the sea to get used to his hands and then his feet.

The woman in the rowing boat moved. Daniel held his breath. She muttered something and went back to sleep. The water was very cold now, and it kept twitching. Daniel whispered to it, the way Be had taught him to whisper to anxious dogs who scented beasts of prey. For a moment he thought the animal seemed to be listening. His hand was floating on the water. It was holding. But then the pelt twitched again. Still, he was satisfied. He would be able to learn this. It would take time, but he would come back to the water every night; he would make the wet pelt grew accustomed to him, and one day he would succeed.

121

He stood up to go back to the attic room where Father lay sleeping. The woman in the rowing boat was snoring. Daniel looked at the mooring line. It was a worn rope, brushy and fraying, that was carelessly looped round a stone post. He wondered what would happen if he loosened the rope. Be was there at once to warn him. He often did things that weren't permitted. Loosened ropes so that people tripped over them, put strong herbs in the food, scared people by painting the white bones of death on his face. Be was never really angry. She would first pull him by the arm, maybe slap him on the cheek, but then she always burst out laughing. She will end up laughing now too, he thought. Carefully he loosened the rope and the boat slid slowly away from the quay. He couldn't manage to stifle a laugh. Since there was no one about, he let it burst out. He laughed straight out into the night as he hadn't done since the day the men came and killed Be and Kiko. He flung the laugh into the darkness, and he knew that they would hear him.

Then he went back the same way he had come. When he reached the hissing lamp where the girl who looked like a bird had stood waiting, he saw that she was gone. Something made him cross the street to the other side. Then he heard her, she was panting somewhere nearby, in the dark, behind some barrels. It sounded like she was having a hard time breathing. He crept deeper into the darkness until he saw her, in the pale light from a window. She stood leaning against the wall with her skirt hitched up, and a man was leaning heavily against her. He was the one who was moaning. Daniel thought at first that the man was trying to slaughter her, that she actually was a bird. Then he realised that they were doing the same thing that Be and Kiko used to do, though they hadn't panted, they had laughed, talked, and then grown silent.

At that moment the woman turned her face to him. Her eyes were open. Then she screamed. The man didn't want to let her go, but she scratched him on the face, pointed at Daniel and screamed again.

Daniel rushed off in the dark with her screams behind him. Somewhere a bell began to toll. He crossed the street again and ran along the cliff so fast that he almost missed the door that led to the staircase and the room where Father was sleeping. He knew that they were hunting him now, all those people who stared at him when he walked at Father's side during the daylight hours.

When he came into the room Father was lying in the same position as when Daniel had left, but he must have been awake, because he had thrown up on the floor. No one was coming up the stairs, no hunters, no dogs. Daniel wiped his feet with a rag and cleaned up the vomit by the bed. Then he crept into bed behind Father's back, curled up and closed his eyes tightly so that the antelope would dare come out. It loosened itself from the rock, took a leap and stood before him with nostrils flaring.

Daniel woke up because someone was crying.

The sound forced its way into his dreams. At first he thought it was one of the many children belonging to Be's sister Kisa. They were always falling down, and they cried often. Then the sand and the heat disappeared and when he woke up from the dream it was Father he saw. He had taken off all his clothes and was sitting naked on a chair, crying with a bottle in his hand. Daniel looked at him through half-closed eyes. It wasn't the first time he had seen Father cry after coming home with shiny eyes. Whatever he drank had weeping in it. Daniel knew it would pass, that he would suddenly stop and then stand for a long time examining his face in the mirror. He would scold the mirror and sometimes shout. Usually he said the first word Daniel had ever learned, *damn, damn*, like a long chant, more and more furious.

Afterwards everything would go back to normal. Father would be quieter than usual today, complaining about his headache and becoming impatient if Daniel didn't immediately grasp what he was saying.

Suddenly Father turned to face him.

'I see that you're awake. I also see that you cleaned up after me last night.'

Daniel sat up in bed.

'I had a strange dream that you were gone,' Father went on. 'But when I woke up you were asleep behind my back.'

He stood up, but did not stop in front of the mirror the way he usually did. He sat down on the edge of the bed and took Daniel's hand.

'Today's an important day. I don't have any money and I can't pay for this room. That's why what I've decided to do has to be a success – what's going to happen this evening. I need your help. I need to be sure you will do as I say.'

123

Daniel nodded. He understood.

'Tonight I'm going to tell people about my journey through the desert. I'm going to display some of the insects and I'm going to display you. They will pay me for this. If it goes well, other people will ask to see both the insects and you. They will pay for it, and we will be able to move to a better room.'

Father was still naked. Daniel saw that he had big blue bruises on one arm. Apparently he had fallen down last night on his way home in the dark when he couldn't make his feet move properly.

'There's nothing difficult about it,' Father went on. 'I'm going to stand up in front of people on a little platform. I'll show the insects, point at a map and speak in a loud voice so everyone can hear. You will sit on a chair next to me. When I say your name you will stand up, bow and say your name. *My name is Daniel. I believe in God.* That's all. When I ask you to open your mouth you will do so, when I ask you to laugh you will laugh, not too long, not too loud, and when I ask you to puff out your cheeks like an animal you will do it. Then you will take your skipping rope and show everyone how skilled you are. And that's all. If someone wants to come up and touch you, you will let them. Believe me, no one wishes you any harm. But above all you must remember that we will get money so that we can leave this damn room and move somewhere better. Do you understand?'

Daniel nodded. He hadn't understood a thing, but Father had spoken in a friendly tone of voice. There was something about him that was reminiscent of Be, when she and Kiko were angry with each other and she wanted them to make peace.

The rest of the day Father sorted his insects. He talked as if there were many people in the room, and when the insects were sorted and packed up in the little case where he usually kept his combs and brushes he practised with Daniel. *My name is Daniel. I believe in God.* He corrected his intonation, asked him to speak louder. He practised the way he would get up from his chair, bow and say his piece.

'My name is Daniel. I believe in God.'

'You're talking too fast. And the word *God* doesn't sound right. It sounds like *Good*. It's *God*.'

'Good.'

'One more time. God.'

'Good.'

'One more time.'

Daniel practised until Father was satisfied.

That day they ate nothing but a little dry bread and water. Father brushed his hair for a long time and made a careful inspection of Daniel's fingernails.

It was already dark when they left their room. Daniel noticed that Father was nervous, and he set his mind to doing exactly as he was told. He didn't know who Father was, or why he had taken him from the desert, but he hadn't done it out of ill will.

He also decided to make his own suggestion about what cliff face they should live in. He had never done that before. Now he would explain that he would feel better if they lived where he could see the big water.

They stopped outside a door where torches were burning. A short man in a tall hat was waiting for them. He stared with anxious fascination at Daniel.

'This will be a great success,' he said. 'The Torch Workers' Association has never before had the opportunity of exhibiting anything like this. Terrifying insects and this black child. A real Hottentot.'

The man leaned in close to Daniel's face to study him. His eyes were yellow and sweat ran down his brow.

'The boy must be treated well,' said Father. 'He may be black, but he's a human being.'

'But of course. A real human being. There is great anticipation for your lecture.'

The man opened the door. They entered a room full of chairs that were still empty. On a podium stood a table with a green tablecloth and next to it a speaker's lectern from which hung the association's banner, a semi-nude woman with a shining lamp in her hand.

'The board members of the association will be here shortly,' said the man, bowing. 'They're eating dinner at the moment.'

'Who is on the board?'

'Head Forester Renström, Baron Hake and Law Clerk Wiberg.

The founder of the association, Colonel Håkansson, has also said he will come. We're expecting many guests.'

'And the workers?'

'They're coming. At least a blacksmith is.'

'But this is a workers' association, isn't it? For the instruction and edification of people of limited means?'

'Naturally. Colonel Håkansson was quite firm on that point.'

'But what if they don't come?'

The man threw out his arms.

'One can hardly blame the colonel for that. He has the best intentions.'

'That sounds like a typical evasion. You form a workers' association to which workers are not admitted.'

'We don't prevent anyone from attending.'

'But you don't encourage anyone either. The blacksmith will be here as an exception. Who is he?'

'He's employed at one of Baron Hake's ironworks in Roslagen.'

'What about the public? It will be a full house, won't it?'

'A number of lieutenants. Women, of course, are not admitted. A journalist or two looking for something useful to write about. It will fill up. There are so many people out and about, and soon they'll be sitting here.'

After half an hour the hall was almost full. Father had set out his insect cases and covered them with a linen tablecloth. Daniel sat on a chair in the corner and practised his sentences. He was in the dark, since Father had put a tablecloth over him too when people in the audience began stamping their feet.

'We're going to surprise them,' he told Daniel. 'I'll uncover you. They can see the shape of a person under the linen. And when I pull off the cover it will make a big impression.'

Daniel could hear people coming into the hall, banging chairs about, laughing and coughing. The smell in the room had changed, it was filled with the odour of dampness and tobacco. He assumed that it had started raining. Now and then Father would whisper to him.

'The place will be full soon. There are just a few empty seats at the back of the hall. Practise your sentences.'

'My name is Daniel. I believe in Good.'

'God. Not Good.'

'I believe in God.'

'That's better.'

Daniel could hear that Father was nervous. He was talking fast and stumbling over his words. It was hard to understand everything he said.

Then the audience fell silent. Someone banged a club on a table right next to him. The man who began speaking kept clearing his throat. Daniel didn't understand what he was talking about. A couple of words were repeated over and over that he didn't know the meaning of: *worker*, *education*, *I give the floor to*, and then a name. He began to grow warm under the linen. Daniel decided to remember that: if it was very cold he could sit underneath a linen tablecloth in a room full of people. Then it would feel as if the sun were rising over the horizon in the desert.

Suddenly he heard Father's name. Some people applauded, briefly, and then Father's voice began speaking. The words came uncertainly at first, fumbling their way out of his dry mouth. Daniel prepared himself but he had to wait. Father had a lot to say about the insects. Finally he heard his own name and Father pulled away the linen.

Daniel wasn't prepared for what he saw: the room so full of people, the faces so close. Father nodded at him and he stood up. It was dead silent in the room and he said his words.

'My name is Daniel. I believe in God.'

He pronounced them all correctly. He could see that from Father's face. He was pleased. That was the most important thing.

Suddenly he thought he saw Kiko's face way at the back of the room, where the light was dimmest. He had to go to him. Kiko had come to get him. He jumped down from the platform and started climbing over the people sitting in their chairs. A tumult broke out; people tried to get out of the way or grab hold of him. But Daniel knew that he had to reach Kiko before he disappeared. He struck at the hands trying to grab hold of him, clawing at the faces in his way.

When he reached the back of the room Kiko was gone.

Someone hit him on the back of the neck and everything went black. He was forced to the floor and the last thing he heard was Father screaming in the background.

CHAPTER 15

When Daniel woke up he was lying on a table covered in green felt. Over his head hung a chandelier on which several of the wax candles had already burned down. He turned his face and saw Father sitting on one of the straight-backed chairs, wiping the sweat from his brow. His memory slowly came back. He had seen Kiko somewhere in the darkness behind all the people staring at him, and he had tried to get to him. It had been like throwing himself into a whirlpool in a river. But Kiko wasn't there, he had vanished into the darkness the same way Daniel was dragged down by the maelstrom, and now he had washed up on a beach consisting of a table covered with green felt.

'He's awake now,' said a voice quite close to his ear.

Daniel gave a start and sat up. The man who spoke was the same one who had met them on the street in a filthy hat and who bowed and scraped as though Father were a man with great power.

Father got up and came over to him. Daniel could see at once that he was disappointed. His eyes were weary and there were white flecks on his lapels from the skin that fell from his scalp whenever he was upset and scratched at his brow. He shook his head.

'I don't understand you,' he said. 'We practised this. They listened when I was talking about the insects. Then I raised the cloth and you went completely crazy. They thought I had let loose a wild ape in the hall. You kicked a cavalry lieutenant in the head and bit a court of appeals judge. There was utter chaos, and I didn't even get paid.'

'Most unfortunate,' muttered the man, who had now taken off his hat and was cradling it to his breast like a baby.

'I still think I should get paid,' said Father. 'That was the agreement.'

The man with the hat hung his head morosely.

'The secretary left with the cash box. There was nothing I could do. The head forester yelled that it was scandalous and demanded that the hall be cleared. The next meeting a month from now will deal with the distribution of free hymnals to the unfortunate people in the poorhouse. Things will be calmer then. The only topic of discussion will be how to determine who is poor enough to be given a hymnal.'

At that moment the doors to the hall were thrown open. Two men came in and marched in a determined column up to the podium.

'The baron,' the man with the hat whispered nervously. 'Now someone will be taken down a peg.'

Father sprang up and stood as if he were about to meet a god. The man marching in front had a long moustache. He struck at the chairs with his walking stick so they flew to either side, and then stopped in front of the table. Behind him stood a man wearing simple clothes, and Daniel looked at his hands, which were very big. Something made him think of an elephant, the one Kiko had shot with three arrows after they had gone without meat for almost a month.

'I don't believe we have ever been properly introduced,' said the man with the moustache. 'Baron Hake. Factory owner and patron of the Torch Workers' Association.'

Father said his name and bowed.

'I beg your pardon. The boy lost his head.'

'Actually it was an amusing sight,' replied Hake. 'But rather bad form. Besides, he climbed on one of my shoulders. I have rheumatism and the pain immediately returned.'

'I beg your pardon once again.'

The man pointed with his stick at Daniel.

'I once saw a Negro in Berlin, but he was full-grown, and a different type. Broader lips and peculiar tattoos on his face. That was in a menagerie. It may have been in Hamburg at Herr Hagenbeck's and not in Berlin. My memory fails me.'

'I can do nothing more than beg your pardon.'

Hake thumped his stick on the floor.

'All these excuses,' he said angrily. 'I've lived my entire life surrounded by excuses. I can't stand them. The boy should have been on a lead, of course.'

Hake kept staring at Daniel.

'What's going through his head?' he asked.

'Hard to know,' replied Father.

'He's wondering why the hell he's here and being put on display,' said the man with the big hands, who had been quiet until now.

Hake turned to him.

'If I chose to do so I might regard that comment as insubordination.'

The man seemed about to leave, but stayed where he was.

'One of my long-time blacksmiths,' Hake explained to Father. 'Nils Hansson. Highly skilled. Made the new wrought-iron gates at Drottningholm Castle, for one thing. That's why he's here representing the workers.'

'I was wondering', said Father, 'whether this really is a workers' association. The hall was filled with lieutenants and foresters.'

'The important thing is not what we talk about,' said Hake. 'The important thing is what we *don't* talk about. We encourage peace of mind in the country. No political preaching, no insubordination. On the other hand, insects are a good topic. If the workers' lot is to be improved, it should be done by deepening the connections among various groups in society, not by changing them.'

'Too bloody right,' said the blacksmith.

Hake didn't seem to have heard that. Or else he chose not to reply. He turned to the man with the hat, who seemed to cringe even more.

'The insects were excellent,' said Hake. 'Being able to hear about and look at fascinating creatures can be useful. But the boy should have been restrained.'

'Naturally,' said the man who had shrunk as much as possible without disappearing entirely.

'I was promised an honorarium,' said Father.

'The secretary will see to it.'

'But he left.'

Hake gave the shrinking man a cross look.

'Herr Wiberg left?'

'He was one of the first to vacate the premises. He has weak nerves.'

'Then he'll be replaced at the next meeting,' Hake said firmly. 'A workers' association must set an example, don't you think?'

This last was directed at the blacksmith, who was trying to cheer Daniel up by smiling at him.

'Naturally,' Hansson replied. 'But if I were black like this boy I would also have felt my soul crack and tried to run for the exit.'

'We're speaking of the secretary.'

'I know. But it's possible to answer more than one question at a time.'

Hake reached into his breast pocket and took out some banknotes, which he handed to Father.

'Finances at the plant are poor at the moment,' he admonished. 'There's too little war in the world. This is all I can give you. And besides, there are the hymnals to pay for.'

He turned on his heel and left. The blacksmith lingered behind.

'How the devil can you exhibit people as if they're in a menagerie?' he said. 'Insects you can stick on pins. But people? No, damn it.'

He placed one of his big hands on Daniel's head before he left. Hake had already vanished from the hall. The man with the hat had now regained his original size.

'Everything worked out,' he said with a satisfied look. 'I have a calling card here, from one of those present this evening. He said he will contact you tomorrow. He has a proposal for you.'

'A proposal for what?'

'Business. What else would one propose?'

Father stuck the card in his pocket. The banknotes had improved his mood. He took his bag of insects and headed for the door. Daniel followed him. They went out into the city, which was dark. Daniel longed for the water. In the darkness he thought he could glimpse Kiko now and then, but it was nothing but weary, huddled people who had never seen an antelope.

Early the next day, as Father was busy shaving and Daniel sat by the window looking down at the street, there was a knock at the door. Father nodded to Daniel to open it. A man who was very fat and had short legs came into the room. He was wearing a red overcoat and was bareheaded. Over his shoes he wore multicoloured spats. Even though he was fat and swollen, he seemed quite agile. His face was childlike, utterly lacking in character.

'Herr Bengler perhaps received my calling card last night?'

Father wiped off his shaving soap and picked up the card lying next to the washbasin.

'August Wickberg, Master of Ceremonies,' he read.

The fat man had already taken the liberty of sitting down, placing his large behind on the only cushioned chair in the room.

'I hope I haven't come too early.'

'The poor do not have the luxury of sleeping in.'

'Precisely. That's why I'm here.'

Father sat down on the edge of the bed. He motioned for Daniel to sit next to him.

'A lovely couple,' said Wickberg. 'If a bit mismatched.'

'What exactly does a "master of ceremonies" do?'

'I handle persons such as you two, who have something unusual to offer but who have no idea how to turn a profit.'

Father shook his head warily. 'So you're some sort of fairground barker?'

'Not at all. I work only with serious propositions. Insects, yes, but not high-kicking dwarfs who turn somersaults. Displaying people who are black is educational, in contrast to seductive ladies rolling about with lazy pythons wrapped round their necks. We live in an age in which serious matters are assuming more and more importance.'

Father burst out laughing. 'That's hardly my impression.'

'You've been away a long time. Things are changing fast. A couple of years ago one could travel about the country and gather audiences who would pay to see a man who poked in the ground for old bronze as a main attraction. That may no longer be possible but some day it will be again. People are not merely looking for diversion, Herr Bengler, but culture.'

'Just like Baron Hake, then?'

'That man is a hypocrite, if you'll pardon the expression. He ingratiates himself with the real friends of the workers, but actually he hates them. Conditions at his ironworks in Roslagen are said to be outrageous. People are treated like slaves. In order not to become a topic in parliament, he undertook to protect the workers' association. A few months ago there was supposed to be a lecture and discussion about "The Meaning of Life". Invited speakers were a journeyman tailor and a Lutheran pastor. The tailor was never given the floor, since the pastor was busy preaching. The lieutenants had called in their orderlies to fill the seats. The tailor's friends had to stand out in the rain and freeze. But Baron Hake had lured one of those radical members of parliament

132

to come, and he later went home and wrote a motion to introduce a bill against irresponsible attacks on the owners of Swedish ironworks.'

Wickberg fell silent, out of breath after his long speech. He pulled out a hip flask and took a swallow and then offered it to Father.

'French cognac.'

Father drank and smacked his lips contentedly.

'It tastes like morning. Especially when the evening before ended in chaos,' said Wickberg.

'You had a proposal of some sort?'

'Most definitely.'

Again Wickberg began to speak. He spoke for a long time. Daniel tried to follow his words, but they rattled out of his mouth and finally became only a pressure in his ears. Daniel had moved close to Father. In the mornings he needed to feel his body warmth to stay calm. Father put his arm around him as he listened. When Wickberg stopped talking he asked some questions and received answers. Then Wickberg handed him some papers which he read through carefully. In the meantime Wickberg pulled out a wad of banknotes from one of his stockings and placed it on the table. From one of the voluminous pockets in his coat he then took out a small wooden box in which he kept an inkwell and pen. Father signed one of the papers. Then they drank again from the hip flask before Wickberg got up, bowed and left. Father picked Daniel up in his arms.

'So, something good came of last night after all. I knew it. When I was in the desert I learned never to lose faith. Now we can leave this damn room and move to decent quarters. But first we have to do a little travelling.'

Daniel knew what *travelling* meant. It made him nervous. Maybe they would head into the forest again, where there was no water.

A few hours later they moved out of the attic room after Father argued with the landlord about the rent. Again their luggage was pulled on a cart through the narrow alleyways. By now Daniel was used to having people stare at him. He didn't look down and he noticed that if he returned their stares they would turn their faces away.

They didn't go far. The alley opened onto a body of water, and Daniel felt his worry ebb away. They went across a bridge and then stopped at a boat by the dock that was puffing smoke from its black smokestack. The baggage was stowed on board and Daniel stood at Father's side when the lines were cast off.

'We're not going far,' said Father. 'We'll be there this evening. This isn't a sea, but a lake.'

Daniel tried to figure out what the difference could be between a sea and a lake. The water looked the same. He wanted to ask, but Father had lain down behind the luggage, pulled his coat over his head and gone to sleep. Daniel stood and looked at the city slowly disappearing behind them. Around him there were always curious people looking and pointing, but he didn't care any more. Father seemed to be content, and they were close to water. That was the only thing that was important.

When Father woke up they went below deck and sat at a table with a white tablecloth and ate lunch. Daniel noticed that Father always acted differently when he had money. He was no longer hesitant, his movements were resolute.

'We're going to display the insects,' he said when they had finished eating. 'Wickberg is a good man. He's setting up a tour for us, I'm being well paid, and if it goes well we can keep doing it. But now you have to promise me not to start climbing on people's heads when I lift up the cloth. Otherwise Wickberg will take back his money and we'll have to move back to the room in the attic. Do you understand what I'm saying?'

'Yes, Father.'

'You promise that it won't happen again?'

'Yes, Father.'

Father reached out his hand and placed it on Daniel's.

'What actually happened? I saw something in your eyes. As if you had discovered something.'

'It was Kiko,' Daniel replied.

He thought that now he could now explain everything to Father, and he wouldn't get angry or shake his head.

'Kiko?'

Daniel realised that Father didn't know who Kiko was. He had never asked about the life Daniel had lived before he ended up in the pen at Andersson's. How was he going to explain that before him there was a man named Kiko?

'Kiko,' Father said again.

'He and Be were the ones who raised me. Kiko painted an antelope on a rock. He taught me about the gods. One day he was dead, like Be.'

Daniel spoke very slowly. He searched for the right words and tried to pronounce them as clearly as possible. Father looked at him in astonishment.

'You're talking,' he said. 'Whole sentences!'

It was as if he had forgotten about Kiko and hadn't heard what Daniel said.

'You're a remarkable boy,' Father went on. 'You've already begun to learn Swedish. You talk like me, with a Småland dialect. And yet you come from a desert far, far away.'

Daniel waited for Father to ask about Kiko, but he went on and on about the language, about the fact that Daniel could speak. *What* he said was of no importance.

Late in the afternoon they arrived at a small town where they put ashore. Wickberg stood waiting on the quay. Next to him were two boys with a cart. Wickberg had turned his red coat inside out so that the grey lining was on the outside. He nodded with pleasure as he shook Father's hand and patted Daniel on the head.

'Everything will be fine. The mayor, who is an amateur botanist, is lending us the meeting room in the town hall. He promises a large turnout. Handwritten posters have been put up. But for Strängnäs they're going to be printed. A ghastly snake swallowing a person. A black man with a spear. To draw people in, it looks like the black man is naked.'

Daniel saw Father frown.

'I'm not showing any snakes.'

'That doesn't matter.'

'I want it to be truthful and scientific.'

'Snakes are good. They bring in the crowds. In Strängnäs we can use a smaller snake.'

Wickberg broke off the conversation and they set off for town.

'It's important to look up,' Father muttered.

Daniel wondered what he meant. He looked up at the rooftops, at the clouds. But he didn't see any danger threatening.

*   *   *

135

That evening Daniel was sitting under his linen tablecloth again. He practised what he was going to say and promised himself not to run towards Kiko even if he was there.

Father gave a better speech that evening. Daniel could hear that. He wasn't nervous and his voice was steady and firm. Sometimes he also managed to get a laugh from the audience. Daniel thought he ought to feel grateful to Father. Even though he had taken him along on this unbelievable journey, kidnapped him, he did have good intentions towards Daniel, although it wasn't clear what they were. On occasion he used to hear the grown-ups talking about trials that made people stronger. Kiko's brother Uk had once been wounded by a leopard, and he dragged himself a long way with a broken leg. That had been a trial. It had taught not only Uk but the others in the family to be even more careful when any of the big cats were in the area. But he had no idea what trial he himself would have to go through. Maybe it was as simple a task as learning something that only one white man had been able to do before: to walk on water.

He felt Father's hand on his head, the firm grip around the cloth. When it was slowly pulled away he was ready. A murmur passed through the hall. He heard a woman laugh hysterically, but he didn't lose his composure. He bowed, said his words and stood quite still. Kiko wasn't in the hall. Father smiled at him and then opened Daniel's mouth so everyone could see his teeth. Father squeezed and pulled on his arms, but not so hard that it hurt. When Daniel puffed out his cheeks the audience applauded. Afterwards he sat quietly when people came forward to look at him.

I wonder what it is they see, he thought. Judging by their eyes I think they see something that fills them with uneasiness. Not fear, not amazement, but uneasiness.

At last it was all over. Wickberg strutted about rubbing his hands. His stockings were bulging with money.

'This is going to go well,' he said. 'Tomorrow in Strängnäs we might extend the performance and stay two days.'

'But no snakes,' said Father, closing his bag.

'No big ones, at least,' replied Wickberg, vanishing out of the door. Father nodded to Daniel.

'Tonight we're staying at a hotel,' he said. 'And now dinner awaits.'

At the same moment the door at the back of the hall opened and a woman came in. She was dressed in black but with a red veil around her hat.

When Daniel saw her face he knew at once that something important was about to happen.

But he couldn't say what it was.

CHAPTER 16

Once Be, who liked to play games, had put a piece of kudu skin over her head and wrapped red strips of cloth around her face so the skin wouldn't blow off. When Daniel saw the black-clad woman walking down the centre aisle between the red plush seats, he thought she was sent by Be. The night before, Kiko had been there in the dark. He must have told Be and now she was the one who came, but not in person; she had sent someone in her place. The woman was young, younger than Father and Be and Kiko. He was sure that she didn't have any children of her own yet. She smiled when she looked at him. Father had straightened up and was flexing his fingers. He was just like Kiko, Daniel thought. If a beautiful woman crossed Kiko's path he would tense his leg muscles and rub his nose. Be always used to laugh at him. Sometimes she would bite him on the arm. Then Kiko would blush and say that the woman walking by might be good-looking but she didn't spark his desire in the least.

Father was just the same. Something happened when the woman with the red veil came up to the podium.

'I hope I'm not disturbing you,' she said. 'I saw your presentation, or perhaps one should call it a lecture. I liked what I heard. And what I saw.'

'Insects are neglected creatures,' replied Father. 'They can teach us a lot about life. And not merely the industriousness of the bee and the strength of the ant. There are grasshoppers that exhibit a good deal of cunning. And a special hymenopteran which has the remarkable ability to transform itself into a stone.'

'And the boy,' said the woman, looking at Daniel, 'he aroused many thoughts.'

Father straightened his necktie.

'My name is Hans Bengler,' he said. 'As I announced before the lecture. With whom do I have the honour of speaking?'

138

'Ina Myrén. I'm a correspondent for one of the newspapers in the capital.'

'Excellent,' said Father. 'I hope you are favourably disposed.'

'Actually I came to hear more about your journey,' said the woman. 'About how you met the boy in the desert. I had a feeling that your story was recounted only in broad outline.'

'Quite right,' replied Father. 'But people tire quickly. One must always be aware of holding their attention, and not go on too long.'

'That's something that preachers should learn.'

Father laughed. Daniel thought it was an ingratiating laugh.

'It's unusual to meet a female correspondent,' he said. 'Before, they were always men. So something seems to be changing after all.'

'Women are seeking positions in society,' she said. 'An old, rotten stronghold is about to collapse. Men are on the barricades, except for the fearless and young, but we shall not give in.'

'I understand that Fru Myrén is a radical, then?'

'Not Fru, Fröken.'

'So, Mamselle Myrén.'

'Not Mamselle either. That's French and shouldn't be used in this country. I am Fröken and thus unmarried. And self-supporting.'

'Are correspondents paid so well?'

'I am also a milliner with seven employees.'

'Here in Mariefred? Can you make a living at that?'

'We fill orders for shops in Stockholm. We have made hats for the Royal Court. That gained us a clientele among the aristocracy.'

Daniel noticed that she pronounced certain words with great emphasis, as if she didn't like what she was talking about. In his ears, the words 'Royal Court' sounded almost the same as when Father said the word 'damn'.

'So Fröken Myrén wants to write an article? Naturally I will be at your service.'

'I would also like to speak with the boy. I hear he has already learned the language, which surprises me.'

'He speaks very little. But of course I can tell you his story. May I suggest that Fröken Myrén accompany us to the dinner that awaits us at the inn?'

'That would not be proper. It could be misconstrued.'

139

'I understand. Rumour spreads quickly in such a small town. Just as it does in a big desert. In that case, we'll have to do the interview right now. We're leaving Mariefred early in the morning for an engagement in Strängnäs.'

The woman removed her hat, opened a small handbag, and took out a notebook and a pencil. Father opened the case with the insects in it, took out the skipping rope, and handed it to Daniel.

'Out in the foyer,' he said. 'And be quiet. I know you can.'

'I would like to talk to him too,' said the woman.

'Then we'll call him in.'

Daniel understood that Father wanted to be left alone. He took the skipping rope and went out into the foyer. An old woman sat asleep with her knitting by the front door. Daniel walked around and looked at things. On the ceiling were paintings of angels playing among the clouds. He thought that it must be just as hard to float among the clouds as it was to walk on water. But neither was impossible. He started to skip. The old woman slept on. His feet scarcely touched the stone floor. He tried to imagine that it was water. One day he would be so skilled that he would not only walk on water, he would be able to skip on it too.

After a while he grew tired. The old woman was still sleeping. He peeked through the door into the big hall. Father was standing there lecturing the woman, who was writing it all down. Daniel entered cautiously and sat down at the back of the hall. He could hear everything Father was saying, because he was speaking quite loudly. Now and then the woman would ask a question. She also spoke loudly enough for Daniel to understand the words. They were talking about insects. Daniel leaned his head against the seat in front of him and closed his eyes. He wondered when he would have time to practise keeping his feet on the surface of the water. Kiko had appeared to him the night before: that had to mean that they were waiting for him.

His thoughts were interrupted when he heard his name. He looked at Father. He was standing still now, and he was talking about him. Daniel began to listen. Then he became confused. Who was Father actually talking about? He was telling about a lion that had been wounded by a gunshot and had dragged an unconscious boy into the bushes to eat him. Was he the boy in the story? Daniel had never in

140

his life seen a lion. Nor had Be. Kiko thought he had seen one at a distance once. Was he supposed to have been dragged off by a wounded lion? He got up and sneaked forward among the chairs to come closer. He sat down on the floor and peeked through the chairs. The floor was filthy. The sailor suit that Father had sewn for him would get dirty, but it couldn't be helped.

There was no doubt. Father was talking about him, and nothing he said was true. According to his story, Father had saved him from the lion and then carried him for four days without water through the desert. There they had been attacked by a band of robbers, but Father had not only saved their lives, he also managed to convert the robbers to the Christian faith, and after that Daniel had been his faithful apostle.

Daniel had heard that exact word before: *apostle*. He understood that it meant he had followed along voluntarily across the sea, that it had been his own wish, a desperate desire to accompany Father when he told him that it was time for him to return with the insects he had collected.

Not a word of what Father was telling her was true! Daniel wondered whether he was talking about some other boy who had followed him across the sea. Someone who no longer existed, whom Father never talked about? But that couldn't be right. Father was talking about him, and what the woman was writing in her notebook was all lies.

Father was lying.

He was making up a story that was not true at all.

Daniel sat on the floor and felt a strong impulse to start screaming. *That's not right, that's not how it happened. I've never even seen a lion.* But he held his tongue. He couldn't scream because he didn't understand why Father was telling this story about him. What he said about the insects was right: there was not one detail that was untrue.

Father finished and wiped the sweat from his brow with his handkerchief. Daniel crept back out to the foyer. There he began skipping, furiously. He slammed his feet against the stone floor as hard as he could. The old woman suddenly opened her eyes and stared at him. But she didn't believe what she saw and went back to sleep. Father came out to him.

'Didn't you hear me calling you?' he asked. 'And didn't I tell you to skip quietly?'

Daniel didn't answer.

'She wants to talk to you, though I've already told her most of the story. Just tell her your name and that you believe in God. That will be enough.'

Daniel followed Father into the hall. The woman had taken off her gloves to write. Her fingers were very slender and white. Daniel wanted to grab hold of them and hold on tight, so tight that Father wouldn't be able to pull him loose.

'I've heard your story,' she said and smiled. 'It's quite a remarkable account, which will thrill many readers. In contrast to all the terrible things we read about slavery and injustice, this is a story that tells us something good.'

'Goodness is necessary,' said Father mildly. 'Without goodness, life is a wasted effort.'

The woman looked at Daniel.

'My name is Ina,' she said. 'Can you say my name?'

'Ina.'

'Do you understand what a remarkable experience this is? To hear my name spoken by a person who was born far away in a desert?'

'I have never seen a lion.'

Daniel hadn't prepared this. The words came out by themselves. *I have never seen a lion.*

Father frowned. 'He thinks that "lion" is the name of a Swedish animal,' he explained. 'Maybe an elk. Isn't that right, Daniel?'

'I have never seen a lion.'

'Now, answer her questions,' said Father. 'Dinner won't wait for ever. We can't go to bed hungry.'

Daniel was just about to commit his third act of rebellion and say again that he had never seen a lion, but he could see in the woman's eyes that she already knew that what he said was true.

'Actually, I don't have anything else to ask you about,' she said after a brief silence. 'But perhaps I can come to Strängnäs tomorrow and listen one more time. If that's all right?'

'You won't have to buy a ticket, of course,' said Father. 'And naturally you are more than welcome. Perhaps I could invite you to dinner? It might not be so improper there.'

'Perhaps.'

The woman put away her notebook, pulled on her gloves and fastened her hat on her curly hair.

'It was a real pleasure,' said Father. 'Permit me to say as well that you are a very beautiful woman. Surely it cannot be considered improper for me to say that?'

'And you are a very remarkable man,' she replied, looking at Daniel.

She has a message for me, Daniel thought. She is sitting behind a rock and whispering to me.

Father stood and watched her as she left the hall. The door closed.

'She is very beautiful,' he said. 'When I saw her I realised that I'm lonely. I have you, of course, but this loneliness is something else. A loneliness you can't understand.'

But Daniel understood. To be lonely was to be without. How could Father say that he didn't understand what loneliness was? He who needed to learn the art of walking on water to find the people who were the most important in his life.

It had rained. They walked along a cobblestone street towards the inn. Daniel usually held Father's hand, but now he didn't want to. Nor did Father seem to want him to. Daniel stole a glance at him. He's thinking about the woman with the slender hands. He thought he could see her in Father's eyes.

The dining room at the inn was empty, but there was a table set for them. Daniel wasn't hungry. The knot in his stomach didn't leave room for any food. He thought about the lion and the fact that Father had told a story about him that wasn't true.

'Why aren't you eating?'

Father gave him a stern look. His eyes were glazed because he had drunk many glasses during the meal.

'I'm not hungry.'

'Are you sick?'

'No.'

'I don't like your tone of voice. You're answering as if you don't want to talk to me.'

Daniel said nothing.

'One can't always tell the truth,' said Father. 'Maybe there wasn't any

143

lion. But she liked it. She's going to write about it. And maybe that will also make her like me.'

Father emptied his glass, shook his head and looked at Daniel.

'Do you understand what I mean?'

Daniel nodded. He didn't understand, but it made Father feel good when he nodded.

'A very beautiful woman,' Father said. 'Unmarried. Perhaps radical, but that usually passes. I have to think about the future.'

So do I, Daniel said silently to himself.

When Father had fallen asleep, Daniel got up, dressed and vanished quietly out of the door. A lone dog barked as he hurried along the deserted street down to the quay where they had landed. It was a clear, moonlit night. Daniel climbed down the side of the wooden pier and took off his shoes. He hated those shoes. Every time he came near the water he wanted to throw them as far out into the dark as he could. He would put stones in them so they would sink. There was a clammy smell from the water. Somewhere further out a fish jumped. The dog kept barking. Daniel rolled up his trouser legs and carefully placed one foot on the water surface. When he pressed down the water broke apart. He tried with the other foot. The surface of the water broke again. I can't do it, he thought furiously. I'm doing something wrong. He closed his eyes and tried to tempt Kiko or Be to come to him. He had to ask them how he should do it. But the desert he carried inside him was empty. The moon was shining there too. He called out for Kiko and then for Be, but all that came back was an echo.

He tried one more time to make the water obey him. First he stroked his hand over its wet pelt. Then he put his foot on the same spot. But the water broke, the pelt twitched.

He began to cry. The tears ran slowly down his cheeks. He wiped them away and dipped his hands into the water. Maybe that would help. But on this night as well the water refused to bear him.

When he came back and cautiously opened the door, Father was awake. He had lit a paraffin lamp and was sitting upright in the bed.

'I woke up and you weren't here,' he said. 'Where have you been?'

'I went out,' said Daniel.

'That's no answer. Don't you understand that I worry about you?'

'I had to pee.'

Father looked at his watch.

'You've been gone for almost an hour. So you're lying.'

'I peed two times.'

'I should really spank you,' said Father. 'If it happens again I'll have to start tying you up again. What did you do?'

Daniel considered telling the truth, but something held him back, something was warning him. Father wouldn't understand. The worst thing that could happen would be for him to start tying him up again.

'I went out to look at the moon,' he said. 'I didn't know I shouldn't. My name is Daniel. I believe in God. I beg your pardon.'

Father looked at him in silence.

'As strange as it seems, you're probably telling the truth,' he said at last. 'But if you do it again it'll be the rope.'

Daniel lay down behind Father's back.

The lamp was blown out.

Daniel no longer felt any safety behind Father's huge back. Now it was like a rock that threatened to fall over on top of him.

In his dreams he finally found Be and Kiko once more. Be had a red veil over her face, she was playing again, and Kiko sat carving new arrows. It was as if Daniel had never been gone. But he had grown, he was older now. Old enough to accompany the men on the hunt. He tried to explain to Kiko that he was still a child, but Kiko wouldn't listen, or else he laughed, and Be slapped him playfully on the back and told him to stop dreaming. Then Kiko shook him by the arm and he woke up, and Father was leaning over him telling him it was time to get up.

'You were yelling in your dream,' he said. 'You were calling for Kiko.'

'Kiko is the man I grew up with,' Daniel said.

'You have no other father but me. Everything that happened back then is gone. It no longer exists.'

'The same way there was never any lion.'

Father's face darkened.

'I won't permit that,' he said. 'I ask very little of you, but if I say that there was a lion, then there was one. That lion will make us money. It will draw the public. More than those real lions that people some- times exhibit in cages or pits.'

He held up Daniel's trousers.

'They're dirty. I don't know what you've been doing. We don't have time to get them cleaned now. We'll have to wait until we get to Strängnäs.'

Daniel got out of bed. His legs were heavy. His feet were still sticky from the muddy water. Father stood in front of his shaving mirror, humming. Daniel could see the woman in his eyes.

They went on board the same boat that had brought them the day before and sailed across a fjord that narrowed and turned into a strait between low islands. On board the vessel were two horses. A boy Daniel's age sat holding them by two ropes. He looked at Daniel but he didn't stare. Daniel sat down next to him. The boy touched his hair and laughed. Daniel pointed at the horses.

'They're going to be slaughtered,' said the boy. 'In Strängnäs they'll get clubbed on the head.'

'Why?'

'They're old.'

'I've seen a lion,' said Daniel. 'A lion that dragged me off to tear me to pieces.'

The boy gave Daniel a close look.

'I don't believe it,' he said. 'I think you're lying.'

'Thank you,' said Daniel, and held out his hand.

The boy took it. His grip was very strong.

That afternoon they landed at a quay and disembarked. Wickberg was waiting for them and further off, behind some stacks of timber, Daniel saw the woman with the red veil.

At that instant he decided that she was someone he could tell the truth to: she would listen to what he had to say.

CHAPTER 17

As soon as they stepped ashore on the quay amid the screeching of gulls, an argument broke out between Wickberg and Father. Wickberg had unrolled the finished printed poster, and Father was furious. There was not only a dangerous snake with a forked tongue, but Daniel was depicted as a grinning, evil wild man with fangs.

'I can't approve this!' Father yelled. 'This goes against everything we agreed on!'

Wickberg seemed to have been prepared for this reaction.

'But it will pull in the public. If it draws a crowd you get a percentage. That's the agreement. If nobody comes the whole thing might go into liquidation.'

'We don't have a company. This is a lecture tour with serious content.'

'What difference does the content make if people don't turn up? As soon as they get there they'll forget about the snake. When they see the boy their hearts will melt. They won't see a wild man but a scared little Negro slave.'

Father gave a start as if Wickberg had stuck him with a needle.

'Negro slave?'

Wickberg drew Father aside because people on the quay were beginning to show more interest in their loud argument than in Daniel.

'You've been away a long time, Hans Bengler. Black people in this backward country are either wild men or slaves. They either boil missionaries or are kept in chains. If you want to change this impression, you have to get them to come.'

Daniel understood that they were talking about him, but he was more interested in the woman who was still hiding behind the timber. He wanted to run over and grab hold of one of her slender hands, but he knew that she was standing there because she didn't want to be seen.

Wickberg rolled up the poster.

'You'll realise that I'm right soon enough,' he said, nodding meaningfully towards the money stuffed in his stockings.

'You're a scoundrel,' said Father. 'But the rest of the contract is all right.'

Wickberg went red in the face.

'Don't ever call me a scoundrel. Anything else, but not that!'

'Everyone is afraid of his real name,' said Father. 'But I'm be content to call you a brigand.'

Wickberg grabbed his heart and then felt his wrist to take his pulse.

'Don't play games with your heart,' said Father. 'There's no queen of hearts inside your coat. There's a spade with a low number. When people start coming by themselves, the snake and the wild man go.'

Wickberg nodded, resigned.

The baggage was transported to a hotel, a building of red brick. Wickberg booked a private room for them. After they got settled in the room, Father took Daniel to a shop that sold sailor suits. The man behind the counter started shaking when he had to measure Daniel's waist. Father was tired and annoyed.

'Damn fumbling!' he shouted. 'The boy is perfectly normal. Narrow waist.'

A pair of trousers was selected, tried on, and they fitted without alterations. They went back to the hotel room, where Wickberg was waiting.

The woman with the red veil was gone. Daniel turned time after time on the street to check if she was there.

'What are you looking for?' asked Father.

'Nothing,' said Daniel.

Wickberg had ordered a large supper. Father's mood instantly improved when he saw the table.

'Tonight we're not working,' said Wickberg. 'It's important to rest up. Besides, Strängnäs is a slow town. People have to have time to think about it, make up their minds, air out their clothes. But tomorrow it'll be a full house.'

'Which hall?'

'The bishop is terrified of everything that doesn't come from on high. He forbade the use of the diocese's large hall. The mayor is afraid of the bishop, so he closed the town hall. All that was left was the Freemasons' hall. It's got poor acoustics, but we'll hang a cloth from the ceiling.'

Father tossed back one of the glasses that Daniel had learned was called a *shot*. He smacked his lips and looked pleased.

'Tomorrow there will be a dinner after the performance as well. A writer named Ehrenhane is the host.'

'What does he write?'

'Rubbish. Heartfelt tributes to the Royal House. But he doesn't take his convictions seriously. He visits whores in Copenhagen, conspires with the radicals, and sometimes invites tramps to dinner.'

'Are you referring to me?'

'Not at all. But not many travellers from foreign lands ever pass through this town. As a young man he was also passionate about pressing plants. He has a colossal collection of oak leaves at home.'

Daniel picked at his food. He still had a knot in his stomach. Somewhere nearby was the woman with the veil, he knew it.

'Aren't you hungry?' asked Father, who noticed he wasn't eating.

'I have a stomach ache.'

'He's tired,' said Wickberg. 'He can have a sandwich in the room.'

'Yes, please.'

Father scrutinised him. 'No going out at night!'

'No,' Daniel replied. 'I'm going to bed.'

He found his way up the stairs by himself. When he entered the room he stood by the window and looked down at the street. There was a single lamp post with a flickering light. He knew that Father would tie him up if he went out. That would ruin everything. The water would be forbidden to him. At the same time he knew that he had to meet the woman who had stood behind the wood and waited. She had come for his sake, he was convinced of that. Maybe she would speak to Father about his travels, continue listening to his lies, but she had understood that there was never any lion. She had come to hear his story, and maybe she would be able to help him walk on water.

He remained standing at the window. A lone dog ran through the light towards some unknown destination. Then a man came staggering by. He leaned against the lamp post and vomited. Then he too disappeared.

149

There was a knock at the door. Daniel gave a start. He thought it was Father testing him to see if he would say *Come in* or if he would open the door without finding out who was standing there. He waited. The knock came again. It was very cautious. Daniel pictured the hand. Without gloves, it was white with slender fingers. He rushed to the door and opened it.

Ina Myrén stood there, and she had no gloves on. Daniel grabbed her hand and pressed it to his face. He couldn't help crying. He suddenly remembered a pain that he had felt long ago when Be had been seized by inconceivable rage and slapped him hard on the face. He had started bleeding, and then she had pressed his face so hard into the sand that he almost suffocated. Someone had grabbed hold of her, torn her away, and afterwards she had vanished and hadn't come back until two days later. She never said a word, never explained what had driven her to hit him. For a long time the whole family had stayed silent. Kiko had retreated. Only later did Daniel understand that Be had been seized by evil demons. No one knew where they had come from. Maybe she had thought forbidden thoughts. Nobody knew. Not until she gave birth to Daniel's little sister did everything go back to normal. Be seemed to forget everything that had happened. Kiko slept close by her side at night, and she caressed Daniel's hair as she had always done.

Now the tears were flowing, but the woman didn't pull away her hand. She closed the door behind her and sat down on a chair, and Daniel buried his head between her breasts.

Afterwards he sat on the edge of the bed and looked down at the floor. She didn't say anything, just sat there waiting. Finally he dared to look at her. She was smiling.

'There wasn't any lion,' he said.

'I know,' she replied. 'But what was there instead?'

'An antelope. That Kiko carved into the rock. An antelope that was about to take a leap.'

'What else was there?'

He realised all of a sudden that he couldn't sit on the bed any longer. Telling a story meant sitting on the ground. Not on the sand, since there wasn't any, but on the wooden floorboards, the dark red carpet. He sat down, and to his astonishment she got out of her chair and sat down facing him with her legs crossed.

'There should be a fire here, I'm sure,' she said.

Daniel nodded. He was dumbfounded. How could she know that?

'I'm sitting facing you. But actually someone else is sitting here.'

He nodded again. She was conjuring with him, saying precisely what he hadn't expected her to say but was hoping for. Still, he wasn't afraid.

'Be,' he said. 'Or Kiko, or Undu, or Rigva who was lame and only had one eye.'

'But there wasn't any lion?'

'No lion.'

Suddenly he was frightened. She knew too much she couldn't know. He had learned enough to mistrust friendly, well-meaning people with slender white fingers. They always wanted something from him that he couldn't give.

'Can you skip?' he asked, to defend himself.

Since he didn't know whether he had been polite enough, he added, 'My name is Daniel. I believe in God.'

'I can skip,' she replied. 'Maybe not with these skirts on, but I can.'

'There wasn't any lion,' he said again.

Suddenly the woman stood up. She grabbed his skipping rope, tied up her skirts so that her stockings and a bit of her naked thighs were showing, and started jumping. Her feet thumped hard against the floor. Daniel saw that it was a long time since she had skipped but she hadn't forgotten how.

She stopped, pulled down her skirts and sat down again. Daniel was disappointed for a moment. He had wanted to lean against her body where her stockings ended, where the skin was just as white as her fingers. She was out of breath. Her chest was heaving and he saw Be again, although she had never had anything covering her upper body. Kiko liked to play with her breasts. He had given them names, and Be had laughed and replied that she was already with child and didn't need to hear friendly words about her breasts. Daniel wondered whether he could ask the woman sitting on the floor to take off her clothes, at least above the waist. Since she had skipped and knew that there hadn't been any lion, maybe it wouldn't be dangerous to ask. He pointed at the black buttons that held her clothes fastened across her breasts. She gave him a quizzical look.

'Those are called buttons.'

Daniel already knew that. Every morning Father would yell at his damn collar buttons, especially if he had been drinking the night before.

'Open up,' he said.

She gave him a long look and straightened her back as she sat there. Daniel already knew he had done something wrong. But then she changed her mind, unbuttoned the buttons, nine of them, one by one, and then unbuttoned her white linen so he could see her breasts. To his surprise they were like Be's breasts. All women had different breasts, the same way all men had different chests, but the woman sitting facing him had the same breasts as Be. Daniel couldn't resist his desire, and he leaned hard against her, and she didn't pull away even though she stiffened.

'I am your mother,' said the woman. 'She is here right now.'

'Be is dead,' replied Daniel. 'She died in blood that ran through the sand. When Kiko came she had already stopped breathing. I was lying behind a hill under a kudu hide and the ones who came with spears and guns never found me. But Kiko came too soon. One of them who was left and cutting the ears off those he had killed saw Kiko and shot him in the head.'

The woman put her arms around him. Daniel felt that Be was very close just now.

'What happened?' she asked.

'I don't know. The men came riding, they were white and had a flag with an eagle. They laughed a lot and they shot everybody and didn't say why. If we had been animals they would have skinned us. If we had been animals they would have eaten us. But the only thing they did was to kill us and cut off our ears. I heard at Andersson's once that our ears were stiffened with tallow and then used as bowls for sugar and chocolate.'

'Who was Andersson?'

'He saved my life. He gave me a crate to live in. Then Father came and took me. He called me Daniel, told me to wear shoes on my feet, and brought me here across the sea.'

Daniel felt a great peace as he told his story pressed against her warm breasts. He could feel her heart beating and smell the sweetish scent of sweat. Something made him remember an experience he had had when he was very small. One night he had woken and gone out to pee in the sand. That night the stars in the sky over the desert were very clear. The stars were eyes that looked at him, saw him pee and saw him yawn. Suddenly he was aware that the stars were looking at him. He had been pulled up from the sand, sucked in as if by an invisible whirlwind towards all these points of light glittering, and he had understood that they were actually very close, the eyes of the gods, and would always be with him. Now he remembered that night as he felt the warmth from her breast, and he knew that he would scream, maybe bite her, if she suddenly pulled away and began to close up her buttons again.

'Then you came here.'

'I came to a town where two girls were skipping in a back courtyard. Father had his bag full of insects, and he used to tie me up when he was afraid I would run away.'

'Where would you go?'

Daniel thought about that. He knew that there was a word for what he was dreaming of. He knew that there was a place where the water would bear him. A short word. He thought for a long time.

'Home,' he said eventually. 'I think it's called home.'

She hugged him tenderly and he pressed against her as hard as he could. One of her nipples came close to his mouth and he grasped it with his lips, not to get milk but to stay calm.

He closed his eyes and dreamed. Her heart was beating. Be was humming somewhere in the background. Kiko had already gone to sleep. The smells were no longer coming from the carpet and Father's shaving lotion. Now he could sense the black coals from the fire burning down, the rancid smell of the old bark from pilko branches.

'I've never held a man close to me,' she said. 'Many men have wanted to, they have grabbed for my buttons and looked right through my clothes, but I've never held anyone as close as you.'

Daniel didn't understand what she meant. He didn't want to, either. He was already deep in his dreams. The nipple he held in his mouth was Kiko's hand that led him away towards the mountain where the antelope waited. There was also sleep, Be's hand against his cheek, the bodies of the whole family pressed tight together, the night that was still long and the dawn that waited beyond all the dreams they would talk about when they were awake again.

'I see your sorrow,' she said. 'But I don't know if you know what that word means.'

Daniel didn't answer. He was dreaming.

'What are you thinking about?' she asked.

'I have to learn to walk on water,' he said. 'I'm going to walk home across the back of the sea and I have to learn to move so carefully that the animal won't be upset and swallow me.'

She asked what he meant. But by then he was already asleep.

A thunderclap came out of nowhere. The lightning and the rumbling crashed right above his head. He gave a start.

Father was standing in the doorway.

He had glazed eyes and stared incredulously at the scene before him. Daniel had raised his head from the woman's breast. She still had her arms around him.

Father started yelling.

'Intolerable!' he shouted. 'A woman is devouring my son. What the hell is this?'

Daniel bored his face into her embrace again. Now her breasts were rocks that could give him a hiding place. Be was still close to him. The warmth came from her, and he thought it would soon catch fire and scare Father into flight the way animals were scared with burning torches.

'I've been talking to the boy,' said the woman. 'I have listened to his story. It isn't the same as what you told me.'

'Then he's lying. He's only a child. A Hottentot from the desert. What does he know about truth and lies? He's telling you what he thinks you want to hear. Besides, he can't tell a story. His vocabulary is too limited. What did he say?'

'The truth.'

'Which truth?'

'His own.'

'What does that mean?'

'That there wasn't any lion.'

Daniel was listening. He could hear from Father's voice that he was uncertain, but the woman was utterly calm. He could feel that her heart wasn't beating any faster than before.

154

'One might regard this situation as extremely indecent,' said Father. 'A grown woman who undresses and seduces a child. A black child, besides, who might be carrying diseases no one knows about. If this came out, a trial or mental hospital would be a likely consequence.'

'I'm not afraid.'

She carefully moved Daniel's head so that it rested on the carpet. Then she stood up and buttoned her dress.

'I call this sick and dangerous,' said Father. 'You have a man close at hand but you are raping a child.'

Daniel heard the smack and he knew at once what it was. She had slapped Father in the face with her slender white hand.

But what happened after that he couldn't have imagined. A man who is slapped by a woman is supposed to collapse, draw back, cringe. But Father cast himself over her with a roar. He didn't try to unbutton her dress, but tore and ripped at her clothes so the seams split open. Daniel got up. He tried to get between them but Father tossed him aside and dragged her towards the bed. Daniel thought he should defend her but at the same time he remembered the men who came riding and killed Be and Kiko and then cut off their ears. Father was the same. He would kill her and cut off her ears, and there was nothing for Daniel to do but hide again.

He rushed out of the room, down the stairs and into the street. It was raining but he didn't feel it. He ran down towards the water and when he came to the quay he waded out.

He would never learn to walk on this water. Father would cut off his ears and then there wouldn't be anything but a dead Daniel far away from those who lay buried in the sand waiting for him.

He waded into the water. He might as well plunge his head under the surface and then be gone.

The cold penetrated his body.

The last thing he thought of was the antelope.

CHAPTER 18

The water spoke to him.

He had expected that death would be a silence, or perhaps the faint echo of rustling grains of sand, but the water had a powerful voice that forced him upwards, forced him to keep breathing. He had walked straight out, deeper and deeper, and he had turned his back to the town and to Father, but when the water forced his head above the surface, his body turned round and he saw the faint lights that still glittered in the darkened streets.

Then came the cold. He was so cold he was shaking. His muscles cramped and knotted up. He waded ashore as fast as he could and hurried back towards the red-brick building where Father had thrown himself at the woman and torn at her buttons. He had no idea what awaited him but he had to get out of his cold, wet clothes. The water had spoken to him and told him he wasn't supposed to die. He had to learn to walk on its surface, return to the desert and tell his strange story to all those who might be dead but were still waiting for him. He was alive and had to keep on living. That's what he understood when his head went under the water. A dead person could never learn to stroke the wet pelt so carefully that he would be allowed to walk on the surface without breaking through. He had to go on living.

When he reached the red-brick building he saw Father standing outside the gate. A covered coach with two horses hitched to it had driven up. Father stared at him as if he were seeing a ghost.

'Into the coach,' he said. 'We're leaving.'

'I need dry clothes,' said Daniel.

Father shook his head. 'You can change later. We have to leave.'

The old night porter stood holding a piece of paper and waited for Father to notice him. Without looking at the paper he gave the man some banknotes. The last of the baggage was loaded. Father looked about nervously.

'We're heading for Örebro,' he told the man who took the money. 'To Örebro. Nowhere else.'

A young boy sat on the coach box. He had an odd-looking fur cap pulled down over his forehead, and Daniel couldn't see his eyes. Father shoved Daniel into the coach, shouting to the boy on the driver's seat.

'To Örebro. The main road.'

Daniel wondered what had happened. A small lamp was lit inside the coach. The flame flickered over Father's sweaty face and Daniel saw that he had a bloody wound just above one eye. He killed her, Daniel thought. He killed her and now he's running away.

Father looked at him. Then he tore open one of the bags inside the coach and pulled out some dry clothes.

'I don't know what you did,' he said. 'Whether you fell into the water or jumped in. Right now I only know one thing.'

Daniel took off his clothes in the rattling coach. The whole time he heard Father muttering. It sounded like some sort of prayer, but he was just repeating that single word, *damn, damn, damn.*

After they had left the town behind, Father pounded on the roof of the coach. The boy stopped the horses. Father opened the door and yelled at him.

'Turn round. We're going to Stockholm.'

'I haven't been paid for that,' replied the boy.

'You will be,' Father roared in fury. 'More money than you've ever seen in your life.'

The boy began to pull the reins so the coach turned round. One of the horses whinnied. Daniel shivered. He was still freezing. Father took out one of the bottles he always carried in his luggage.

'Drink this,' he said.

Daniel tasted it. It was strong and burned his throat, but he swallowed it and felt the warmth quickly come back into his body. Father wrapped him up in a blanket. His hands were rough and shaking. The coach picked up speed. Now and then they would hear the sound of a whip cracking. Father kept muttering and hissing between tight lips. Daniel waited. What had happened? Why did they have to leave in the middle of the night? He knew it had something to do with the woman, with the buttons that Father had torn off.

'Where are we going?' he asked.

Father didn't answer. Daniel pulled the blanket over his head so that he was completely enveloped in his own body heat. Inside the warm darkness he imagined that Father was far away. He was sitting next to him but he was in a completely different world. The coach that shook and rocked gave him the same feeling he had during the long voyage across the sea. The horses were transformed into sails that were stretched taut, the boy on the coach box held not reins in his hands but a wheel. He heard the clink of a bottle. Father was drinking. The whip cracked. The coach shook.

Daniel didn't know what time it was, but what Father usually called *a long time* must have passed before the coach came to a stop. Daniel unwrapped himself from the blanket. It was still dark. Father had opened the door of the coach.

'Why are we stopping?' he shouted.

'The horses need rest. They need to eat and have some water.'

'We don't have time.'

'I can't run them to death.'

'I know about oxen. They could do it.'

The boy would not relent.

'Oxen and horses aren't the same thing. In half an hour we'll drive on.'

Father slammed the coach door furiously. But he said nothing. He looked at Daniel. His eyes were glazed, but there was something else too, a fear that Daniel had never seen before.

'I did something I shouldn't have done,' said Father. 'I tried to touch her. She scratched me and broke free. We had to leave in a hurry.'

Daniel waited for more, but it never came. Because he had to pee he climbed out of the coach. The ground was cold under his feet. They were deep in a dense forest. The trees stood black, watching him. He peed. The boy was busy watering the horses.

'Why are you black?' asked the boy. 'Were you burned? Or are you made of coal?'

Father flung open the door.

'Don't talk. Give the horses what they need so we can get moving.'

The boy came over to the door. He was short but broad-shouldered. He had taken off his fur cap. Daniel saw that his hair was cut short and very light.

'I want to see the money,' he said. 'Or else I won't go on.'

Father held up a fistful of notes. The boy tried to snatch them but Father was ready and held them high.

'When we get to Stockholm,' he said. 'Not before.'

The boy kept staring at the money.

'I've never seen that much money in my life. So much money and in such a hurry. What's going on here?'

He walked back to the horses. Daniel climbed into the coach. Father leaned towards him and whispered, 'Everything will be all right. I made a mistake, so we had to change our plans. You can't always follow a path you plan in advance.'

'Did she die?' asked Daniel.

Father stared at him.

'She ran,' he said. 'And she might report me. It will be a scandal. I'll be hunted down. So the plan had to change.'

Daniel tried to pronounce the name of the man in the red coat. He couldn't do it. There were too many letters. But Father understood.

'Wickberg will be chasing me too. I don't know which is worse, ripping off a woman's clothes or breaking an agreement.'

He drank from the bottle again. Daniel could see that his hand was shaking.

'We have to start a new life,' Father said. 'That life starts tonight.'

'Where are we going?'

'I'll tell you when I know.'

The coach began to roll again.

'Try to get some sleep,' said Father. 'I have to think.'

Daniel wrapped himself in the blanket again. He soaked up his own warmth and stroked his face and imagined it was the woman with the slender hands who was touching him.

Daniel woke up because the coach had stopped. He was alone. Father was standing outside talking to the boy. It was beginning to get light. They were still in a forest, but it was more open now. He could see fields and pastures. A lake glimmered between the trees. There was fog. Daniel felt cold and wrapped the blanket tighter around him. He had been dreaming. The antelope had been inside him. But Kiko wasn't there. It was as if the antelope had been searching for him, searching for someone who could finish the work, paint its eyes and finish carving the last strokes in its leap.

Father opened the coach door.

'We're getting out here,' he said. 'The baggage is continuing on to the harbour, but we're getting out here.'

Daniel climbed out. His body was stiff. Father seemed just as frightened as he was earlier that night but his eyes were no longer glazed, and Daniel knew that he had made a decision. The boy took down one of the bags that was tied onto the roof.

'I'll follow you all the way to hell if you don't do as I told you,' Father said to the boy.

'For that much money, anyone will do as he's told.'

'Now off with you.'

The boy clucked at the horses and the coach vanished down the winding road.

They were alone. Daniel was shivering. Father was in a hurry. He yanked open the bag, tossing clothes and combs and brushes onto the ground. Finally he found what he was looking for: a white shirt, which, to Daniel's astonishment, he began tearing apart. He didn't stop until he had shredded the whole shirt into strips. The collar lay like a dead bird on the ground. Father sat down on the bag and wiped the sweat from his brow.

'When this is all over I'll explain,' he said. 'But now we have started a new life. As quickly as possible, we have to put some distance between us and everything that happened before. We're travelling through a desert again. In order to reach our destination you have to do as I say.'

Daniel waited for the rest. He still couldn't understand what had happened.

'People will come and try to catch me,' said Father. 'They know that you and I are travelling together. And you are black. That's why you have to let me do what is necessary. I'm going to wind these strips of cloth around your head and just leave holes for your mouth, nose and eyes. You have been severely injured in a fire. You have to keep your hands inside your coat. We'll put a cap on your head. Then nobody will be able to see that you're black. And no one can find me either.'

Father didn't wait for him to answer, but began winding the rags around Daniel's head. All at once he had the feeling that Father was going to suffocate him and started pulling at the cloth to get it off.

'I'm only doing what I have to do,' Father shouted. 'It's only for a few days. Until we escape. I once saved your life. So you can do this for me.'

Daniel suddenly noticed that Father was not only scared and sweating but he also had tears in his eyes. Daniel stopped pulling at the cloths. No matter what had happened, he had to help Father now. There was no other way out.

Father cut holes for Daniel's eyes, nose and mouth with a little knife that he kept with his brushes and comb.

'Pull in your hands,' he said.

Daniel did as he was told.

'No one can tell that underneath all this you have black skin. Now we have to get moving.'

They started walking. Daniel could feel his skin beginning to itch underneath all the material. Father walked fast with his bag in his hand. He was panting. It was morning now, and the sky was heavily overcast.

'As long as it doesn't rain,' Father said. 'I'll lose my mind if it does.'

Daniel didn't answer. He couldn't talk. He could breathe through his mouth but couldn't move his lips.

The forest grew thinner and soon there were open fields all around them. Father stopped now and then to catch his breath. At the same time he was listening and kept turning round to look behind them. Daniel wondered who was following them.

They had reached a crossroads when Father saw a wagon approaching. He raised his hat and yelled. The man sitting at the reins stopped the horses. Big sacks of flour lay on the bed of the wagon.

'My son has had an accident,' Father said. 'He has terrible burns on his face. We're on our way to the city to see the doctors.'

The man holding the reins stared aghast at Daniel.

'Whine,' Father whispered. 'Whimper and moan.'

Daniel whined. The man shook his head.

'So the boy has burned his face, eh? Then he won't have long to live.'

Father lifted Daniel up onto the sacks and climbed up after him. The man clucked at the horses and urged them into a trot.

'Of course I can pay you for your trouble,' Father said. 'If possible we'd like to go down to the Stadsgård Harbour.'

The man turned round in surprise. 'Are there doctors there? Are there hospitals among the dockers?'

Father didn't reply. Instead he took out a banknote and stuffed it into the man's coat pocket.

When they entered the town Father told Daniel to lie down and pull his coat up around his head. He did as he was told. The man with the reins looked at him.

'Is he dead?' he asked.

'He'll be all right,' replied Father. 'But I'm too tired to answer any more questions.'

'My name is Eriksson,' said the man. 'My horses are called Stork and Giant. Not very good names, but I've never been good with names, even though I've had a lot of horses.'

'My name is Hult,' said Father. 'I come from Västerås, where I sell hardware. My son, my only son who's lying here, is called Olle.'

Daniel listened, but nothing Father said surprised him any more. After he had left the desert and travelled across the sea he had become part of a story: the story that Father had in his head, in which nothing was really true. Daniel wondered what would happen if he stood up in the wagon and tore off all the strips of cloth. Then there wouldn't be any more story. Then he would be himself again.

But who would Father be?

He lay there looking up at the sky. Kiko had taught him that a hunter always had to have patience, always had to be prepared to wait until the right moment. Daniel imagined that he was a hunter who was waiting. Some day the moment would come when he could finally teach himself to walk on water.

It was already evening by the time they arrived. When the horses stopped, Daniel could smell the water, but when he tried to sit up, Father pushed him back down.

'It's best that you lie down,' he said softly. 'At least for a while longer, until it gets really dark.'

The man with the reins gave him a worried look.

'I think he's paler now,' he said. 'Is he dying?'

'How can you see that he's paler?' asked Father. 'His face is covered with bandages.'

'It's just a feeling,' said Eriksson. 'But I won't ask any more. I have to get going now. The flour has to be unloaded. And I have a way to go yet.'

Father took a few more banknotes out of his pocket. Daniel had a feeling that the money he had received from Wickberg would soon be gone. He wondered how these pieces of paper could have such great value.

'I need help,' said Father. 'In a few hours there's a passenger ferry leaving for Kalmar. We need a cabin.'

'Kalmar?'

'There's an excellent skin doctor there,' said Father. 'The best in the country. He's often called to the royal residences all over Europe.'

The man shook his head doubtfully. 'Will the boy be able to manage the trip?'

'He has to. I'll watch the horses and the flour if you would be so kind as to procure a cabin and tickets.'

Eriksson vanished into the darkness.

'Soon it will be over,' Father said. 'Just as long as we get out of here.'

'It itches,' said Daniel.

'I understand. But soon. Just as soon as we get on board and close the door to our cabin. Then I'll take off the bandages and explain what has happened. Everything will be all right. We have started a new life.'

When Eriksson returned he had the tickets in his hand. Father gave him another banknote and asked him to drive them to the gangway. The boat was illuminated by paraffin lamps.

'I said they were for Herr Hult and his son,' said Eriksson.

'Excellent,' replied Father. 'You're a clever man. And your horses have lovely names. Unusual, but lovely.'

When they reached the boat Father told Daniel to wait by the wagon. A man in uniform was standing by the gangway and checking the passengers' tickets. On the foredeck they were busy stowing baggage. Father went up and spoke to the man in uniform. Eriksson stood stroking one of his horses on the back while he looked at Daniel.

'It can't be easy,' he said. 'It must hurt a lot. But you're very patient.'

'My name is Olle,' said Daniel. 'I believe in God.'

Eriksson nodded slowly. 'That's probably for the best,' he said, 'even though it doesn't help. But in the end it's all you've got. Hope. And someone called God.'

Father came back. 'Keep your hands inside,' he whispered.

Eriksson lifted Daniel down from the wagon.

'I hope all goes well,' said Eriksson.

Father nodded and gave him one of his last banknotes.

The man by the gangway shook his head in alarm when he saw Daniel's bandaged face.

'There might be rough weather south of Landsort,' he said. 'Can the boy stand the rough seas?'

'I've given him some medicine,' said Father. 'He'll be asleep.'

They went down to their cabin and Father locked the door and sank exhausted onto the bunk. The cabin was cramped. Daniel remembered how it had been on the ship during the long journey from the desert.

Suddenly his heart began beating very fast. Could it be possible that they were on their way back to the desert and he wouldn't have to learn how to walk on water?

'You've been good,' said Father as he loosened the cloth stuck to Daniel's sweaty face. 'You've been very good, and I'll never forget it.'

Daniel waited. But Father still didn't say anything about where they were going.

The boat gave a lurch. There was a snap of mooring lines and the sound of commands. Then the boat began to vibrate.

Daniel sat down next to Father.

Now he'll tell me, he thought.

But Father just put his hands to his face and began to weep without a sound.

CHAPTER 19

They had tickets to Kalmar, but they got off the evening before in Västervik when the boat landed at Slottsholmen. Because it was dark, Daniel didn't have to put the bandages over his face. While Father ventured into the night to find someone with a horse and wagon, Daniel sat and watched the baggage. A lone dog wandered about by his legs but then vanished into the darkness. A light misty rain was falling but there was no wind at all. Only a few people were boarding or leaving the boat. An argument arose by the gangway when a drunken man was refused passage even though he had a ticket. Finally he left, cursing, and he too disappeared into the darkness that seemed to swallow up everyone.

Daniel felt a cold breeze from the sea. It brought with it the same smell he remembered from the evening he had walked into the water and hoped he would die. It was only a few days ago, but it felt as though he had dreamed it.

During the boat trip Father didn't say a word. His silence finally hardened into a mask over his face. It was a silence that Daniel could not penetrate. He had no idea what Father was thinking. Now and then he would burst into tears but only for brief spells. Daniel merely waited. He still didn't know where they were or where they were headed. During the journey he was not allowed to leave the cabin and no one but Father came in. He brought Daniel food and then took away the empty plates.

The boat rolled heavily the first night, and Father got seasick and threw up several times. Daniel lay in his bunk and imagined he was a very small child rocking on Be's back, wrapped in a piece of cloth that smelled of her body. Occasionally the boat shook violently when it was struck by a big wave. For a few hours they hove to and waited for the wind to die down. Daniel heard cows mooing on deck and people moaning in the cabin next door, but he was completely calm. He was waiting. His only thought was that they were on their way back across the sea.

Their departure happened very suddenly. Daniel was sleeping and dreaming about the smell of roasted meat when Father shook him awake.

'We have to get off soon,' he said. 'You'd better get dressed.'

Daniel looked out through the gilded porthole. Outside it was black. Waves sloshed up towards his face and broke against the glass. He suddenly developed a stomach ache. The trip had gone too quickly, they couldn't be there yet. Besides, it was much too cold. When he pressed his hand against the glass with the drops of water running down the outside, he could feel the cold. He turned and looked at Father, who was busy closing one of their bags.

'Are we there yet?' Daniel asked.

'We're going to get off,' said Father. 'In a town called Västervik. Then we'll continue our journey.'

He put down the bag and stood up. Daniel could see from his eyes that he'd been drinking.

'We've begun a new life,' he said. 'But now we have to get off this boat. Everything will be all right.'

Father vanished into the night. The gangplank was pulled up and the boat turned slowly in the small harbour basin and then disappeared into the darkness. The last thing Daniel saw was the white lantern that sat atop the foremast. The quay was now deserted. He pulled the blanket round him and huddled down. Father was gone. The lone dog came back and sniffed his legs, but when he tried to pet it, the dog gave a twitch and went away.

Daniel was struck by the thought that Father might have left him, just as the dog and the boat had done. Vanished completely into the night. He was alone now. Alone with the baggage and the dark and the misty rain. He thought about the old ones who died in the desert. When they felt that it was time, they went away. Some lay down in their huts, others in the shade, and Daniel remembered one old man whose name he had forgotten who had leaned against a rock wall. There he had sat, without eating or drinking or speaking for more than a week before he died. Maybe Daniel should prepare himself for the

166

same thing to happen to him. When the sun came up he would sit on the bags and do nothing but wait for his heart to thump one last time and then he would be dead.

The thought terrified him. He jumped up from the baggage, threw off the blanket, and began running in the direction Father had gone. He didn't want to die, not yet, not here. Without Father he would never get back to the desert. He would die without anyone knowing about it. Be and Kiko would search in vain and never find him.

He ran straight into someone standing in the darkness: Father. Behind him came a clattering horse-drawn wagon.

'I told you to watch the baggage. What are you doing here?'

'I heard you coming.'

Father grabbed him hard by the arm.

'We have to leave right now. We must be far away from here by daybreak. We're already late. I couldn't find anything but this horse, and it doesn't look too strong.'

The man sitting on the driver's seat had only one eye. He was old and his lower lip hung down. He looked at Daniel as if he didn't really exist. Father loaded the baggage and Daniel climbed up and sat among the bags. Father sat next to the driver and pulled an old fur around his shoulders.

They left the town and after a few hours stopped to rest in a forest. Whenever other wagon-drivers came down the road, Father would take Daniel with him to hide in the woods.

'Where are we going?' Daniel asked again. By then it was already afternoon.

'We'll be there soon,' replied Father. 'Tomorrow night. As long as this damn horse doesn't fall over.'

They kept going even when it got dark. Now and then Daniel glimpsed the sea on the left side of the road, but it was so far away that he couldn't smell the water. The only thing he smelled was the fear from Father's body as he sat in silence on the driver's seat. When Daniel looked at him from behind, at the fur wrapped around his shoulders, he thought that Father was slowly turning into an animal.

* * *

Daniel was asleep when they drove into Simrishamn. He woke when the wagon stopped. He sat up, his body sore all over, and in spite of the darkness he recognised the house where they had spent their first night after they left the coal lighter and came ashore. He wanted to shout. He was right. They were on their way back. There was a ship waiting here that would take them back across the sea. Father turned round. Daniel couldn't resist the impulse to throw his arms around his neck. He had never done that before. Father shrank back as if afraid that Daniel would bite him. He pushed him away.

'I'll see if they have a free room,' he said. 'I can't pay, but I'll tell them that you're sick.'

He took the bandage out of his pocket.

'Moan like you're in pain when anyone looks at you. I'll carry you inside.'

Daniel nodded. He had understood the words, but not what they meant.

Father paid the man with the horse. The baggage was lifted down and the wagon rolled off. Daniel wrapped his head in the cloths. When Father came out he had the proprietor with him. The man had his shirt off and was carrying a lantern in his hand.

'Did he fall?' he asked.

'From a cliff.'

The man with the lantern was worried.

'He's not going to die, is he? Places where people die can get a bad reputation.'

'No, he's not going to die.'

'But he's moaning like he'll expire at any minute.'

Daniel understood and stopped groaning at once.

'What he needs is sleep,' said Father. 'I guarantee he won't die.'

The man with the lantern nodded dubiously. Then he shouted and a boy sleeping underneath the staircase came stumbling out.

'Put the baggage in the room with the wood stove.'

They had the same room as last time. Father sat down heavily on the bed after carrying Daniel up the stairs. Daniel could see that he was very tired.

'When do we travel more?' he asked.

Father gazed a while at him before he replied.

'Tomorrow,' he said. 'Tomorrow we'll set off. Take off the bandage. Lie down and go to sleep.'

Daniel curled up close to Father's back. Everything was different now. He didn't know what had happened with the woman and the buttons but it must have been something good, since it made Father realise that they had to return to the desert.

That night Daniel had a hard time sleeping. He kept getting up and standing by the window and looking down into the courtyard where the two girls had been skipping. A single lantern hung by the gate out to the street. He felt completely calm now.

'I'm coming soon,' he whispered. 'I'm coming home soon.'

When Daniel woke up the next day, Father was gone. A heavy rain was falling and the drops drummed against the windowpane. Daniel stayed in bed. He imagined Father was searching for a ship and a captain. Soon they would be on their way. He jumped out of bed and went over to the window. The cobblestone courtyard was flooded. Daniel went back to bed. It was as if the whole building was being turned into a ship. The bed moved, the curtains fluttered as if the ship were slowly starting to roll. He tried to remember everything that had happened since he had lain in this bed the first time. But the memories were gone. He could already see himself wearing only a loincloth, on his way with his family through the desert.

He fell asleep and when he opened his eyes Father was standing by the bed. Next to him stood another man who smiled with kindly eyes.

'This is Dr Madsen,' said Father. 'He works at the hospital here. We met in the city where we visited a man lying in bed who gave us money. Do you remember?'

Daniel remembered vaguely. Not the man in the bed but a woman who slammed the door too hard.

'We're going to take a trip together,' Father went on. 'We'll leave as soon as it stops raining. We'll be there before evening.'

'On the sea?' asked Daniel.

Dr Madsen smiled. Father shook his head.

'No,' he said, 'not the sea. Once again we have to ride behind a horse. But it's not a long trip.'

Daniel got out of bed and dressed. The rain had stopped. When he looked out of the window he saw the two girls. He waved at them, but they didn't see him. They didn't have a skipping rope.

Once again they sat on a wagon. It rolled out of the town, and Daniel wondered where they were going. All around him lay brown fields. Here and there stood some lonely trees full of screeching flocks of black birds. In some of the fields he saw wagons with horses, and people creeping about in the mud. Father shook his head.

'Can you imagine anything worse? Slogging through mud up to your chin, picking turnips?'

'Many of them are Poles,' replied Madsen. 'They come here for the season. Live with the pigs in the barns. Get the same food. And yet they're eager for the work.'

'Mud,' Father muttered. 'All that mud they have to crawl around in. From morning to night.'

'I thought you were going back to the sand,' said Madsen.

Father looked at Madsen, who nodded without saying anything more. Daniel wondered why. Something gave him a sudden pain in the stomach. Why didn't Father want to talk about the desert?

They continued on in silence. The flocks of birds were fighting and screeching above the trees. The people were crawling in the mud. Church bells could be heard in the distance. Daniel realised that the landscape scared him. There was no water anywhere. Only this sticky clay that clung to the bottom of his shoes and made them even heavier on his feet. This was what made this journey unlike all the others.

Daniel tried to think about what Father had said. *They were going to start a new life. A life that would be better.* The only life that could be any better was in the desert. That's where they would have to go. Daniel knew that he would find Kiko and Be again. Even if they were dead, he would search for them, and there would be other families he could follow on their nomadic wanderings.

He hopped down from the wagon to stretch his legs. The clay began to clump under his shoes so he took them off and ran barefoot.

'It's too cold,' said Father. 'You might catch a chill.'

'The boy is healthy,' said Madsen. 'He'll be fine.'

Daniel stopped and looked at a bird of prey hovering motionless on the wind. It dived and caught a mouse only a few metres away from him. The horse gave a start when the bird dived and the driver pulled on the reins. The bird, which was brown, flapped away with its quarry in its beak.

'A buzzard,' said Madsen. 'There's good feeding here. There are more of them every year.'

'Right now I feel more like the mouse,' said Father. 'A few days ago it was just the opposite. Everything can change very fast.'

Madsen nodded but didn't reply. Daniel waited in vain for Father to say more.

That afternoon they turned off the main road and came to a town where the houses were low and the mud seemed to creep all the way up their front steps. Madsen pointed and they made another turn onto a track that was barely navigable. They stopped next to a low house that was only just standing. Madsen climbed down and went into the cobblestone yard and banged on the door. A man with his shirt unbuttoned opened it. Madsen went inside and the door closed. The driver had hopped down from his seat and went behind some bushes to take a piss. Daniel climbed up onto the driver's seat and Father let him hold the reins.

'Now we just have to wait,' said Father. 'Dr Madsen loves people. That's why he became a doctor. He could have been a professor at a university. But he wanted to go out into the countryside and take care of sick people.'

'Is someone sick?' asked Daniel. 'In the house?'

'He's talking to them,' replied Father. 'We'll wait till he comes back out.'

'Then we're going on?'

Father didn't answer. He climbed down from the driver's seat and started off along the track. Soon he was so far away that he looked like a lone tree out in the field. Daniel held the reins and followed him with his eyes. He still couldn't get inside Father's thoughts. Something was very different, but he didn't know what. The driver came back and took the reins. His flies were unbuttoned and he smelled like piss.

'You little black devil,' he said with a menacing smile. 'You're not going to hold *my* reins.'

Daniel quickly moved off the driver's seat. Father was still standing out in the field. Slowly, as if he were searching for something, he looked all around. Daniel jumped off the wagon and ran over to him. Father held out his hand and Daniel grabbed it eagerly. It was several days now since Father had voluntarily offered his hand.

'It's lonely here,' said Father. 'Lonely like in the desert. It's as if heaven and earth are merging. You can't tell where one begins and the other ends.'

Daniel didn't understand what he meant. He knew what the words meant, *heaven* and *earth*, but not what Father was trying to tell him.

The farmhouse door slammed. In the distance they could see Madsen coming out. Father kept holding Daniel's hand. When they reached the house Madsen was not alone. By his side stood a man and a woman. They were wearing grey clothes and had pale faces, but they smiled at Daniel.

'Everything is fine,' said Madsen. 'Ten riksdaler per month. They're good people. Edvin and Alma Andersson. I helped Alma once when she had the quinsy.'

'I could have died,' said the woman. 'But he cut it out without killing me.'

Father let go of Daniel's hand.

'Go and fetch your skipping rope.'

'I don't feel like skipping,' Daniel replied.

Now he was starting to get scared again. Father was far away, even though he was standing right next to him.

'Do as I say,' said Father impatiently. 'It will only take a moment.'

'Then will we keep going?'

Father didn't reply. 'Fetch the rope,' he said. 'You've been sitting still far too much the past few days. That's not good for a child.'

Daniel went and fetched the rope from the wagon. The driver stood stroking the horse's mane.

'You little black devil,' he snarled. 'I know what the Devil's children look like.'

Daniel took the rope and went off along the track. He watched Father shake hands and knew that a great danger was approaching. But where it was coming from he didn't know. He tried to skip but stumbled and fell. The rope wound like a snake around his legs. His feet were black with mud and he was freezing cold.

Father called to him and he went back. He yanked on the rope and hoped it would snap.

Father smiled, but the smile was dangerous.

'I have to go on a trip,' he said. 'A short trip. I'll be back soon. In the meantime you will live here. With Edvin and Alma. They are good people and they will take care of you. What did I teach you to say?'

'*My name is Daniel. I believe in God.*'

'That's right. And you will live here until I come back.'

Daniel felt the terror growing.

'Tomorrow?' he asked.

His tears began to flow. It was the secret river that broke through all the dams; the river of pain that everyone carried inside, the one Be had told him about.

'Maybe not tomorrow. But soon.'

Suddenly it was clear to Daniel that Father was leaving right now. They wouldn't even have time to say a proper goodbye. Madsen had gone over to the wagon and was standing there waiting.

Daniel yelled and clung to Father. If he left, everything would come to an end. Father was leaving him, and he was lying when he said he would come back. He had driven him here, as far away from the sea as possible.

'Control yourself,' said Father. 'It's for your own good.'

Daniel screamed. He was like an animal being led to the slaughter. When Father tried to prise his arms away he sank his teeth into his wrist. Father jerked away and they both fell over in the mud. The man named Edvin pulled at Daniel, but he wouldn't let go. His teeth were the last hold on life he had left.

But he couldn't keep it up. Father got up from the mud. Blood was running from his wrist.

'This won't work,' said the woman, upset. 'The boy is grief-stricken.'

'It will be fine,' said Father. 'Parting is always dramatic.'

'You ought to tell him the truth,' said the man holding Daniel's arms. 'You ought to tell him the truth about how long you'll be gone.'

'He knows I'll come back. When I'm gone he'll settle down.'

Daniel could feel the grip around his arms slacken. He tore himself loose and clung tight to Father again. He knew his hands weren't enough; he had to sink his teeth into him, act like a desperate animal, hold on tight, and he tried to get to Father's throat with his teeth. But Father hit him hard in the face so he fell to the ground. The blow had struck his nose and he started to bleed.

'Now calm down!' Father yelled. 'I'm doing everything for your sake. I want you to live here until I come back.'

'It's not going to work!' shouted the woman.

'It will work,' said Father. 'As soon as I'm gone he'll calm down.'

Then he turned and started towards the wagon. He pressed a handkerchief to his bleeding wrist. Daniel tried to run after him, but the man named Edvin grabbed his arms. The wagon rolled away. Father didn't look back. Daniel had stopped screaming. Now he was wailing, but softly, as if he had already crept off into a thicket to die.

He closed his eyes.

The last he saw of Father was an image inside his eyelids. He was holding a rifle in his hand and sighting at an antelope that was taking a leap.

The rifle fired.

The antelope was gone.

Daniel opened his eyes.

The wagon had vanished.

A flock of birds was fighting above a solitary tree far out in a field.

The fog came rolling in and enveloped everything in its white silence.

PART III

SON OF THE WIND

CHAPTER 20

One morning Daniel awoke to find the ground completely white. At first he thought it was a dream, that he was still asleep and back in the desert. But when he saw the black birds fighting above the piles of manure and went outside into the yard and stepped barefoot onto the cold white blanket, he knew that he was still with Edvin and Alma. He walked across the yard. The cold penetrated his body quickly, and his footprints looked like those he had left behind in the warm sand.

He left tracks in both the cold white and the warm white. He didn't understand how that was possible.

Alma had come out in the yard and discovered him.

'You can't go barefoot in the frost!' she shouted. 'Put on your shoes!'

During the time that had passed since Father left, Daniel had realised that Alma was afraid of him. She liked him, sometimes stroking his head, especially when no one was looking, but she was afraid. Daniel didn't know why. She avoided looking him in the eye, and when she didn't think he would notice she kept watch over him.

Daniel and Alma shared a secret. He was sure of that. But as yet he didn't know what it was.

Edvin came out on the steps.

'The boy's standing here barefoot in the frost,' he said. 'Why don't you tell him to put on his shoes?'

'I did, but he won't move.'

By the time Edvin came out, Daniel's feet had already turned into frozen clumps. He wanted to hurry inside and curl up by the fire burning in the kitchen, but something made him stand still. The cold whiteness under his feet was tugging at him. The earth desired him, wanted to have him.

'He can't just stand there,' said Alma. 'He'll freeze to death.'

Edvin shook his head. 'How can we work out what he's thinking?'

He walked through the whiteness and stood next to Daniel.

'You can't walk outside in the frost barefoot,' he said. 'Can't you feel how everything is freezing?'

Daniel was shaking all over. He tried to be still but couldn't do it.

'We're going back inside,' said Edvin.

He took hold of Daniel's hand but Daniel didn't move. Through the kitchen window Daniel could see the two milkmaids and the hired hand eating breakfast. They were looking out at what was happening in the yard with curiosity.

'You'll have to carry him in,' said Alma.

'He has to learn to obey. If we tell him to go inside he has to do it. I don't understand why he won't wear shoes.'

'What difference does it make if you understand it or not? He can't stand out here freezing to death.'

Edvin lifted Daniel up and carried him inside. In the kitchen Alma wrapped him in a blanket and began rubbing his feet. She had strong hands. Daniel liked it when she grabbed him hard. It was almost as if Be's hands were touching him.

'What he did outside?' asked the milkmaid whose name was Serja and who came from Poland. She spoke poor Swedish. Several times Daniel had heard Alma scolding her and calling her lazy. She ought to take lessons from Daniel, who already spoke much better than she did, even though he was black and came from very far away.

'Don't talk so much,' said Edvin. 'The cows are waiting.'

The girls and the hired hand left. Alma rubbed Daniel's feet. Edvin sat on a chair by the deal table, staring at his hands.

Daniel gazed into the fire. Far inside among the flames there was another world. He could see Be and Kiko, he could see the snakes gliding through the sand, and the clouds and the rain and the rock face where the antelope had frozen in its leap.

He gave a start at the thought. The antelope was caught in its leap there on the rock the same way that he had started to freeze solid in the white stuff that covered the ground. It must mean that the gods were very close to him. Somewhere underneath his feet. They were the ones who had tugged at him and slowly tried to change him from a human being into an image carved in a mountain wall.

He pulled away from Alma, threw off the blanket and rushed out into the yard again. This time he also took off his clothes and was standing naked by the time Alma and Edvin came after him. Daniel tried to resist when Edvin grabbed hold of him, but Edvin was strong. He lifted the boy up and carried him inside. Daniel tried to bite him on the neck, but Edvin held him far enough away that he couldn't reach him. He put Daniel down on the floor by the fire.

'Now you're not going out again!' he shouted. 'Not without clothes and not without shoes. You live here, and we are responsible for you until Bengler comes back.'

Daniel didn't answer. He knew that Father would never come back. He also realised that if he ran outside again Edvin might hit him. And he didn't want that. He let Alma wrap the blanket around him again and rub his feet.

'If only I understood,' said Edvin, who had sat down in the chair again. 'But I can't see into his head.'

'We have taken on responsibility for him,' Alma said. 'It doesn't matter whether we understand or not.'

'But how can you raise a child you can't understand?'

Alma didn't reply. Daniel thought about being the only child in the house. Alma and Edvin didn't have any children of their own, even though they were already starting to get old. Maybe the children were already dead or were so big that they had left. He wanted to know, but he didn't dare ask.

'We'll have to talk to the pastor,' said Alma. 'Maybe he can give us some advice.'

'What will Hallén understand that we don't?'

'He is a pastor.'

'He's a bad pastor. Sometimes I wonder if he really believes in what he preaches.'

'Don't blaspheme. He's a man of God. Besides, he's not stuck-up.'

'Somebody said he was the son of a town whore up in Småland.'

'Don't blaspheme. I want you to talk to him.'

Edvin got up from the table. 'Things might get better when he starts school. It's not working the way it is now.'

Alma kneaded and rubbed. 'We must have patience,' she said. 'And we have to give it time.'

Daniel looked into the fire again. The flames were dancing. When he closed his eyes the dance continued inside his eyelids. The cold had made him tired. Every night since Father left, Daniel had woken up in the darkness. He had dreamed that Father was standing outside the house, but nobody heard him knocking. But when he opened his eyes there was no one at the door. There was only the snoring hired hand, the milkmaids, and himself sleeping alone in a corner of the kitchen.

Edvin went outside. Daniel closed his eyes. Alma kept rubbing his feet. Daniel tried to imagine Father's face, but he was gone. Maybe he wasn't even alive any longer. Then Daniel would have lost two fathers. First Kiko and then Father. Daniel often tried to work out what had happened that evening when the woman with the buttons was alone with Father. Everything that took place after that, the plans that were changed, had been affected by something that happened then. Daniel searched for an answer that he couldn't find. How could Father just leave him here? In a place where there wasn't even any sea? There were only the ponds in the beech woods and the puddles in the fields after a long rain.

Daniel didn't know how long Father had been away. He knew that days, weeks, and months had passed. The only thing he was sure of was that the moon had been full four times since he left. It had grown colder, and the earth had changed and turned white.

For the first few days Daniel thought that he had been left far from the sea so that he would die. Maybe he had also hoped during that time that Father might come back. But late one evening, when Edvin had been drinking and was tipsy, Daniel had listened to a conversation between him and Alma in the bedroom. They were talking about Father. The first payment of ten riksdaler had arrived. It had been sent to Hornman the organist, who often handled estate inventories and was an honest man. Edvin had said that Father would probably never come back, but as long as the money arrived on time they didn't have to worry. Alma asked about the future. What would happen when Daniel was bigger? And Edvin replied that he would be a farmhand like the others.

In that instant Father had vanished for good. He had been transformed into a shadow. And Daniel started to hate him. He was an evil man behind all his friendly words.

*   *   *

180

That was also when Daniel started to make a plan.

It had come to him from a bird.

Every morning when the hired hand was working with Edvin out in the fields and the girls were milking, Daniel went up onto a hill behind the house. From there he could see the horizon. Black birds that always seemed restless were riding on the updraughts or screeching in a clump of trees in the middle of the nearest field.

On this particular morning a lone seagull had joined the flock. The black birds chased it off, and as it left, the gull sailed right over Daniel's head. He remembered that bird. There had been flocks of them around the ship that brought him here. Whenever they approached land the birds had appeared. Daniel realised that the gull had come to remind him that the sea was still there, even if he couldn't see it.

He had to prepare for his escape. Without attracting attention, he had to find out in which direction the sea lay. Then he would take off. He would find somewhere he could be alone and learn to walk on the water. No one would find him, even though they would surely look for him.

There was no danger from the two milkmaids and the hired hand, but Edvin and Alma were always trying to see inside him and read his thoughts. He had to build a shell around himself that their eyes could not penetrate.

The most important thing was for him to act friendly and humour them. Even though he hated the shoes he was forced to wear, he would try to avoid showing his disgust. Only when he was alone would he kick them off and walk barefoot on the ground, which was growing colder all the time. He would do as he was told. Whenever Alma or Edvin asked him for help he would do more than they asked of him.

But this morning he was unsuccessful. He woke up and saw all that whiteness and he couldn't control himself. Now he had to be careful so that Edvin and Alma would not discover his secret.

Alma finished rubbing his feet. She had bad teeth but he liked her smile anyway.

'Are you warm now?'

Daniel nodded.

'Then you can get dressed and go and play.'

Daniel went outside. The white on the ground had been trampled. He stood completely still in the yard and looked at the smoke that came out of his mouth every time he breathed. As soon as the girls were finished milking he would go into the barn. It was warm in there. He would have liked to sleep there with the animals, bedded down in their straw.

One of the piglets had escaped from its pen and was snuffling around in all the white. Daniel didn't like the pigs, though he didn't know why. He liked their smell but he was afraid of their eyes. They looked at him as if they wanted to do him harm. He was sure that they had once been people who had died and now had come back to live another life. But they must have been evil people, since they didn't come back as horses or cows.

He looked at the pig snuffling closer and closer to him. He took a step to the side. But the pig followed him. Suddenly it began to change. It had a human face now, a face that Daniel had seen before. He jumped out of the way but the pig kept following him. He yelled. It was Kiko who had taught him that loud noises could keep beasts of prey away. He also knew that you should never look a beast of prey in the eye or it might attack. Kiko had taught him that animals had to be handled in different ways. If a snake raised its head to spit poison, you should stand motionless and hold your breath.

But Kiko had never seen a pig. Daniel's shouting didn't help. The pig kept coming closer. Daniel searched his memory in vain for where he had seen this face before.

Then he knew.

It was the man who had killed Kiko. The pig was the same man who had shot Kiko and then kicked his dead body. Daniel looked around for a weapon, but there was nothing in the yard apart from him and the pig that kept coming closer and closer. He tore off one of his wooden shoes and slammed it hard on the pig's head. It shrieked. He hit it again. Now the pig's legs began to give way. The yard was slippery. It tried to get away but Daniel kept hitting it. Somewhere behind him he heard Alma yelling. Then the hired hand and Edvin came running up. The milkmaids stood in the doorway of the barn. And Daniel kept hitting. He didn't stop even when Edvin tossed him aside. By then the pig was dead. Its blood had run out onto the white ground. In the moment of death the pig had shut its eyes. Daniel knew that he had conquered the man who killed Kiko. He now had his revenge. Kiko would have been proud of him.

Edvin stared in astonishment at the dead animal.

'He beat it to death with his wooden shoe,' said Alma.

'But why?'

'I don't know.'

Edvin looked at Daniel. Daniel could feel that he had his shell on now. Edvin couldn't see into him.

'Why did you do it?'

Daniel didn't answer. Edvin wouldn't understand anyway. No one would understand.

'Why did you do it? Why kill a little piglet with a wooden shoe?'

'He's crazy,' the hired hand blurted out. 'He's crazy and he doesn't belong here.'

'He lives here,' shouted Edvin. 'I'm getting ten riksdaler a month for him. He lives here and he will stay here.'

The hired hand spat but didn't dare reply.

Edvin looked at Daniel again. Daniel moved away.

'He saw what you were thinking,' said Alma. 'He saw that you were thinking of hitting him. And you did.'

'I haven't touched him.'

'But he could feel the blow you were thinking of giving him.'

Edvin motioned the hired hand to take away the dead animal. Alma called to the milkmaids to go back inside the barn.

'This won't do any longer. We'll have to talk to the pastor. Maybe he can get him to say why he did it.'

'He wants to go home,' said Alma. 'It can't be anything else. He wants to go home.'

'But he doesn't have a home, does he? Aren't they all dead? That's what Bengler said.'

'That man is a big windbag. I didn't believe half of what he said.'

Edvin looked at his hands. He said no more. Then he went back out in the field.

'What harm did the pig do you?' asked Alma.

From her hand Daniel could feel that she wasn't angry with him. He put his fingers cautiously around her wrist to feel her pulse and sensed that it beat just as calmly as Be's heart used to do. But at the same time he knew that he couldn't answer her question. He could say something that wasn't true, of course, that he didn't know why he felt compelled to kill the pig, but she would never understand that the evil man who had once killed Kiko had searched for him and changed himself into a pig.

So he said the only words he knew would never be misunderstood. *'My name is Daniel. I believe in God.'*

He put on his wooden shoes and left Alma. One shoe was bloody. He could feel his foot sticking to it. Alma stood and looked at him. She's the one who can see inside me, Daniel thought. I have to watch out for her. But at the same time she's the one who understands that I'm not actually here, I am somewhere else.

He went up onto the hill behind the house. Far out in the fields he could see Edvin and the hired hand. They were busy moving away a large stone. The wind had begun to blow. The black birds sat motionless and silent in the clump of trees. Daniel searched for the seagull. He listened. Sometimes he thought he could hear drums in the distance, but then he realised that it was only the wind that blew across the fields and then was gone.

He was cold and his nose was running. No matter how much he sniffled, his nose was always full. In the desert he had never had a cold. There he was sometimes struck by fever or had a stomach ache, but he had never had a runny nose.

He kept on gazing at the horizon. Edvin and the hired hand had managed to get the stone onto a wooden sledge. The two horses were pulling and straining at the sledge. Daniel had noticed that Edvin never hit his horses. Father had whipped his oxen. Sometimes he had loosed some unknown wrath on them, even though they were pulling as best they could, but Edvin never struck the horses. He might slap the reins, but never so hard that it hurt the animals.

Daniel continued to scan the horizon as he slowly turned round.

He saw something moving on a cart track on the other side of the hill. It led to a neighbouring farm where a family named Hermansson lived. Soon after Father had left, people from this farm had come to have a look at him. He had shaken hands, bowed and avoided looking

184

them in the eye. They were young people, and they stood silently with mouths agape, watching him. Finally it was too much for Alma, who told Daniel to go out to the barn, and then served coffee to the guests. He had stayed in the barn until he heard the clop of hooves in the yard. He had peeked through a crack in the barn wall, and when the neighbours were gone he came out.

'They'll get used to you,' Alma said. 'But it's terrible the way people can stare.'

Daniel fixed his gaze on what was moving along the cart track. At first he thought it was an animal. Then he saw that it was a person. A woman. She was running. He hadn't seen her before. She was heading towards the hill. He moved aside and hid behind some bushes.

When she reached the top of the hill he saw that it was a girl. He guessed that she was older than the girls who had skipped in the court-yard in Simrishamn. He lay motionless behind the bushes and watched her. Her clothes were dirty and she had clumps of mud in her blonde hair. Daniel wondered what she was up to. She was squatting down and scratching with her fingers in the mud. After a while he realised she was searching for something. As she dug she muttered, but he couldn't hear what she was saying. He could see that she was in a hurry. She gave up on the first hole she scratched. Then she put her ear to the ground and crawled about until she stopped and began digging again.

Daniel sneezed.

It came on him so quickly that he couldn't stifle the sound. The girl gave a start and saw him at once behind the bushes. She's going to scream, he thought. It'll be the same way as with the pig. Edvin and Alma will come dashing over and this time Edvin will do what he's thinking of doing. His heavy hand will fall like a stone on my head and it will hurt.

Daniel stood up. But the girl didn't scream. She didn't even stare. She smiled and started to laugh. She got up out of the mud and came over to him. He could smell the urine and dirt on her. On her fore-head along the hairline he saw dried mud.

'I've heard about you,' said the girl. 'But they wouldn't let me come along and see you. They thought I'd behave badly.'

She spoke rapidly and her words sounded mushy in her thick dialect. Yet he could still understand what she said.

She grabbed hold of his hand.

'You're completely black,' she said. 'In the church there's a devil on the wall. He's black too. Do you come from hell?'

'I come from the desert.'

'I don't know what that is. But your name is Daniel?'

'I believe in God.'

'I don't. But you can't tell anyone that.'

The girl was still holding his hand. He took hold of her wrist, just as he had done with Alma. The girl's heart was beating hard.

'What were you searching for?' Daniel asked.

'Sometimes I hear voices in the mud. As if someone is trapped down there. I try to help them. But I never find anyone.'

She let go of his hand and spat out some pebbles.

'I like to chew on pebbles. Sometimes I can make them clack. Do you chew on pebbles?'

Daniel shook his head.

'My name is Sanna,' said the girl. 'And I'm crazy.'

Then she ran off. Daniel watched her go. For the first time since Father left him he felt like laughing.

She ran along the cart track.

He watched her until she disappeared.

CHAPTER 21

Every morning David Hallén repeated the same ritual. Just after seven he would leave the dilapidated parsonage and walk across the road to the church. Inside the sacristy he swept out the mouse droppings that always awaited him. During the night the mice usually tried to nibble at the hymnals and the Bible on the table in the whitewashed room.

Then he would stand in front of the mirror with his head bowed, take a deep breath, and look at his face. Every morning he hoped that it wouldn't be his own face that met him, but the face of the God he served. But it was his own features that looked back at him with eyes wide, a nose that was growing redder all the time and those pale cheeks that were always poorly shaven.

This morning too he encountered his own face in the mirror. Since he still hadn't given up hope that a miracle might occur, he felt the same disappointment he had felt so many mornings before. He had now been the pastor of the congregation for eighteen years. When he was young he had dreamed of the mission, that his poor congregation far out on the wind-lashed plain of Skåne would be one step on a long journey. But he had never gone any further. The fields had become his ocean. He had never reached the foreign lands where the heat was strong, the diseases perilous and the black people thirsted for salvation. He had remained here. The children had come too quickly and there were far too many of them. The years had passed before he actually noticed and now he was too old to start over. The mud would hold him here until he dropped.

David Hallén was a stern pastor, and he had an energy that could sometimes drive him to rage. He was impatient, couldn't stand the inertia he felt all around him, and often wondered whether there was actually any difference between saving black souls and dealing with these dull farmers. Sometimes he felt like giving up, but the face he met in the mirror each morning reminded him of why he was standing there. He was a servant who could finish his service only when he was dead or so paralysed that he could no longer climb into the pulpit.

He heard the church door close and knew who had come in. Alma, who never fell asleep during a sermon and always sang loudly even if she was off-key, had stood and curtsied in the doorway of the parsonage and told him about the black boy who was living with her and Edvin. Hallén hadn't met him yet. He knew that the boy had come, he knew Dr Madsen well, but he had been away on a long trip to Dalarna to bury his sister when the boy had arrived. Alma had stood there and asked for help. The boy had killed a pig, he refused to wear shoes, and nobody knew exactly what to do with him.

Hallén had told Alma to send the boy to the church by himself. He had also admonished her not to frighten him, just say that the pastor was a friendly man who wanted to meet everyone who lived in the parish.

He stepped out of the sacristy. The light filtering in through the windows was still faint. It was hard to see in the gloom. Then he noticed Daniel standing at the very back by the church entrance. He started down the centre aisle. The boy didn't move. Hallén saw that he had shoes on his feet. When he had almost reached the boy he saw him raise his hand and knock as if there were a door.

'Come in,' said Hallén. 'But you don't need to knock when there's no door.'

Daniel fell to his knees and grabbed hold of one of Hallén's muddy shoes.

'You don't have to kneel down either,' said Hallén. 'Get up.'

Daniel did as he was told. Hallén looked him over. The boy's eyes were alert. He seemed to be ready for something to happen to him. Hallén hadn't heard the whole story about why the boy had been lodged with Alma and Edvin. All he really knew was that the boy had been adopted by a man who was searching for rare insects and who suddenly felt compelled to set out on a long journey.

'So you're Daniel,' said Hallén.

'My name is Daniel and I believe in God.'

Hallén looked at the boy thoughtfully. The boy seemed to be taking his measure. His gaze made him uncertain for a moment. The boy wasn't looking directly at him, but slightly to the side. Hallén turned round. It was the altarpiece the boy was looking at. The image of Jesus had hung there since the 1700s. A chip of wood had come off one knee but it had never been repaired.

They walked forward to the altar rail. Daniel wanted to climb inside the choir but Hallén held him back.

'Not yet,' he said.

Daniel looked at the cross. Hallén watched him from the side. The boy was searching for something that was missing.

'What are you looking for?'

'The water.'

'The water?'

'He could walk on the water.'

Hallén nodded. Actually the boy's knowledge didn't please him. He had wanted to exercise his power by converting this black child: transform the savage into a human being. Now someone seemed to have already begun this work.

'Did you see him in the desert? Was there a church there?'

'My name is Daniel. I believe in God. Where is the water?'

Hallén tried to read his thoughts. He could understand that a person from the desert would talk about water, but what was Daniel actually looking for? Hallén decided to proceed carefully. In the drab monotony that was his daily work the boy might still offer him the challenge he had been missing for so long.

'I'm going to tell you about the water, but first I want to hear about you. Where you come from. And why you don't want to wear shoes on your feet.'

Daniel didn't answer. He kept searching for the water. Hallén waited.

'I'm very patient. There's no hurry. Why don't you want to wear shoes?'

'They're heavy.'

'Shoes are indeed heavy. But if you get cold you might get sick.'

Daniel said nothing more. Hallén kept asking questions but got no more answers. Nylander, the sexton, came in.

'I have a visitor,' said Hallén, who detested Nylander. They had been chafing at each other for far too many years. He often looked forward to the day when he could bury Nylander.

'I've seen him. People are wondering what he's doing here.'

189

'The church is here for everyone. The paths that lead from on high are inscrutable. Also, I don't want you to keep storing your aquavit underneath the baptismal font.'

Nylander did not reply, but left the church. Hallén could hear the clatter of spades. Nylander had to dig a grave for an old farmer who had died of gangrene.

Hallén kept waiting, but Daniel remained silent. He was looking everywhere for what was missing.

Hallén waited for half an hour, then he decided to show the boy even greater patience. It would take a long time to get close to him.

'Come back here tomorrow,' he said. 'If you answer my questions I'll tell you about the water.'

Daniel bowed, took his clogs in his hand, and went out of the church door. Hallén went into the sacristy and sat down. Through one of the narrow windows he could see Nylander digging. Hallén immediately felt himself growing irritated. Nylander was lazy. He worked far too slowly. A man digging a grave should do his work with power and tenacity.

He closed his eyes and imagined that he was in a desert where black people were gathered around him for prayer. He had a white pith helmet on his head and he was very young.

Daniel ran from the church to the hill behind the house. When he got there Sanna was sitting and digging in the mud. He was happy to see her.

'I saw you. You were at the church. What were you doing there?'

'I asked the pastor about the water.'

'What water?'

'The water Jesus walked on.'

Sanna stopped digging. Her fingers were caked with dried mud. Daniel couldn't tell whether she had heard what he said. She took his hands and ran her finger over the back of one of them. She cautiously scraped at his skin.

'You're black. I can't scrape it off. Wasn't he afraid?'

'Who?'

'The pastor! He must have thought you were a real devil who had climbed down from the wall.'

Her hands were rough with clay, but Daniel liked the way she held his hands. She didn't want anything from him, like everyone else who held his hands. She just wanted to hold them. For the first time since he had found Kiko and Be dead in the sand he had discovered something that really made him elated. Father had betrayed him, leaving him as far from the sea as he could, but maybe the girl named Sanna would help him find it again.

She kept examining his hands. She searched in the lines of his palm, flicked at his fingernails, squeezed hard.

'If we had children they would be grey,' said Daniel.

She gave a loud, shrill laugh. 'We can't have children,' she shrieked. 'You're only a child and I'm crazy.'

She leaned in close to him. She smelled of sweat, but there was also something sweet that reminded him of honey.

'I hear voices in the mud,' she said. 'All those people down there are whispering. I can't help it. I hear them. Only me. Do you hear anything?'

Daniel listened.

'You have to put your head to the ground.'

Daniel pressed his cheek and ear to the ground.

'Not your ear,' she whispered. 'You can only hear the people down there if you listen with your mouth or your nose.'

Daniel pressed his face to the ground. But he could only hear through his ears. The wind was whining and the birds shrieking.

'You'll have to teach me,' he said.

'I'm too stupid to teach anything.'

'Who told you that?'

'Everybody.'

Daniel wondered what stupidity actually meant. The girl who sat holding his hands made him feel quite calm. Even though he still couldn't see the sea, her eyes seemed to glisten with seawater. Maybe she could tell him what direction to go in to find the sea. A person like that couldn't be stupid.

'Actually I'm not supposed to be here,' she said all of a sudden.

'Why not?'

'I might get lost.'

Daniel didn't understand the word *lost*.

'I don't know what that is.'

191

She laughed harshly again.

'Then you're even stupider than me. If you go away and can't find your way home, you sit out in the dark and scream for help but nobody hears. Then you freeze to death. When they find you, you're so stiff that they'd have to break off your legs to get you into the coffin.'

Daniel sat silently pondering what she had said. Finally he had found a word for what he felt. What she was describing applied to him. He didn't know where to go. Even though it wasn't dark and he hadn't frozen to death, he was still lost.

He decided to memorise that word. Some day, when he was old and moved away from the others in the desert, he would remember it. Everything that had happened the time he got lost. Everything that by then might have fallen away and become a mysterious memory.

'I like being quiet,' said Sanna.

She still hadn't let go of his hands. Daniel was starting to get chilly because the ground he was sitting on was cold, but he didn't want to move. He didn't want Sanna to let go.

'I do too,' Daniel said.

'There are so many kinds of quiet. When you're just about to fall asleep. Or when you're running so fast that all you can hear is your own heart.'

She leaned her head against his chest and closed her eyes.

'Do you have a heart too?' she said in surprise. 'I didn't think the Devil did. Damn! I thought there was only a sooty chimney inside the chest of Satan.'

Daniel gave a start. She had said the word that Father always used when he was angry or impatient. He didn't like it. The word scared him.

'What are you thinking about?' she asked.

'Nothing.'

She let go of his hands and began to slap him in the face. When he tried to protect himself she stopped.

'I don't like people who lie. You lied. You were thinking of something.'

'I was wondering where the sea is.'

'What do you want with the sea?'

'I want to go home.'

'You can't walk on the sea like it was a road. You'd sink, you'd drown. And float back up with eels swimming out of your eyes.'

Daniel could tell that Sanna was starting to get restless. She looked around, kicked at the dirt and spat. He thought that she too was a stranger, who came from somewhere far away, even though she wasn't black. She didn't look like any of the people he had met when he was with Father. Maybe she was on her way somewhere too, even though she didn't know that it was possible to walk on water.

Suddenly she pulled up her dress. She was naked underneath. There was thick black hair between her legs. She pulled down her dress again.

'Now it's your turn,' she said.

Daniel stood up and pulled down his trousers. Since he was cold, his member had shrunk. He pulled on it.

'You shouldn't do that,' Sanna shrieked. 'You shouldn't touch yourself or it will fall off. On me it would turn into a big wound.'

Daniel quickly pulled his trousers back up. Sanna stared at him. Then she turned round and ran off. Daniel ran after her. Sanna stopped, picked up a rock and threw it at him.

'You can't come with me,' she shouted. 'Or I'll get a beating.'

The rock hit Daniel on the cheek and made a cut that bled. She was holding another bigger rock in her hand.

'I'll throw it,' she yelled. 'Don't follow me.'

She turned and kept running. Daniel stood looking after her. He didn't know what had happened. If Father had thrown a rock at him, he would have been afraid, but he wasn't now. She wasn't angry with him. She was angry with somebody else.

The next day the wind was blowing hard across the brown fields. During the night he had had a dream about the oxen who had pulled him and Father through the desert towards the city where the ship was waiting. The animals were buried in sand. Only their heads were visible. They had bellowed in terror and then the sand had slowly covered their heads too. He stood looking at the animals. He wanted to help them, dig away the sand with his hands, but his hands were gone. His arms were like dry branches hanging down from his shoulders.

The dream had yanked him out of sleep. At first he didn't know where he was. Then he heard the milkmaids sniffling and the hired hand muttering and passing wind. He lay utterly still in the darkness and tried to understand what the oxen buried in the sand were trying to tell him. Without being able to explain why, he knew that Be was behind the dream. She was the one who had sent it to him. But he couldn't understand it. Restlessness drove him out of bed. The floor was cold. He stood carefully on one of the milkmaids' dresses that had fallen from the end of the bed. For an instant he thought he was surrounded by all the people who had lain dead in the sand when Kiko and Be had left him. Their whispering voices were still there, with someone laughing quietly and the smell of freshly slaughtered meat. He tried to grab their bodies. But it was impossible – there was only the darkness and the voices.

Afterwards he slept fitfully until dawn. When they had finished breakfast he helped Edvin harness the horse. Alma called him into the kitchen and laid out the soiled ABC book that she had borrowed from Master Kron, who would soon be Daniel's teacher. Daniel looked at the pictures and tried to learn the alphabet. Usually he thought it was fun, but the anxiety from the dream made it hard for him to concentrate. When Alma left him alone for a moment, he closed the book, wrapped a scarf around his neck and went outside. The cold wind almost took his breath away, but he ran towards the hill that was always waiting for him. When he got there he found Sanna sitting and digging in the dirt. It made him happy. He thought that he would tell her about his dream. Maybe she could explain it to him. When she saw him coming she stood up and waved. She looked at his cheek.

'I didn't mean it,' she said. 'I never do.'

'It didn't hurt.'

'I prayed to God last night. I asked Him to forgive me. I think He listened to me.'

Daniel told her about his dream. He grew annoyed when he couldn't find the right words, but Sanna listened. She listened to him in a way that Father had never done.

'I don't understand any of it,' she said. 'I don't even know what a desert is. So much sand?' She pointed out towards the brown fields. 'Would all this be sand? And hot?'

'You would burn your feet.'

She rested her head in her hands and thought. 'So it would be like burying two horses here in the mud,' she said. 'And they would be whinnying like the butcher was standing in front of them.'

She threw a dirt clod at Daniel. It didn't hurt and she laughed.

'You're making it up. There aren't any dreams like that.'

'I dreamed it just like I told you.'

'You're just as strange as I am. But at least I don't tell lies.'

Then everything happened very fast. Daniel saw Sanna react to something and get up. There was something behind him, but he didn't have time to turn round before a big hand grabbed hold of his coat and jerked him to his feet. The man standing there was big and rough and there was tobacco juice running out of the corner of his mouth. He let go of Daniel and gave him a box on the ear so he fell over. Sanna tried to run away but he grabbed hold of her arm. He slapped her hard in the face several times. She screamed.

'Didn't I tell you to stay home at the farm? Now I find you with that damn troll that Edvin brought here.'

He released Sanna, who huddled in the dirt with her hands over her head as if afraid she would be hit again. The man gave Daniel a withering stare.

'She's retarded,' said the man. 'She doesn't know what she's saying or what she's doing. It's a pure pity! That's what it is! No parents, nothing. But we let her live with us. A pity! But the little bitch won't do as she's told. So she has to get slapped. That usually works. At least for a while.'

The man dragged Sanna up from the dirt and pulled her along with him down the hillside. He had a strong grip on her hair. Daniel thought she looked like a chicken on its way to have its head cut off.

Then he noticed that he had started to cry. It was as if Sanna's pain were inside him too.

He looked all around. The fields were deserted.

Except for the shrieking black birds.

CHAPTER 22

The next day was Sunday. Daniel woke up early as usual. On Sundays the milkmaids took turns sleeping in. Even the hired hand could stay in bed an hour longer than normal. Daniel got up and quietly dressed. The floor was cold under his feet. The hired hand lay watching him with one eye open. He motioned to Daniel to come over to the bed. Daniel didn't like him, but he didn't dare disobey.

'Pull the covers off her,' whispered the hired hand. 'If we're lucky, her nightgown will be hitched up.'

This scene repeated itself every Sunday morning, no matter which of the girls was sleeping in. Daniel had never understood why the hired hand enjoyed spending his free time looking at the girls' naked legs. But he did as he was told. She stirred a little but didn't wake up. The nightgown had slipped all the way up to her waist. The hired hand would be pleased. Daniel hurried out of the kitchen.

It was raining. The fog lay thick over the brown fields. The black birds sat motionless in the grove of trees. Alma stood at the well hoisting up water. Edvin stood next to her, staring straight out into the fog. From far off they could hear a cow bellowing. Daniel had his shoes in his hand. He hurried to the barn where the milkmaid was milking. When he entered the warm building, one of the cats rubbed itself on his leg. He lay down in the straw and covered his body so only his face was visible. During the night he had dreamed that Sanna was calling his name. He had searched for her. Suddenly he was on the ship, rolling heavily in a storm. Sanna was sitting at the top of one of the masts, waving at him. But when he tried to climb up there, someone grabbed him by the scruff of his neck and held him back. He tried to turn his head to see who it was but there was nobody there. Nothing but the wind holding his neck in an invisible grip.

Daniel lay in the straw and thought about his dream. It was easy to understand what his night-time messenger had wanted to say. Daniel wanted to be close to Sanna but it wasn't possible. Something was always coming between them.

He curled up in the straw to keep warm. The horse stamped in its stall.

As it was Sunday, everyone in the house would soon be going to church. The hired hand would slick his hair down with water, the milk-maids would wrap their best shawls round their shoulders and then they would all set off, with Edvin and Alma in the lead. On the way they would meet others heading in the same direction, and they would all look at Daniel and he would see at once which ones were curious, which ones didn't like him, and which ones were jealous because Edvin got paid to have Daniel living in his house.

Hallén was going to preach. He would say a lot of words that made Daniel sleepy because he couldn't understand them. But Alma would make sure that he didn't fall asleep and would keep an eye on the hired hand and the milkmaids as well. They would sing, and Daniel would look up at the man who hung nailed on the boards in front of them.

He had already visited the pastor on two mornings. Daniel was still waiting to hear about the water. Hallén had asked the same question each time he had come. *What was he thinking about?* And Daniel had refused to answer. He didn't want to talk about his plan. He was afraid that Hallén might tell Edvin, or forbid him. Daniel was still having a hard time learning what was forbidden. It was a word that he understood was one of the most important for people like Hallén, Edvin and Alma. The others were: *damn* and *may I*. Everything that happened between dawn and twilight was controlled by what people were allowed to do and what was forbidden. Going barefoot when the ground was white was one of the things that was most forbidden. Nor could you piss anywhere and especially not if someone was watching. There were rules about everything, and Daniel tried to learn them but without understanding why.

Sanna would also be at church. She sat right at the back, and Daniel knew that Alma would give him a disapproving look if he turned round to look at her. At church you had to look down or forward. Looking back was one of the things that was forbidden.

Daniel moved restlessly in the straw. He wondered whether Sanna would come to church, or whether the man who dragged her away would lock her in at home. Maybe he was like Father and tied her up.

The milkmaid was clattering the pails. She was singing. It sounded terrible, but he still liked her voice. Sometimes she would laugh and pat him on the head. She wasn't like the other milkmaid, who never touched him and flinched if he happened to brush against her.

He got up from the straw. The girl was milking the last cow. He sneaked out of the barn. The yard was empty. He ran out onto the cart track. When he turned round he was surrounded by the fog. He tried to catch it in his hands. Then he listened. Sounds were louder in the fog. He turned round slowly and tried to listen for the sound of drums. From somewhere he thought he could hear beasts of prey growling or somebody laughing, but if he headed in the direction the sound was coming from they would move.

He was just about to go back when he stopped short. On the road in front of him lay a snake, frozen stiff. It was brown and had a pattern on its back. At first he thought it was dead. He took a few steps backwards without taking his eyes off it. It didn't move. Then he realised that it was so cold that it couldn't move. It had come up out of the ground too soon. Maybe it had dreamed of the sunshine and then, when it woke up, could not go back to sleep.

It was Father who once told him about the snakes. There weren't any really dangerous snakes in this country. One of them was poisonous but people rarely died from its bite. From his description Daniel gathered that it was a snake like the one that lay before him on the road. He took a stick from the ditch and poked at the snake. It moved sluggishly, but didn't whip about or coil. He hit it with the stick, but it still didn't move.

He thought about the visit they would soon pay to the church.

He made a quick decision, ran back through the fog and fetched a wooden pail that no one was using from the barn. When he came back the snake was still lying there. Cautiously he bent over and grabbed it behind the head. When he lifted it up its body moved weakly. He shivered from the cold and dropped the snake in the pail. Then he hurried back to the barn, where he set the pail behind some spades that the hired hand used for mucking out. He covered the pail carefully so that the snake couldn't escape if it livened up from the warmth.

He went in the house and sat down by the fire. Alma looked at him.

'You're not walking about with no shoes on, are you?'

Daniel shook his head.

Edvin stretched as he sat on the stool near the fireplace. 'He's learning fast. And now it's time to go.'

Daniel got up quickly and ran out to the barn. The snake was still stiff. He wrapped it up in a piece of old burlap and stuffed it in his pocket.

The fog was as thick as ever when they reached the church. Daniel had a tight grip on the snake in his pocket. It hadn't moved. He looked around for Sanna. Finally he saw her, standing behind the man who had dragged her off by the hair. She cast down her eyes when Daniel looked at her. She had a big bruise on one cheek. Daniel felt a violent urge to rush up to the man and stuff the snake down his shirt. Maybe the snake wouldn't be able to bite and inject its venom, but the man would have a good fright and understand that there was someone who was prepared to defend Sanna. When the church bells began to ring Daniel tried to shift closer to her, but she moved away and shook her head almost imperceptibly. Daniel understood. She was afraid. The man who had pulled her by the hair had a firm grip on her arm.

Daniel sat between Alma and Edvin. The snake still lay motionless in his pocket. He wondered if he had been mistaken after all, that it wasn't just frozen stiff but dead. Snakes were cold-blooded though. And he knew that when you least expected it they could sink their fangs into a person or an animal.

Hallén climbed into the pulpit. He looked at Daniel and smiled. Daniel looked down. Then Hallén began to talk about grace. It was a word he almost never used. Grace and sin. Daniel tried to comprehend what he was saying, but the snake in his pocket and the man with the chipped knee hanging on the cross in front were more important. He understood that someone had placed the snake on the road. It hadn't got there by itself. Someone who knew where snakes hid had found it and laid it at his feet. No one had been as good at knowing where to find snakes as Be. She was the one who usually dug them up and caught them. Once she caught a snake that was more than twice as long as he was and as thick as Kiko's arm. They had eaten it, and it was enough to feed everyone in the group for a whole day.

Be had placed the snake before him, and since it was Sunday that could only mean that she wanted him to give it as an offering. In this country people didn't eat snakes. So there was only one possibility, and he knew what he was supposed to do.

He looked at the man hanging motionless on the cross. He too was an antelope frozen in the midst of flight, but he wasn't about to take a leap. He was nailed fast and someone had stuck a sword in his chest. He had frozen at the moment of death, in the middle of his last breath. While Hallén was speaking, Daniel tried one more time to understand. Why did these people have a god that they nailed to planks? Why did they treat him like an enemy? Why didn't anyone take him down from the cross and fix his chipped knee? But he could find no answer.

Hallén finished speaking and left the pulpit. Everyone stood up and prayed. Daniel had almost learned the entire prayer by heart. Then they sat down again. The whistling and wheezing organ began to play. Daniel felt the snake. The moment would soon arrive. Alma sat with her eyes closed. Cautiously he took out the coiled snake and held it below his knees. The two men who were carrying the long poles with bags at the end would appear soon. Edvin already had a coin in his hand. When the pole was thrust towards him Daniel quickly dropped the snake into the bag. He did it so quickly that no one noticed.

Then he felt that Be was right next to him. He closed his eyes and felt her warm breath against his neck.

Edvin gave him a poke.

'I'm awake,' said Daniel. 'I believe in God.'

At the same moment he heard a loud howl. Hallén, who was kneeling before the altar rail, gave a start and stood up. One of the men with the poles came rushing up the centre aisle.

'There's a viper in the offering pouch!' he yelled.

He held out the bag so Hallén could see. The organist had stopped playing. There was total silence in the church. Hallén stared. The man dropped the bag to the floor. The snake was no longer frozen; it wriggled out of the bag onto the stone floor. The man who had yelled was standing behind the pew where Daniel was sitting. He pointed at him and kept on yelling.

'He was the one who put it in there!' he shouted. 'It looked like a rag. I thought there was money wrapped inside it. But it was a snake.'

Daniel's stomach was churning. He hadn't expected this. He had thought that the offering he gave, the fact that he had caught a poisonous snake, would be greeted with joy.

The snake wriggled slowly across the stone floor. People rushed out of the pews and the church door was thrown open. Finally a man who Daniel knew was an old seaman brought a spade and chopped the snake in two. Daniel had seen snakes cut in half many times before. The two halves usually kept moving very fast, whipping back and forth. but the viper just kept moving slowly and soon it was quite still. Hallén had come down from the altar and stood in front of Daniel.

'Did you put the snake in the offering pouch?'

Daniel didn't answer. He got ready to kick off his shoes and run out of the church.

'You must answer,' said Edvin. 'The pastor is asking you a question.'

Daniel leapt up from the pew. But he didn't get past Edvin, who seemed to be ready and grabbed him.

'We'll take him into the sacristy,' said Hallén.

Edvin held him tight. When Daniel tried to bite him to get loose, Edvin shouted at him to settle down. The man who had carried the offering pouch and pointed at Daniel and accused him now took hold of his legs and held him so hard that Daniel screamed in pain. He managed to get his legs free and kicked the man in the face so his nose started to bleed. But Edvin didn't release his grip until they were in the sacristy. Alma followed, but Hallén told her to wait outside.

'I didn't see any snake!' she shouted. 'It must have been somebody else.'

'He'll confess soon enough.'

'I don't want you to hurt him.'

Hallén shooed Alma away without replying and pulled the heavy door shut.

'Let the boy go and give him a box on the ear,' said Hallén. 'That'll calm him down.'

Edvin did as he was told. The blow was so hard that Daniel fell to the floor. His cheek burned and his eyes began to water.

Hallén bent over him. He was breathing hard, panting as if he had been running.

'Did you put the snake in the offering pouch?'

Daniel thought that Hallén was a beast of prey and he had to avoid looking him in the eye at all costs. Next to him was a window and outside he caught a glimpse of Sanna, with her nose pressed against the glass.

For the first time since Father left he felt that he wasn't alone. It gave him the same power as when he was small and Be or Kiko sat next to him. That was the first thing he had learned, that a human being who is alone is not a real human being. Sanna was waiting outside, his pain was hers, and he was no longer afraid to look Hallén straight in the eye.

'I was offering to the gods.'

Hallén promptly stood up as if Daniel's reply had given him a jab in the chest.

'Did you put a snake in the collection pouch as an offering?' Hallén shook his head and looked at Edvin. 'This was the Sunday we were taking a collection to support the mission in Africa, and so this little black devil puts a snake in the offering pouch.'

Edvin stood with his cap in his hand. Daniel could see that he was afraid of Hallén.

'He probably had no idea what the collection was for.'

'He put a snake in the bag!'

Hallén was talking very loudly, as though he were in the pulpit letting his words hail down over the congregation. Edvin shook his head.

'I'm sure he doesn't understand.'

'A snake in the offering pouch is not merely blasphemy. It is a mark of shame for you and Alma, who have not succeeded in teaching him how to behave.'

'He probably doesn't even know what *behave* means.'

Hallén pointed at Daniel's feet in a rage.

'He doesn't have shoes on his feet. Even though it's winter. He goes to church barefoot. And you allow this?'

Edvin tried to hold his head high when he replied. 'He had shoes on when we came. He must have kicked them off in the pew.'

Hallén shook his head. 'I've tried,' he said. 'I've spoken to him several times. But he says nothing. He only asks about the water.'

Daniel was sitting on the floor looking at Sanna. Each time Edvin or Hallén moved, her face disappeared, but then it would pop up again.

Hallén stood with his back leaning against the big wardrobe and regarded Daniel.

'Next Sunday he will have to make a full confession in front of the congregation. He will have to beg their forgiveness.'

'Perhaps we should realise that he doesn't understand,' said Edvin. 'He comes from a place where there's nothing but sand. Here we live in mud. Perhaps a person like him thinks differently.'

Daniel thought that Edvin was right. He had understood something that even Father had not grasped.

'What do sand and mud have to do with snakes?' Hallén enquired. 'The boy must be disciplined. He does indeed come from a desert. But the mission has shown that people can become civilised. The most important step on this path is to give testimony and beg for forgiveness.'

'I'll try to talk to him. But I must still ask the pastor to help.'

'I shall talk to him. Tomorrow. You can go now.'

They left the sacristy. Alma was waiting in the centre aisle. The man Daniel had kicked in the face lay on a pew with a rag over his nose to stop the flow of blood.

The snake was gone.

'His shoes,' said Edvin.

Alma looked under the pew where they had sat. She bent down and pulled out his clogs. Daniel bowed to the shoes and then put them on.

Alma looked at Daniel's cheek. 'Hallén hit him.'

'No. It was me,' said Edvin.

'Was that necessary?'

'How should I know what's necessary? How can I make sense of what I don't comprehend? Where are the hired hand and the milkmaids?'

'I sent them home.'

'And the church green?'

'It's probably full of curious folks.'

Edvin tossed his cap to the floor and sat down heavily on one of the pews. 'Then we'll have to run the gauntlet.'

Alma gave him an astonished look as she stroked Daniel's hair. 'Surely *we* don't have anything to be ashamed of?'

'I might get so angry that I punch some of them on the nose.'

'There's been enough hitting here today. We should be able to walk home without thinking of falling to the ground in shame, shouldn't we?'

Edvin kept shaking his head. Daniel waited impatiently to go outside with them. He longed for Sanna. Even though he couldn't talk to her, she would at least see his face.

Alma took Daniel's hand. 'We're going now,' she said. 'You can either sit here or come with us.'

Edvin gave her an entreating look. 'What shall we do? Maybe it was a mistake to take him in.'

'We'll talk about that later. Right now we're going home.'

Edvin bent down to pick up his cap. The man lying on the pew sat up. He was holding the rag to his nose.

'He just about kicked off my nose,' he said in a thick voice.

'There's a doctor in Simrishamn,' replied Alma. 'If you hadn't yelled and pointed so much this never would have happened.'

Daniel had never heard Alma speak so firmly before. The man on the pew said no more and lay back down.

When they came out of the church the green was full of people. Edvin groaned and Alma took a deep breath. A silent path opened before them as they walked, led by Alma. Daniel looked around for Sanna. When he didn't see her he began to worry. Had he been imagining it? Was it not her face he saw outside the window?

When he finally found her she was standing on the churchyard wall. She waved cautiously to him. Daniel raised his hand but Alma pulled it back down. The people around them were silent. Edvin trudged along behind. He didn't catch up with them until they reached the road.

'Did you see?' he asked.

'I saw,' said Alma. 'And I felt it. But I don't care. I care about understanding why he did it.'

Edvin stopped. 'A viper in the middle of winter? Where did it come from?'

'I don't know,' said Alma. 'But I don't want you ever to hit him again.'

Daniel wondered what had actually happened. He thought that Sanna was the only one who would be able to explain it.

Slowly he could feel himself filling with joy. He had found someone who pushed away his loneliness. Someone who might understand him.

He thought about the water, about the wet pelt that would grow accustomed to his feet.

Suddenly he was certain.

Sanna could show him where the sea was.

CHAPTER 23

A fierce storm was passing over the plain of Skåne. It was the night after Daniel had put the viper in the collection pouch. He woke up when Edvin shook the hired hand and said that the straw roof was starting to blow off the barn and that the animals were frightened. Soon afterwards Alma came in and woke the milkmaids. They had to help with the animals so none would be injured. When Alma leaned over Daniel with a candle in her hand he pretended to be asleep.

'I don't know why,' she said. 'But you're not fooling me. I can see you're awake.'

Daniel opened his eyes.

'Are you afraid of the storm?'

Daniel shook his head.

'I would dearly like to help you. But how can I help someone that nobody understands?'

The wind tore at the walls of the house. Daniel felt the draught coming through the ill-fitting windows.

'The sky is restless,' Alma said.

Daniel sat up in bed.

'You don't need to help. You're too little.'

Daniel stayed sitting on the edge of the bed and watched as Alma busied herself at the stove. He squinted his eyes so hard that his vision grew blurry. It might have been Be moving about in front of him. He whispered her name to himself but the roaring wind was too loud. He couldn't hear whether she answered or not.

The next day the storm was still raging. It came in squalls. Ragged clouds raced across the sky. Edvin and the hired hand struggled to keep the straw on the roof of the barn. Daniel wasn't allowed to go into the barn because the animals were skittish. He didn't have to go to church either. Hallén could wait until the storm had passed. One of the trees blew down in the grove where the black birds perched. The birds screeched. Daniel stood and watched them. Sometimes it looked as if they were writing letters against the sky. He tried to decipher them but could not.

Edvin climbed down from the roof to piss. When he had buttoned his flies he went over to Daniel.

'Alma says you aren't afraid of the storm, is that right?'

'I'm not afraid.'

Edvin touched the cheek where he had slapped him.

'I won't hit you again,' he said. 'That will never happen again. Even if Hallén tells me to.'

Then he clambered back up the ladder. Daniel watched him go and decided that Edvin meant what he said. If he raised his hand again the blow would never leave his arm.

Daniel ran towards the hill. He held out his arms so that his coat was like a sail behind him. Many times Kiko had told him that a human being could not fly but Daniel had never thought that he sounded quite sure of what he was saying. He kicked off his shoes and tried to take off, but his feet kept striking the ground.

When he reached the hill he was disappointed. Sanna wasn't there. He looked towards the house where she lived, but the path was empty. He wondered whether the man who had pulled her by the hair had tied her up, the same way Father had done with him. He decided that he would try to find her if she didn't show up the next day.

He ran back and sat down with his ABC book in the kitchen. Alma was out with the milkmaids in the barn. He read the letters aloud to himself. Neither Kiko nor Be had known how to read. They would often draw with sticks in the sand. Not words, but signs, faces, paths. Daniel put down the book and knelt on the wooden bench by the window. The windowpane was steamed up. With his finger he tried to draw Be's face, but it didn't look like her. He puffed new fog onto the window and tried Kiko's instead, but that didn't turn out any better.

Then he tried to draw the antelope. He imagined that his finger was the stick that Kiko used had. But the fog-covered glass windowpane was no rock face. He grew angry and had to hold himself back from smashing his fist through the glass.

*   *   *

207

By the next day the storm had abated. The straw lay still on the roof of the barn. Just after seven in the morning Daniel went to the church. The door to the sacristy was closed. He knocked and Hallén answered. Daniel opened the door, entered and bowed. Hallén was sitting on a chair in the middle of the room. He nodded to Daniel to come forward.

'First you killed a piglet with a shoe,' Hallén said. 'I heard all about it. And now you put a snake in the offering pouch. All this tells me that you are still a savage. It will take time for you to learn what it means to be a human being. I will show patience, but patience has its limits. If you obey me, good will come to you. If you do not obey, you will be punished. Do you understand what I'm saying?'

Daniel nodded.

'I want to hear you say it.'

'I understand.'

'What is it you understand?'

'Wear shoes on the feet when there is frost, do not kill pig, and do not put snakes in the offering pooch.'

'The words are "pigs" and "offering pouch".'

'The words are "pigs" and "offering pooch".'

'Offering pouch.'

'Offering pouch.'

Hallén got up from his chair. 'Let's go and look at Jesus.'

They stood before the altar rail again. The sunlight shining through a window glittered in one of the eyes of the nailed-up man. Daniel gave a start. The same glint had been there in the antelope's eye.

'Jesus sacrificed his life for you,' said Hallén. 'No one can become a true human being without believing in him. But one must also know how to behave oneself.'

'That must hurt,' said Daniel.

Hallén gave him a questioning look. 'Hurt?'

'To be nailed to a board.'

'Of course it hurts. His suffering was appalling.'

Daniel thought that now he could ask his question again.

'I want to learn walking on water.'

'Nobody can walk on water. Jesus was God's son. He could do it. But no one else can.'

Daniel knew that the man standing at his side was wrong, but he didn't dare talk back. The slap from Edvin still burned on his cheek.

'This is where you will stand next Sunday,' said Hallén. 'In front of the whole congregation. You will beg us all for forgiveness because you violated the holy church by putting a viper in the offering pouch. Do you understand what I'm saying?'

Daniel realised with dread what Hallén meant.

'Will I be nailed up on boards too?'

Hallén grabbed the collar of Daniel's coat and raised his hand, but he did not strike.

'You have the gall to compare yourself to our Saviour? You have the gall to compare yourself to the One who suffered for all our sins?'

Hallén let him go and stepped aside, as if he couldn't stand to be too close to Daniel.

'You are still a savage. I keep forgetting that. The path you must walk is long. We shall walk it together. You may go now. But I want you to come back tomorrow.'

Daniel stood motionless until Hallén had vanished behind the tall altarpiece. Then he rushed out of the church. He ran all the way home, and he was soaked with sweat when he reached the hill behind the house. He knew that there were five days left until it was Sunday again. Then he would be nailed up on boards. Before then he had to find out where the sea was. He had to set off, and even if he still couldn't walk on water he had to stay hidden until he had learned how to do it. He called out for Kiko and Be. He yelled as loud as he could, but no reply came except for the unsettled sounds of the black birds.

He fell to the ground and curled up with his head between his knees. The long run had made him tired. It was cold, and he felt exhausted.

When he woke up, Sanna was standing beside him.

'I heard you yelling,' she said. 'Why are you lying here sleeping? You could freeze to death.'

He didn't know how long he had been asleep. In his dream he had been hanging on two crossed boards. It was the hired hand who had nailed him up, and the milkmaids were lying at his feet, asleep with the covers pulled up to their necks.

'They will nail me up,' he said.

'What do you mean?'

'They will nail me up on boards. And put me in the church.'

Sanna shook her head. 'Who told you that?'

'Hallén.'

'So the pastor is going to nail you up on boards? He can't do that. It's forbidden. It's permitted to chop off people's heads, but not to nail people up on boards.'

'He said so.'

Sanna gave him a pensive look. She chewed on her lip while she thought.

'Maybe it's not the same for people who are black,' she said. 'Maybe they're allowed to nail up people like you.'

Then she shrieked so shrilly that the black birds lifted off from the treetops.

'He can't do that!'

'I'm going to leave.'

'Where can you go? They'll come after you. They'll catch you.'

'I'll hide.'

'But you're black. You can't hide.'

'I'll make myself invisible.'

Sanna started chewing on her lip again. 'Can you do that?'

'I don't know.'

She sat down close to him and took his hand.

'If you start to scream when they nail you up, I promise I'll scream too. Then it might not hurt as much.'

'Thanks.'

'But you can't hang there too long. Because you're a human being and dead people smell bad. But I can put flowers on your grave.'

'Thanks.'

Sanna sat in silence for a moment. Daniel tried to decide when he should make his escape. Should he wait or should he leave tonight? He realised that Sanna would never dare come with him. She certainly didn't have the patience necessary to learn to walk on water, either. But he would still tell her about it. He had to share his thoughts with somebody. Maybe she could help him by steering the people who would be searching for him in the wrong direction.

He told her the truth. He was going to leave. Maybe even that very night. He would find his way to the sea, and when he had learned what he had to do for the water to support him, he would walk until he reached his home. Sanna listened with her mouth hanging open.

'You're crazy,' she said when he was finished. 'I don't understand half of what you're talking about. But I know this much – you're just as insane as I am.'

'What does it mean to be insane?'

'Like me. I'm stupid in the head. I don't understand what people say to me. I can't learn to read or write. Sometimes they say that I'm stupid, sometimes that I'm retarded, but I'm not dumb enough to be locked in a madhouse.'

'Why did your pappa drag you by the hair?'

Sanna pinched his nose so hard that he got tears in his eyes.

'He's not my pappa. My pappa is dead. My mamma too. I live with them because I was auctioned off.'

Daniel didn't understand the word.

'Is he your pappa's brother?'

'His name is Hermansson and he grabs me under my skirts when Elna isn't looking. At night he comes and grabs me under the covers. I don't want to but he tells me I can't say anything. Otherwise I'll end up in the madhouse and have to lie all day long in a tub full of cold water.'

Daniel didn't understand the meaning of her words. But he could see in her face that she bore a pain that reminded him of his own. He thought that when he finally got home he would remember her and he would certainly dream about her at night.

'I will carve your face in the rock wall,' he said. 'Next to the antelope.'

'What's that?'

'An animal.'

Daniel got up from the dirt, crossing his arms over his head like the crown of a kudu buck.

Sanna laughed. 'That looks like an animal.'

'The antelope *is* an animal.'

'But you're a human being. Even though you're just as crazy as me.'

As she talked she kept looking around. Suddenly she pointed.

'Someone's coming up the path.'

Daniel saw that it was Edvin.

'I'll come back tonight,' he said. 'I want to see you one more time before I leave.'

'But they'll find you! They'll send dogs after you.'

'They will never find me.'

Sanna ran off down the hill. Daniel went to meet Edvin.

'Who was that you were talking to?'

'Nobody.'

'You don't have to lie to me. Was it Sanna?'

Daniel didn't answer.

'Dr Madsen is here,' said Edvin. 'He has two gentlemen from Lund with him. They want to meet you.'

Daniel stopped short.

'It's nothing dangerous. They just want to draw you. They're going to write about you in a book.'

The two men waiting in the kitchen were both young. They stood up, shook Daniel's hand and smiled kindly. He noticed that they weren't staring at him. They looked at him with a curiosity that held no fear. Then they said their names. The shorter one, who had a pale face and yellow hair, was named Fredholm, and the other, who was bald with a moustache, was named Edman. Dr Madsen, who frightened Daniel since he was to blame for Father's departure, squatted down in front of him.

'Herr Fredholm and Herr Edman are students,' he said. 'Do you know what a student is?'

Daniel shook his head. When Madsen was there he didn't want to say too many words. Every time he spoke he revealed his thoughts. He didn't want Madsen to know what he was really thinking.

'They study at the university in Lund,' Madsen went on. 'I don't suppose you know what that means either. But you have been there, and you have certainly heard that people go there to seek knowledge. A biology professor there, Professor Holszten, studies people – why we're all different. The noticeable differences between the races. Those that are inferior, dying out, and the races that have a future ahead of them. It was Professor Holszten who sent these gentlemen to visit you.

The results will be published in a journal of racial biology that has just been started.'

Dr Madsen led Alma and Edvin out of the kitchen. The man named Edman with the bald head took out a drawing pad and began to sketch a likeness of Daniel. Fredholm wrapped a measuring tape around Daniel's head. Daniel felt like laughing but knew that he should be serious. He couldn't understand why it was so important to measure his nose or the distance between his eyes. The two men reminded him of Father. They devoted themselves to actions that were difficult to comprehend. Father had almost lost his life in the desert, searching for beetles and butterflies, and here stood grown men measuring his nose in all seriousness.

'I wonder what he's thinking,' said Edman, taking up a new position to draw Daniel's profile from the left side.

'If he thinks at all,' replied Fredholm, noting down the length of Daniel's left ear.

'It's odd to stand before a creature from a race that's dying out. I wonder if he's aware of it himself? That soon he will no longer exist?'

Daniel listened absent-mindedly to what they were saying. Suddenly he had an idea. Maybe they could tell him where the sea was. Since they were alone in the room, neither Alma nor Edvin would know that he had asked. He would wait until they were finished, then he could ask, and he would do it in such a way that they wouldn't realise the purpose of his question.

'Open your mouth,' said Fredholm.

Daniel obeyed.

'Have you ever seen teeth like this? Not one cavity.'

'Cavities are caused by bacteria. But the whiteness of his teeth seems brighter because he's black.'

Fredholm tugged at his teeth. 'As strong as a beast of prey. If he bit you it would be like having a mad cat hanging from your wrist.'

Daniel remembered that this was the second time he had been drawn and measured. He wondered whether it was a custom in this country to put a measuring tape around the heads of people who came to visit.

Fredholm kept measuring. Now he pulled on Daniel's lips. It hurt, but Daniel didn't flinch.

'I drew the head of a fox once. Presumably it had rabies and its head had been cut off. I have the same feeling now, that it's an animal I'm drawing.'

Fredholm blew his nose in his handkerchief and then asked Daniel to raise his arm. He sniffed at his armpit.

'Bestial,' he said. 'Very strong. No normal peasant sweat.'

Edman put down his pad and smelled Daniel's armpit. 'I don't notice any difference.'

'In what?'

'The odour of my own sweat and the boy's. You have to be careful to stay faithful to the facts.'

'Then I shall note that he perspires the same odour as a human being.'

Edman laughed. 'He *is* a human being.'

'But of a dying race.'

Fredholm put down his measuring tape and sat on a chair. 'Just imagine this boy a few years older. Copulating with a rosy-cheeked peasant girl.'

'The thought is repulsive.'

'But what if? What would be the result?'

'A mulatto. With low intelligence. Holszten has already written about that.'

Fredholm scratched out his pipe and then lit it. 'But what if that's all wrong?' he said. 'If the very premise is incorrect. Where does that leave us?'

'Why should the premise be incorrect?'

'What if Christian teachings are telling the truth after all? That all human beings are created equal?'

'Species of animals die out. Why not less successful human races as well?'

'I have a feeling that he understands everything we're saying.'

Edman put down the drawing pad. 'Perhaps. But he doesn't fully comprehend what he understands. If you're finished I would like to go outside. It smells rank in here.'

Fredholm shrugged his shoulders. 'I admit that he reminds me of an ape. But I can't keep thinking that nevertheless he doesn't seem like a human being who's about to die out.'

'Take up that discussion with Holszten. He doesn't like being contradicted. He believes that racial biology is the future. Whoever doesn't follow his path will have to find different ones.'

Fredholm said nothing more, but put his measuring tape and calipers back in a little bag.

'Where is the sea?' asked Daniel.

The two men looked at him in astonishment.

'Did he say something?' asked Fredholm.

'He asked about the sea.'

'Where is the sea?' Daniel repeated.

Edman smiled. Then he pointed. 'In that direction is Simrishamn. And that direction is Ystad. In that direction is Trelleborg. And that way is Malmö. The sea lies all around you like a horseshoe. East, south and west. But not north. There is nothing but forest up there.'

Just as Daniel had hoped, they didn't ask why he was wondering about the sea. They packed up their bags and opened the door to the room where Dr Madsen was waiting with Edvin and Alma.

'I hope that five riksdaler will be enough,' said Dr Madsen, placing a banknote on the table. Edvin nodded. 'More than generous.'

Then he and Alma accompanied the three men out to the waiting carriage.

Daniel was still standing in the middle of the kitchen. He closed his eyes and thought he could hear the roar of the waves.

Now he knew in which direction *not* to go.

CHAPTER 24

Two days later Daniel set off. Just after one in the morning, when he was sure that everyone was asleep, he silently got dressed and slipped out of the kitchen with his wooden shoes in his hand. He had packed a bundle containing the sand that was left in Father's insect cases, and some potatoes and pieces of bread. When he reached the courtyard the cold hit him hard. He hesitated, wondering whether he would survive his walk to the sea. He didn't know how far it was, or whether the plains would be broken by mountains or bogs. He wrapped his scarf round his head and started off. He sensed that Be and Kiko were calling him. There was no wind and it was overcast. He had decided to head south. The night before he had gone outside and taken a bearing on a star in that direction. He followed the cart track past the house where Sanna lived and ran straight out into a field when a dog started barking. He didn't stop until it fell silent. The cold stung his lungs.

He had explained to Sanna that he had to leave. They were sitting up on the hill and he told her about it while she dug and searched for the invisible people under the mud. She repeated the same thing she had said before, that he was crazy, that they would find him and bring him back. A person who was destined to be nailed up on boards could never escape.

In the end he realised that she didn't believe what he was saying. Then he knew that she would never consider coming with him.

When she ran home he watched her until she disappeared. Then he imagined his own disappearance. He would run through the night and he would be gone when Edvin and Alma woke up in the morning. He had poured a little sand into his bed and hoped they would believe that he had turned himself into those grains of sand.

The darkness surrounded him. The cold tore at his chest. He made his way along the narrow tracks that wound through the fields. The soil was frozen and no longer stuck to the bottom of his shoes. Now and then he would stop to catch his breath, but he grew so cold that he forced himself to keep moving.

The plain seemed endless. He felt like he was moving in a trance. The cold had stopped stinging him. Now it burned inside him. He knew that he had to keep going until dawn. Only then could he search for a place where he could get warm and sleep. If he stopped now he would be buried in the darkness, and when the sun returned only his stiff, frozen body would be left. All night long he thought about Be and Kiko. They were inside him and they were as cold as he was. Sometimes he stretched out his arms and asked Kiko to carry him. But Kiko would only shake his head and say that he had to manage for himself.

The dawn came.

At the same time it began to snow. At first scattered snowflakes, then so thick that he couldn't make out the horizon. He was in the middle of a field. Off in the distance he saw a house surrounded by trees but he couldn't see the sea anywhere. At the top of a small hill stood the ruin of a windmill. Its sails hung like the remains of a dead bird above the crumbling walls. He walked towards the hill. When he looked back the field had already turned white, and his tracks were clearly visible. He kept on heading for the windmill. He glimpsed a fox, and then it was gone. One corner of the ruin still had part of the roof left. On the floor lay some old sacks. He wrapped the sacks around his body and huddled in the corner. Then he ate one of the pieces of bread and a potato. He wondered why he wasn't thirsty. If he had walked all night long in the desert he wouldn't have been hungry, but he would have wanted water. Now it was food he needed.

Did he dare go to sleep? Would the sacks keep him warm enough, or would he freeze to death? He tried to make a decision, but he was already asleep. Kiko lay by his left side, with one arm under his head as usual. Be was somewhere behind him. Without seeing her he knew that she had curled up and was sleeping with her hands clasped under her belly.

He dreamed that his heart was beating more and more slowly. With a huge effort he kicked himself up out of the dream. He was so cold he was shaking. He had no idea how long he had been asleep. To his surprise he noticed that he was crying. The tears had run down to his mouth. That had never happened before; he had never started to cry while he was asleep.

At first he didn't know where he was. It was still snowing. He struggled to stand up and tried to determine from the thickness of the snow how long he had been asleep. He measured with one finger and then looked up at the clouds. He couldn't see where the sun was. He took a little snow in his hand and put it in his mouth. Now he realised how thirsty he was.

Before he left the ruin he tore the sacks into strips and stuffed them inside his trousers and shoes. Then he continued heading south.

He knew that he wouldn't be able to survive another night. He had to rest, and he had to get warm. Otherwise he would die. Just before dark he reached a farm with big barns and a red-brick house with a tower in the middle. He hid behind some boulders in the field and waited. Now and then he could hear voices in the distance and the sound of buckets clanking. When it got dark he cautiously approached one of the barns. At the back there was an old manure trench that he could creep inside. The barn was full of cows. Some moved restlessly as he trudged forward in the dark. He smelled the aroma of milk. He found some in the bottom of an unwashed pail and drank it down. He kept looking and found another pail of milk. All the while he was listening for voices, but he was alone with the animals. He went back the way he had come and crept into the straw next to the cow that stood closest to the manure trench. The cow sniffed at him. Daniel felt its warm breath on his face. He ate the bread and potatoes he had left and then burrowed into the straw. One hand was slippery with manure. He wiped it off against the wall and then curled up. Slowly he could feel his body's warmth coming back. Tonight he would not freeze to death.

He woke up when he heard someone screaming. He had slept so soundly that he hadn't noticed when the milkmaids came in, clanking their pails. Now a skinny girl with a pockmarked face was standing outside the cow's stall and screaming him awake. He stood up and she fled, dropping her pail. He sneaked out through the manure trench and ran as fast as he could. It had stopped snowing but it was colder. He slipped and fell but got to his feet and kept running. He expected to hear shouts and dogs barking behind him. He noticed that he was running uphill. If only he could make it over the top he would be safe.

When he reached the top he stopped short.

Far off on the horizon lay the sea. He closed his eyes hard and then looked again. It wasn't his imagination. The sea was there, far ahead of him, and when he turned round the fields were empty. There were no people and no dogs.

He continued walking and reached a wider road. Already he could see the smoke rising into the air from many chimneys. Maybe he was on his way to the same town where he had once arrived with Father. He carried on. When he saw two horse carts in the distance he left the road and hid in a ditch. The driver behind the first horse was asleep. Behind the reins of the second cart sat a woman. The thought crossed Daniel's mind that it was Be in disguise, wanting to show herself to him and tell him that he was on the right track.

He kept hiding until it began to get dark again. He had come close enough to the town to see that it wasn't the same one he and Father had visited. There were no cobblestone streets here, only a few muddy lanes winding between low houses.

But he had discovered something that was more important. There was a harbour. And in the harbour were several ships. Perhaps he would be able to get aboard one of them and not have to learn to walk on water.

Hunger was gnawing at his stomach. He tried to imagine what had happened when Edvin and Alma had discovered that he was gone. Alma probably thought that the sand in his bed was all that was left of him, but Edvin would be doubtful and they would start looking for him. By now a whole day and two nights had passed. They would think that he was lying dead somewhere, buried under the snow.

Just as darkness fell the wind began to blow. Daniel was worried that the ships would leave before he managed to get aboard. He went a roundabout way past the houses and down to the harbour. The wind picked up. The ships scraped against the quay. He was surprised that there were no lights in the cabins. Where were the sailors?

The quay was deserted. The only light came from the window of a hut near the end of the jetty. He walked past the ships without running into anyone. His disappointment made him angry. Why were they lying here in the harbour like dead animals? Why weren't any sailors waiting for dawn to set sail?

He stopped near the biggest ship. The clouds were beginning to shred in the wind. The moonlight made it possible to see. He hopped over the railing and felt how the deck moved beneath his feet. Suddenly he gave a start. It felt as if Father were somewhere among the shadows. He didn't want Daniel to board a ship. He wanted to grab him by the scruff of the neck and take him back to Alma and Edvin. But the deck was empty. There was nobody there. Again he felt how hungry he was. If he didn't find some food he wouldn't be able to think clearly. He walked along the deck and tried the door to the aft cabin. It was unlocked. Without knowing why, he knocked. No one answered. He opened the door and went in. It smelled of wet clothes inside. There was a candle on a table. He pulled the curtains over the portholes and lit the candle, capping his hand over the flame to shield it. On the table stood a butter tub and a plate of hard tack. He began to eat. He spread the butter on the bread with his fingers. There was also a bottle there, the same kind Father used to drink, which he called *beer*. It tasted bitter, but he drank until the bottle was empty.

When the bread was gone he was full. He put out the candle and sat down on the bunk behind the table.

There were voices all around him now. He could feel their breath and sense their bodies in the darkness as the ship scraped and bumped against the quay.

'What shall I do?' he whispered into the darkness.

But the answers were lost in the whining and screeching from the draughty portholes and from the lines slapping against the masts outside.

He lay down and pulled up the blankets. They smelled acrid from tobacco and urine. He knew that he ought to make a decision, but he was too tired. He couldn't even think about finding a hiding place.

In his dreams he saw Be, who had flown up into a treetop. There was no sound around her, only water. She was alone up there in the tree, and the water was rising up the trunk. He saw that she was giving birth to a child. She called for Kiko but no one answered. Daniel wanted to climb up to help her, but he couldn't, and finally he understood that he was the one being born up there, as the water slowly rose. He saw Be bite off the umbilical cord of the bloody child and he felt himself being torn away from her. Soon the water would reach all the way to the top of the tree and the waves would sweep them away. Then he noticed that Be had wings. She unfolded them and lifted off from the tree just as the waves began to snatch at her feet.

He awoke with a violent start. A ray of light was hitting his eyes. A man stood leaning over the bunk with a lantern in his hand. He was unshaven, and one eyelid hung halfway over his eye.

'Now I've seen *all* the devils,' he said. 'Who are you?'

Daniel sat up.

'My name is Daniel. I believe in God.'

'If I was drunk I'd run right out of here. A little black person in the aft cabin?' The man shook his head. 'I hear the wind picking up and decide to get dressed and go down to check the moorings. Something makes me take a look in the cabin. And here lies a person in my bunk.'

Daniel could tell at once that the man wasn't dangerous.

'I'm on my way home,' he said. 'I'm not afraid of climbing up masts. I don't eat much. I can sleep on deck. Just so long as it's warm.'

The man set the lantern on the table without taking his eyes off him.

'You are really black,' he said. 'A young black man from Africa. Who speaks Swedish. Who eats hard tack. And drinks Pilsner. And lies down to sleep in my bunk. If I told anyone about this they'd say I was crazy. Maybe I *am* crazy.'

He reached out his hand.

'Take my hand so I can feel that you're real.'

221

Daniel reached out his hand.

'You're real, all right,' said the man. 'And you're cold. You're freezing. And your name is Daniel?'

'I believe in God.'

'That's not so important. But you have to understand that I'm wondering where you came from. And how you wound up here. In my cabin, in the middle of winter.'

The man sat down on the edge of the bunk and pulled the blankets over Daniel's legs.

'My name is Lystedt,' he said. 'This is my ship. Her name is *Elin of Brantevik.*'

He paused and pulled the lantern closer to the edge of the table.

'You probably don't know where you are, do you?'

'No.'

'But you came from somewhere?'

'From Alma and Edvin.'

'Alma and Edvin? Do they have a last name? And where do they live?'

Daniel thought he had said too much. Even if the man with the droopy eyelid wasn't dangerous, he might still think that Alma and Edvin ought to come and fetch him.

The man waited. He had brown eyes and deep furrows in his brow.

'You don't want to say where you came from? And you say you're on your way home? That can only mean one thing. That you're on the run. How long have you been walking in this weather?'

'Two nights.'

'Where did you sleep?'

'With the animals.'

'And you're on your way home? Where is that?'

'It's called the desert.'

Daniel remembered something that Father had often said: *The boy comes from the far-off Kalahari Desert.*

'I come from the far-off Kalahari Desert.'

The man nodded pensively.

'Once when I was young I sailed on a Dutch vessel that was going to Cape Town. We almost capsized in a storm off the Skeleton Coast. I recall the captain saying there was a desert called the Kalahari.'

He leaned over and pulled the blanket up to Daniel's chin.

'Are you cold?'

'No.'

'How did you come to Sweden, boy? Who was cruel enough to drag you way up here?'

'Father.'

'Your father?'

Daniel was forced to search through his weary and distressed memory for the name that Father used.

'Hans Bengler.'

'A white man? Not your real father?'

'Kiko died in the sand. My mother was named Be. She could fly. Her arms turned into wings when the water went up around the tree. That's where I was born.'

Daniel sighed. He only had the energy to give short answers. Most of all, he wanted to go back to his dream and fly away with Be.

'I don't understand much of what you're saying. But I know you're on the run and that you were brought here by some madman who probably wanted to exhibit you at fairs. Is that how it was?'

'Father showed insects. Then he lifted a cloth. There I sat.'

The man leaned forward and stroked Daniel's face.

'I understand that you want to go home,' he said. 'Why should you be here in the cold winter when you're used to the heat? What was it he was called, the man who brought you here? Hans Bengler? Do you know anyone else here in Skåne? Because you've been living in Skåne. I can tell by the way you speak.'

'Dr Madsen.'

'The doctor in Simrishamn? Then it's not only unpleasant people that you've met. He helps people even if they have no money.'

Daniel could feel that he was slipping into sleep again. The man sitting on the edge of the bunk made him feel utterly calm.

'I can raise the sail,' said Daniel. 'And I don't get sick when the waves are high.'

'No doubt you're a good sailor, even though you're only a boy. But first you have to get some sleep. I think you should stay here. The old woman at home would go crazy and shriek that the Devil had come into her house if I took you there. She doesn't have much patience with things that aren't familiar.'

Daniel could no longer understand what the man was talking about. Or else he didn't have the strength to listen.

'When do we sail?' he asked.

The man gave him a long look before he replied.

'Maybe tomorrow,' he said at last. 'It depends. If the wind holds.'

'I can sleep on deck,' Daniel muttered.

'You can sleep here. You don't need to run any more.'

The man put his hand on Daniel's forehead.

'Well, you haven't got a fever from the cold, at least. Go to sleep now, and we'll see in the morning which way the wind is blowing.'

Daniel sank quickly deep inside himself.

At one point in the night he opened his eyes. The man was still sitting on the edge of the bunk looking at him. Daniel thought that he would probably sit there until he woke up the next day. He felt completely safe now. He wouldn't have to learn how to walk on water. And he wouldn't be nailed up on any boards either.

He would go home.

But when he woke up it was Dr Madsen who stood there looking at him. Lystedt waited by the door and avoided looking Daniel in the eye. Madsen was grave.

'You've caused Alma and Edvin a great deal of worry,' he said. 'We're going home now.'

Daniel looked with horror at Madsen. And then at Lystedt.

'I had no choice,' he said. 'The ship is unrigged for the winter. I won't be sailing until spring. But I understand why you want to go home.'

'The boy will stay in Sweden,' Madsen snapped.

'I'm saying what I think,' said Lystedt. 'The boy has the right to go home to the desert. What business does he have staying here?'

Dr Madsen didn't answer. He just pulled off the blankets.

'Get up,' he said. 'I really don't have time for this. There's a serious case of gangrene waiting at the hospital. But I will see to it that you get back.'

They came out on deck. It had started to snow again. Daniel looked up at the sky. Be was there, but he couldn't see her. Dr Madsen held his arm and shoved him on ahead. Daniel wriggled loose. Instead of hopping over the railing to the quay he ran across the deck and jumped straight into the harbour.

The last thing he thought of was the antelope, which had finally managed to free itself from the rock and take its leap.

CHAPTER 25

The rest of the winter, which was stormy and cold in Skåne, Daniel lay in bed. He had no idea what had happened after he jumped into the harbour. When he woke up he was lying in his bed in the kitchen again. Alma was sitting on a chair next to him, and he saw that she was happy when he opened his eyes. She called Edvin and he came in, but when the milkmaids and the hired hand wanted to see him too, she angrily shooed them out. Edvin stroked his cheek and shook his head. Daniel was warm and his heart was pounding as if he had been running in his sleep.

Then he started coughing. Edvin took a step back, while Alma did the opposite. She leaned towards his face and fluffed up the pillow behind his head.

Afterwards, when Alma explained to him what had happened, he realised that he had been asleep for a very long time. She held up a mirror so that he could see why his face hurt and he saw that he had big wounds on his forehead and across his nose that had not yet healed.

'You hit an ice floe,' said Alma. 'It cut up your face. But you didn't sink. For that, I have thanked God every day and every night.'

Daniel tried to recall what had happened. He wondered where all his dreams had gone. He couldn't remember a thing. The last thing he had seen was the black water coming towards him like the open mouth of a beast of prey.

He stopped talking during the months he lay in bed. The hired hand moved out to a room that was hastily prepared in the barn. Alma set up two screens in front of the milkmaids' beds. Even though she strictly forbade it, they used to peek at him from behind the screens. Daniel didn't mind. He listened to his heart, which was still in flight. Even though his legs had stopped, his heart kept on running. Now and then

Dr Madsen would come to visit. He felt and listened to Daniel's chest and rubbed salves on his face. Daniel always closed his eyes when he came into the room. He didn't want to see the doctor's face because he hadn't let him stay on the ship.

At the end of each visit Dr Madsen would repeat the same words. 'The boy has a bad cold. And a cough that I don't much like.'

The fever made Daniel tired. Most of the time he slept.

What was hardest for those around him was his silence. Even though he didn't want to make Alma sad, he couldn't speak. In his dreams, which slowly returned, he had reverted to his old language.

Pastor Hallén came to visit once a week. Daniel knew when he was coming because Alma always cleaned beforehand. Hallén would sit down on a chair a short distance from the bed and ask to be left alone with Daniel. Then he would fold his hands and say a prayer. Through his half-closed eyelids Daniel would try to see if he had a hammer and nails in his pocket, but the fact that he was sick and lying in bed seemed to have saved him from the boards.

Hallén prayed that Daniel would get well and regain his ability to speak. Each time he asked Daniel the same question, whether he wanted to hear about the time when Jesus walked on the water, but Daniel closed his eyes and lay motionless.

He thought he had heard enough. Only Be or Kiko could give him the words he longed for.

The only person he really wanted to see during those months he lay in bed never came. That was Sanna. Once he heard Alma whispering to Edvin that maybe they ought to ask the girl to come, since Daniel obviously liked her. But Edvin was hesitant. Dr Madsen had said she was not suitable company for him. She might make him upset because she was unpredictable.

Daniel slept during the day and lay awake at night when the house was quiet and the milkmaids were snoring behind the screens. Sometimes he would get up, especially when the moon was out, take his skipping rope and silently skip in the kitchen until he used up all his strength.

One night Alma opened the door. She saw him skipping but didn't say a word, just closed the door again, and he knew that she would never tell anyone, not even Edvin.

Spring was already on the way when Daniel got out of bed one day and moved to the barn. He could no longer stand the snoring of the milkmaids. Alma and Edvin were standing in he yard when he came out of the door early one morning and walked straight over to the barn. He made himself a bed underneath the stairs that led up to the hayloft and lay down. After a while Alma came in. She chased out the curious milkmaids, and for the first time Daniel heard the way she yelled at them.

'You don't have to stare as if you'd never seen him before!' she shouted.

When the milkmaids were gone, she squatted down beside Daniel. She had a bad back and her knees were stiff.

'You can't sleep here,' she said. 'If you do, you'll never get rid of your cough.'

Daniel pulled the blanket he had taken with him over his head. He refused to answer. Then he heard Edvin come in.

'Why does he have to sleep out here?' said Edvin. 'And how can we find out if he won't answer, and we have no idea what he's thinking? He isn't lonely. He seems to be surrounded by people I can't see.'

'There's nobody else here but you and me. You're imagining things.'

'Can't you feel it? It's like a fog around him.'

'He's dying of longing,' said Alma. 'Bengler has to take him back to the desert.'

'That man is never coming back,' Edvin said. 'We can't even be sure that he's still alive.'

Daniel jerked the blanket down from his face.

'At least he can still hear,' Edvin said. 'Just don't ask me to carry him inside, or he'll sink his teeth into my throat.'

'The hired hand can move back into the house and the boy can take his room.'

'If he lay down here then it's because this is where he wants to be.'

Daniel turned his head and looked into Edvin's eyes.

'I feel like I'm looking at an old man,' said Edvin. 'And yet he's only nine or ten years old.'

228

'He's dying of longing.'

'But what is it he's longing for? Parents who are dead? Sand that burns under his feet?'

'He's longing for home. Whatever it is, that's where he longs to be.'

The hired hand moved back to the kitchen but his room remained empty. Daniel continued to sleep underneath the stairs to the hayloft. Alma came and gave him food, and shouted at the milkmaids when they were too inquisitive.

Daniel still slept during the day. At night when he was alone with the animals, he would get up and skip between the stalls. Edvin had hung up two lanterns in the barn, which he lit every evening. Sometimes, when it rained, Daniel would go outside and feel the raindrops striking his face. The fever was gone but he still had the cough. And a strange weariness that never went away no matter how much he slept.

The nights had gradually grown lighter and shorter. Daniel started going up to the hill when it was quiet in the house. He had a feeling that Alma was standing like an invisible shadow behind a window, watching him. But he trusted her, her and Sanna, and maybe even Edvin. All the others had betrayed him. He still hoped that Sanna would come back. He left signs for her on the hill, wrote his name in the dirt, left his shoes there, but whenever he returned there was never any trace of her. One night he ventured down to the house where she lived. He tried to look in through the low windows, find the place where she slept. But the only thing he could hear through the wall was someone snoring, and Daniel knew it was the man who had dragged her off by the hair.

He calculated that three full moons had come and gone by the time he felt able to think again. He would run away one more time. If he didn't succeed in getting home he would die. If they caught him again he would be tied up and he would never have the strength to get loose.

He thought that death might not be so frightening. Kiko was dead, and Be too, but he could still talk to them. Even though they lay buried in the sand, they could still laugh. He also remembered how Be had given birth to him in the treetop and then changed her arms into wings. He decided that he wasn't afraid to die, even though he was still just a child. The cough that never left him was a sign that death had already hidden away in some corner of his body. Kiko had once told him about all the caves there were inside a human being. Somewhere in a hole, death was hiding, and one day it would drive the living spirits out of his body. Daniel knew that the cough didn't come from his lungs; it had the musty smell of a secret grotto deep inside him.

What scared him was not death. It was the thought of having to be dead for so long. And even longer if he was buried here in the mud, by the church where Hallén preached. Kiko and Be would never find him. He couldn't imagine anything worse than lying dead surrounded by strangers. Who would he talk to? Who would he have for company when he set out on the long migration through the desert?

The most important thing of all was the antelope that had never been completed.

He couldn't leave it. Kiko had said that he was the one who had to finish it, see that it lived on. The gods would also abandon him if he died here in the mud.

He no longer believed that he would be able to learn to walk on water. The death he carried inside him made him too heavy. He also didn't believe that he would be able to find his way back to the harbour where the ship was waiting.

The thoughts he was thinking were so heavy that he could barely manage to carry them. He was still too little for all that was loaded on his shoulders. And the weight wasn't only on his shoulders, it was inside him too.

One night as he was sitting on the hill he realised that he would never succeed if he didn't get some help. The only ones who could help him were Alma and Sanna. Maybe Edvin too, but Edvin was afraid of Hallén. He almost never dared look up at the sky. His gaze was always fixed on the ground. He was afraid of everything that was unexpected. Even the fact that he had taken Daniel in might be a sign of fear about staying in Dr Madsen's good graces: some day the doctor might refuse to help him or Alma if they fell ill. But Alma was different. The only thing she was afraid of was that Daniel might be treated badly. But he couldn't ignore the fact that she was old. She had pain in her back and her legs were stiff.

That left only Sanna. And she had disappeared. Despite the fact that he had left signs for her on the hill, she didn't reply.

Maybe she was dead. Maybe the man who had dragged her by the hair had killed her. Sanna wasn't like anyone else. She might have done something dangerous and then been punished with death. Maybe Hallén had nailed her up on the boards instead of Daniel.

He had to find out whether Sanna was still alive. Without her he might as well lie down and die. Then he would vanish into the depths of the brown fields, and anyone who searched for him would search in vain.

And the antelope would weep.

That night he walked up the long path to the church. The big door was locked, but he managed to prise open a window to the sacristy and climb in. He lit a candle and shivered with cold. Hallén was there in the darkness, breathing towards him. Daniel growled like an animal and Hallén's shadow disappeared. He went into the sanctuary. He found no boards anywhere with Sanna nailed up on them. For the first time he dared go inside the altar rail. He stood on tiptoe and stroked the chipped knee of the figure hanging there. When he felt it with his fingers he noticed that a sliver of wood was coming loose. He carefully pulled it out and put it in his pocket.

He blew out the candle and left the church.

It was already starting to get light. Mist was drifting across the field.

He ran as fast as he could along the road. Somewhere in the distance he heard a cock crow. When he reached Alma and Edvin's house it was still quiet. He turned off the road and continued along the cart track until he reached the top of the hill. He could see at once that Sanna hadn't been there. He took the piece of wood out of his pocket and buried it. As he ran all the way from the church he had decided to make use of his memories. Memories from the time when he was so small that Be still carried him bound to her back; the memories of her movements when she danced. With his bare feet he drew a circle around the place where he had planted the piece of wood from Jesus' broken knee. Then he began to search in his body for Be's rocking motions.

Even though he started to cough, he danced around the circle. He also wanted to sing, but thought that Edvin would hear him. A hare sat motionless out in the field watching him. He danced until the coughing fits were about to choke him.

When he rubbed his hand across his mouth he found blood on it. The cold wind from the grotto of death had come all the way out to his mouth. He squatted down and spat onto the ground. Now both the piece of wood and his blood were there. He sat on the ground and fought for breath. It ripped and tore at his chest, but now he was sure. Sanna would come back. And she would understand that he was searching for her.

As he came down from the hill he was struck by a sudden weakness that made him collapse. He lay there on his back and looked up at the sky, which was covered by low clouds. His heart was beating fast, and his lungs were fighting to take in air. I have to make it, he thought. I can't die here in the mud.

After a while he got up and continued home. There was still no smoke coming out of the chimney. He went into the barn, curled up in the straw, and fell asleep.

He woke up when the hired hand poked him.

'Vanja is sick,' said the hired hand. 'Alma is taking care of her. Here's your food.'

Daniel didn't reply. He merely took the dish and began to eat his porridge. He didn't like the hired hand. Jonas had never dared look him in the eye. Even when he said his name it sounded as though he were saying something that wasn't true. Daniel assumed that Jonas hated him because his skin was a different colour. Jonas had red hair and his skin was almost as white as snow. Several times he had heard Edvin complaining about him to Alma, that he was lazy.

Vanja was the older of the two milkmaids, and the fatter one, compared to Serja who was very thin. As he ate he thought that Vanja must be seriously ill for Alma not to bring him his food. Serja had always been the one who stared at him, the one who most often made Alma cross. Vanja moved slowly and heavily, and would suddenly break out in violent laughing fits that no one understood and then sit silently and rub her hands over her heavy breasts. The hired hand always wanted

Daniel to pull the covers off her when she lay alone in bed. It was her big body that he most wanted to see.

Daniel put down the dish. The cows were waiting impatiently to be milked. A hen came near his blanket pecking the ground. The door slammed. It was Serja coming in. She had pails in her hands and stopped before Daniel with tears in her eyes.

'Vanja sick,' she said in broken Swedish. 'She raving.'

Daniel didn't know what *raving* meant, but he could tell that Serja was scared. He decided to break his silence.

'Does she hurt?'

'It is in her throat. She cannot breathe.'

'Does she hurt?'

'She cannot breathe! Hurt can one. But if one cannot breathe one die.'

Then she began to clank the pails against each other as if she were losing her mind.

'I have to milk!' she screeched. 'But Vanja sick. And I am afraid. I sleep in same bed. Maybe it catching.'

She vanished among the cows. Daniel could hear her crying. Late in the afternoon Jonas came back with more food.

'She's even sicker now,' he said, and Daniel could see that his shivers of fear were somehow mixed with glee.

'The doctor has come,' he went on. 'But not even Madsen can do anything.'

Jonas left. Daniel pushed the plate away. He wasn't hungry. Nearby lay someone who was very ill, who might die. And he knew that it had something to do with him.

That evening Alma came out to the barn. She was pale and moved with extreme difficulty.

'You know that Vanja is sick,' she said. 'The illness has progressed quickly, and we don't know if she'll survive. She has an abscess in her throat. Dr Madsen can't cut it out because she might bleed to death.'

'Why is she sick?' Daniel asked.

Alma seemed not to hear.

'The girl is only nineteen years old. That's not an age for dying. That's a time to live.'

Alma left him. Serja was doing the evening milking. Daniel waited. When everything was quiet he left the barn. Through the window of the house he could see Alma sitting on a chair next to Vanja's bed. Alma had fallen asleep. Her hands were resting in her lap, and her head had drooped forward. Carefully he opened the door and went in. Vanja was breathing with a wheezing sound. There were brown medicine bottles on the table. Daniel looked at her face. She was both pale and red at the same time. Her breast was heaving violently. He carefully lifted the covers. He had to know if her knee had swollen up. Whether she was about to die because he had pulled a splinter of wood out of the wooden body that hung on the cross in the church. Her knee looked normal. The abscess in her throat had nothing to do with him. And yet he knew it was a warning. Death was searching, and soon it would find him.

Two days later Vanja died. It was Alma who came out to the barn and told him. She was crying. Daniel thought that he didn't have much time left. If he was ever going to make it home it would have to be now.

That same night he went up to the hill. Sanna still hadn't been there, but he knew that she would come soon.

On Saturday the coffin was taken on a wagon to the church. It was raining. Alma brought food for him out to the barn. She was dressed in black. Daniel reached out his hand and took hold of her wrist. He hadn't done that in a long time.

'The girl was so young,' Alma said. 'So young and now she's dead.'

Daniel waited until the wagon was gone, then he got up. While the funeral was in progress he would leave Alma and Edvin's house for the last time. He walked around in the barn and patted the cows.

When he reached the top of the hill, Sanna was sitting there waiting for him.

CHAPTER 26

Sanna hadn't noticed the splinter of wood. She hadn't come to the hill to wait for him – she had gone there to be alone.

Daniel could see at once that something had happened. All her restless energy was gone. She sat still, huddled up, and she hardly noticed when he appeared. He sat down next to her and waited. Even though time was short, he knew that he couldn't leave without her. He couldn't talk to her, either. All the invisible doors surrounding her were closed. For once the black birds were quiet. They perched in the tree out in the field, unmoving.

Daniel waited. On Sanna's face he could see the traces of tears. He sensed that it had something to do with the man who had dragged her off by the hair.

Not until Daniel had a coughing fit did she come to life again and look at him.

'Who died?' she asked.

'Vanja.'

'What happened?'

'She got something in her throat that poisoned her and made her stop breathing.'

'I saw when they drove off with the coffin. First I thought you were the one who was dead. Then I saw that the coffin was big.'

'I'm leaving. I have to go now. I can't stay any longer.'

She gave a start. 'Do you still want me to come with you?'

Daniel was dumbstruck. Was she answering his question before he even had a chance to ask it?

'Yes,' he said. 'I want you to come too. But we have to leave now. Before they come back from church.'

Instead of replying, Sanna began to cry. She seemed to cast herself headlong into a sobbing fit, filled equally with rage and sorrow.

'He raped me!' she shrieked. 'That damn devil of a man raped me! And he was supposed to be my father!'

Daniel didn't know what the word meant. *Raped*? He had never heard it before.

'What happened?' he asked cautiously.

Sanna pulled up her dress to the waist. She was naked underneath and Daniel saw that there was dried blood on the inside of her thighs.

'Did he beat you?'

'You're stupid, you're a child, you don't understand a thing. He told me to help him move a calf to another stall. Then he threw me down and stuck it in. I couldn't even scream. He shoved straw and cow shit in my face. I almost suffocated. And then he said he would kill me if I said a word.'

She suddenly started to scratch and tear at the hair below her belly. Daniel still wasn't sure that he understood what had happened.

'What if he got me pregnant?' she yelled. 'Then they'll lock me up in the madhouse in Lund.'

She let her skirt fall and sank back to the ground. Daniel took her hand. She squeezed it so hard with her fingernails that he had to make an effort not to pull his hand away.

Just as suddenly as it began, her fit was over.

'I'll come with you. But I'll never be able to walk on water. I'm too stupid and I'm too clumsy.'

'We're not going to walk on water. It's too late for that now. We're going to find a boat.'

'I can't swim.'

'We'll find a boat that won't sink.'

'I've never seen the sea.'

Daniel dug up the sliver of wood from the mud.

'This will protect us.'

He told her about his night-time visit to the church.

'It will protect us from the waves if they get too high.'

She got up and pointed to the road on the other side of the hill.

'I'll wait for you there. I just have to run home and fetch something I want to take with me. There's nobody there now, so I can do it.'

Then she was gone. At the same moment the birds took off from the treetop. They circled around a few times and then vanished across the fields. Daniel followed them with his gaze as long as he could. It occurred to him that they had been there the whole time he had lived with Alma and Edvin. Now they were leaving. Earlier he had walked in the direction they had flown. Now he understood that he had to go in the other direction.

He looked at the house one last time. Then he went down to the road and waited for Sanna.

She came as she had promised. She had wrapped a red shawl around her head. In one hand she had a bundle, in the other something that Daniel couldn't make out.

'I took everything he had,' she said as she came close and opened her hand. There was a bunch of banknotes like the kind Father had often sat and counted.

'Everything he had,' she repeated. 'He didn't think I knew where he hid the money. In an old hymn book behind the corner cupboard. But I took everything he had.'

'I don't think we need any money,' said Daniel. 'I know that somewhere a boat will be waiting for us.'

'It's important to have money. Otherwise it's impossible to survive.'

They started walking but stopped after a few steps.

'Where are we heading?'

Daniel pointed in the direction of the road. 'To the sea.'

'I think it's called Copenhagen,' said Sanna. 'It's on the other side of the water. A city that's very big.'

They began walking again. Sanna walked so fast that Daniel couldn't keep up with her. She didn't stop until he started coughing.

'You're sick,' she said. 'You might die.'

He shook his head and wiped away the tears once the violent coughing fit was over.

'I have to go home,' he said. 'Then I'll be well again. And you're going with me.'

'I would much rather it had been you who stuck it in,' she said. 'Even if it turned out to be a grey baby.'

'I can't have babies,' Daniel said. 'I'm too little.'

'Me too!' Sanna yelled. 'If I walk as fast as I can, maybe I can shake it loose.'

That afternoon they reached a small town. While Daniel waited behind a barn outside the town, Sanna went in to find them some food. She came back with milk, bread and a fistful of dried fish. When they had eaten, they took a detour around the town. Daniel could feel his fever had come back. He didn't say anything to Sanna, and tried to keep up with her even though she was almost trotting. When evening fell Sanna still didn't want to stop. Daniel saw her turn round often and then walk even faster. He could tell that she was very frightened.

That night they crept in under a bridge. Sanna felt that Daniel was feverish.

'Crawl in here,' she said, wrapping her shawl around his shoulders. Then she drew him close to her.

'Can you hear it?' she asked.

'What?'

'The sea.'

Daniel could hear only the fever pounding between his temples.

'Tomorrow,' he replied. 'Tomorrow.'

No woman had held Daniel so tightly since he was with Be.

'You've got a fever,' she said. 'But you mustn't die.'

'I won't die. I'm just tired.'

She began to rock him as if he were a little baby.

'They won't find us,' she said. 'Are there apples in the country you come from?'

Daniel didn't dare tell her the truth.

'Yes, there are apples,' he said. 'And they're just as green as the apples you have here.'

'Then it doesn't matter if there's a lot of sand. As long as there are apples.'

Daniel thought that Sanna probably didn't understand what a long journey they had before them, and how different everything would be. But he also knew that she couldn't go back. The man who had dragged her by the hair had hurt her and Sanna had stolen his money. There was no going back now. Hallén would nail both of them up on boards.

'I'm scared,' Sanna said suddenly, when Daniel was almost asleep.

'But at the same time I feel happy. For the first time I'm doing something that nobody told me to do.'

She burst out laughing. Daniel woke up. Her happiness made his fever feel lighter to bear for a moment. We're going to make it, he thought. Tomorrow we'll find the boat. Then everything that has happened will become a dream, and soon I won't remember any of it.

'Tomorrow we'll reach the sea,' he said. 'But there's still a long way to go. So we have to get some sleep.'

Several times during the night Daniel awoke because Sanna got up and went onto the bridge to look back the way they had come. He understood her fear, but he knew that nobody was there. The people following them would go in the same direction the birds had flown.

They set off at daybreak. They drank their fill from the stream that ran under the bridge and then shared what was left of the bread. The road was narrow and wound through groves of trees and across open fields. Late in the afternoon they reached a hill. On the way up Daniel had to stop and catch his breath. Sanna ran ahead, racing the last bit to the top. Then he heard her shriek and saw her jump up and down as if she had an invisible skipping rope in her hands.

When he rubbed his hand across his mouth he saw that there was blood again. He wiped it on the inside of his coat sleeve before he went up to the hilltop where Sanna was waiting impatiently.

The sea lay at their feet.

'Is that where we're going?' Sanna asked, pointing.

Daniel was worried that it wasn't the sea but one of the lakes he had seen so many times on his travels with Father. On the other side of the water was a strip of land. But when he followed the line of the land with his eyes he could see that it disappeared in a haze. There the sea continued. Then he knew that they had come the right way.

'Where's the boat?' asked Sanna. She kept looking back over her shoulder.

'I don't know,' Daniel said. 'We have to find it.'

Sanna looked at him and flew into a rage.

'If only you weren't so damn black!' she shrieked. 'They're going to find us.'

'Not when it's dark. Then they'll see me less than they will you.'

Sanna started walking down the slope. Daniel followed her.

Sanna did the same thing she had done the day before: left Daniel and came back later with some food. They hid in a grove of trees and waited for the sun to set. Daniel slept. When he woke up it was already almost dark. Sanna was sleeping by his side. She had stuck her thumb in her mouth like a little baby. Daniel tried to remember what he had dreamed, whether there was any message for him, but his head was silent. He touched the sliver of wood in his pocket.

He woke Sanna cautiously. She gave a start and held her hands in front of her face as if he might hit her.

'We have to get moving,' he said.

Sanna shivered. 'How are we going to find a boat when it's nearly dark?'

Daniel didn't know. But somewhere there had to be a boat. If they had reached the sea, they had also reached the boats. The wind had already begun to flutter in the masts that Daniel bore inside him.

They passed through a village that lay silent. A dog barked. Then everything was quiet again. All Daniel knew was that they had to walk straight towards the water. Now he was the one leading the way. Sanna followed close behind, holding onto his coat.

They followed a ridge along the water, which roared in the dark. The wind felt colder now that they were so close to the sea.

'Where's the boat?' Sanna nagged. 'Where's the boat?'

Daniel didn't reply.

They reached some wooden steps that led down to the water. Daniel smelled tar, so there had to be boats nearby. When they got down to the beach they found themselves standing in the midst of some over-turned rowing boats. By a little stone wharf lay some bigger boats with sails wrapped around their masts. Daniel was disappointed. The boats were small.

Sanna pinched him anxiously on the arm.

'What are we going to do now?'

Daniel looked around. He was like Kiko now, on the hunt for prey; not an animal, but a ship.

'Wait here,' he said. 'I have to search.'

'No,' she replied, pinching his arm hard. 'You're not leaving me.'

She kept holding onto his coat as if she were blind. She stumbled often, and Daniel realised she was really quite clumsy.

Suddenly he noticed the glow from a fire far out on the little wharf. A man was sitting by the fire with a mug in his hands which he lifted to his lips now and then.

He's waiting for us, Daniel thought. That's the only reason he would be sitting there.

They walked out onto the stone wharf. Daniel stamped hard with his clogs so that the man wouldn't be afraid. He looked in their direction with his mug in his hand. They went up to the fire. The man was old. He had a long beard and a worn-out cap on his head.

'Do I have trolls paying me a visit?' he said.

'We need a boat,' said Sanna, 'that can take us away from here.'

The man looked them up and down. He wasn't in the least afraid, Daniel thought. That was the most important thing. Sanna held out the money they had left. The man leaned forward and looked at it. Then he squinted at Daniel's face.

'Come closer,' he said. 'So I can see you.'

Daniel squatted down by the fire. The man threw a few twigs onto it so that the flames flared up.

'You really are completely black,' said the man. 'I saw a person like you once on a street in Malmö. Was it you?'

'I don't know. My name is Daniel and I believe in God.'

'And the girl?'

'I have no name,' she said. 'But people call me Sanna.'

'And you want me to take you across to Copenhagen? Because you've run away from somewhere?'

Sanna promptly began to cry. She pulled her jumper over her face.

'I don't care why you ran away,' said the man. 'Children have a hard time. I ran away from Älmhult myself, and I wound up here.'

'We have to go now,' Daniel said.

The man shook his head. 'There's no wind. And I certainly won't be rowing you across the Sound.'

241

'It's not totally calm,' said Daniel. 'Your boat is small. It doesn't need much wind.'

The man burst out laughing. He had almost no teeth. Then he snatched up the money that Sanna had in her hand.

'We can always drift across,' he said. 'Help me up. My bones are stiff.'

Daniel took hold of his arm. The man kicked the burning twigs into the water, where they hissed and went out.

'Climb aboard,' said the man. 'You sit in the middle. There's a blanket there.'

Sanna had stopped crying, but she hesitated to climb into the boat.

'It'll sink,' she said. 'The fish will swim into my body and eat me up.'

'It won't sink,' Daniel told her. 'Remember what I have in my pocket.'

Sanna stepped clumsily onto the boat.

'There's water in it!' she shouted. 'We're sinking already.'

'Only a few drops,' said the man. 'There's a bailer somewhere.'

Daniel stepped down onto the boat. When he felt it move, relief washed over him. The man cast off the moorings and shoved the boat out. Then he raised the triangular sail and sat down at the tiller. They drifted slowly across the water. Now and then a gust of wind would catch at the sail.

'Will we sink?' Sanna asked.

'We're on our way now.'

Sanna giggled. Then she whispered in Daniel's ear, 'He didn't get all the money. I have two notes left.'

The boat drifted away from the shore. The water lapped softly against the sides.

'My name is Hans Höjer,' said the man at the tiller. 'I'm a thousand years old, I fish, and I know that if I sit by the fire out on the wharf somebody will always come, either to keep me company or to ask me to take them over to Copenhagen. I respect freedom. I don't care whether it's thieves or whores or counterfeiters who want to cross. I don't take murderers on board. But I assume that you haven't killed anyone.'

'Somebody killed me,' replied Sanna.

'Not quite,' chuckled Hans Höjer. 'You're still alive.'

*   *   *

242

And then he died. Daniel saw him suddenly grab his chest, grunt, try to draw air into his throat, and then fall forward. Sanna didn't see what happened because she was busy wrapping the blanket around herself.

'Damn, what a smell,' she said.

Daniel didn't answer. He reached out his hand and felt for one of the big blood vessels in the man's throat. He couldn't feel a pulse.

The boat had begun to turn in the wind. The sail was flapping back and forth. Sanna sat with her head sticking out of the dirty blanket and closed her eyes.

'He's dead,' Daniel said.

Sanna didn't reply.

Daniel tried to think. Why had he died? There could only be one explanation: Daniel was meant to take over the tiller. Hans Höjer had really been sitting by his boat and waiting for them.

'He's dead,' Daniel said again.

Sanna opened her eyes and looked at him.

'Who's dead? I know that Vanja's dead. Is someone else dead?'

Then she noticed that there was no longer anyone sitting in the stern at the tiller. She got up on her knees.

'Is the man dead?'

'He just fell over and stopped breathing.'

Sanna pinched him hard on the arm. 'Then we're going to sink.'

'I'll steer.'

'What are we going to do with him? Is he just going to lie here and be dead?'

'I don't know,' Daniel said. 'First I have to sit down and steer.'

He crawled over the dead man and sat down by the tiller. The line to the sail was loosely lashed. Sanna started digging in the dead man's coat for the money.

'If he's dead he won't need any money.'

She stuffed the roll of notes inside her blouse and then threw the dirty blanket over the man.

'Will we be there soon?' she asked impatiently.

'Not yet,' said Daniel. 'Not quite yet.'

*   *   *

243

They sat in silence. Sanna dozed. Daniel could hear her snoring. He waited for daybreak. Only then would he be able to see which direction to sail in. Then he would also decide what to do with the man who lay dead at his feet.

CHAPTER 27

The lookout yawned. He was standing by the railing and scanning the horizon with his binoculars. Daybreak had come slowly across the Sound. At the stern a deckhand was hoisting the three-tongued blue-and-yellow Swedish naval flag in which the coat of arms of the kingdom of Norway was inset. The morning was cool, the water calm. On the east side lay Malmö, to the west Copenhagen. They were steaming slowly northwards. King Oskar had come down with a headache the evening before, and Captain Roslund had hove to during the night. Now they were continuing their slow progress towards Gothenburg, which was the first stop on the journey to Kristiania.

The lookout kept looking though his field glasses. A lone seagull sat bobbing on the waves. In the distance some fishing boats were on their way north, perhaps heading for the rich fishing banks beyond the Danish coast.

Suddenly the lookout spied a boat floating still on the water. It was a very small fishing skiff. He rested his elbows on the railing to steady his gaze. It looked as though someone was preparing to set a net or perhaps a buoy. Then he realised to his shock that someone was tying weights around a human body. He called to the deckhand, who had finished with the flag. Captain Roslund, who was always up early in the morning, stuck his head out from the bridge and shushed him. The Swedish King was sleeping and did not want to be disturbed. The deckhand looked through the binoculars.

'They're tipping someone overboard,' he said in amazement. 'Could it be a murder?'

They took turns looking through the glasses again and were convinced. A lifeless body was being wrapped in a blanket with stone sinkers. In the boat were a young girl and a boy who was completely black.

The deckhand shuddered. 'We have to tell Roslund.'

Together they went up to the command bridge of the *Drott*. The captain listened to what they had to say, shook his head, but then put his own big telescope up to his eye. He gave a start, lowered the glass and then raised it again.

'We'll have to go over there,' he said. 'If the King wakes up, let's hope he understands that it was necessary.'

Roslund gave orders to increase their speed slightly. The white-uniformed helmsman was given the new course. Roslund estimated the distance at eight hundred metres.

'One of them is black,' Roslund said. 'Could it be a coal stoker?'

'It's a boy,' replied the deckhand.

Daniel saw the large ship approaching. Earlier it had not been moving at all. He was having a hard time fastening the two stone sinkers he had found in the boat. Sanna refused to help him. She had turned her back, playing with one hand in the water and humming, as if what was going on behind her was of no consequence.

When Daniel finally tipped the body into the water the large ship was already quite close.

The body did not sink. It remained floating near the boat.

Someone shouted to him, a man with a peaked cap and gold buttons on his coat. Daniel didn't listen. He tried to force the body under the surface, but it was no use. A lifeboat was lowered over the side and some seamen rowed quickly over to their skiff. Sanna had pulled the dirty blanket over her head, but she kept on humming. Daniel could hear that it was a hymn. The man with the peaked cap grabbed hold of the gunwale.

'What the hell is going on here? Did you kill him?'

The seamen began to pull up the body. There was another boat next to the lifeboat. Two seamen had guns in their hands.

The body was now halfway out of the water. Hans Höjer's face had turned yellow. One eye was half open, as if even in death he wanted to know what was going on around him.

'This man has been murdered,' said Roslund. 'I've seen plenty in my day, but never a little black devil like this all alone out on the Sound. Why is the girl hiding under the blanket?'

Daniel thought he ought to say something. but Sanna, who kept humming underneath the blanket, upset him and made it impossible for him to find the words.

At that moment there was a whistled signal from the big ship. It cut through the dawn and scared some seagulls from the water.

'Hell,' said Roslund. 'What's the King doing up so early?'

He turned round and saluted. A man with a grey beard was standing at the railing. Next to him were two men dressed in black and white. One had a tray in his hand, the other a towel.

'What's going on?' asked the man with the grey beard.

'I don't know, Your Majesty. But we discovered someone trying to throw a corpse overboard.'

People had begun gathering at the railing of the big ship. A woman appeared but the man with the grey beard waved her away.

'Who's hiding under the blanket?'

One of the seamen pulled off the blanket. Sanna closed her eyes and held her hands in front of her face. She kept humming, louder now, and she was rocking back and forth.

'Bring them aboard,' said the King. 'But perhaps it would be best to tie up the Negro boy. Quite a remarkable wake-up call, I must say. The sun comes up in the mist and the first thing one sees is a little black boy who has committed a murder.'

Roslund pointed to two of the seamen. One of them took off his belt and tried to grab Daniel's hands, but Daniel sank his teeth into the man's wrist. The seaman yelled and let go of Daniel, who began climbing overboard. There was nothing else to do now. Once again his journey home had been interrupted. Now he was surrounded by men in white who wanted to tie him up, so he might as well die. He would then drift deep in the sea until he finally reached home. That would be better than being buried in the earth behind Hallén's church, where nobody would ever find him.

He made it only halfway into the water. The person who caught him was not one of the seamen but Sanna, who suddenly cast herself over him. He tried to pull himself loose, but she held on, and she was strong. He bit and struggled, but she didn't seem to care.

'I won't!' he screamed. 'I want to go home!'

Somewhere inside him his old language welled up and cut through all the words he had been forced to learn. Be and Kiko were inside

247

him, their voices shouted at Sanna, and they struggled as much as he did. They didn't want to let go of him now that he was so close.

'We're not going to drown!' Sanna screamed. 'We're going back home, no matter what happens. We're going home.'

Daniel realised that Sanna had betrayed him. She wouldn't let him die. She forced first Be and then Kiko to release their grip. Two of the seamen dragged him aboard and tied his hands behind him with the belt. He no longer resisted. He just closed his eyes and tried to go to sleep, to force his heart to stop beating. He felt himself lifted up and carried off and then he lay utterly still.

When he opened his eyes the man with the grey beard was standing watching him. The whites of his eyes were bloodshot.

'Hardly one of my subjects,' he said. 'Not even in the remotest villages in Norway can one find the like. A Negro.'

The man looked at Captain Roslund, who stood next to him.

'What does the girl say?'

Roslund snapped to attention and held his arms rigid at his side.

'To be honest the girl doesn't seem very bright, Your Majesty. She says that they were sailing to the desert. And that the man just died. Dr Steninger was unable to find any wounds on the body. He asks for permission to carry out an autopsy.'

'On the *Drott*? Are corpses to be cut open on the King's yacht? On my holiday trip to Kristiania? Permission denied!'

Roslund stamped on the deck, saluted, turned on his heel and left.

Daniel lay on a sail that had been spread out. Someone had placed a pillow under his head. All around people stood looking at him, but it was the man with the grey beard who was the most important. He stood closest, and there was a distance between him and the others. Daniel thought that he recognised his face. He had seen him before.

'I think he recognises Your Majesty,' said a man with a short stubby moustache.

Then Daniel remembered. In Alma and Edvin's sitting room there was a picture on the wall. The picture was of the man who was now looking at him. Once Daniel had asked who he was, and Alma had said he was King Oskar and then a number that he didn't recall.

He sat up at once. The grey-bearded man took a quick step backwards.

'Careful,' he said. 'It's possible the boy cannot be trusted. What does the girl say?'

'She's crying, Your Majesty.'

'But before – what did she say about the boy?'

'She said that his name is Daniel and he's from an African desert.'

'But I definitely heard him speaking Swedish, in a Skåne dialect.'

'She said that they come from a village near Tomelilla.'

'And they were just off on a sailing trip?'

'He wanted to go back to the desert.'

The man who was the King held out his hand and was given a handkerchief. He wiped his mouth and then dropped it on the deck.

'A peculiar dawn,' said the King. 'One awakens too early and immediately one has the most remarkable experience. Bathe the boy and put some clothes on him. They need food. See to it that the girl stops crying. Then I want to hear their story. What's happening with the dead man?'

'He is being taken ashore, Your Majesty.'

The King nodded and turned to go. A woman leaned over towards Daniel. She smelled strongly of perfume. She looked at him and then burst out laughing.

Daniel passively submitted to everything. He was bathed, given new clothes and a coat with yellow buttons. Then he was led into a room where Sanna was waiting. She was wearing a dress and her mouth was wide open.

'The King!' she shrieked. 'We're on the King's boat.'

'You should have let me drown. Why didn't you let me sink to the bottom?'

She didn't hear him. She tugged on her dress, her eyes still big with disbelief.

'It's the King,' she said again, and Daniel saw that she had tears in her eyes, but whether they were from fear or joy he couldn't tell.

Sanna had pulled him back into the boat. She had been stronger than Be and Kiko and she had betrayed him.

He knew that he must have revenge, but he didn't know how.

The door opened. A man with a gold ribbon over his shoulder came in.

'His Majesty awaits,' he said in a wheezing voice.

He motioned for them to stand up and turn round. He straightened Daniel's coat.

'No one sits down until His Majesty gives permission. No one says anything unless His Majesty addresses one of you. You reply briefly and clearly, using no curse words, of course, and do not sit with your legs crossed. If His Majesty laughs, it may be suitable to join in with a brief laugh, or rather a smile with a little sound. No improvisations are acceptable. Is that understood?'

'Yes,' said Sanna, curtsying.

'No,' said Daniel. 'I want to die.'

'His Majesty expects answers to his questions and no digressions. Is that understood?'

'Yes,' replied Sanna, and curtsied even deeper.

'I want to die,' said Daniel again.

They went down a narrow corridor, up some stairs and stopped before a double door.

'His Majesty will receive you in the aft salon. It is proper to curtsy and bow at the exact moment when I close the doors.'

They went inside. The man with the grey beard, from the portrait on Alma and Edvin's wall, sat leaning back in a chair upholstered in red. He had a cigar in his hand. Behind him stood the man who had given the King the handkerchief. Otherwise the room was empty. Sanna curtsied and Daniel bowed. He remembered what Kiko had once told him, about the kings in olden times – you were supposed to fall to the ground and place your neck under their feet as a sign of submission.

I'm standing before a king, thought Daniel. He is my last chance.

He took a few steps forward, threw himself prostrate on the floor and then grabbed one of the King's patent-leather shoes and placed it on his neck. The King flew out of his chair and the man with the handkerchief nervously rang a bell. Daniel was instantly surrounded by men who seemed to have come in through the walls. They held him tight.

The King sat down again.

'Careful,' he said. 'Let us take a cautious look at the Negro child. It is clear that the girl is less than intelligent, but the boy must have a remarkable tale to tell.'

They were allowed to sit on low stools of the same red fabric as the King's chair. Sanna immediately began to weep. But she did it silently. It was only Daniel who noticed the tears running down her cheeks. Maybe it was because she was sorry, maybe now she realised that she should have let him sink into the deep where Be and Kiko were waiting. He understood, and yet he hated her.

'What's your name?' asked the King.

'My name is Daniel. I believe in God.'

The King regarded the smoke curling from his cigar.

'A good answer. But it seems practised. Let me hear the story. About how you came here.'

Daniel told him. Maybe the King would understand how important it was for him to continue his journey. Sanna sat in silence, tugging at her dress. Now and then the King would ask a question, and Daniel tried to answer without losing the thread of his story.

When he was finished, the King looked at him for a long time. Daniel saw that his eyes were kind. But they didn't see him. They looked past him, just like Father's when he was thinking about something important.

'A peculiar story,' said the King. 'But filled with good intentions. You ought to stay and live your life where you have ended up. You should forget the desert. And besides, it's much too hot there.'

He nodded to the man with the handkerchief. The man in the gold livery who always stood in the background came closer.

The King stood up and held out two photographs. His name was written on them. The photograph was the same one that was on the wall at Alma and Edvin's house. Sanna made a deep curtsy. Daniel took the photograph but dropped it on the floor. He bent down to pick it up thinking that somebody was going to punish him by hitting him on the head.

'In truth, quite a remarkable dawn,' said the King and left the room.

They were allowed to keep the clothes, and their wet ones were put in a sea bag. The boat with Hans Höjer's dead body had already gone.

Daniel noticed that two seamen were always at his side in case he tried to jump overboard again. But he had given up. They went down a ladder and then sailed to the shore. A wind had blown up over the Sound. They came to the city called Malmö. Sanna held the picture of the King tightly. Daniel did as he was told. A carriage was brought up, and the coachman was instructed where to go. When they were sitting in the carriage, Sanna leaned against him.

'Now he won't dare hit me any more,' she said. 'He won't dare throw me down on the ground and stick it in. Not when I have a picture of the King.'

Daniel didn't reply. Sanna had betrayed him. He could never forgive her for that.

Late that evening the carriage rolled into the yard. It was Sanna who had directed the coachman. Alma and Edvin came outside. Daniel said nothing. He went straight into the barn and lay down in the straw. Outside he could hear Sanna explaining, leaping from one word to another as if the words were a skipping rope. When she stopped, Daniel burrowed into the straw. He heard Alma and Edvin come in and sensed that Alma had squatted down by his side. She put her hand on his brow.

'He's hot again.'

'How will we ever understand him?' said Edvin.

'Go now,' said Alma. 'I'll sit here a while.'

Daniel pretended to be asleep. He breathed slowly and deeply.

'What makes you so restless?' said Alma. 'How can we make sure that you won't kill yourself with longing? How can a child carry around so much sorrow?'

The next day Daniel stayed silent. His coughing fits worsened. Dr Madsen came several times to examine him, but Daniel no longer answered any questions. He was mute. Afterwards Madsen had a long conversation with Alma and Edvin, talking in serious whispers. That evening Alma came to Daniel and asked him if he wanted to move back into the kitchen. They hadn't found a new milkmaid to replace Vanja and he could have a better bed. His cough wouldn't go away if he stayed out here with the animals.

Daniel could hear that she meant what she said. His cough had begun to crack him open inside.

Two weeks after his last attempt to return to the desert, Daniel woke up in the middle of the night. He was very hot. When he rubbed his hand across his forehead he could feel that he was sweating. It was Kiko who had woken him. He stood with his hand over his face to shield his eyes and laughed. He hadn't said a word, but Daniel understood what he meant. He got up from his bed in the straw and searched for the tip of a scythe that the hired hand had broken off. Then he headed out into the night. He ran barefoot through the dark. The sky was clear, and he didn't stop until he came to the church. He squatted down and coughed. When he touched his mouth with his hand he saw that there was blood.

Daniel picked a stone in the wall of the churchyard that was completely smooth. He carved an antelope into it. It was hard to do, and he made many mistakes. The legs were different lengths, the animal's back much too straight. But the most important thing was the eye. He took great care to make it completely round.

Then he sat down to wait.

When the cough came he drew the index finger of his right hand across his lips and then dabbed the blood in the antelope's eye. In the darkness he couldn't see the colour, but he knew that the antelope's eye would shine bright red in the daytime when the dawn came.

CHAPTER 28

Someone had seen him in the night.

By early morning the rumour had started to spread, and just after nine o'clock people began gathering at the churchyard wall. The wind was blowing hard that day and the rain came in heavy squalls. Hallén woke up with a sharp pain over one eye. He was lying in bed with a cold facecloth on his forehead when his serving woman came in and announced that people had begun gathering at the church and that someone had carved a picture on the churchyard wall. Hallén had long suspected that the serving woman was growing senile, but he got out of bed because she didn't seem confused in her usual way. Something had happened or was happening at the church. Hallén pressed one fist against the pain above his eye and left the parsonage. As he walked towards the gate he could see the crowd by the west corner of the churchyard. Hallén wondered anxiously, and with some annoyance, whether a suicide might have chosen this unfortunate place to end his life. The thought was not unreasonable because the old belief that suicides should be buried outside the churchyard was still embraced by many of his parishioners. He grimaced at the pain above his eye and at the thought. If it was a suicide, he hoped that there wasn't too much blood. He stopped, took a few deep breaths and tried to think of a glass of cognac. He always did this when something unpleasant awaited him. He had never been able to derive the same strength from the Holy Scriptures as he could from the thought of a glass of cognac.

The crowd parted as he approached. To his relief there was no corpse lying by the wall. What he found there was a poorly carved picture of an animal. Actually it was only an outline with strange proportions and a big eye.

The eye was red, or really almost black. But it was blood, he could see that at once. The eye stared at him and the pain over his own eye grews sharper. One of the richest parishioners, an unpleasant man by the name of Arnman, stood and pounded on the wall with his stick. The year before he had donated an ugly, heavy, but expensive bridal crown to the parish. Hallén suspected that it was stolen goods that he had acquired on one of his many trips to Poland. Arnman lived there with his mistress on a run-down estate very close to the port where the ferry connection from Ystad reached the Continent. He boasted openly that almost every year he begot a Polish brat, even though his wife in Sweden kept bearing him new children. Hallén felt sad when he gazed from his pulpit at fat Arnman and his skinny wife. Sometimes he also permitted himself the unpleasantness of imagining them naked together. It seemed amazing that Arnman hadn't crushed his wife to death in bed long ago.

'The Negro,' said Arnman in his thick voice. 'It's the Negro's doing.'

There was muttering and buzzing among the crowd. They sounded like angry bees, thought Hallén.

'The Negro,' Arnman repeated, and Hallén wished he could get rid of him. But Arnman had great influence in the parish. He sat on the church board and nobody could deny that in spite of everything, he had contributed to the needy church with his donations.

'How do you know that?' asked Hallén, thinking about the boy from the distant dark continent, the boy he had tried to teach manners but who had thanked him for his efforts by putting a viper in the offering pouch.

Arnman waved his stick. From the dark-clad crowd of people, one of Arnman's hired hands stepped forward. He was always drunk but according to rumour had a way with sick horses.

'I saw him,' said the hired hand.

'What did you see?'

'He was sitting here and chipping at the wall.'

'When?'

'Last night.'

Arnman rapped the hired hand on the back with his stick, and he slunk off.

'He's been drinking,' said Arnman. 'But you can't deny what he saw. It was the Negro who sat here chipping away, and cut himself and rubbed blood on the wall. He doesn't belong here. We know about witchcraft.'

Hallén gave Arnman a searching look. The pain over his eye increased.

'What is it you know?'

'That people should be careful about who they allow into their community.'

Arnman uttered these last words in a powerful voice. A murmur of agreement came from the crowd.

'I shall attend to the matter,' said Hallén. Then he turned to the sexton. 'Try to scrub this off,' he said. 'And the rest of you can go home.'

Arnman marched down to the road and the carriage that was waiting for him. The crowd dispersed slowly. Hallén knew that he should talk to Alma and Edvin right away, but the pain above his eye made that impossible. He went back to the parsonage and lay in bed for the rest of the day.

The next morning his serving woman came and told him that the animal with the red eye was back on the wall. Hallén had just woken up, relieved that the pain over his eye was gone.

That same day he paid a visit to Alma and Edvin. They had heard about what happened. Alma had asked Daniel about it, but she got no reply except a few words in his own strange language. They all went out to the barn together where Daniel lay curled up in the straw.

'He has a fever,' Alma said. 'But he refuses to sleep in the house.'

Hallén observed the boy in silence.

'It's possible that he should be moved to a mental hospital,' he said. 'There are many indications that he has gone insane. It's not normal to carve animals on churchyard walls. Did he cut himself to get the blood?'

'I think he coughed it up,' said Edvin.

'He's killing himself with longing for home,' Alma said firmly. 'What business does he have among lunatics?'

'You don't know anything about these matters. You heard what the pastor said,' said Edvin.

Hallén tried to catch Daniel's eye, but he kept looking away. Every time Hallén looked at the boy he had an eerie feeling that there was something he ought to understand that was escaping him. The child lying there in the straw had a message for him that he couldn't comprehend.

'It's causing unrest in the parish, the way he's carving the wall and daubing blood on it,' Hallén said. 'If it happens again we'll have to consider sending him to St Lars in Lund.'

'Is that a church?' Alma asked.

'You know quite well that it's the madhouse,' said Edvin.

'He doesn't belong among those people.'

They left him in the barn. The milkmaid who had been alone since Vanja died went about among the cows, weeping. Daniel thought of Sanna. He still couldn't grasp how she could have betrayed him. He had felt happy with her, and she had shared her warmth with him. But she had deceived him about who she really was. She had acted the same way as the man who had hit her and dragged her by the hair.

He lay there until far into the night and tried to understand why she had acted as she did. He didn't touch the food that Alma brought him.

'I don't want you to be tied up,' she said. 'I don't want you to end up with crazy people. Can't you stop going to the church?'

Daniel didn't answer. But when Edvin came in she told him that Daniel had promised he wouldn't go out that night.

'We could always put the boy in the house,' Edvin said. 'Or I could stay out here myself.'

'That's not necessary. He won't go.'

Edvin shook his head. 'The hired hand said that Arnman has stationed some of his boys outside the church.'

'That man is disgusting. He probably told them to attack Daniel if he shows up.'

'If only we knew what he was thinking. He sees something that we don't see. He's surrounded by people again. They're here, I can feel it.'

'Nobody wants to put *you* in the madhouse,' Alma replied. 'But you want to put *him* there?'

'I'm just trying to puzzle him out, that's all. It's as if he's telling a story. Sometimes I feel like all this mud is being transformed into sand, and that it's getting hot. But then it's gone again.'

*   *   *

Daniel listened to what they were saying. By now he understood most of their speech, but his old language had taken over almost all his consciousness.

Alma put her hand on his forehead.

'He's much too hot,' she said. 'I don't know why Dr Madsen can't do something. He can't catch a fever from being homesick, can he?'

'It's the cough,' Edvin said. 'You know that as well as I do. And there's nothing to be done about that.'

'I don't want him to die,' Alma said. 'I want that man named Bengler to come back and take him home.'

They left Daniel alone. The cows stirred in their stalls. A rat rustled in a corner. One of the hens fluttered its wings. Daniel kept thinking about Sanna. At last it seemed there was only one possibility. One explanation for why she had let him down. She was an evil spirit. He had no idea who had sent her to destroy him.

He dozed off and in his dream he saw Sanna sitting among the black birds in a tree out in the field. At first he thought it was Be, who was waiting there so that she could fly off with him, but then he saw that it was Sanna and that black soot was running out of her nostrils.

He woke up with a start and thought about what he had dreamed. Whoever had sent Sanna into his path had done it to prevent Be and Kiko from reaching him. Suddenly it all became clear to him: as long as Sanna existed he would never be able to go home. He was never meant to learn to walk on water or to sail with a ship the long way back. Be and Kiko were right next to him.

And yet he was unsure. He was too small to know everything about the evil spirits who possessed people's souls. The only thing he could do was to try to trick Sanna into revealing who she really was and who had sent her.

Daniel slipped back and forth between sleeping and waking. Sometimes he would reach out for the mug of water that Alma always set beside him.

At dawn he ate all the food he had left untouched the night before.

If he was going to find out who Sanna really was, he would have to eat and build up his strength.

It took him a few days and nights to work out a plan. He searched his memory for everything that Kiko had taught him: about how evil spirits had to be tracked the same way as animals.

Finally he found the solution.

In his coat he still had the sliver of wood he had taken from the knee of the Jesus statue.

The following night he would put his plan into action. As if to convince himself that he was doing the right thing, that he had understood the invisible powers who were preventing him from returning to the desert, his fever suddenly abated, although he was still coughing up blood. Dr Madsen, who came to visit Alma, said that perhaps he might still get well.

It was completely calm when Daniel left the barn. He stopped in the yard and listened. Everything was quiet. He had taken along one of the lanterns that Edvin lit every evening in the barn. He had put it out, but he had matches with him.

When he reached the hill he stopped and listened. He opened his nostrils wide as Kiko had taught him to do when he was scenting a spoor. Sanna often smelled bad – she was dirty and her clothes smelled sour. But he didn't notice anything. He crept cautiously up to the top of the hill, lit the lantern and screwed down the top. At the spot where Sanna most often sat, either still with her eyes closed, or rocking impatiently and digging in the dirt, he stuck the piece of wood into the ground. Then he did as Kiko had taught him, imitating a hyena and laughing out into the darkness. Hyenas always followed the trail of death. They ate not only animal carcasses but also dug up people who had been buried. That was how they drew the spirits of people inside themselves, both the evil ones and the good. Daniel whispered the words in his language that were the most important: that in the piece of wood lived a spirit who would be able to lead Daniel back to the desert. Then he blew out the lantern and went back to the barn.

*   *   *

259

In the morning when he woke up, the hired hand stood looking at him.

'There was somebody laughing last night,' said the hired hand. 'It sounded like a pig, but also like a person. It must have been you.'

'No,' Daniel said. 'It wasn't me.'

The hired hand stared at him. Then he ran to fetch Alma and Edvin.

'I heard him,' he said excitedly. 'I heard him speak.'

'What did he say?'

'He said, "No. It wasn't me."'

'Is that all?'

'Yes.'

Alma squatted down next to Daniel. 'Is it true that you've started to speak again?'

Daniel stayed silent. Alma asked him again.

'It's no use,' said Edvin. 'The hired hand must have been imagining things.'

'I heard what I heard.'

Edvin gave him a shove. 'Work is waiting.'

That afternoon Daniel crept out through a hole in the wall at the back of the barn. Before he set off he stuffed the broken-off scythe point into his pocket. He crouched down when he ran across the fields. A fog bank was slowly shrouding the landscape in white. He could feel his heart begin to pound faster when he saw Sanna sitting up on the hill and digging in the mud. When she caught sight of him she was happy. She jumped up and grabbed hold of him. Daniel saw that she had been digging right where he had put the stick. There was no longer any doubt. She smelled like an animal – her clothes were like a pelt – and when she laughed she sounded like an animal, not a human being.

'I thought you were never coming back,' she said.

The fog covered the landscape. Sanna squatted down in the mud. She had the photograph of the King with her and traced his signature with her finger. Daniel carefully pulled the scythe point out of his pocket and plunged it into the back of her neck. She fell forward without a sound. When he turned her over she stared up at him with her eyes wide open. He rubbed mud onto her face until her eyes couldn't see him any longer. So that she wouldn't be able to talk either, he shoved as much mud into her mouth and throat as he could. He was out of breath and sweaty when he rubbed off the blood that had spattered on his clothes. Then he took the scythe point and the photograph of the King and buried them in the mud.

The trees where the birds used to perch could not be seen in the fog. Daniel took hold of Sanna's arms and began to drag her down the hill. Several times he had to squat down. He coughed so violently that he threw up. His mouth was full of blood, but he didn't care. Soon he would be home again. He dragged Sanna's body until he reached the trees. He covered her body with a thin layer of fallen branches and old brushwood. When the birds came back they would peck at her body until nothing was left. Even though he had the fever again, he felt strong. Now he didn't need to do anything but lie down in the barn and wait. Kiko and Be would come soon.

That evening he began carving on one of his wooden shoes. He wanted to give Be and Kiko a gift when they came to get him. Above all, he wanted to show Kiko that he had grown better at carving figures. When Alma came in with the food he hid his whittling knife and the shoes. He started eating at once.

'Not too fast,' she said. 'Your stomach won't stand such haste.'

Daniel did as she said. For an instant he felt an urge to tell Alma that everything was going to be all right now. Soon he wouldn't have to lie out in the barn any more. They wouldn't need to worry about him at all. Yet he thought it was probably best not to say anything. Dr Madsen and Hallén had both spoken about a house where people were locked in. He never wanted to be tied up again.

That night, when he was alone with the animals, he took off all his clothes and washed his whole body. Even though the water was cold he rubbed himself hard until all the dirt was gone. He found flecks of blood on his clothes. He scrubbed them with the brush Edvin used for the horses. Then he put his clothes back on and lay down for a while, whittling on his wooden shoe. He took care not to be impatient. He wanted Kiko to be pleased and say that he had begun to learn.

*   *   *

261

At daybreak he went out into the yard.

Thick fog lay over the fields. In the distance he could hear the birds screeching. Edvin came out onto the steps and stood there taking a piss. He didn't see Daniel until he was finished. He buttoned his trousers and went over to him.

'Are you starting to get well?' he asked.

'Yes,' Daniel replied. 'I will be well soon.'

CHAPTER 29

Daniel divided up his last days alive by carving notches on his other shoe, the one he wasn't trying to turn into a sculpture. Each time he put down the whittling knife and each time he picked it up to continue his work, he would cut a notch on the shoe.

He was waiting. Now that he had tested his powers against all the evil that surrounded him and shown that he was stronger, time had lost its significance. His waiting involved something different to seeing the light of dawn creeping in through the windows of the barn or seeing the twilight fall. His waiting meant that he was listening. No matter what direction Be or Kiko came from, he would hear them. Their voices would be faint, almost whispering. Maybe they would sound like the cows snorting in their stalls, or like a hen flapping its wings. He didn't know, and that's why he had to pay attention to any sounds that might signal their arrival.

His cough had grown worse from the effort of dragging Sanna's body through the mud. The fever that came and went made him tired. He slept a lot in these last days.

When he opened his eyes after dozing off one afternoon, Dr Madsen was standing in front of him. He was smiling. In his hand he held a letter.

'Your father has written,' he said. 'A letter has come for you, postmarked Cape Town.'

Daniel no longer had many memories of the man he called Father. They had faded and turned into vague phantoms. Only with difficulty could he remember how he looked. His voice was already completely lost. The images in his mind were shadows.

'He wrote to me and asked me to read the letter to you.'

263

Behind Dr Madsen stood Edvin and Alma. They kept their distance as if the letter demanded great respect.

Dr Madsen read:

To my son Daniel far away in Sweden,

I will always think of you as Daniel Bengler. Sometimes I think the name befits a grown man better. But what surname is actually suitable for a child? At present I am in Cape Town, the city where you and I began our journey. Do you remember? The high mountain that looked like a table? The day we walked along the beach and saw dolphins leaping in the sea? The journey here took a long time because I rode in an inferior carriage through almost the whole of Europe in order to board a ship in a French city called Marseille. I have been in Cape Town four months now. At first I lay ill. I had eaten something that bothered my stomach for a long time. For several weeks I was afraid that the illness would get the better of me. But I am healthy now. Soon I will complete all my preparations to return to the desert. But this time I shall travel in a more north-easterly direction. There are large areas that are mostly unknown, and of course I hope to be able to find insects which will later be a pleasure to exhibit to people in Sweden. My journey commenced abruptly, I know. But it was necessary. Now everything is fine, however. I don't know when I shall be coming home. Father.

'An excellent letter,' said Dr Madsen when he had finished reading and stuffed the paper back in the envelope.

'He doesn't even ask how the boy is doing,' said Alma, upset. 'He doesn't even ask how he is.'

'But now we know he's alive, at least,' Edvin said. 'We didn't know that before. Now we know that it will be a long time before he returns.'

Dr Madsen placed the letter in the straw next to Daniel's head.

'A very fine letter,' he said.

Then he pressed his hand against Daniel's forehead. He looked into his eyes and listened to his chest. There was a rattling sound when Daniel breathed.

'It would have been best, of course, if we could have taken him to a sanatorium,' he said to Alma and Edvin when he finished his examination. 'But that's out of the question.'

'If it will make him well I'll sell the horses,' replied Edvin firmly.

Dr Madsen shook his head. 'We can always find the money,' he said. 'Many people would be moved to tears by a black child who is sick. Besides, he has met the King. But it's not a question of money. It's a matter of whether he could stand being moved again to a place that's completely foreign to him.'

Dr Madsen regarded Daniel lying in the straw.

'Naturally he should be sleeping in the house. The vapours from the animals may not be dangerous, but neither are they healthy. In addition, he ought to have a diet that consists of only eggs and milk.'

'That will be easier than moving the animals into the house,' said Edvin. 'He'll stay out here whatever we do. And I refuse to tie him up.'

'You should still think it over,' said Dr Madsen as he left.

Daniel heard the conversation continuing in the yard. He took out his wooden shoes, which he had hidden behind his head, and went on whittling. The wood was hard and his arm quickly grew tired. The whole time he kept listening for Be and Kiko. They had come closer, he could feel it, but he still couldn't hear them.

Two days after Dr Madsen's visit, Alma came to see Daniel at a time when she rarely went to the barn. He saw immediately that she had been crying and was afraid that she was sick. She sank down into the straw, and he wondered whether she was going to start sleeping there too.

'I have to tell you this,' she said. 'And it's better that you hear it from me than anyone else. Sanna is dead. Something horrible has happened. One of Nilsson's boys found her out in the field. Somebody killed her.'

Daniel nodded cheerfully. He couldn't understand why it made Alma so sad. She gave him an appalled look when he couldn't help laughing.

'Are you happy that I've told you the girl is dead? I thought you liked her, even though she was retarded.'

Daniel didn't want Alma to be angry with him and stopped laughing at once.

'Somebody killed her,' Alma went on. 'Someone stabbed her with a knife, violated her and buried her under some bushes out in the field. Somewhere there's a murderer and no one knows who it is.'

Daniel didn't know what the word *murderer* meant. but he thought that it would be best not to tell Alma the truth, that Sanna hadn't been a human being but an animal, a dangerous animal, which they should be happy to be rid of. There was so much that Alma and Edvin and perhaps even Dr Madsen didn't understand, about the powers that could conceal themselves in the earth, among the trees, and above all in human beings.

For the next few days no one talked about anything else. Everyone seemed to be afraid of what they called *the murderer*. Several times Daniel nearly told them, but something held him back.

One morning Edvin stood before him as he lay in the straw.

'There's a man sitting in the kitchen,' he said. 'He wants to talk to you about Sanna. He's from Malmö and has come all the way here to search for the damn person who did Sanna such harm.'

That was the first time Daniel had heard Edvin say the word that was so important to Father. *Damn.* Daniel could see that he was furious.

'It was me,' said Daniel.

Edvin stiffened. 'What did you say?'

'It was me.'

'Who did what?'

Edvin's questions made Daniel confused. He immediately regretted that he had begun to speak again.

'I'm glad you're talking. But I don't understand what you're saying.'

'I'm going home soon.'

Edvin shook his head. 'You're sick,' he said. 'And you won't get well as long as you sleep out here in the barn. You're raving, but I still have to bring in the man who wants to talk to you.'

The man who came into the barn was young with only a few patches of hair on his head, and he moved quickly, as if he were in a great hurry. Edvin brought over a milk pail for him to sit on. He gave Daniel an inquisitive look.

'I've read about you in the newspapers,' he said. 'About your trip with the dead girl on the Sound. And about how you got to meet the King. But I expected you to be bigger. And I didn't expect that I would meet you like this.'

He moved the pail closer to Daniel and leaned forward.

'You know what has happened. Someone killed Sanna in a very brutal way. We have to catch the man who did it. Then he will probably be executed in Malmö prison. A man who has committed such a horrible crime might do it again. That's why we have to catch him. Do you understand what I'm saying?'

Daniel's face was immobile.

'He understands,' said Edvin, who stayed in the background. 'But he's ill and doesn't speak very often.'

'I have to ask some questions,' the man went on. 'Did you see Sanna after you both came back here?'

Daniel didn't like the man sitting on the pail. He smelled of shaving lotion and tobacco and would never understand what had happened. He had come to get Daniel and then chop off his head. He didn't have time for that. Soon Kiko and Be would arrive. Each morning when he woke up he knew that the moment would soon be here. He quickly decided that the best way to get the man to leave him in peace was to answer his questions.

'No.'

'You never saw her?'

'No.'

'Do you know if Sanna ever met someone who was not from around here?'

'No.'

'She wasn't afraid of anybody? I'm not talking about her stepfather, she was terrified of him, I know that. But he didn't do it. I've questioned him hard and he can prove he didn't do it. Anyone else?'

'No.'

The man rubbed his hand over his bald head without taking his eyes off Daniel.

'The two of you tried to leave Sweden,' he said. 'I can understand that you wanted to go back to Africa. My only question is how you managed to lure Sanna into going along. Or did she want to escape from someone she was afraid of?'

'He dragged her by the hair.'

'Who?'

'Her stepfather.'

The man shook his head thoughtfully. 'I don't understand it,' he said. 'The two of you came back. And suddenly somebody kills her.'

He stood up quickly from the milk pail. 'We're going to catch him,' he said, smiling. 'A man who commits a crime like this cannot go free.'

Edvin followed the man out. Daniel was overcome by a great weariness that seemed to press him roughly into sleep. He tried to fight it without success.

When he woke a few hours later he had a high fever. His heart was beating very fast. He was sweating and had to squint his eyes to make out Alma, who was anxiously watching him. Behind her stood Edvin and the hired hand.

Alma leaned over close to his face.

'You will sleep in our bed,' she said. 'You'll be alone in the room.'

Daniel was too tired to resist when Edvin and the hired hand lifted him up. As they carried him across the yard he could feel that it was raining. He opened his mouth and felt the raindrops landing on his tongue, but by the time they put him to bed he was asleep again.

That night his condition grew worse. Only once during the time that remained did he get up from the bed and go out into the yard. It was when he dreamed that Be and Kiko had come and were waiting for him. When he went outside and felt the cold from the ground seep into his body, there was no one there. He went back into the barn and searched for the wooden shoes that he was carving and the knife that lay in the straw. He stuffed them under his nightshirt and returned to the yard. He called out to them, shouted their names, but got no reply. Alma and Edvin came out, roused from their sleep. After he had moved into the bedroom they slept in the kitchen with the milkmaid. He didn't resist when Edvin lifted him up and carried him back inside.

*   *   *

268

That was the only time he got out of bed. It was a brief interruption in his decline, which would not end until he was dead.

Now and then he was struck with severe coughing fits that bloodied the sheets, but most of the time he lay quietly in the borderland where dreams and reality meet. He never said a word, never met anyone's eyes, and recognised only Alma and Edvin. Hallén came to visit regularly, as did Dr Madsen. On one occasion Alma also called in a wise woman from Kivik who, it was said, could cure people of consumption by greasing their chests with cow fat. But Daniel continued to decline. He was not in pain, felt no hunger, had no idea whether it was day or night.

As his condition worsened, he discovered that the way back did not go towards the horizon but inwards, downwards, towards a deep that was drawing him in. There Be and Kiko were waiting. In his dreams he could already glimpse the sand that was completely white in the blazing sun. He was utterly calm now. Nothing would keep him from returning. Be and Kiko had not abandoned him. Kiko would be angry because he had taken so long to come, but not even this worried him. For a few hours every day he managed to keep carving the wooden shoe. He thought that Kiko would be pleased. He had become a better carver. One day Kiko would be able to entrust the antelope and the rock wall to him.

In the last days, after he had already slipped very far towards the desert that awaited him, he finally began to hear their voices. Now they were quite close to him. Gradually he was able to distinguish their faces as well. A boy who was a few years older than Daniel was the first to come up to his bed. Daniel no longer remembered his name, but there was no doubt that it was him, the third son that was born to one of Kiko's older sisters. When Daniel asked his first question, – whether it would be long before Be and Kiko came – the boy replied that they were out hunting, but they would be back soon.

Just as the boy reached him, Edvin opened the door and carried in a wooden mug of milk. He set it on the table next to the bed and stood there. Then he went over to the door and called Alma in a low voice. Daniel explained to the boy who they were, Edvin and Alma, and when Alma came in the boy was sitting on the bed by Daniel's feet.

'They're here again,' said Edvin.

'Who?'

'The voices! Can't you hear them? He isn't alone in here.'

Alma listened. 'You're imagining things. There's nobody here.'

'Can't you hear them? He isn't alone here. Damn it all.'

'You're tired,' Alma said, taking Edvin by the hand. 'You're not sleeping well because you're worrying. I'm worried too. But we have to trust in God.'

'God?' Edvin said angrily. 'What does he know?'

'Don't blaspheme.'

They left the room. The boy got up from the bed, waved to Daniel and vanished. Daniel closed his eyes and continued to sink. He could feel the warm sand under his feet. If he shaded his eyes with his hand he could see some zebras moving in the shimmering sunlight. Even though he wasn't hungry, he had an urge to sink his teeth into some meat again from an animal that Kiko had killed.

Only once during these last days did he think that he saw Father again. By then he had already sunk so far that he was surrounded by sand and low bushes. Near a dried-up stream lay a whitened skeleton scraped clean. Right next to one hand, where the finger bones were splayed, was a little wooden box. Daniel recognised it at once. It was the same box that Father had asked Daniel on several occasions to guard because it contained the insects that Father would give his name to one day. Daniel opened it and found a desiccated butterfly that had once been blue. When he touched its wings it disintegrated into a bluish powder. He put the box back next to Father's skeleton and hoped that someone, maybe the woman with the buttons, would one day find Father and take him back home.

At last he was there. First he saw the hills with the cave where the antelope was carved. In the distance two people were approaching. He waited. Finally he saw that it was Be and Kiko, and Be was carrying a new baby on her back, and she told him that a sister had arrived while he was gone. Kiko wasn't angry. Daniel held out his present and at the same moment forgot that his name had been Daniel. Now he was Molo again. Nothing more. Kiko admired for a long time what he was holding in his hands.

'You have gained patience,' he said then. 'You have grown up.'

Molo smiled. He was home now. Everything that had happened would soon vanish from his mind.

Daniel died early one summer morning. By then he had lain in a coma for several weeks. Dr Madsen hadn't been able to do anything for him. There was no hope.

Not until they were about to lay him in the coffin did Alma discover the wooden sculpture. She showed it to Edvin.

'He carved a deer out of a wooden shoe,' he said. 'Why did he do that?'

'We'll put it in the coffin with him,' Alma said. 'He won't be lonely any more.'

They placed the sculpture next to his head and then screwed down the lid. Many people came to the funeral. Hallén chose not to speak from a Bible text but instead propagandised for the importance of supporting the mission work under way in Africa.

No one knew that the coffin they buried was actually empty.

EPILOGUE

KALAHARI DESERT,
MARCH 1995

On the road between Francistown in Botswana and Windhoek in Namibia, he spent the night at a hotel in Ghanzi. The village consisted of a collection of wind-tormented houses that lay strewn in the middle of the desert. The hotel was full of sand. Even though the menu at the restaurant offered a great variety of dishes, they consisted mostly of sand. It crunched between his teeth even when he drank water. In the hotel's desolate bar two men sat concluding a deal. They were taking their time and there were frequent long silences before they continued the conversation. In the desert there was no reason to hurry. Since there were no other guests in the bar and the barman had disappeared, he couldn't avoid hearing what they were talking about. One of them had got his lorry stuck just past the Namibian border and was now trying to sell both the vehicle and the load, which apparently included bicycle tyres and various wares, such as children's clothing, stockings and a carton of peaked caps that the man had acquired at a bargain price. The negotiations proceeded slowly, and he didn't stay long enough to hear whether the two men reached an agreement or not.

Just before dark he took a walk along the only street. Everywhere the desert was present. He went into a shop, mostly to see what there was to buy. The woman behind the counter, who was black and quite young, asked him at once whether he would marry her and take her away. He had a strong feeling that she was serious, and he quickly left the shop.

In the evening, after eating eggs, potatoes, vegetables and sand, he lay awake in his hotel room fighting with the mosquitoes. The desert that surrounded him roared in the darkness, as if he were actually on an island in the middle of an endless sea.

*   *   *

When he awoke in the morning he was covered with mosquito bites. He lay in bed and counted the days. If he had been infected with malaria during the night, it would take about a fortnight before the illness broke out. By then, if everything went as planned, he would already be far away from the desert.

He continued his journey towards the Namibian border. He had been warned that the road was very poor, sometimes almost non-existent, but the jeep with its four-wheel drive and powerful engine drove him on. He wondered when he would pass the lorry that should be out there somewhere, like a shipwrecked boat in the sea of sand.

Before he got that far he stopped to take a piss. The desert was flat, not like the desert he had seen in pictures, with dunes that rose up in soft ridges, hiding all the sand that lay beyond them. Here there were no hills. The sand was grey, and there were a few isolated low bushes. At the horizon, heaven and earth met in a colourless mist.

When he had buttoned up his flies and turned round to get behind the wheel again, he discovered a group of people walking towards him across the desert. They moved very quickly in single file, and it took a while before he was quite sure that he was seeing people and not animals. He went back to the jeep and leaned against it so that the driver's side gave him shade. He squinted and counted the people approaching. He came up with the number thirty-one.

The first to reach him was a skinny old man who had grey hair and bow legs. The man regarded him with inquisitive eyes.
'I know how to speak English,' he said.
He was surprised. He had been told that the nomads in the desert, the Bushmen, didn't speak any language but their own, which comprised the strange clicking sounds that were almost impossible for others to master.
The jeep was now surrounded by the nomads. All of them gave him friendly looks, and not even the little children seemed afraid of him. Suddenly he realised that he now had an opportunity that might never come again. It was impossible to make an appointment with a nomad. One could never specify a time with a group belonging to the San

people. But here he had happened to meet one of these groups, and there was even a man who spoke English.

He asked the old man whether they had time to stop for a while and let him tell them a story. The man turned to the others and began speaking the language with the clicking sounds. They all seemed quite intrigued that someone wanted to tell them a story. They sat down in the sand, and even though it was quite hot, none of them wanted to sit in the shade next to the jeep.

Then he told the story of a boy who was given the name Daniel and who had come to Sweden about 120 years before. The old man translated his English and he noticed that the people grew very quiet as they sat before him in the sand. It was a quietness that came from within, a concentration that he had never experienced. He told them everything he knew, all the details he had managed to find out about the boy who now lay buried in a churchyard in the southern part of the faraway land called Sweden. He also told them that he was now making the long journey to Windhoek to search through the old German archives, which were now the National Archives of Namibia, to see whether he could find any documents about the people who had taken the boy named Daniel to Sweden.

When he had finished telling the story, he handed the old man the photograph, taken in the photography studio in Lund, that he had managed to find. It had been in the possession of the relatives of Hans Bengler, who were very reluctant to part with it. He had never been able to understand their reluctance, or perhaps it was anguish. The story of Daniel seemed enveloped in a shameful silence.

Now the photograph was passed among the people in the sand. He had a feeling that what was playing out before him was a religious rite.

As he handed back the photograph, the old man began to speak. He searched a long time for the words, as if it was important to him that everything he said was correct.

The old man thanked him. For coming the long distance in the jeep from the land whose name he couldn't pronounce and restoring Daniel's spirit to the desert, to the place where he should have lived and also been buried.

When the man stopped a woman stood up. She was carrying a tiny baby on her back and she came and stood in front of him.

'Her name is Be,' said the old man.

He looked into her eyes and thought that Daniel's mother might have looked just like her. He also knew that from this moment on she would always think that she was the mother of that boy, the boy who lay buried so far away.

Afterwards they got up and walked away. Soon he could hardly see them, only a drawn-out line of black dots in the dazzling sunlight.

In the archives in Windhoek he found no documents that could tell him anything more about Daniel and Hans Bengler, or about Wilhelm Andersson; nothing that he didn't know already. On the other hand, he spent the whole day leafing through huge folders full of photographs that an English photographer named Frank Hodgson had taken during his travels in what was then called German South-West Africa in the 1870s, the period when Daniel had made his long journey to Sweden.

One of the photographs depicted a man, a woman and a boy. They were posed stiffly in front of the photographer's camera. The boy stood in the foreground. He was much like Daniel, the way he looked in the photograph taken at the studio in Lund. He thought that they might have looked like this, Be and Kiko and Daniel, who at that time had an entirely different name – which no one would ever know.

Then he left the National Archives. The hot, dry wind outside the cool air-conditioned building library hit him like a wall.

Two days later he drove back the same way he had come. When he reached the spot where he had told his story, he stopped and got out of the car. In Windhoek he had bought a telescope. He looked through it, scanning the horizon, but the desert was empty. He couldn't see any people anywhere. He didn't dare wait too long, since he wanted to make it to Ghanzi before dark.

The desert stayed empty. He drove on. Just before sundown he arrived in Ghanzi.

Several years later he wrote this book, which has now come to an end.

AFTERWORD

This is a novel. That means that the events and characters depicted in this book have no direct models in real life. It also means that any similarities with historical events or persons should be considered pure coincidence.

The novel does not necessarily depict what actually happened. The task of the novel is to portray what might have happened.

Henning Mankell
Mozambique, April 2000